THE EMERALD WAVES 1

THE EMERALD WAVES

THE SILVER PEAKS SERIES BOOK TWO

NIKKI ASHTON

Copyright © Nikki Ashton 2025 All Rights Reserved © The Emerald Waves
Published by Bubble Books Ltd

This book is licensed for your personal enjoyment only.

This book may not be re-sold or given away to other people. If you would like to share this book with another person, please purchase an additional copy for each recipient. If you're reading this book and did not purchase it, or it wasn't purchased for your use only, then please return to your favorite book retailer and purchase your own copy. Thank you for respecting the hard work of this author.

All Rights Reserved ©

This is a work of fiction. Names, characters, places, brands, media and incidents are either the product of the author's imagination or are used fictitiously. The author acknowledges the trademark status and trademark owners of various products referred to in this work of fiction, which have been used without permission. The publication/use of these trademarks is not authorized, associated with, or sponsored by the trademark owners.

Cover design and formatting by – Lou Stock of LJDesigns

For my grandmothers, Emily (Cissie) and Jenny. I miss you both even after all this time.

ACKNOWLEDGMENTS

Thank you Mum, for all your belief and help when I needed it. I know I'm not the mushy kind of daughter, but I love you. There you go, that's enough of that now.

To everyone who took the time to read The Lilac River and told me they couldn't wait for more. You will never know how much I appreciate it and the love you showed for it. It means you now get Gunner and Wilder's stories.

To Lou for her incredible covers and formatting. How the hell do you manage to make everything so pretty?

Emily, Lou's sister, for an incredible, banging country music playlist to give me inspiration.

Lana and Tash for your eagle eyes over all three books.

Finally, Luke Grimes, for being my muse for Gunner, actually and also for Nash and Wilder – Cole Hauser who?

THE EMERALD WAVES
Some rivalries spark fire.
Some hearts get caught in the blaze.

She can't forgive him. He can't forget her. After one disastrous date and years of mutual irritation, Cassidy Turner and Gunner Miller have perfected the art of avoidance. But when a troubled student brings Cassidy to the gates of Last Creek Ranch, old sparks reignite and not all of them are angry.

Gunner's got enough on his plate, ranch expansions, land disputes, and a headstrong woman who gets under his skin in more ways than one. Cassidy's just as infuriating as he remembers... and twice as captivating.

As tension gives way to truth, something unexpected grows between them. But in a town where secrets simmer and loyalty runs deep; love might not be enough to survive the storm of tragedy.

Set against the green hills and rumbling skies of Silver Peaks, *The Emerald Waves* is a story of stubborn hearts, slow-burning redemption, and a love that refuses to back down.

Some grudges run deep.
Some truths can't be ignored.
And some sparks were meant to burn.

Cassidy & Gunner's Song

Fire Away – Chris Stapleton

Do I Wanna Know - Arctic Monkeys

PROLOGUE
Gunner

Three years ago.

I'd dreamt about her nearly every night, for a whole damn week.

Not that I was losing sleep over Cassidy Turner. And the dreams weren't anything sentimental. They were the kind of dreams you don't mention to your brothers. The kind that makes you wake up annoyed with yourself, and hard as hell.

It was stupid, she was just a teacher. An impossible-to-ignore teacher who dressed like summertime, all the time, and looked at me like I was the punchline to some private joke. And yeah, she showed up in my head sometimes. So what?

I leaned against the hood of my truck outside Bertie's school and told myself I hadn't volunteered to pick up my niece just so I could see Miss. Turner.

The late afternoon sun was low and sharp, turning the blacktop to liquid and making every kid scream twice as loud, or so it seemed. Parents clogged up the curb, hollering names, honking, waving and trying to out-do each other in the warmth of their greeting for their kid. Next semester would be different because the principal was introducing a pick-up line. Fucking A.

Wanting to stay out of the rumpus, I stayed where I was. Still. Quiet. Watching the door.

Then I saw her.

Cassidy crouched near the flagpole, zipping up a kid's backpack and then adjusting the strap on it, like she had nowhere else to be. Her hair was up, for a change. Usually it was down, cascading over her shoulders and nearly hitting her ass. Straight but a little messy like she didn't take herself too seriously. She stood, brushed her hands off on her red and white checkered skirt and started to walk back toward the double doors.

She didn't see me.

She never did.

Some days I convinced myself she did it on purpose. Ignored me. Like she knew exactly how I looked at her when she wasn't looking. Other days I figured she just didn't think about me at all.

Maybe one of these days I'd ask her out on a date. Then she'd think about me every damn day. I'd make sure of it.

Bertie exploded out of the building, like she'd been shot from a cannon, arms flailing, backpack jiggling, hair looking like a bald eagle had nested in it.

"You're late," I said as she skidded to a stop in front of me.

"Uncle Gunner, can you not complain? This heat is killing me."

God this kid was too dramatic and funny for seven years of age.

Once she was safely buckled into her seat in the back of my truck, I took one last look at the school as I rounded the hood.

Cassidy was gone.

It didn't matter, though. No doubt I'd dream about her again and maybe tomorrow I'd ask her out for dinner. It couldn't hurt. Right?

Complicated – Avril Lavigne

CHAPTER 1
Gunner

I leaned against the paddock fence, watching as Songbird nudged her foal with her velvet nose. The mare's eyes caught mine for a moment, deep, knowing eyes that could see every storm in my head. She didn't bolt, even though everything in her probably wanted to protect her baby. She just stood there trusting I wouldn't hurt either of them. I wondered what that kind of faith felt like, to give someone your fear and hope they held it gently.

That was just one of the things I loved about horses. That and how they carried their wildness just beneath the surface yet chose to offer gentleness instead. Like me, I suppose. The need to run free battling against the desire to belong. That need to bond with everyone, for them to like me, yet at the same time, the desire to stay wild and untethered.

Nearby, Ariel, my old horse, grazed lazily under the wide oak tree, her chestnut coat catching the low morning light. She was a good horse, steady, patient, the kind you'd trust with anyone, kids, beginners, even stubborn ranchers like me. There was something about her, though, something fierce and loyal beneath the calm. She'd run through a storm if you asked her to. She was retired now but had been mine since I was eight years old and barely a day went by where I didn't talk to her. She was my constant. My tether to the past.

Watching Songbird and her foal graze, and Ariel just beyond them, a great sense of calm settled over me. No background noise, no mental buzz, just steady breaths and the whisper of the breeze. The sky was heavy with spring storm clouds, the kind that carried more than just rain. It mirrored something in me, unspoken, brewing, waiting to break open.

The usual morning chaos was unfolding in the house, so I'd escaped outside for a little peace. Not that I didn't love the noise, I did, but sometimes, I just needed space to think. Hell, I always needed to think. The subject just varied.

"Hey." Nash's voice sounded behind me as he handed over a coffee. A pink barrette stuck out from his dark hair at an odd angle.

"What the hell?" I gestured at his new accessory.

"Bertie thinks I need a haircut 'stat,'" he said, rolling his eyes.

My ten-year-old niece, Bertie, was sunshine in all our lives, her and her brother, Billy. Bertie lived every day like it was a dance party. Billy was more Yoga Zen, everything done at his own pace, which was great except when you had somewhere to be. I'd lost count of how many times Nash and Lily were late because Billy wouldn't shift out of park.

"How's the foal doing?" Nash leaned against the fence, mirroring my stance.

"She's good. Strong. Always feeding. Almost ready for weaning." I took a sip of the coffee, strong enough to tingle my tastebuds. "Did I tell you I love your wife?"

Nash snorted. "Good coffee?"

"The best." I glanced back at the house. "Breakfast still going on in there?"

Nash exhaled heavily. "About that. I know the noise and chaos isn't ideal."

"Better than the alternative," I said. "Just us three boys and Dad popping in whenever he damn well pleased."

"You mean you enjoy the shouting and chaos."

"Yeah, actually, I do. So don't sweat it."

Truth was, it had been a long time since I'd seen Nash so animated. Before Lily came back, he'd been a shadow of himself. All that promise he had in high school was stripped away after she left. Now, he was the main source of laughter around here. Even the knee he'd busted playing college football was feeling better after another surgery, one we could finally afford after the settlement with Dad. If he'd had the chance back then, he might have made it all the way to the NFL like he'd dreamed.

"But I do worry," Nash continued. "That my kids are ruining your peace."

"Don't. It's better than the silence."

Nash fell silent for a beat. Then: "Got me thinking."

"Breakfast?"

"Breakfast, bathtime, cartoons blasting when you just want to watch Friday Night Football," he said, raising a brow.

I swatted a fly buzzing past.

"I've been thinking about you and Wilder," Nash continued.

Songbird, the mare, wandered over, nuzzling my hand. I pulled a mint from my pocket and fed it to her, scratching her mane as she turned away.

"What about us?"

"You know how much land we have."

I nodded. "Thousands of acres. Why?"

"Enough that we could build a couple of cabins. One for you and Wilder. Maybe even houses."

My heart sank, a lump forming in my throat. Stupid to feel like that because I was twenty-seven, not a kid.

"Do you want us to leave?" I asked. "Does Lily?" A breath caught in my chest. I hated how small the question sounded. Like a kid asking if he'd overstayed his welcome. It made me feel…temporary. Replaceable. Like maybe this ranch might not be home anymore, just land that I worked.

"God, no." Nash clapped a hand on my back, fear in his eyes. It was as if he'd read my mind and he hated what he'd seen. "She doesn't want you to leave. She especially doesn't want Wilder to leave. He's her favorite."

I wanted to believe him. He was my brother, and I knew he loved me. But some part of me was always braced for the door to slam shut. For everything to get ripped away again, like it did when Mom died. Ever since Lily came back, that fear had crept in, whispering that maybe things were too good. That any second now, the other shoe would drop. It was stupid. I knew better. Wilder and I mattered to Nash just as much as he mattered to us and I needed to stop overthinking.

"You want us to leave, then?"

"Absolutely not. I'm thinking of your future. You might get married someday."

"Hmm, not likely." Hookups were more my speed. Less likely to get hurt.

"You never know. Look at me."

At the slam of the house door, we both turned.

"Here we go," Nash said, leaning against the fence.

Bertie stomped toward us, hands on her hips. "Mom said I have to go to school today."

"And you do." Nash looked down at her. "It's Friday."

She squinted up at him. "You grownups always stick together."

"What's with not wanting to go, short stuff?" I ruffled her hair.

"I've grown two inches," she huffed. "And we have math today. I hate it. Plus, Dorcas Gailen gets lonely without me."

Dorcas was her puppy, naturally named after a *Seven Brides* character, just like many other animals around the ranch.

Nash laughed. "Nice try. You still have to go. Uncle Gunner's taking you." He raised a brow. "You still okay to take her?"

"No problem," I said, finishing my coffee. "It's on my way to Clementine.

Need to see Deacon."

"What for?"

"He acquired a retired barrel horse. Wants me to take a look. Thinks it's been mistreated."

"Ask him about that new feed we heard about," Nash said.

"Will do." We watched Bertie race up the porch steps, shouting about the unfairness of life.

"Oh, and just so you know," Nash added as he followed, "Lily packed some cookies and cupcakes that need delivering."

"No problem," I said.

"To Cassidy."

I cursed under my breath as he disappeared inside.

Meddling fucker.

You're So Vain - Carly Simon

CHAPTER 2
Cassidy

Opening my classroom door, the last person I wanted to see was Gunner Miller heading toward me, carrying baked goods. At least he came bearing gifts. Still, Lily Miller would feel my wrath next time I saw her.

"Gunner." I held out my hands for the plastic boxes, but as I went to take them, his fingers grazed mine, lingering a fraction too long. The jolt that zipped up my arm was immediate, stupid, and completely out of line. I snatched the boxes faster than I meant to, causing one to tilt precariously.

"Careful now," he drawled, steadying the top with his thumb. His touch brushed mine again. Brief, but enough to make my pulse lurch.

"Tell Lily thank you, and I'll be calling her." I ground out, my voice tight, my chest even tighter.

"Don't I get a thank you for bringing them?" His tongue flicked slowly over his bottom lip as he folded his arms across his chest, making his biceps strain against his white T-shirt. It shouldn't have made my stomach flip, but it did. And why wasn't he cold? It wasn't exactly balmy outside.

"Thank you, Gunner." My tone was tight, my chest even tighter. Being near him always did that to me. Made breathing harder.

"My pleasure, Cassidy." His gaze skimmed over me. "Looking very demure today."

I knew what he was getting at. He'd mocked my clothes a couple of weeks back, and I'd 'accidentally' spilled a strawberry milkshake all over him. We hadn't crossed paths since, and I preferred it that way.

"I'm thrilled you're satisfied with my attire. Now," I said with a sigh, mirroring his stance, "if that's everything..."

"Not quite." He turned to leave, then swiveled back around. "I forgot something."

"What now?"

His grin was wicked. "That stick up your ass."

I slammed the door harder than I intended once he was gone, instantly regretting the sound echoing down the empty hallway. I leaned my forehead against the wood and closed my eyes. The sound of his laughter lingered behind him. Too smug, too sure. But it was the look he'd had in his eyes that stuck; like he saw something in me that no one else had noticed. That smirk. *Why did I let it get under my skin so easily? And why was his arrogance so annoyingly attractive?*

It had been a long day even before Gunner's ambush. Two of the boys in my class had decided to settle a football argument with their fists during lunch break. In trying to split them up, I took a glancing blow to my side. Not hard, because how much force could a ten-year-old manage? Still, it smarted. And it embarrassed the hell out of me when both boys burst into tears afterward, each blaming himself.

The rest of the day had passed without further drama but now came the next hurdle: parent pick-up.

Jordan's mom showed up, heard what had happened, and grounded him right there on the sidewalk. But Lucas' mom? Nowhere to be seen.

I watched Lucas out of the corner of my eye. He sat on the bench by the lockers, methodically unpacking and repacking his backpack, over and over. *Waiting. Hoping.*

"Everything okay, Lucas?" I asked, keeping my tone casual.

He shrugged but didn't meet my eyes. "Mom said she'd try to come early today."

The way he said 'try', my heart ached.

"I'm sure she just got held up," I said gently.

"Yeah. Work, probably." His voice was small.

"That's a good reason," I said, ruffling his hair lightly. "Want to read for a while until she gets here?"

He nodded, pulling a book from his bag and curling up in the reading corner like it was his own little island.

When Mrs. Keller finally arrived, she barely glanced at me, mumbling something about traffic. Lucas followed her silently out the door.

I exhaled slowly, locking up my classroom and heading to the office for the meeting Mrs. Wright had scheduled.

Mrs. Wright, Silver Peaks Elementary's principal, pinched the bridge of her nose as I finished explaining the fight. "Have you seen any bruises or signs of... anything worrying on Lucas?" she asked.

"No," I said. "We had PE on Monday, I would've noticed. But... his lunches aren't great, sometimes he wears the same clothes all week. And this isn't the first time he's been late getting picked up."

Mrs. Wright sighed. "Any similar issues with Jordan?"

"No. His mom's very involved. She was mortified."

"It's not usual behavior from either of them," she stated.

"No, it isn't. It was just a dumb argument about who the best Bronco ever was," I said, trying to inject some light into the heavy.

Mrs. Wright chuckled. "Who were the contenders?" She opened her drawer and pulled out a Tupperware box of cookies and pushed it toward me. "Gunner dropped them off for me, from Lily."

I bristled. "How kind of him," I ground out. Seemed he'd been quite the girl scout today. "Von Miller and Champ Bailey." Taking a bite of the cookie I'd taken, they were so good I almost forgave Lily for sending Gunner with them.

She laughed. "Please. John Elway. Kids are so naïve."

The laugh burst out of my mouth along with a smattering of cookie crumbs. "God, sorry. I didn't mean to…" Leaning forward I brushed clean the pile of papers on her desk.

"It's fine. Okay," she said, serious again. "Let's call Mrs. Keller in for a formal meeting. See if there's something going on. If we're still concerned afterward, we'll escalate to CPS."

"Agreed," I said.

I stood to leave, but she stopped me.

"Cassidy, you fostered kids, right?"

My chest tightened. "My mom was," I said carefully. "After she passed, I kept the certification active for a while...helped transition some of the kids we were fostering. But I haven't taken a placement ever."

"If it came to it," Mrs. Wright said, "would you consider fostering again? There's a shortage here. If Lucas had to go into care, he'd be sent out of town and then move school."

I swallowed the lump rising in my throat.

"I don't think it'll come to that," I said quickly. "And I'm not sure I could..."

"Just think about it," she said gently.

I nodded, fleeing the office before the pressure building inside me could explode. Before I agreed to something I wasn't sure I wanted.

Outside, the late afternoon air was cool and heavy with the scent of spring rain, and my skin still buzzed from the accidental brush of Gunner's hand when he passed me the cookies. It was nothing. It was barely a second. So why did it feel like he'd let something loose in me?

Trying to ignore the thought, I dug out my phone and called Lily as I walked toward my car.

"Hey, did you get your cookies this morning?" she asked, laughter in her voice.

"Mmm, yeah," I muttered. "Delivered by the spawn of Satan."

She laughed louder. "You two really need to get over yourselves."

"Unlikely." I blew out a long breath. "Can you meet me at Downtown tonight?"

"Tonight? I promised Bertie we'd watch *Singing in the Rain*."

"She's finally moved on from *Seven Brides*?"

"We're expanding her horizons," Lily said. "Why don't you come over instead? Bring wine. Stay over if you want."

"Will he be there?" I asked, knowing the answer already.

"I'm not answering that," she said. "Bring the wine. Wear pajamas. Prepare for Bertie commentary."

She hung up before I could argue.

I smiled despite myself, the heaviness in my chest easing just a little.

Meddlesome woman.

Look What You Made Me Do - Taylor Swift

CHAPTER 3
Cassidy

"**D**inner was great, baby." Nash kissed the top of Lily's head. "You and Cassidy go and have your girl's chat before Singing in The Rain, and we'll clear the dishes."

"Me too, Daddy?" Bertie asked, swinging her legs.

"Did you eat the dinner that your momma made?"

"Yep. And the broccoli and she knows I hate broccoli."

Nash shrugged his broad shoulders. "Then yep, munchkin, you, too."

"Me too, Daddy?" Wilder asked, pouting.

I liked the youngest Miller brother. He was funny and much more carefree than his brothers. They all had this rhythm, teasing, laughing, cleaning up together like they'd rehearsed the dance a thousand times. I was just a guest, watching from the wings, wondering if there'd ever be room on that stage for me. Besides, he was far less obnoxious than Gunner that was for sure.

"You're washing," Nash told his youngest brother.

"We have a dishwasher," Wilder complained.

"Yep and it's called Wilder." Gunner flicked his brother's ear and pushed out of his seat. "Come on Bertie girl, you can help me to wipe, Dad will put it away."

"You have them well trained, Lily."

"I know." She beamed at me and patted my hand. "Get your glass, we'll go and have our chat." As she passed Nash to get another bottle of wine from the refrigerator she patted his ass, gaining a tender smile and a wink for herself. When I looked away I saw that Gunner was watching me. A shiver rolled up my spine as his eyes met mine. I told myself it was distaste, nothing more. But there was no denying how the low lighting created shadows beneath his cheekbones, or how his jaw tensed when he caught me looking. Gunner Miller had mastered the art of looking down his nose at people, especially me, with an aristocratic disdain that somehow made him even more infuriating. "Gladly," I told Lily and followed her out.

"We'll go to the lounge. The boys will want to go into the den to watch football."

The warmer weather still hadn't arrived so there was a log fire roaring, adding to the coziness of the room. I'd never been in there before Lily moved in, but it was clear that a lot of her had been added to the room. Cushions, throws, beautiful black and white photographs of them all, it even smelled like Lily, cookies and lavender.

"Okay," she said, throwing herself onto one of the sofas and pulling her legs up. "Spill the beans, chickie. Or don't you want to tell me that you've finally realized that Gunner is for you?"

Sitting on the other sofa, I reached for a cushion and threw it at her. "Stop with the me and Gunner thing."

"One bad date a million years ago doesn't mean you have to hate each other forever." She winked at me. "Didn't you say it was going great, lots of sexual chemistry until he suggested you couldn't understand country kids because you weren't from Silver Peaks."

Thinking about that still smarted. "He knew nothing about me. Still doesn't. You haven't told him have you?" Lily shook her head. "Because he made assumptions about me, and you know what assume means."

"Yeah, I do." She rolled her eyes. "Make an ass out of you and me. He's a good guy, though, Cass. If you just gave him an opportunity."

I shook my head. "Nope. Anyway, it's not about him. It's about Lucas Keller."

Lily slumped. "Is his mom still not stepping up?"

"She didn't seem to care about him fighting in my classroom today."

"Bertie told me what happened?" Lily shook her head. "That's not like Lucas. He's been here a few times for parties and play dates. Always polite. Was a dream when I taught him."

"Same, but to be honest, it was something and nothing that turned to fists. I got one to the ribs."

"Cassidy!"

I waved her away. "It's fine. It was accidental and I barely felt it, but I didn't tell Mrs. Wright that part so we keep it between ourselves, okay?"

"Are you sure it was accidental?"

"Absolutely. They both burst into tears when they realized what had happened." I couldn't even feel the start of a bruise, so I wasn't concerned. "But I do need to talk to you about the meeting I had with her."

Lily reached for the bottle of wine she'd placed on the floor and filled her glass. She then held the bottle out to me. "Fill up."

Once I'd filled my glass, I settled back and let out an exasperated sigh. "I know I don't talk about my family much, but my mom fostered when I was a kid."

"Wow, really? That's an incredible thing to do."

Thoughts of my mom filled my heart with love, the memories bringing a smile. "I know it was. She did it right up until she died."

The familiar slice of grief cut through me remembering my mom, with her deep raucous laugh and no nonsense attitude. "When she died, Social

Services asked me to keep the kids we had until they could find somewhere else for them. I was only eighteen and was working the farm with just two part-time hands helping me out."

"That's a lot of responsibility, Cass."

"It was. One I didn't want, but," I shrugged, "I ended up loving every minute of it."

"How many kids were there?"

"Three. Meghan aged eleven, Savannah, who was eight and her little brother, Max who was six. It was hard work, difficult at times but so rewarding. Savannah loved Mom so it took her a while to let me in, but we got there, and I loved those kids so much by the end of the six months. We loved each other."

Lily's expression was full of sympathy for me, her eyes shining as she placed a hand over her heart. "That must have been awful, saying goodbye to them."

"It was." Coughing to clear the lump in my throat, I continued. "But I knew it was the best thing for them. And now they're all thriving. Meghan is working as a wedding planner in LA, Savannah is starting college this year, studying finance while Max is doing well in high school." I smiled softly, a familiar sting to my eyes whenever I thought of the kids. "I remember Max crying himself to sleep for the first two weeks after he and Savannah came to us. Mom used to sit outside his door, whispering fairy stories just so he wouldn't feel alone. After she passed I did the same, for as long as he needed. Even though some nights all I wanted to do was cry, too. When I did, it was quiet, so the kids wouldn't hear. I just needed to do it right for them. Be enough for them."

"Did they all get permanent families?" Her tone was hushed like she was waiting for bad news.

"Savannah and Max did but not Meghan. She stayed with a great foster family until she was eighteen and went to college. Savannah and Max were adopted by a lovely middle-aged couple who live on a ranch in Montana. They've had the best life they could have asked for. Four older brothers in their late teens and early twenties who are even more protective than their parents."

"How come you've never told me any of this before?" Lily asked.

"I don't know. It was ten years ago and they're happy. I speak to them every birthday and Christmas and we all have a video call once a year for a catch up."

"So, what happened with Mrs. Wright?"

"She wants me to agree to foster Lucas, Lily. If it's necessary."

"And you don't want to?"

I shrugged. "It isn't that I don't want to, it's just…"

"It hurt letting them go and you don't want the same to happen with Lucas."

There was a good reason why Lily Miller had become my best friend over the last couple of years. She understood me and knew exactly how my brain worked.

"That's it exactly. What if it becomes clear his mom can't take care of him, and I have him for a few months and then goes somewhere more permanent?"

"Do you think things are that bad at home for him?"

"I have no clue. I wouldn't say it's neglect exactly, maybe more apathy on her part. Maybe she's just struggling." The whole thing brought back memories of some of the poor kids that Mom took in. They were in a much worse condition than Lucas.

Lily dropped her feet to the floor and leaned forward, her hands cradling her glass of wine. "One of the things I know about your past is that you left the farm to become a teacher, because you wanted to help kids. Right?" I nodded. "And you taking Lucas in would be helping him. If that's what is needed. Because can you imagine how he'd feel being taken from his mom and sent to live with someone he doesn't know?"

Damn meddlesome woman.

"Ah fuck you, Lily." I shook my head at letting myself be emotionally blackmailed by her. "I'm going to say yes, aren't I?"

She smiled softly and nodded. "Of course you were."

So What – P!nk

CHAPTER 4
Gunner

When I padded into the kitchen at almost three a.m. I hadn't expected to see Cassidy sitting there. Especially not wearing some skimpy little silky shorts and matching top. She was at the table with one foot up on her chair scrolling through her phone. It was dark in there, bar the light from the screen reflected in her glasses, and she was reading a document of some kind. Her chin was resting on her knee while she chewed on her thumbnail.

"Something interesting?" I asked.

She jumped and slapped a hand against her chest. "You scared the life out of me. Sneaking up on me like that."

"I was hardly sneaking. What are you reading, anyway?" Moving past her I went to the refrigerator, casting more light into the room and pulled out the jug of iced water that Lily always kept filled. The cold air mixed with a lingering scent of something light and floral. It was her. Shaking my head of thoughts that shouldn't be there, I closed the refrigerator door.

"Just something for work." She sounded distracted and when I looked back over she was still reading.

"Interesting?"

Her head shot up. "Yes actually," she flashed me a tight smile. "It's all about getting to know country kids so you can be a better teacher."

"Oh, come on, Cassidy, I apologized. I told you I worded it all wrong."

Her eyes narrowed on me as she dropped her leg to the floor and put a finger to her lips. "Hmm, let me think your words were, 'How on earth do you think you can teach country kids when you haven't lived in Silver Peaks?'. That was it, wasn't it?"

Groaning, with my eyes adjusting to the dim light, I pulled two glasses from the cabinet. "Those weren't my exact words Cassidy, and you know they weren't." I poured water into both glasses and slammed one down on the table in front of her. "You should stay hydrated if you're not getting enough sleep, and you and Lily drank two bottles of wine."

"What were your exact words, then," she snapped, turning her phone face down and ignoring the water.

She was so fucking exasperating, why couldn't she just accept that I'd made a clumsy comment, and it wasn't even aimed at her personally. And why the hell couldn't she just drink the water so that I could watch her swallow, watch that delicious neck of hers stretch while she tipped her head back to drink.

"It doesn't matter what my words were, Cassidy," I sighed. "You've clearly made up your mind about me."

Her gaze followed me as I walked around the table to pull out a chair, so when I sat down I made a show of stretching. Wearing only low slung pajama bottoms of course I was going to entice her to look at my body. But the truth was, I didn't need her to look because for some reason I needed her to *see* me the way no one else ever tried to. And damn that was scary, so it was much easier to act like my ego could give a shit. When I scratched one of my abs I heard a sharp inhale. Tiny and quiet as it was, it was there. She'd taken the bait.

"Are you going to tell me the truth now about what you're reading?" I reached across the table and placed a finger on her upturned phone and dragged it closer.

Cassidy slammed a hand on top of mine. "Nothing that would interest you."

"How do you know unless you let me read it." I could easily have shrugged her hand off mine, but I liked having it there. I liked torturing us both.

"Because it's not about horses, cows or hay." Her fingers curled around the edge of my hand. "Let me have my phone back."

Our hands touched, hers warm, mine unsure. The contact was fleeting, but it set something in motion. A flicker of something that wasn't anger or banter. Something far more dangerous. Something that short-circuited my brain. I brushed it away, telling myself it didn't matter but the skin on my hand burned where my gaze lingered.

"No, not until you tell me what you were reading."

"What do you care?"

I shrugged. "Just want to know." Whatever Cassidy was reading didn't matter to me, but the fact she was engrossed in it did. I was curious as to why she'd been so lost in it she hadn't heard me come down the stairs, across the foyer and into the kitchen. Why was I curious? Who the fuck knew. "Oh, and for your information I like more than horses, cows and hay."

Cassidy's tongue darted out and licked along the cupid's bow of her top lip as her nostrils flared a little. After a couple of seconds of staring at me, she removed her hand and sat back in her chair.

"Fine, keep it then."

Scrutinizing her so closely, I saw the goosebumps pebbling on her soft skin. The pale, fine hairs on her arms stood up and I wondered why. It wasn't cold in the house, it was always temperate somehow, which was why I questioned why Lily insisted on having hundreds of throws around the place.

"You cold?" I asked.

"No." She frowned and then instantly looked down at her tits.

That just drew my attention to them and my dick twitched in my sleep pants. It wasn't so much morning wood; it was her. Always her. The way she looked half-furious, half-fierce, like a storm I never saw coming but kept walking into anyway. Whatever it was that had caused my middle-of-the-night stirring, there was enough movement for me to pull my chair closer to the table. My hand was still on her phone, and it was growing warmer under my touch. It was a stupid game I was playing with her, but I liked to push her buttons. Loved the back and forth and the way her earlobes went pink when she was angry. As much as she irritated me, it felt good being in her company because she challenged me in a way no woman ever had before.

I was a Miller brother, and we were popular amongst the girls in town. Seeing as Nash had been off the menu for a long time, even before Lily came back, Wilder and I were never short of company. Girls threw themselves at us, offering us whatever sort of relationship we were willing to have with them. That didn't mean we were disrespectful to them. I, for one, always made it clear that it would never come to anything. Was pretty sure Wilder did, too, yet it didn't seem to matter to them. Cassidy wasn't like that, though, from the moment I'd fucked up on our date got up and walked out we'd barely had a decent conversation since.

"Why are you awake?" She asked me, crossing her arms over her chest.

"I don't always sleep through, especially when I've had too much coffee the night before." I hadn't had coffee; I was irritated by our houseguest. Irritated and horny. But that was another issue I needed to deal with on another day. "What about you? What are you doing awake?"

"Too much going around my head." She took her glasses off and rubbed her eyes. "School stuff before your ego starts to think it might be you."

"Never went there. I don't think anyone has an ego big enough to consider they'd keep you awake at night."

Her lips pursed as her brows pushed together, her body stiff with annoyance. "What does that mean?"

"Whatever you decide, Cassidy," I told her, reaching for my glass of water. "Now I'm going back to bed, I have to be up in a little under three hours."

"You're actually more annoying than I thought," she bit back, watching me stand.

"Shit, really, that's great. My work here is done then." I gave her a two fingered salute. "See you soon, Miss. Turner."

"Not if I see you first."

I chuckled. "You know you've been spending too much time with those kids you teach. That's a fourth grade response if ever I heard one."

As I reached the door I heard a heavy sigh.

"You mean those kids I don't understand?"

"Your words, not mine, Cassidy." I waved a hand over my shoulder. "Night, night, don't let the bed bugs bite."

When I heard her glass slam on the table I smiled, knowing that I wouldn't be the only one tossing and turning.

Since U Been Gone - Kelly Clarkson

CHAPTER 5
Gunner

The gray block road curved past the main house, splitting at the old oak to lead either left to the training paddocks or right toward the winter barn. We'd laid it two years ago, replacing the dirt track that had served us for years. Now our pride and joy - the new indoor training arena - stood where an old machinery shed had been.

Clutching my Stanley mug of coffee, pride swelled at my chest as the sound of horses whinnying blew in on the breeze along with the smell of hay and manure. White fences lined the lush green paddocks where horses grazed and in the distance a day of work was beginning. A couple of the younger ranch hands were brushing the horses, Ariel in her usual spot, leaning into the curry comb like she couldn't get enough of it. She always knew how to sweet-talk the new hires into spoiling her. Others were washing down the stalls, a couple watching the farrier shoe a horse, and I could bet that Charlie, my head stable hand was in the office brewing coffee. I could rely on her for that at least. She'd been off her game a little lately, forgetting to put meetings in the diary, missing issues with horses that I'd expect her to see and then trying to bluff her way out of it. I was beginning to wonder if I'd been too hasty in promoting her when we expanded.

A couple of years back, we extended my horse training and breeding program, investing a whole load of money in it. Money that we'd got back after it had been stolen from us by our dad. I'd expected Nash, as unofficial head of the family, to want to spread it across the whole ranch. He was convinced, though, that horses were the best way for us to move forward and be successful, seeing as the best-bred horses went for millions of dollars. It was my dream, always had been, so I jumped at the chance. Now we had the best facilities in the whole of the state and while it was hard, every day was a joy to come to work.

"Hey, Gun."

I stopped walking and turned to see Nash jogging toward me. "Hey, did I forget something?" I felt my back pocket for my phone and could feel my keys in the front one.

"No, it's about what we talked about yesterday. The houses for you and Wild."

"Okay," I said, frowning. "You desperate to get rid of us?"

Nash laughed. "Fuck no. I mentioned it to Wild and he liked the idea and I'm going into town so thought I'd call at the town council and see whether any permissions are needed even though it's on our land. I wondered if you wanted to come with."

"Sure. What time are you thinking of going?" I looked down the road toward the stables, mentally working out my schedule for the day.

"Three suit you?"

"I can make that work." Nash scratched his stubble. "Have you been out to the far south edge of the land recently?"

"Not for a couple of weeks, when I helped bring the calves in for branding. Why?"

"I went out there yesterday and there's some stakes in the ground, around twenty feet from our boundary."

I frowned. "You think maybe it's the county doing some sort of assessment?"

Nash shrugged. "No idea, but I'm going to ask when we go and visit the council." He started to walk away but then turned back on his heel. "Oh, I've had another idea, too. Thought we could talk about it in more detail later, but what do you think about turning the old hay barn into a wedding venue?"

I looked across the paddock to the old barn that was nestled behind a cluster of trees. It was close to the house and had run into some disrepair since we built a new one about six years ago. "What's given you that idea? Not that I'm saying it's not a good one, because I've been thinking for a while that we should do something with it."

"When Lily and I went to Sweet Maple Falls last week for dinner, we bumped into Rose Anderson."

"Our vet?"

"Yeah. She was having dinner with a friend, a wedding planner, and she was just saying there are a lack of venues around here. On the way home Lily said it was a shame the barn wasn't in better condition as it would be a good revenue earner."

Nodding, I looked back over to the barn. "I agree, but it's in pretty shit condition."

"I know, but we have enough money to spend on making it a top class venue."

"And so, what are you thinking? Asking about permissions when we go into town?"

He shrugged. "May as well. What do you think?"

"I agree. Let's go for it. Spoken to Wilder about it?'

"Mentioned it when I asked about the house, and he said he needed a shit so just do what I thought best."

We both burst out laughing. That was typical of our youngest brother.

Who knew that he could be such a whizz at accounting and wrangling cows!

"Right, I'm going to get to work." I gave my brother a nudge. "I'll see you back at home at three."

He saluted me and then turned back to the house and as I watched him go, I saw Bertie running around with her puppy Dorcas Gailen while Lily looked on with Billy on her hip, and my heart swelled. My brother deserved the good after the years of manipulation from our dad. He'd been the one who'd made Lily leave town and Nash for ten fucking years. All that shit was over now, and Lily had brought so much to all our lives. Satisfied that all was good in life, I turned and went to start my day.

"Charlie, how's things going with Momma's Pride?" I asked, searching on my desk for a packet of gum I knew was there somewhere. When she didn't answer I looked up.

She picked at her bottom lip and sighed. "Dick Hazel keeps calling in and trying to tell me what we should and shouldn't be doing. He was trying to force me to put a saddle on him yesterday."

The anger blew through me like a summer grassfire, heating my veins until it felt like they might set me alight. "Who the fuck does Hazel think he is? I know he's the owner, but for fuck's sake. Why didn't you come and get me?"

"You were in Clementine, at the feed store." Her tone was defensive and spiked concern in me. "I knew Nash was busy interviewing for the new cook."

"What about Wilder? Did you try him?"

"I did, on the radio, but he was on the far west side of the property, and I couldn't contact him."

Her cheeks pinked and I shook my head. My damn brother. If I was guessing right I'd say he'd hooked up with her. If I thought that he'd ignored her radio call on purpose then I'd rip him a new one.

"How did you handle it, then?" I perched on the edge of my desk, watching as she twisted her fingers together. I wasn't a hard boss, I was fair and listened to what my staff had to say, so why the hell did she look so nervous and why did I feel apprehensive. "What did you do, Charlie?"

"He wouldn't stop, Gunner. He was insisting and yelling at me."

Exhaling an infuriated breath, I dug my fingertips into the edge of the desk, gripping it like I might fall off if I didn't. "Did you put a saddle on that horse, Charlie?"

"You have to understand, Gunner it—"

"Don't even try to explain it away. You know how long I've been working with that horse. How damaged he was and how slow I wanted to take it." I pushed off the desk and hung my hands from my hips. "And you've put a saddle on his back when he wasn't ready." Another fortifying breath didn't calm my anger; this was too important for me to brush off as a silly mistake. "You know better, Charlie. You've worked for me long enough to know that when I set out a rehabilitation plan for a horse, it's with good reason. I don't just make them up as I go along."

"I know, and I'm sorry, but God, it was one time." The stubborn jut of her chin told me I wasn't getting through.

"Don't give me attitude, Charlie. That's not how we do things around here, you know that."

"Well, if you'd been here then—"

"No." I pointed a finger at her. "Don't you dare do that. If you think you need me here every second of every day then we have a problem. Maybe that means you're not ready to be my deputy."

"I am, you know I am," she protested. "I work hard, you know I do."

"Everybody on this damn ranch works hard, that doesn't mean they're qualified to handle million dollar horses. Whereas you." I widened my gaze, leaning the top half of my body closer to her. "You are supposed to be, but that's not what I'm getting from this situation, Charlie."

"I did equine management at college, Gunner. You didn't."

Now that made me pissed. I'd taught her everything she damn well knew, because the college had only given her the basics.

"Don't even try with that," I warned her. "I've lived on this ranch all my life and worked with horses since I was seven years old, so don't tell me that a piece of paper from the college makes you more qualified. I respect the work you put in at college. I respect the knowledge you bring to this place, Charlie, because I will always listen to your point of view. I do not respect you going against everything we agreed on for that horse. That plan, that schedule of rehabilitation wasn't written off the top of my head. It was written through years of experience, reading and researching and talking to other trainers. Do you know how hard it is to get Jesse Connor to mentor you? I do and I learned more from that man than twenty years at college will ever teach you."

She bowed her head and looked remorseful enough that I felt my blood pressure lower. "Just go and get Sinbad in the indoor school and check if he's still limping after the heat treatment."

"Fine."

The door slamming made me groan. "Fuck."

Pinching the bridge of my nose, I looked down at the floor, wondering for the hundredth time whether hardwood floors had been the best option. They were scuffed to hell. I hated yelling at people, but this had been something I couldn't let go. Charlie knew how finely tuned our training and rehab programs were. I could only hope it hadn't affected Momma's Pride's progress.

Stewing over the last half hour and how we moved forward, I was startled by a knock on the office door.

"Christ, Charlie, I'm not that mad, just come in," I yelled, walking back around my desk.

The door creaked open and just as I sat down she walked in, and my mouth dropped to the floor.

"Cassidy, what the hell are you doing here?"

We Don't Talk Anymore - Charlie Puth ft. Selena Gomez

CHAPTER 6
Cassidy

What was I doing there? I'd been asking myself that with every step I'd taken from the house to the stables. I'd woken after everyone else, seeing as they all woke at a stupid hour every day. Lily, thankfully, had left me to sleep but once I woke I went back to thinking about Lucas and how I could help him. That was what I was doing there.

"I need your…your expertise," I said, keeping my tone neutral. Professional. This wasn't about us, it was about Lucas.

Gunner straightened, his usual smirk fading into something more thoughtful. "What kind of expertise?"

"Your help. The professional kind." I cleared my throat and forced out, "Please."

He lifted a brow and smirked, making me second guess what the hell I was doing. When he stretched his legs out in front of him and crossed his arms over his chest, the air of superiority and confidence boiled my piss, as my Granny Lizzie used to say.

"You know what, it's fine. I'll ask someone else." I turned to leave but Gunner laughed and that had me turning back around to face him. "What is so funny?"

"You are. Pretending to be all pleasant and polite." He leaned forward. "Just because you want something."

"I can be pleasant, even if I don't want anything."

"Really?" he scoffed. "I'm not sure I've seen that side of you. Ever."

My teeth felt like they might splinter, I was grinding them together so hard. I hadn't worn ugly braces for almost two years in high school to wreck them now. "Well, that's probably because we're not really friends and don't spend much time around each other."

"And the one time we did it didn't end well." He looked at me with a raised eyebrow, like it was my fault he'd insulted me.

"What did you expect when…" Gunner shifted his position, crossing his legs at the ankle and tilting his head to one side. He still didn't think he'd said anything out of turn. Stupid idiot. But I did need his help. "Let's just forget about that. For now," I muttered the last part because I couldn't help it. He boiled my piss more than anyone I'd ever known.

With a stupid smirk, he braced his arms back on his desk, probably to show off his biceps. "Okay, just tell me how I can help."

"I can't go into too much detail, but there's a little boy in my class who I think needs some attention.."

"And you want me to…" He sat forward and rolled his hand, encouraging me to continue.

"I wondered if he could spend some time here. You know, maybe clean out some stables, feed some horses or something. I was reading last night that working with animals can be like therapy. I thought it would be good for him. Seeing as I was here, I thought I might as well just come out and ask you."

He didn't say anything but just looked at me, his gaze pinned to my face and his head still on one side. The silence was deafening, unnerving, his stare heating my veins yet giving me goosebumps at the same time. I felt like I wanted to run but was desperate to stay. I disliked him intensely, yet he fascinated me.

"Okay, if you don't want to help it's fine."

"Never said that, Cassidy." He pushed himself off the edge of the desk and stood in front of me. Inches from me. "Lucas Keller the kid?"

I tipped my head back to look up at him, seeing as he was a good foot taller than me. "How did you know?" How could a man who only seemed to care about horses be so perceptive?

"I know he's in your class and Bertie told me about the fight yesterday. Plus, he's been here a few times, parties and play dates with Bertie and his mom was always late picking him up. One time she didn't turn up at all. I took him home and she was out. The kid had to let himself in."

"And did you tell anyone? Did Lily know?" Anger sparked as I thought about Lucas being home alone. About Gunner knowing and not doing anything about it. "God, Gunner, he's just a little kid. Did you not think that someone should know?"

He blinked slowly and held up a hand. "Do you want to stop right there and listen to what I have to say?"

"Like what?"

"Like I went in with him and stayed for ten minutes until his mom arrived home. I told her it was unacceptable. Knowing he was going to be coming home she should have been there for him."

"And what did she say?"

He worried his jaw and inhaled deeply. "She told me that her boss at the call center she works at in Montrose kept them all behind for an unplanned meeting."

"She works in *Montrose*?" That was almost an hour and a half away. It explained so much.

"She does. And on weekends she works from home for an answering service."

"She has two jobs?" The poor woman, no wonder she never had time for school meetings or events.

"She does. It appears Mr. Keller left them about six months ago. Went off with some woman he met through work. He lives in Montana now." Gunner sighed and moved around his desk and pulled open a drawer. He searched around it until he pulled out a packet of gum. He took a piece and then held it out to me. I shook my head. "Anyway," he continued, throwing the gum back in the drawer, "he sounds like a dick to me. I asked if I could help in some way, but she said it was fine. She's working on finding somewhere in Montrose to live."

He'd offered to help her. Wow, that surprised me, and it made me feel a little strange. In my stomach. Like I'd eaten something bad.

"How would you help her?" The words were out before I could stop them. It was none of my business but the unease in my belly was growing.

Gunner raised an eyebrow as he scratched at the stubble on his chin, an amused twinkle in his eyes. "Not in the way that you're thinking."

"I wasn't thinking anything," I replied too quickly.

"Hmm I'll bet." His tongue licked slowly along his full bottom lip and the unease suddenly felt like something different. Something I didn't want to think about but made me realize that I really needed to get laid soon. It had been too long.

"I was going to offer her a job here. In my office." He swept a hand over his desk. "You can see me and Charlie aren't really ones for admin. Nash and Wilder are always complaining that I take too long to get everything on the computer."

There was a tower of three trays, each one full of paperwork, with more covering the desk.

"You should just do it straightaway." I rolled my eyes. "And who still sends actual paperwork anyway?"

"Ranchers, farmers and old guys who've worked the land for the last forty years."

As he chewed his gum I couldn't stop my gaze from wandering to his

Adam's apple, watching it bob with each chew.

Shaking my head to erase the images threatening to push through, I sighed heavily. "Okay, so about Lucas. Do you think you'd be able to help him?"

"I think I could find work for him to do. I'm sure Nash and Wilder could, too. If things work out with his mom finding a place in Montrose, though, it might not be necessary."

My heart sank. "He's doing so well at school; it would be a shame if he had to move to the city. There might be malls and movie theatres, but there's no mountains, or beautiful landscapes like there is here."

Gunner's expression was one of awe, like I'd just told him the secret of how to find a pot of gold at the end of the rainbow.

"What?" I asked.

"You really do love living here, don't you," he said, shaking his head slowly. "And there was me thinking you townie's hated the great outdoors."

"That would be because you don't really know me, Gunner." I took a step away and looked out of the window, to the lush green paddock beyond the stables with the sliding doors which had been pushed open. I turned back around and gave him a flat smile. "Thanks for telling me about Lucas' mom. I'll let Mrs. Wright know and now we have the full facts we can come up with some ideas."

"No problem. Glad I could be of help and just so you know, I've been trying to figure you out since the second I met you." He pulled the chair out at his desk. "And maybe I'll speak to his mom about that job, that way they won't have to move to Montrose."

As Gunner turned back to his paperwork, I didn't immediately leave. I hovered by the door, watching him work. When he glanced up, our eyes met and held for a moment longer than necessary.

"You know," I said quietly, "I misjudged you."

He set down his pen, giving me his full attention. "Yeah?"

"I thought you were just another arrogant rancher who didn't care about anything but his horses." I shifted my weight, suddenly vulnerable. "But you do care. About Lucas, about his mom, about doing the right thing."

Something shifted in his expression. "And you thought I'd do what, let them struggle?"

"I don't know what I thought." I touched the door handle but didn't turn it. "I'm sorry."

The apology hung between us, and for a moment, neither of us moved. Then Gunner's voice, softer than I'd ever heard it: "We both got it wrong, didn't we?"

I nodded, and my heart stumbled a little as he flashed me a warm smile. I tried to ignore how his eyes crinkled at the corners or how his whole face transformed when he wasn't being a jerk. Why did he have to be so attractive when he was being nice? Being…vulnerable.

"Thank you," I managed to say.

"Don't need to thank me, Cassidy. Just next time maybe get the full picture before you accuse me of not giving a damn about something."

"I didn't say that," I told him as he dropped into his chair. "Did you not just hear me apologize?"

"I did but you only had to because you wanted to hate me so badly, you didn't even stop to notice that I was trying." He swiveled away from me and picked up a pile of papers. "Anyway, I need to get back to work, so…"

Damn it, for a man with a good heart he could be a real douchebag.

Problem – Ariana Grande

CHAPTER 7
Gunner

"Who pissed on your grits?" Nash asked, a stupid grin on his face. "Or do you have a hard on you can't get rid of?"

"No, I do not. My honkers are under control, thank you. It's you, tapping the steering wheel in time to this shit music you're listening to."

His whole body shook as he chuckled and started tapping harder, adding a little hum. We drove like that for another couple of minutes before he leaned forward and turned off the radio.

"Come on little brother, tell me all about it."

As we turned into the town hall parking lot, I remained silent. As Nash parked up I remained silent. When he turned off the ignition and then nudged me, I finally spoke.

"Cassidy."

My brother, the stupid num-chuk, burst out laughing. Loud and deep from his belly.

I turned in my seat to face him. "What's so fucking funny?"

"You and Cassidy. It's about time you both figured out that you're thirsty for each other and just do something about it."

"I'm not thirsty for her," I scoffed.

"In the words of Bertie, liar, liar, panties on fire." He reached for his wallet, tucked in by the windshield. "You could cut the sexual tension with a knife when you're together. So, when the fire goes out on them, pull up your big boy panties and ask her out on a date."

"Hah, no way. You're clearly delirious through lack of sleep." I swung the truck door open. "Stop talking shit and let's get inside."

As I walked across the parking lot, all I could hear was Nash laughing, stupid prick.

The meeting with the town planning office was not going well. It wasn't the issue over building two more houses on our land or converting the barn. Pete McCallister didn't see there being a problem for either, as long as we followed some rules on certain restrictions on size. The barn should be good to go, too, but there were a lot more hurdles to clear on that. We had a much bigger problem. The whole town had a bigger problem.

"They can't just do that, surely." I fisted my hands at my hips, as Nash and I looked down at the plans.

"I know." Calvin Taylor, our town mayor, was breathing heavily as he paced up and down his office.

He'd seen us passing his office on the way out and so called us in.

"I'm only showing you this because phase one backs onto your land. You can't tell anyone about this yet." He looked up at the ceiling and cursed.

"If you didn't agree with this, who did?" I asked.

"Marissa Joseph, the County Mayor. She'll do anything for fucking money, including selling off county land to developers."

"What about the other town mayors? Don't they have a say in it?" Nash asked.

Calvin shook his head. "None of us do. County has the final say. They're reasoning is that the towns are running at loss and are also in disrepair."

"Disrepair!" I cried. "What fucking disrepair? Silver Peaks is immaculate. There's not a bit of litter; every store front is painted and tidy. What the hell are they talking about?"

"Gunner is right." Nash leaned closer to the blueprints and stabbed a finger at it. "What the hell is that going to be?"

Calvin sighed. "A meat packing factory."

"What!" I thought my eyes were going to pop out of my head. "A what now?"

"You heard." Calvin braced his hands on the desk and groaned. "I'm speaking to Ron Matthews and Grace Rogers tonight."

"Do you think we have a chance of getting them to change their mind?" Nash asked.

Calvin shrugged. "We're going to discuss how we do that tomorrow, but wildlife has to be a big factor."

"Fuck yes," I agreed. "If there is any chance that any of it is going to be displaced then this development can't be allowed to happen."

"Gunner is right. This meadow that it's going to butt up against." Nash drew along the border of our line with his finger. "Well, we have weasels in there, right up against the edge of the land. If they build anything there, houses or a meat packing factory that will be really bad for them."

Calvin nodded. "That's something we could use, but that might only stop the building near your land."

"The whole area is full of wildlife," I responded, feeling my gut twist. I loved the land we lived on; it was beautiful. Spectacular. With its jagged peaks that silhouetted the amber sky at sunset, to the dense forests and patchwork of emerald meadows, it had my heart. I didn't think I'd ever be able to live without the silence and peace or the way the soft glow of the moon turned the mountain peaks silver. That was why I would never go to

Montana like Nash seemed to think would have been good for me.

"Then that'll be our main angle. We'll get the state environmental board involved before permits are issued. If we can prove there's protected wildlife or a major water contamination risk, we can force a review." Calvin slapped my shoulder. "I'm sorry guys."

"No problem, we just appreciate the heads up." Nash scrubbed a hand down his face. "And the day seemed like it was going so well."

"What were you doing here, anyway?" Calvin asked.

"Nash is building me and Wilder a house." I grinned at my brother. "He wants us out of his love nest."

"I'm not building them. I'll be getting a contractor, and I do not want you out of my damn love nest as you call it. I told you; it's for your benefit."

Calvin laughed and moved to behind his desk. "Sounds like a great idea. Imagine having your own little *love nest*, Gunner."

"Yeah, Gunner," Nash added. "Your own little love nest that you could take Cassidy to."

"Cassidy, Lily's friend Cassidy?" Calvin wiggled his eyebrows. "I knew it."

"No, you didn't because he's wrong." I pointed at my brother. "And I'm sick of him stirring the pot. There's nothing happening with me and Cassidy."

"I'll ask Bertie when I come for dinner on Tuesday."

Calvin was seeing Ella, Nash's mother-in-law and had been coming around with her for dinner a lot recently. It seemed things were going well between them.

"Short stuff won't tell you anything," I replied. "She's Team Uncle Gunner."

"We'll see about that." Calvin winked and opened a drawer in his desk. He took a card and handed it to Nash. "This guy is a contractor. He built my sister's house in Telluride."

Nash took the card. "Markus Gruber. I think I heard of him."

"You have," I told him. "He was the one who turned Dad down for the refurb on the house."

Nash laughed. "The one who told him it was a fucking travesty to such a beautiful home."

"That's the one."

"He's hired." Nash pocketed the card and held out his hand to Calvin. "Thanks again and see you for dinner next week."

As we walked down Silver Peaks corridors of power, Nash groaned.

"What are we going to do about this development?" I asked him.

"Fight it, Gun. What else can we do? Let them screw up the land with ugly apartment blocks and a meat packing factory?"

"Fuck, no."

"So, we fight." He slapped me on the back. "Now, let's go to Missy May's to get a coffee so you can tell me what's going on with you and Cassidy."

He strode off chuckling to himself, not giving me a chance to reply. Fucking meddlesome dick.

Shake It Off - Taylor Swift

CHAPTER 8
Cassidy

Knowing what I did about Lucas' mom, I felt like I should have gotten the full story before I went to Mrs. Wright. The poor woman was doing a round trip of a hundred and twenty miles every day just to keep food on the table and pay the bills. Not only that she worked weekends. No wonder she had no time for her son.

"Do you think Gunner was serious about offering Ruth Keller a job?" I asked Lily at lunchbreak.

She peered inside her sandwich and frowned. "I was sure I made chicken salad."

"And what have you got?"

"Cheese salad." She shook her head. "I still have a baby brain. And yes, Gunner always keeps his word."

"It would be a shame if he had to move. He's such a quiet, kind, thoughtful boy and a huge city high school might change him."

"I'm not sure it would, but I understand you're thinking." She took a bite of her cheese salad and frowned. "God, I was looking forward to chicken."

"Mrs. Wright said that she's going to call her and get her to come in for a meeting." I picked up a piece of celery and chewed on it.

"Why are you eating that?" Lily asked, "It's practically water and tastes like watery string."

"I didn't go grocery shopping this weekend. I was too distracted."

"By Gunner?"

"No. Not by Gunner, by the Lucas situation. I'm worried about him and his mom." Who was I trying to kid. Of course, I was also distracted by Gunner. Once I left the ranch and went home, I couldn't stop thinking about the job he'd been willing to offer Ruth. He'd done that before I'd even spoken to him about Lucas. He'd figured out for himself that they needed help.

"At least you know that he's not being neglected willfully." Lily threw her sandwich down. "I'm so disappointed that it's not chicken." She brushed the crumbs from her lap and then wiped her hands on a napkin. "I feel bad for her. It must be hard doing it all alone. That journey to Montrose is a trek in itself."

"I know. Lucas is a good kid, but we know that even good kids can be a handful." My gaze turned to the kids all running around enjoying their lunch break. They should all be carefree and happy and that can only come from being made to feel secure at home. Poor Lucas had to be picking up on the strain his mom was feeling.

"You think that maybe we should do more for those we teach?" I asked Lily, my gaze still on the excited children.

"Every day," she replied with a sigh. When I turned to face her she was watching them, too. "When they seem upset when they come into class, when it's clear their parents don't understand the definition of a nutritious lunch, when they're too shy to talk to their peers." Her eyes were bright with compassion and empathy, the reasons why Lily was a great teacher.

"I think I might have an idea."

She frowned. "About what?"

"About how we can give more to the kids."

"Apart from the hours of prep, teaching and marking assignments. We are both supportive, there when they need us to be."

"I know, every teacher in this school does an incredible job, but I think we can do more. Not more as such, but we can offer them something different. Well." I winced. "Gunner can."

Lily busted out a laugh. "Hah, I knew it. You've been thinking about him all weekend."

"No, I haven't. This is about the kids."

"But it involves Gunner?"

I chewed on my bottom lip. "Maybe Nash and Wilder, too."

Lily's eyes narrowed as she moved closer to me. "Go on."

"The ranch. Gunner said that he could give Lucas some stuff to do, and I was reading that horses, well animals in general, can be good for kids. It can help them with trauma and stress."

"I don't think many of the kids we teach are traumatized, though." She patted my hand. "I'm not saying it's not a good idea, though, because it is. In fact, I love it." Sitting back, she looked thoughtful as she pulled her phone from her pocket. "Let me message Nash and get him to organize with Gunner about us all having a conversation."

I watched as her thumbs tapped out a message, a cute little smile played on her lips.

"You're sexting him aren't you?" I tried to grab her phone, but she moved it out of my reach.

"Maybe." She definitely was because a message immediately came back, and she gave a contented little sigh. "All good. Come around tonight and we'll talk it through."

"Just like that?" My chest swelled with gratitude. That 'just like that', after one short conversation, Nash was willing to listen to what I had to say.

I'd not had a lot of dealings with him before Lily came back as I wasn't Bertie's teacher, but I knew he was unapproachable and grumpy. He was a totally different kind of man these days. A happy man.

"Just like that." She giggled. "Although, I did have to promise something in return."

"Ugh," I groaned and threw a stick of celery at her.

***

When I knocked on the door of the ranch house, I half expected Gunner to be the one to open it, just to mess with me. Thankfully it was Wilder.

"Well, if it isn't Miss. Turner." His voice slid over my name like molasses and moonshine. He winked as he opened the door. "Come on in, sunshine. Try not to fall too hard for me. It's a family trait."

"Hey, Wilder, how are you?"

"I think I'm okay, although I'm worried about this meeting that you've requested."

"God, you make it sound so formal." I followed him across the foyer, noticing he had a slight limp. "What happened to you?"

"Sorry?" He asked.

"The limp."

"Oh, you don't want to know."

Without saying anything else, he pushed open the lounge room door to the sound of laughter and the heat from the open fire. Nash and Lily were on one sofa, with Nash massaging her feet which were in his lap. Gunner was on the other sofa, his arms waving around as he regaled some tale about horse manure.

As I walked to the doorway, Lily looked up and smiled. "Cass, hey. Come in, sit down." She waved me in but if I thought she was going to move her legs so I could sit next to her, I was mistaken. "Sit next to Gunner and Wilder will get you a drink."

"Yeah," Wilder said, throwing his hands into the air. "Wilder will get you a drink, even though he's limping. Coffee, sweet tea, coke, OJ?"

I grinned at him. "An OJ would be great."

"Anyone else?" Wilder asked, halfway through the door. "No. Okay. Great."

"Why do we keep him?" Gunner asked.

"Because he's Lily's favorite," Nash said at the same time that Lily chimed in with, "He's my favorite."

"Hey." Gunner gave me a head nod and moved further up the sofa.

I sat as far away from him as I possibly could and turned my gaze on Lily and Nash. He looked at me expectantly, still massaging Lily's feet, while she grinned with one brow raised.

"What?" I asked.

"You said you had an idea and wanted to tell the guys." Lily pulled her foot away from Nash and sat up. "I didn't tell them much, just that it was about the kids at school."

I didn't have a chance to respond because Wilder came back into the room and handed me my drink. He then limped over to the armchair, sat in it and reclined it.

"I can't believe you made me do that seeing as I'm injured," he complained.

"Shouldn't have hooked up with Monique Porter and then told her 'it's not you, it's me'."

Wilder's usual grin faltered. "You can't force feelings that aren't there," he said, and for the first time, there was something hollow in Wilder's voice. Like maybe *he* was tired of pretending he didn't want more. Even if he didn't know what that 'more' looked like yet.

"Which is why you should have made it clear from the start," Gunner said, "At least she doesn't work for us, but you'd be best avoiding The Crafty Corner for a while."

"But Bertie likes it when I take her to buy her crafting stuff," Wilder protested.

"Yeah well," Nash said. "You should have thought about that before you hooked up with the cashier."

I looked over at Wilder and the smirk from before had vanished, replaced with something else. He looked disappointed, like a kid who opened their biggest gift at Christmas only to find it was home knits from Grandma.

"You okay?" Lily asked, clearly seeing the same thing I had.

In an instant Wilder's wistful look was replaced with a cocky smirk.

"Yeah, just remembering how it felt when she stood on my foot with her damn boots on." He groaned dramatically. "I might be maimed for life."

"Here's hoping," Nash muttered. "Now, Cassidy, what can we do for you? Lily said you had an idea about the ranch."

"I must have missed when she became a shareholder," Gunner said, his tone dripping with sarcasm.

I turned my head to see expressive brown eyes staring at me, clearly displaying his dislike for me. "I'm not demanding anything," I told him. "I had an idea and wanted to run it past you. It doesn't mean you have to say yes." I turned in my seat to get a better look at him. "If you must know, you were the one who gave me the idea. You're the one who told me that it was good for kids." I turned my head to Lily. "Did you tell them anything?"

"No honey, it's your idea. I just told them you had one."

"Okay," Nash said, leaning forward, resting his forearms on his thighs. "Tell us all about it."

I took a sip of my orange juice, unsure why I felt so nervous. It wasn't like this had been a dream of mine for a long time, or my future was depending on it, but it was important. The more I'd thought about the kids, the more I'd researched it, the more I'd known it was the right thing to do.

"I've been reading about how working with animals, specifically horses, can help troubled kids." I looked at each of the Miller brothers in turn, trying to gauge their initial reaction, but they simply looked at me with interest. Even Gunner's head was tilted, listening carefully. "We don't have too many troubled kids at our school, I know that, but I feel like we could do more for some of them. Lucas Keller for example. His mom works every hour she can and is probably meeting herself coming backwards trying to keep two jobs going as well as being there for him. And she just can't do it, so I thought that maybe we could set some sort of afterschool or holiday program up, where they come and work on the ranch." I licked my lips, sure that they were going to say no, but carried on regardless. "I'd do all the planning and get all the paperwork sorted, organize health and safety checks. You wouldn't have to do anything."

"Except spend time out of our busy days with these kids," Gunner replied.

Already feeling frustrated, I huffed out a breath. "I should have known it would be you who dismissed it." My stomach clenched at the idea of them hating the idea. Now I had it in my head I didn't want to let it go. Which was typical of me, probably my biggest downfall in life.

"Gunner does have a point, Cassidy," Wilder said from his recliner. "We have a lot going on."

"I know, and I know I'm asking a lot of you all." I looked at each of them. "This is a huge ask, but I think it would be good for the kids of this community. Lucas could be a trial run, if his mom agrees and if it doesn't work out for you then I'll think of another option. Another ranch maybe."

"Aside from Calvin's ranch the only other one close enough would be Brad Jenkins." Nash linked his fingers together between his open legs, looking up at me through his thick lashes. "Aside from the cattle he only has a few horses and pigs, but even so I wouldn't want any kids on a ranch that has the Dupree brothers working there. As for Calvin, well he's cattle only and there wouldn't be much the kids could do other than odd jobs."

"Oh, my goodness," Lily exclaimed, her eyes going wide with excitement. "Ariel would be perfect for the kids."

Gunner groaned, clearly aware of the levels of excitement Lily reached when she liked an idea.

"Lily's right," Wilder added with a smirk with a mutual understanding. "She'd be great. She's calm, she knows when to stand still, and hell, she'd probably teach the kids a thing or two about patience.

"So basically, what you're saying is, you want me to give up my horse and my time," Gunner said with a long sigh.

Breathing in so deeply my nostrils flattened, I turned to him. "Do you practice being so negative all the time, or is it just a natural talent?"

His grin didn't quite reach his eyes. "Pure talent, sweetheart. Some of us are just blessed I guess." He turned away, but not before I caught the flash of something deeper, regret maybe, crossing his face.

My chest tightened. These moments when he let his guard slip were the most dangerous, reminding me of that first date when he'd been different. Before everything went wrong. "Children please stop," Wilder said, adjusting a cushion behind his head. "You're making my ankle ache."

Nash cleared his throat. "Okay, so how big of a thing are we talking, Cassidy? Just a couple of kids, one at a time or bigger groups?"

I grimaced. "Sorry, I haven't thought that far ahead. Maybe Lucas at first but then," I shrugged, "small groups of four or five maybe."

"Hey, you know what," Lily said, excitedly. "Instead of turning the old hay barn into a wedding venue, what about a bunk house for kids. Where they can come and stay for a few weeks and work on the ranch."

"So, we've gone from afterschool club to a mini dude ranch," Gunner scoffed.

"It's better than fucking weddings and bridezilla's," Wilder stated. "Kids are much more fun."

Nash sat back in his seat and slapped his hands on his thighs. "I don't think we can say yes or no yet," he said. "Let us have a think about it, but I must admit, I like the idea."

"You do?" Gunner sounded surprised.

"We turned out okay living here and we had Dad as our dad." Nash raised an amused brow. "Bertie and Billy are thriving living on this ranch. It would be good to let other kids have that."

"I thought you wanted to make more money?"

"I do, Gun, and I think we could make money from that, too." Lily gave a little gasp and Nash slowly turned to face her, an amused smile on his face. "I'm not all soft and squidgy, Lila, I'm a businessman as well."

She rolled her eyes and leaned in to kiss his cheek. "Okay, but I like the soft and squidgy best."

Them thinking about it was the best that I could hope for, and I was more than grateful for that.

"Right." I placed my glass on the coffee table, mind already racing with plans despite their noncommittal response. "Thank you for listening."

"Hah, like we have a choice when you're talking," Gunner murmured loud enough for me to hear.

I chose to ignore him and stood up. Nash did too. "I'll see you out, Cass."

"Bye honey." Lily gave me a finger wave. "I'll see you tomorrow."

When we got to the door, Nash didn't open it straight away. Instead, he turned to me.

"I think it's a great idea, we just need to talk it through first." He leaned in and kissed my cheek. "You're a good person to want to do this."

I shook my head. "No, you will be if you agree."

Nash chuckled and opened the door. "Gunner is the one who'll be giving up most of his time, so I think you could say he's the good guy."

I didn't say anything but got in my car and drove away, because I wasn't sure I could disagree.

Need You Now – Lady A

CHAPTER 9
Gunner

The morning after Cassidy's visit, light snow fell outside landing on the thin layer that had fallen through the night. It was the tail end of the snow season, but we often got flurries, or the odd snowstorm, before the month was out. The weather didn't stop us working, though, which was why we were grabbing a few minutes before breakfast to talk about ranch business.

Nash leaned forward in our father's overpriced leather chair in the home office. "What are you thinking about the kid's project?"

Wilder swiveled around on the visitors chair like a nine year old, while

I leaned against the windowsill.

"Do we get a choice?" I asked, grinning. "Lily loves the idea, and you love Lily, so…"

The smug bastard smiled like the cat who got the cream and clearly he'd got something the night before, if the giggles and banging of the damn headboard was anything to go by. No grown man should have to listen to that.

"You know what, I think I like the idea of us having a house each," I told him.

His brow furrowed. "Okay, but what about the project? Contrary to what you think, it's ultimately your decision."

"Oh great, make me the bad guy who says no."

Wilder laughed and did another three-sixty on his chair. "You can't say no to Cassidy any more than he can say no to Lily."

"I can say no to her," I scoffed. "I can say a lot of things to her, none that she actually likes."

"You two should just fuck and be done with it," Wilder suggested. He pointed a finger at Nash. "I think I told you the same about Lily and look how right I was."

Thinking about fucking Cassidy momentarily increased my pulse, until I remembered you had to ultimately like someone to have sex with them.

"Unless you really don't like her and then maybe I could—"

"Don't finish that fucking sentence," I told him, my chest clenching tight. "The point is if I say no then I'm going to be the one breaking those kid's hearts."

"They have to know about it for you to break their hearts, Gun." Nash slapped a hand on the desk. "I like the idea, a little more than the wedding venue one. It'll probably take just as many hurdles to jump, if not more, and may cost us more money to set up, but it's a good idea and will make us some bank."

"Why not do both?" Wilder suggested. "Limit the kid's ranch to certain dates and build some bunk houses for the kids instead of using the barn. I mean we don't really have to limit the dates for the kids, but it'd just be more work to have the two run at the same time."

"I looked into it some more last night," Nash said, clicking on his Mac and bringing a saved search up on the screen.

"What, you had time with all that sex?" I asked wryly.

"When you get the same stamina that I have you'll understand, Gun. Now," he said, reading the screen. "If we do a kid's camp, ranch, whatever you want to call it we can get a little funding. Either a government youth grant or a supply grant from local business'. Lily said that Cassidy mentioned something about crowd funding as it's going to be helping local kids as well as out of towners."

"So, most of our cash will go to the wedding venue?" Wilder asked.

"If we do as you suggest and do both. The friend of Rose's who I was talking to, the event planner, said we just have to provide the venue and the appropriate safety certificates. Staff, decoration, tables, chairs and so on would all be down to her as she has a regular supplier."

"So, the renovation and upkeep of the bar is it?"

"Yep, Gun. And then we get a fee each time she uses us. Although, I think we'll have to add a kitchen, but I also had an idea about that."

"Wow," I said blinking slowly, "you had a real busy night, didn't you?"

Nash just smirked and folded his arms. "The bunk house kitchen is basic at best. Especially since we expanded the bunk house and we're employing Ruby as cook."

"Okay," Wilder replied, finally stopping swiveling. "And your idea is?"

"We build a kitchen big enough for both Ruby and outside caterers to use. If we build it in the east pasture, it's equal distance between the bunk house and the barn. There's no room to add it on to the bunk house so it would be a good resolution. The current one, inside the bunk house, could be made into a dining area or lounge area."

"They're ranchmen, Nash," I mocked. "Not sorority girls."

"And some of them are living away from home months at a time, so let's give them a little comfort."

"Nash is right," Wilder agreed. "They should have decent facilities."

I knew they were right, but I was feeling grumpy as fuck. Listening to your brother bang his wife while you struggled to get a certain woman out of your head, did that to you.

"We can think about that more once we decide about the kids camp."

"Nash," I replied. "Why are we even thinking about it? As much as I hate agreeing with anything that woman says, it's a great idea. I'd love to share my love of horses with kids, teach them what magnificent animals they are. It'll be good for us and them." I shrugged. "We'll need more stable hands and maybe some ranch hands." Over the last couple of years, we'd doubled our workforce, but it still wouldn't be enough. "We'll need help in the office, too, although I have someone in mind for that. But we can talk about that later down the line."

"So, we agree with the kid's camp then?" We both nodded at Nash who then sighed. "Good. Now we have to talk about the land development and what we do about it."

The idea of people building a factory and businesses, not to mention ugly apartment blocks, made me feel sick. This land was beautiful, a patchwork of jewel colors, from the land to the sky, we didn't need the ugly stitches of grey concrete marring its beauty.

"We have to do whatever we can to stop it." I pushed off the windowsill and paced across the office, stopping in front of Nash. "I can't believe the County let this happen."

"Me neither, but according to Calvin they're determined to push it through as fast as possible. He's trying to find out who is buying the land so we can get a meeting with them. The three mayors are meeting tonight to talk about the next steps."

"Well, let's hope we can stop the bastards. Now, anything else?" I growled. "Because I have things to do."

Nash clicked on the mouse and changed what was on his screen. I groaned inwardly at the sight of our quarterly report. "Do we have to?"

"I'll be quick." My big brother smirked and highlighted a row of figures. "Training program's up thirty percent from last year. Your reputation's growing, Gun."

"Yeah, but so are our costs." I tapped the screen on the section that said, 'Feed Supplier'. "Price of oats has doubled since spring. We need either more clients or higher rates."

"Or both," Nash said. "Especially with this development threat looming.

We can't afford to look vulnerable right now."

"Which is why my idea of the Kids ranch, and the wedding venue is the best." Wilder cocked an eyebrow. "You can thank me later."

"Whatever." I turned to Nash. "Can I go now and leave you with Business Brain of the year?"

"Bye, bye, Gunner," Wilder said and gave me a finger wave on his way to another three-sixty turn.

***

My day had really gone to shit and lack of sleep was the least of my worries. I'd tried to do some work with Momma's Pride in the indoor school. It was the horse that Charlie had messed up with and the fact she had messed up meant that the whole session had gone badly. As soon as I'd gone near him, he'd bucked and kicked, stressing himself out until he was frothing at the mouth. He'd gone back weeks in his progression. Weeks that I didn't have the time for and certainly wouldn't have the money because I doubted Dick Hazel would pay. Fucking dick by name and dick by nature.

When I got to the stables, I looked inside but couldn't see who I was looking for.

"Bailey," I yelled down to one of the hands who was brushing down one of the ranch horses. "Where's Charlie?"

"Not sure, but Soloman turned up as he had a spare afternoon, so maybe she's with him."

I didn't answer but stormed over to the pool, our latest addition to the facilities. Soloman, a qualified equine hydro therapist, came in twice a month to work with the horses. Charlie was fascinated by it and spent any time she could over there.

Pulling the door open so hard I almost yanked it from its hinges, I tried to get my anger under control. I didn't want to spook the horse in the water being massaged by Soloman after its swim.

Charlie was where I expected her to be, standing on the parapet leaning against the rail and watching. Her head turned as I approached, and she flashed me a tentative smile. I hadn't stayed mad at her over the saddle incident, but it didn't mean I'd forgotten it. Charlie was fully aware that I'd been disappointed and had kept her distance, limiting her time in the office with me. She had still brewed the coffee every morning at least.

"Hi, I've just been watching," she said, her eyes going back to the pool. "Soloman said that Chipper is doing really well, getting the muscle back."

"Good." My jaw tensed as I looked over at the water. "Have you got a minute?"

Not waiting for a response, I turned and stalked out of the pool and across the yard to my office. I knew Charlie was following because I could hear her boots on the concrete, quick steps desperately trying to keep up with mine. Flying into the office, I strode into the middle of the room, stopping in the space between our two desks. My hands went to my hips, and I stared up at the ceiling, still unsure of how much anger I was going to unleash. When the door opened again and Charlie stepped inside I wondered if I should have left it until the following day, but it was too late.

"What's wrong?"

Inhaling slowly, I turned to her and silently counted to ten. "You need to let Dick Hazel know that he's going to have to pay for another couple of months of rehab for Momma's Pride."

"Sorry? What do you mean?"

"What I said, Charlie. He needs another couple of months of rehab and you're going to have to let Dick know." I tensed as I looked at her. There was a curl to her top lip and an aggressive jut to her chin.

"That's not my job. That's yours."

"I'm your boss. You went against my wishes for that horse. He now needs further rehab, so I'm telling you that it's your job to tell the owner."

She folded her arms and the lip curl became a full on snarl. Instantly the frosty atmosphere in the room dropped to freezing.

"I said I was sorry. I told you that he was hassling me."

"And he doesn't pay your salary, I do. Of which I think I pay you very well."

"Debatable."

Oh no, she was not going there. "I pay you a damn good salary and you know it. You have the use of a ranch truck, which is serviced regularly so I know you're safe driving to town or to and from ranch business and you get health insurance. So, do not come at me with that one, Charlie because I will win every time."

"Okay, but he—"

"We talked about this a few days ago, I'm not raking over the dead embers of it again. Because that horse had a saddle put on him before he was ready, his rehabilitation has not only stalled but gone backward. That means I need to keep him here longer. Therefore, I want you to call Mr. Hazel and tell him that and how much he needs to pay for another two months board and rehab." I took a beat, realizing I was on the verge of raising my voice and I'd been determined not to do that. "Alternatively, he can keep him at his own place and horse box him in every day. Up to him."

"Why am I getting the blame for this?" she argued. "He was the one who insisted."

I shook my head. "Like I said, we discussed it and now we have to face the consequences." My phone started to buzz in my pocket, but I ignored it. This was more important, plus whoever was on the other end of the phone probably didn't deserve the results of my anger. "Before you call him I need you to check on Momma's Pride and make sure he's okay. It's taken me almost an hour to get him in his stall and calm."

"What happened? What did you do?" she said in an accusatory tone that got my spine going straight as a rod.

"What I did was put a light hand on his back. Something even the skittish of horses should be able to withstand. Now, seeing as only last week he would take a blanket, I don't think a hand is too much to ask. Unless of course he's had a saddle on his back. A saddle that he's not ready for." My chest was rising and falling so fast I was either on the brink of a heart attack or full on rage. Either one was unwelcome. "Just go and see to the horse, Charlie and then call Dick Hazel." She opened her mouth to argue but I'd had enough. "Now, before I say something I might regret." Like fire her damn ass.

She didn't second guess what that might be because she scuttled out of there like a rat up a drainage pipe. As soon as the door closed behind her, I was able to let out a breath. Things between us would not be good after this, because now I couldn't trust her and that did not bode well for my business.

Maybe a bunch of kids would be a damn sight easier, then I realized that would mean seeing more of Cassidy and I wasn't sure I could handle that either.

Fighter – Christina Aguilera

CHAPTER 10
Cassidy

"Lucas, honey, honestly you're not going to get into trouble." Pain twisted in my chest as his little body shook with sobs.

"But we're going to see Miss Wright." Tears dripped off the end of his chin, soaking into the gray—should-be-white—shirt he wore.

"We are, honey, but only because we're worried about you."

Two things had made the emergency meeting a necessity. First, Lucas had no lunch and no money on his lunch card. He tried to hide in the boy's bathroom, but Bertie had tattled. How she knew, I didn't want to know, but I was grateful she did. Then, while I taught the class about Henry VIII and his unfortunate wives, Lucas had fallen asleep, his head lolling on the desk, soft snores drawing giggles from the others.

"Be quiet," Bertie had hissed at them. "He's tired." Bless her sweet heart.

When Lucas's mom called to say she'd be late picking him up again, Mrs. Wright decided it was time for a meeting.

"Is my mom in trouble?" Lucas whispered as I led him along the corridor.

"No, sweetheart. We just want to make sure she's okay and that you're okay too."

He looked up at me, brown eyes swimming, chin trembling. It was almost too much to bear. I chewed the inside of my cheek, wondering if I'd have chosen teaching had I known how often it would bruise my heart.

When we got to Mrs. Wright's door, it was already open. She smiled warmly and waved us in.

"Hello, Lucas. Come on in." She patted one of the visitor chairs. "I think I've got some cookies in my drawer. Would you like one?"

Lucas shot me a cautious look. I shrugged. "If you don't think it'll spoil your dinner."

He accepted a cookie with tentative fingers and nibbled at the edge. As he swung his legs under the chair, his gaze traveled around the room; certificates on the walls, a vase of tired flowers, a couple of softball trophies gathering dust.

"She's five minutes away," Mrs. Wright mouthed to me over Lucas's head.

I nodded and took the seat beside him, offering a reassuring smile when he glanced up.

"Another?" Mrs. Wright asked, rattling the packet.

He shook his head solemnly. "I'm good, thank you."

The silence was thickening awkwardly when Ruth Keller practically ran into the room, breathless.

"I'm so sorry, the traffic was awful." She dropped to her knees in front of Lucas, hugging him tight. "Are you okay?"

"Yes, Mom. I'm good." A small smile bloomed on his face, and it was obvious that love wasn't the thing lacking in Lucas's life.

"Mrs. Keller, please take a seat," Mrs. Wright said, her tone calm and kind.

Ruth sat down and smoothed Lucas's hair, her other hand wringing in her lap. "Is this about me being late again?"

"It is," Mrs. Wright said gently, "but it's also about a couple of things that happened today."

Ruth's gaze sharpened, darting to her son. "You didn't get into a fight again, did you?"

"No, Momma. I promised I wouldn't." His sincerity nearly broke me.

"Lucas." Mrs. Wright tapped his knee. "Why don't you go down to the cafeteria? I believe Miss Goody has some mac n' cheese that needs a brave taste-tester."

Lucas lit up. "Can I, Mom? It's my favorite!"

Ruth looked stricken. "I have food at home—"

"We know," I said quickly. "But Miss Goody's very nervous about her recipe. She'll be grateful for his opinion."

"Okay, sweetie," Ruth said with a watery smile. "And use your manners, please."

He bolted from the room so fast, he nearly left a vapor trail behind him.

Mrs. Wright clapped her hands lightly. "Right. Let's talk about how we can help you and Lucas."

"I know I've been tardy," Ruth said, twisting her hands. "My job's in Montrose, and sometimes the traffic, or my boss keeping me late…"

"We're not judging," I said softly. "We just want to help."

"What happened today?" she asked, her voice cracking.

Mrs. Wright nodded for me to continue.

"He had no lunch money, and he tried to hide in the boys' bathroom."

Ruth gasped, her hand flying to her mouth. "I thought he had money on his card. That was why I didn't worry about giving him some lunch."

"And later, he fell asleep in class," I added gently.

Shame and worry chased across her features. "I worked extra hours at my second job last night. I didn't get a minute to check he was asleep." She drew in a ragged breath. "I'm such a terrible mom."

"No, Ruth, you're not."

"You're doing your best," Mrs. Wright reassured her, reaching over to squeeze her hand. "But it's clear you're struggling."

"And the general state of his clothes…" she added carefully.

Ruth sagged in her chair. "My washer broke. And the cost of gas alone eats up any extra."

God, the poor woman was drowning and dragging Lucas with her.

"We just want to figure out a way forward," Mrs. Wright said kindly.

Footsteps echoed in the hall before there was a familiar voice: "Knock knock."

I turned, and there he was. Gunner Miller, leaning against the doorframe like he was posing for the cover of some Wild West heartthrob calendar. His hair was damp, his biceps straining the sleeves of a faded Wrangler tee, and, of course, no jacket.

Mrs. Wright all but fluttered her eyelashes. "Mr. Miller, we're in a meeting."

"Yep. Know that. Bertie told me." He pushed off the frame and sauntered in, hands tucked into the pockets of his worn jeans.

"How did Bertie know?" I asked, folding my arms, trying to armor up against the sight of him.

He gave me a lazy grin. "How does Bertie know anything?"

"Hey, Ruthie," he said warmly, tipping an imaginary hat. "Good to see you."

Mrs. Wright blinked. "How can we help you?"

"I came to offer Ruthie a job," he said casually, like offering salvation was just a thing he did on Wednesdays.

My eyes flew to Ruth, who was already shaking her head.

"Gunner, I can't. I'm moving to Montrose."

"That's the beauty of it, Ruthie." He rocked back on his heels. "You won't have to."

"But the pay—"

"You don't know what I'm offering yet."

"Gunner," I cut in, unable to stop myself. "We appreciate it, but—"

He glanced at me, his blue eyes sparkling with something I couldn't quite name. "Maybe you should hear the offer first."

There was a hard thud against my ribs.

He turned back to Ruth. "Come out to the ranch after this. Bring Lucas. We'll have dinner, and I'll lay it all out for you."

She opened her mouth to protest, but he barreled on.

"It's a good, steady job. Use of a ranch truck and gas. Health insurance. A salary you'll like. And…" He flicked a glance at me. "There are two new projects in the works that I think you'll be excited about. Isn't that right, Miss. Turner."

My pulse quickened. Was he talking about—

"I'll let y'all get back to it." Gunner clapped his hands together and backed toward the door. "Just wanted to throw my hat in. Pleasure seeing you ladies."

He winked as he left, whistling some cheery, irritating tune that somehow still made my knees a little wobbly.

Mrs. Wright looked like she was about to swoon. Ruth was crying quietly. Me? I was torn between wanting to hug Gunner…and wanting to kick him in the shin.

"I'll be right back," I said, pushing up from my chair before I could change my mind.

I caught him just as he reached the front entrance.

"Gunner!"

He turned smoothly, arms open. "Well, hey there, Cassidy. Couldn't stay away, huh?"

God, that grin. Somebody should outlaw it.

"I just wanted to thank you," I said stiffly. "For what you did for Ruth."

He shrugged; all easy charm. "Nothing to thank me for. I just threw a rope. She's the one who's got to grab it."

"And the somethings?" I narrowed my eyes.

His mouth curved wickedly. He leaned down, tapping my nose with his finger. "Nosey, nosey."

"I'm sure Last Creek Ranch isn't my business, but I was wondering…"

"If it might be your kid's club."

"It's a little more than a kid's club."

I scowled. He chuckled.

"Maybe, but like you said The Last Creek Ranch *isn't* your business," he said softly. "*Yet.*"

Before I could demand he explain, he gave me a salute and sauntered out the door, the fading whistle of the stupid tune behind him.

Damn him. Damn him for being the most aggravating, swoon-worthy man I'd ever met.

And damn those jeans for making me forget which one mattered more.

Hot N Cold - Katy Perry

CHAPTER 11
Cassidy

As I walked back to my classroom after the meeting, Gunner's casual kindness troubled me. The way he'd sauntered in to help Ruth without any fanfare or expectation. It wasn't the actions of the man I thought I knew. The man who pissed me off royally that night three years ago.

Standing at my desk, packing my stuff away, the memory hit me with unexpected force.

Three Years Earlier

"You really don't understand what these kids need, do you?"

The words sliced into me like a knife, changing the atmosphere of what had been a surprisingly great first date into something else entirely. Something sharp-edged and tense.

I set my glass down, taking a breath to calm my anger, feeling the heat rising in my cheeks. "I think I understand exactly what they need. That's why I became a teacher."

Gunner's jaw clenched tight. "A teacher who wants to change everything about how we do things here." He leaned back in his chair, the easy charm of earlier replaced by something harder. The patio lights of Downtown cast shadows across his face, making him look like a stranger. "These kids don't need your fancy city ideas. They need to understand the land, their heritage."

"Who said that I was trying to change everything?" I gripped the arms of the chair, afraid if I didn't I might throw my drink in his face.

"You're not teaching them about their heritage."

"Bringing in new teaching techniques and organizing a few trips to the City isn't going to change them. And that isn't all I'd like to do, I'd like to—"

He cut me off with a dismissive wave. "You can't change everything that makes this place special." He scoffed. "But then you wouldn't know that would you, being an out of towner."

He had no idea because I'd grown up much like these kids - early mornings helping with chores, learning to drive a tractor before a car, understanding that the rhythms of farm life waited for no one. But he hadn't bothered to ask about my background. I guess he'd just assumed when I said I'd lived in Bloomington that was where I was brought up. It wasn't, it was where I went to college. I'd lived on a farm in a small town nine miles from Durango with a close community. Well, I wasn't going to tell him.

My veins heated with anger. "Not that you'd care, but I was trying to tell you that I want to blend traditional knowledge with modern opportunities," I'd said, my voice tight. "Give these kids every possible advantage while honoring their way of life."

"By teaching them that your big city vision is better and that they need to change?" His laugh was cold. "That what they know, what their parents know, isn't good enough anymore?"

"That's not what I—"

"Listen, I'm sure your ideas work great in the city." He threw enough cash on the table to cover both our meals. "But out here? We don't need fixing."

I watched him walk away, my half-eaten dessert growing warm in the summer heat. It wasn't just his dismissal of my ideas that stung, it was his complete refusal to even hear them. To see me as anything more than some city teacher with grand plans to 'fix' his world.

Present Day

The janitor's footsteps in the hallway brought me back to the present and the fact that three years later he was championing a program that wasn't so different from what I'd suggested that night. The same man who'd dismissed my 'city ideas' was offering jobs and opportunities to help local kids.

Closing up my purse, my gaze caught on the artwork my students had made. The pictures were all about what they loved about their present and what they wanted for the future. Every single one, bar none, had illustrated Silver Peaks in some way alongside pictures of veterinarians, teachers, ranchers, astronauts. It was proof that the kids didn't see any contradiction in loving where they came from and wanting more. They understood something Gunner hadn't that night.

Maybe he did now and that was what made it and him all so confusing.

Slow Hands – Niall Horan

CHAPTER 12
Gunner

The contract in Ruthie's hands was shaking as she read it for what seemed like the tenth time. Each time she finished, she looked up at me with watery, moss green eyes and took a deep breath. Her hand went to her chest, and she clutched the sweater she was wearing.

"Are you okay, Ruth?" Nash asked.

Her gaze raised to his and she licked her lips. "This is the same salary as I'm already getting," she announced.

Wilder nodded. "Same salary but no travel, the use of a ranch vehicle, health benefits and as much beef as you can fit in your freezer."

"It's too generous."

I laughed. "You have no idea how much work there is yet. I'm not the best at paperwork."

"He's not wrong," Nash added.

We were in the study, while Lily took the kids over to the stables to see Bertie's new pony, Caleb Pontipee—we were all hoping Bertie ran out of Seven Brides for Seven Brothers characters soon. None of us had ever pushed her, but she'd finally decided that she wanted to learn to ride so her daddy tasked me with buying her the horse best suited for her. He was a gentle soul, patient and well-behaved under instruction. He could also run like he had the devil at his heels, not unlike my niece, so they were the perfect match. Ruthie had chatted animatedly during dinner, mainly to Lily, but it was obvious she wondered why she was there. Everything told me she was going to refuse the job offer, but looking at her now, I wondered if I'd been mistaken. Her eyes were on the contract again but this time a huge smile stretched her lips.

"Are you sure?"

Nash lowered his head to look up at her through her hair hanging down in front of her face. "Hey, Ruth, we wouldn't have offered it if we weren't sure."

"There's a lot of new stuff going on down here soon, too." Wilder slapped the desk. "Exciting stuff."

"Once it's finalized," I warned. "There's a lot to be decided yet."

Ruthie's head shot up. "Does that mean you won't need me if it doesn't happen?"

"God no." I patted her hand. "We desperately need you, honestly."

"What are the plans?" She looked at each of us in turn. "Can I ask? If I'm going to be working here..."

"Part of your job would involve helping coordinate this new project we're planning." Nash pointed at me. "You tell her, it's going to be your rodeo brother."

"A rodeo?" Ruthie blinked rapidly. "I don't know anything about rodeos."

Chuckling, I shook my head. "No, it's not a rodeo. It's a kid's camp, after school, school breaks and so on. In fact, it was Cassidy, Miss. Turner's idea."

"It was?" Swallowing, she looked out of the window where Lily and the kids were walking back to the house in the dimming light of the early evening, their breaths misting in the cold. "She's been good for Lucas. Not that Lily wasn't. She was too."

Nash laughed. "It's fine, I know how great my wife is."

"It was yours and Lucas' situation that gave her the idea." Something started to build in my chest and my stomach felt weird.

"What do you mean?" she asked.

"You having to work such a distance and Lucas having to wait at school." Her bottom lip trembled as she swallowed. "She wanted to help you." That feeling in my chest grew as I continued telling Ruthie about the kid's camp. "Her idea was that we become a place that the kids can come to and work with the horses. Like therapy as well as teaching them things, giving them an experience of working."

"We haven't discussed the finer points yet," Nash added. "We need to speak to Cassidy about what her vision of it is, but it's going to happen seeing as Gunner is on board."

I respected that it had been ultimately my decision, but it had felt like I was carrying a big weight. Thinking it through, though, it had been a no brainer. How could I not want to help kids out while doing a job I love.

"But we would like you to start working here as soon as you can." The mounds of paperwork on my desk was a clear sign of that.

"The camp sounds amazing," Ruthie replied, wrapping her arms around her middle. "I just feel bad that Miss. Turner was worried about Lucas enough to create something like this. A good mother shouldn't need help like that." Her voice cracked. "But I'm grateful. So grateful. It's just... you work so hard to give your kids everything, and sometimes it feels like you're just failing them anyway."

"And that's why we want to set up the camp," Nash said softly. "Because life is damn hard for parents, no matter how hard you try."

"The camp will be great, and Lucas will benefit from it along with a whole other bunch of kids," Wilder added. "Cassidy had a great idea."

It was then that I realized what the feeling in my stomach was. Pride. And it wasn't for me it was for the woman who incensed me more than any other had or probably ever would. The same woman whose ideas about mixing tradition with progress I'd once dismissed so easily. Looking around the ranch now, I could see exactly what she'd meant that night - this wasn't about changing our way of life, but about sharing it. About giving kids like Lucas both roots and wings.

***

As the horse trotted around the schooling ring, I watched his form carefully. "He's still got a limp," I told Charlie.

She was watching from her perch on top of the fence and taking a video. "It's only slight"

"Yeah, but it's still there." I blew out a frustrated breath. "I think maybe we have to up the hydrotherapy. Can you ask Soloman if he can come next week? I know he's not scheduled, but I think it would help."

"Really? Not call Rose instead?"

I shook my head. "Nah. I don't think it's anything too serious that a little more time in the water won't solve." I guided him around another loop of the ring and was confident that I was right. He was limping because he was afraid to put his foot down. Soloman would encourage him, with a massage, that it was fine.

"Want me to call her anyway?"

My head whipped in her direction. "No," I snapped. "Contact Soloman."

"Rose is the best vet in three counties," Charlie pushed, a challenge in her voice. "Unless you're avoiding her for some reason?"

The insinuation in her tone made my jaw clench. Charlie had been hinting at things she knew nothing about ever since the Momma's Pride incident. "The horse needs hydrotherapy, not a vet. Take him back to his stall and call Soloman."

She had the nerve to sigh but I chose to ignore it. Her attitude since the argument about Momma's Pride was getting worse by the day, and I was starting to wonder if there was more behind it than her own wounded pride.

Charlie walked over to me and grabbed the lead rope from me without saying a word. For a second I almost told her to change her attitude, but I didn't have the energy for a fight. Plus, I needed to meet Wilder and Nash. Charlie was a battle that I'd fight another day.

The ground was hard underfoot as I walked toward my brothers. They were laughing loudly, and it made my chest burn. Nash had been sad for so long until Lily came home and now he never stopped smiling. It was all I'd ever wanted for him to be happy and now he was. I wondered if I'd ever want what he had or whether I'd always be happier with my horses.

"What's got you two giggling like toddlers?" I asked, pushing my hands into the pockets of my denim jacket. "And why are you dressed like it's the middle of winter?" They were both wearing thick Shearling jackets with gloves, Wilder wearing a wool cap and Nash his usual ball cap.

"Because it's fucking cold." Wilder clapped his hands together. "We can't all be warm blooded like you."

"Warm blooded, incredible personality, huge dick, I'm just the gift that keeps on giving." I did a full three-sixty. "So, is there where we're going to build our houses?"

"It's just one of the options," Wilder said.

"Wild thought here because it's closer to the stables for you."

I looked around and nodded. "I like it. Do we have enough room for both houses here, though?"

Nash shrugged. "Depends how big you want them. It wouldn't give you much of a yard but then we live on a ranch, so…"

"I think my biggest problem would be having to hear Wilder hooking up with different women all the time."

"How close do you think these houses are going to be?" Wilder cried. "How loud do you think I am when I'm having sex?"

"Too fucking loud. I heard you when we went on vacation to Cabo. To name just several occasions."

"The alternative is one of you here and one over on the east side of the house, adjacent to the lavender farm. I've already checked with Shane and Felicia, and they don't have a problem with that." Shane used to manage our lavender farm, until we found out that Mom had signed it over to him before she died. A fact Dad had kept secret.

"That someone being me, seeing as Gun will prefer to be near the stables." Wilder took a couple of paces back and looked around. While he looked I considered the options. Having him close by might feel less of a change than living in the house. The idea of feeling alone with only the horses close by didn't worry me, though. "I also quite like the idea of being near the south pasture. I'll think about it as either would give us both more outside space," my youngest brother finally said.

"There is an alternative," Nash said, his eyes creased like he was scared to say it.

"What?" I asked.

"We build for us and you both stay in the house."

"Do you want to do that?" Wilder frowned. "The kids have their rooms and Lily just redecorated and furnished all that shit of Dad's out."

Our dad had refurbished the main house a few years back, with money he stole from us, and filled it with all kinds of garish furniture. Thanks to Lily it was finally looking more like a family home again.

Nash rubbed the back of his neck. "Can't say as I want to, but Lila pointed out that I didn't even ask if that was what either of you wanted to do."

"Not me," Wilder offered, holding up a hand. "I'm looking forward to a brand new bachelor pad."

"Got to be honest, I agree with Wild." I looked over to the stables, in perfect view of where I imagined my porch to be. "I like this spot. Happy to have Wild alongside me but I also think more outside space would be great." Liking the idea of an herb garden and maybe some raised beds to grow some roses like Mom used to like to do. There was a soreness in my throat and lungs as I thought about her. It had been almost two decades since she'd been killed in a car accident, but I still missed her, still remembered the gentle touch of her hand on my head. Sometimes I was sure I could also remember her smell, but who knew. I'd been nine years of age and devastated by her death. We all had, except for Dad maybe. He'd played the grieving widower, but we found out a couple of years back he'd been having an affair for years and Mom had started divorce proceedings when she died.

"Okay, we build two separate houses," Nash said, slapping his hands together. "One here and one adjacent to the lavender farm."

We all shook on it and as soon as we had a small fire was lit in my belly. As much as I loved us all living together, it was an exciting prospect.

"I'll contact the contractor," Nash told us as he started to walk away, when Wilder stopped him.

"What the fuck is that?" he asked, grabbing Nash.

He and I turned to look and at our boundary line, about half a mile in the distance, a convoy of trucks could be seen.

"That can't be the developer's." I looked to Nash who was taking his phone out of his jacket pocket. "They can't have all the right permits yet, can they?"

"No idea." He tapped at his screen and then held the phone to his ear. "I'm calling Calvin."

"Want to reconsider where you build your house?" Wilder asked, moving up alongside me.

"No, he doesn't," Nash snapped, "because those fuckers will not be building there if I have my way."

I looked at the convoy of trucks, thinking about the kids' camp plans. "That meadow would have been perfect for teaching the kids about local wildlife. Part of what makes this land special is how untouched it is. The weasels are there."

"Exactly," Nash agreed. "And think about the noise from construction. How are you supposed to work with skittish horses when they're blasting and drilling next door?"

If I knew my brother he'd move heaven and earth to stop them. I just hoped it didn't put paid to our other plans, because Cassidy's plan for the kid's camp had me more excited than I thought possible. It was exactly the kind of program this land was meant for, not concrete and machinery.

Counting Stars – OneRepublic

CHAPTER 13
Cassidy

I was nervous. Stupid because I'd been on the ranch before. I just hadn't spent time with Gunner on the ranch. Not just me and him, anyway. We were going through some of the details that I'd envisaged for the kids' camp. Lucas was with me, but he was spending the time with Bertie and Mikey, one of the stable hands, learning how to groom Bertie's pony. We wanted to see if he liked the horses and if it would be a good fit for him until Ruth started working on the ranch. It seemed her current employer was being a stickler about her notice period. It was decided because of that, if today went okay, Lucas would come to the ranch whenever she was working.

Gunner placed a mug of dark, rich coffee on the desk in front of me and flashed a smile. "Creamer no sugar."

"Thank you." We were in his office on the same side of his desk, close enough that I could smell his subtle cologne mixed with leather and…man. A very manly man and it was distracting in a way I refused to acknowledge. "What's the plan for today?"

He took a seat next to me, resting his ankle on his opposite knee, fingers steepled under his chin. The epitome of cool and chilled. Annoyingly so. Three years ago, that same casual confidence had both attracted and infuriated me. Now it just made me wary.

"We need to get a full picture of your vision and decide how we move forward."

The word 'vision' triggered an echo of that disastrous night—him dismissing my 'city vision' for ranch kids. I pushed the memory aside and opened my purse, taking out a folder that had everything I'd prepared. Everything that I'd spent hours poring over and collating about similar camps and institutes across the country. Taking out the contents, I spread it across the desk.

"These are all examples of existing camps. This one," I pointed at the images I'd printed, "in Michigan is the one I think we could base the Last Creek model on. It's mainly for terminally ill kids but we could apply the same principles."

Gunner picked up the paper and started to read it. My nerves spiked again because ultimately this was his decision. They were his horses. The irony wasn't lost on me. Here I was again, presenting ideas about helping ranch kids to the man who'd once told me I couldn't understand them. It felt like an age watching him, holding my breath to the point that my lungs started to burn. When I couldn't hold it any longer I slowly exhaled.

"Well?"

Gunner looked up at me and his shining eyes stunned me as he swallowed. The hardness I remembered from that night was gone, replaced by something that made my chest tight. "Those poor kids." He shook his head. "Call me selfish but I'm not sure I could work with terminal kids, knowing that…"

Blowing out a ragged breath, he placed the piece of paper back on the pile and looked at me. Not with doubt, but with something deeper. "It's a great model, I agree. If anyone can do this," he added softly, "it's you."

I placed a hand against my chest, the emotion he was showing felt like it was pushing its way into my heart. Making it swell to the point of pain. This wasn't the dismissive man who'd walked away from our date. This was someone else entirely. He was showing belief in me and for a second I couldn't breathe.

"I should have picked something else," I whispered. "I'm sorry."

Gunner shook his head. "No, this is perfect. It's the idea of losing Bertie or Billy like that, it, well," he blew out his cheeks, "makes me feel sick."

"I know it's a terrible thought. Any child who has to go through that, any parent that has to go through that."

We both fell silent for a beat, the air filled with a palpable fear. Gunner eventually cleared his throat and picked up the rest of the papers, flicking through them.

"I like this," he said pointing at the outside movie theater. "We could easily set that up. I know a guy in Clementine Hill who has all the gear. He hires it out so if we could come up with some sort of schedule in advance then we could be sure to have it."

I nodded. "Or maybe we could do a crowd fund to buy our own equipment. In fact, I was thinking a crowd fund would be great anyway."

"Nash looked into it and thinks we can get a whole load of grants, from local government and businesses." He looked sideways at me. "Crowd funding might be a good idea, though," he muttered.

"Gee, thanks." I flounced back in my seat. "Your belief in my ideas is much appreciated."

His gaze shot to mine. "What's with the attitude?"

"I don't have an attitude." I had an attitude because of his damn *attitude*.

"You do. What did I say?"

"That crowd funding *might* be a good idea. It's a great idea."

Gunner sighed heavily, with more than a hint of sarcasm in it when he slapped on a smile. "Wow, Cassidy, the idea of crowd funding is an absolutely great idea."

"There's no need to be so caustic."

"Ooh big words, Cassidy, did you think I wouldn't know what it meant?"

My fingers gripped the arms of the chair, mainly to stop me poking him or worse. "I know you're not stupid, Gunner. I know you know big words like egotistical, narcissistic, conceited, egocentric."

He smirked. "I think you forgot a bigger one like, Gunner's dick."

"You're a dick, and anyway," I scoffed, "I doubt it's that big, you were blessed with a huge head, so I doubt you'd get a dick to match."

He let out a loud roar of laughter and shook his head. "How little you know." He stepped closer, his voice dropping low. "But you only have to say the word."

"Yeah and that word would be one I'm too ladylike to repeat." I reached for the file and the papers, but Gunner slapped his hand down on top of mine."

"Just stop."

"No, if you can't be polite then I don't want to stay here." I tugged at my hand, but he wouldn't let it go. "Get off me and give me my papers back."

Lifting his hand from mine he grabbed the arms of my chair and swiveled me to face him. He leaned in, closer to me. "I'm sorry that you think I'm a dick, but we need to do this. If we can't even have an initial meeting then how do you envisage the whole damn thing working?"

"I don't know," I shrugged. "I'll pass it on to someone else."

"No, you won't, Cassidy. This was your idea and contrary to what you think, I believe it's a good one. One that you deserve to see through." He scrubbed at his stubble, his posture rising and falling slowly as he exhaled. "I have to be involved because these are my horses and call me egotistical, narcissistic and what was the other one?"

"Other two. Conceited and egocentric."

"Yeah, call me those, too, but no one else will be able to help you pull this off. No one else will know what will help those kids the same way I will.'

I had to stop myself from rolling my eyes because now was not the time to be childish. I chose to clear my throat instead, because everyone knows a throat clear says everything.

Pushing his chair back, he linked his fingers over his stomach. "When my mom died, I was nine years old. The age when you still need your mom's hugs, her touch, her soft words, her reading me a bedtime story." He scoffed. "Although, that one was getting to be less needed. The point is, when she was killed my whole world fell apart. I had Nash and Wilder, but they weren't her." He shrugged. "My dad was less than hopeless. Always had been with the emotional stuff. So, the only thing that got me through it, still gets me through it, are the horses."

I slumped back in my chair, a weight pushing against my chest as I saw my own grief mirrored in Gunner's eyes. The kids I'd fostered helped me, the kids I taught still helped me, but that crippling pain and realization that she wasn't coming back was always with me. Just like it was with him.

"Horses," Gunner continued, "are non-judgmental, you see. So, any shit I pulled because I was hurting, they never told me what a dick I was and that I'd never amount to anything if I didn't get a fucking grip." He paused and drew in a slow breath, pressing his hand down onto the desk, like he was pushing down all his emotions and thoughts. "They picked up on my moods and were just quiet and soothing while I cried and raged."

Footsteps outside came closer but no one came to the office, and seconds later they walked away. Something metal clanked on the ground, like a bucket or something, and then I heard water running followed by the ringing sound of water on vibrating metal.

Gunner glanced to the side, to the window, and sighed. "This ranch, this land, those horses have probably saved all of us in some way or another." He barked out a laugh. "Apart from my father, seems it wasn't quite such a healing environment for him."

"It must have been hard for all of you, finding out how he'd stolen from you over the years." When he raised an eyebrow I felt my cheeks burn up. "It was all in the local newspaper, Lily didn't tell me or anything."

"Oh, I know it was common knowledge and you're her best friend, so I would expect Lily to tell you. You know that he hid the fact that mom had signed the lavender farm over to Shane and Felicia?"

"No. They didn't report that." Jeez the man was a real piece of work.

"Yeah, he hid the deeds that mom had signed over to them as a thank you for their loyalty. Hid her will, too, which left him nothing. Hence why every penny he took from this place was theft. He was a shit dad anyway. You know he was the one who forced Lily to leave town all those years ago?"

"Yeah," I whispered. "I did. She told me all about it." When Lily first came back to town and we became friends, Nash was more than hostile to her. Thank god they'd managed to get through that and get their happy ending.

"So, you see why I needed the horses." His laugh was hollow. "Anyway, you ready to get back to this?"

I nodded. "Yes, I'm ready. Let's organize a kids' camp."

When he turned back to his desk and picked up a pad and pen, I watched him for a moment. After that first date, I'd written him off as just another stubborn rancher who thought he knew better than everyone else. Who'd dismissed my ideas without really hearing them. But this Gunner, the one who understood exactly why kids might need more than just traditional ranch life, who'd found his own healing with these horses - was someone entirely different. Or maybe he'd been there all along, and I'd been too quick to judge after that disaster of a first date.

Just Give Me a Reason - P!nk ft. Nate Ruess

CHAPTER 14
Gunner

Cassidy and I had managed to thrash out the basic details of the camp. It had been a little fraught at times. She didn't appear to like my natural charm, but at least we managed to get through a couple of hours of work without drawing any blood.

"Hey Uncle G. You look nice." Bertie stood with her hands on her hips, looking me up and down. "Got a date?"

I looked down at my white button down and the clean jeans. Nothing special. "Do I look like crap usually?"

"Nope." Her little brow furrowed as she pursed her lips. "Just not as good as you do today." She lifted her chin and sniffed. "Smell nice, too." Her eyes narrowed on me. "Am I going to get another teacher in the family? I mean having my momma as a teacher is one thing, but an aunt, too. Jeez."

"What are you talking about, short stuff?" I knew what she was getting at, and it was making me feel distinctively uncomfortable.

"You and Miss Turner. I've seen you making eyes at her. You smile differently when she's around."

"I have not! I do not!"

"Have so. Do so." She grinned and leaned forward to poke me in the stomach. "Just like I told Daddy when he and Momma made out they didn't like each other, that's the best fairytale I've ever heard." She then patted where she'd poked. "Anyways, you have fun now. Come on Dorcas! We're going to see Ariel and then play in the tree house!"

"Short stuff," I called after her. "Do not take that puppy up the tree."

She waved at me over her shoulder. "How stupid do you think I am, Uncle G. Uncle Wilder rigged up a lift for him with an old basket. And don't you forget to have fun."

As I watched Bertie skip away, her puppy following, Lily started to chuckle behind me. I spun around to see her leaning against the doorway with Billy on her hip, him playing with her hair.

"You are so deluded," she said with a huge grin. "She's deluded, too."

"Who, Bertie?"

"No and you know exactly who I'm talking about. Cassidy." She shifted Billy whose head had started to lol against her shoulder, her hair wrapped around his tiny fingers.

I walked to her and dropped a kiss to my nephew's soft hair, inhaling the smell of baby powder and milk. "There's nothing to talk about where Cassidy and I are concerned," I whispered so as not to disturb Billy. "I'm not going to give you the 'we're just friends' line, because we're not even that."

"You know what they say about love and hate, Gunner?"

Damn meddling woman. "Lil, don't get things in your head that don't need to be there." My stomach felt weird again. "We'll be building up the camp together and that is just about it."

As I walked past her, Lily followed me and gently placed Billy on the sleep mat inside his playpen. It was now a permanent fixture in our large kitchen and provided Wilder with hours of fun. Yep, Wilder!

"Why do you two dislike each other so much?" Lily asked as she ran a hand over her baby's head.

"You know this story," I told her as I took a glass from the cabinet. "We had a shit date. A huge difference of opinion about how kids around here should be taught."

"You thought she was trying to bring her big city ways where they weren't wanted." She rolled her eyes. "Blah, blah, blah. You know now that isn't what she meant." When I didn't respond she blinked slowly. "Oh, come on, Gun, do you really think that Cassidy doesn't want the best for the kids of this town? Still? Even after having the idea about the camp."

I ran the cold water for a few seconds before filling my glass. Before answering I took a long sip, delaying having to admit that maybe I'd been wrong. Maybe I admired the woman who I'd spent all this time disliking. And that didn't sit well with me because I always gave people the benefit of the doubt; just not Cassidy Turner it seemed.

"Whatever happened on our date all those years ago, *was* all those years ago. It was what it was." I turned and leaned against the sink. "Now, because of that and the time that has passed I'm sure we can only ever be colleagues on the camp and then acquaintances after."

Lily's hand went to her throat as she gasped softly. "Gunner, no. Don't just dismiss it like that."

"I'm not, Lil, because there's nothing there."

Even as I said it, I remembered how she'd leaned over my desk earlier, pointing out details in her plans, the scent of her shampoo mixing with her perfume. How her voice had softened when we'd talked about the kids, about loss. How different she was from the woman I'd dismissed three years ago. Yes I was attracted to her. No, she wasn't the person I'd thought she was. Yes she was a much better teacher and person than I'd ever given her credit for. The way she'd talked about helping those kids today, the passion in her eyes when she'd laid out her plans... I'd been dead wrong about her, and that was harder to admit than the attraction. That didn't mean I should pursue something that probably wouldn't last anyway. We were too different, too stubborn, too set in our ways. And yet every time she challenged me, now I found myself wanting to push back just to see that fire in her eyes.

"I wish you would both realize that you'd be great together." Lily moved closer and placed a cool hand on my cheek. "Firey but great." She gave me a little smirk. "And think about all the makeup sex."

The idea of that was tempting but…

"Lily, leave it be, okay?" I kissed her cheek. "Now, I have a town meeting to go to and find out what those trucks are doing near our land."

She looked me up and down, just like Bertie had done. "Dressed up like that. For a town meeting."

"Yep I am. Nothing wrong with being smart for your adoring public." I gave her a wink and then sauntered out to the foyer. "Nash," I called up the stairs. "You coming or not? We don't want to be late."

One thing I hadn't told either Bertie or Lily, was that a certain brunette might be there. And that maybe, just maybe, I'd chosen this shirt because I knew exactly how her eyes lingered when I wore it. Not that I'd ever admit that to anyone, especially myself.

***

The town hall was packed to the rafters with townspeople wanting to know the same thing we did about the development. There were also some faces that I recognized, including my buddy Deacon and his brother Joe, who was Sheriff of Clementine Hill. No sign of Cassidy, though.

"Deacon is here," I told Nash, ignoring the rolling of my belly.

He looked over. "There's a few faces I've never seen before. I spoke to Calvin, and he said that the front row are all from Sweet Maple Falls."

"We've got five minutes, let's go and see what Deacon knows."

Nash followed me over, greeting locals as we passed. More than one of them asked what he planned to do about the development, like he was the Mayor and not Calvin. I wasn't surprised because he'd always given off an heir of responsibility. He'd been captain of every football team he'd played in, spokesperson for all his friendship group whenever one was needed. He was our cheerleader when we needed it and the head of our family, even before Dad turned to the dark side and got sent to prison.

"Hey guys." Deacon lifted his battered old cowboy hat and grinned. "Great turn out."

"Shows you how much it's not wanted." Nash held his hand out to Joe. "Been a while, Joe. How you doing?"

"Good, thanks, Nash. As long as my brother doesn't lose his cool tonight." He gave Deacon a skeptical look.

"Which I will if they can assure us that fucking monstrosity is going nowhere near anyone's land. Especially people with animals."

I slapped him on his shoulder. "Appreciate you, because it's too damn near my horses for comfort."

"There's only us here from Clementine, because even though it doesn't affect us yet this thing is only going to get bigger. So, I promise you most of the town is against it."

"Most?" Nash asked.

Joe rolled his eyes. "There's the odd one or two in Mayor Rogers' pocket, but that's another story."

"Hah," I scoffed. "We know that feeling, don't we brother?"

Nash sighed, his frown a window into his own thoughts of our dad. "I guess we do." He patted my back. "We should go and take a seat. Great to see you guys."

"You too," Deacon replied and then held up his phone. "Oh, and I have a guy who I think would be a good fit as architect for your construction projects. I'll send his number over."

"Great, thanks buddy." We shook hands and then Nash and I went and took our seats.

"This could get tasty." Nash nodded over to a group of people standing at the side. In the middle of them was Dudley Granger, local busybody and owner of Dud's Marvelous Motors. I'd had one of Dud's motors when I was eighteen, let's just say they were more duds than marvelous.

"You think he's for or against?" I asked, leaning forward to look down the row of people.

"Knowing that bastard he's all for the development. Think of all the new residents that could buy one of his shit vehicles," Nash replied wryly. "Plus, I do believe he's been having sexy times with Mayor Rogers."

"How do you know that?" I glanced over at Sweet Maple Falls Mayor, sitting on the stage reading through something on her phone. Her long legs were crossed, tucked in next to each other and pointing away from her body like she'd been to etiquette school or something. It couldn't be further from the truth, seeing as her dad and brothers were well known, blatant cattle rustlers. Word was not one of the cattle on their ranch had their brand, and if they did then the original one had been burned off. She was a year into her first term and had already caused friction by handing her dad a large portion of town land. She'd done it under some bullshit excuse about incorrect town rezoning years before.

"How do I usually get my info'; Peggy."

I laughed. Lily's grandmother liked her gossip and was rarely wrong. "Think you're right, Nash, things could get tasty."

The buzz of conversation continued around us as I scrolled through my phone and Nash chatted to the guy on the other side of him.

"Quite a crowd."

The soft voice startled me. I whipped around to see Cassidy settling in the seat next to me. She was wearing her glasses, and her hair was up in a high ponytail. With the soft gray sweats that she was wearing she would have easily passed for a high school senior. Her face was clear of makeup, except for some shiny stuff on her lips. I couldn't tear my eyes away from it. Couldn't stop wondering what it might taste like.

"Surprised to see you here."

Cassidy frowned as she dug her hands deep into the pockets of her sweats. "Why?"

I shrugged. "Would have thought you'd welcome the development. Seeing as you like the big city life."

She rolled her eyes and turned to face the stage. "You talk so much BS it smells like your ranch in here."

"Just saying." I laughed emptily. "I know how much you like the excitement that Silver Peaks just doesn't bring."

She didn't answer but took a pause with a huge inhale. When she inched her chair away from me, I thought the conversation was over, but then she nudged me hard in the ribs.

"Hey, that damn well hurts."

"Good. It was meant to." She scowled at me. "You know nothing about me, so don't ever try and tell me how I think, or what I feel. I'm here because I hate the idea of some ugly ass buildings ruining the beauty of this place. Those mountains are like the backbone of this state. When I look at them I'm in awe at the way their peaks seem to pierce the sky. And how impossibly blue is that sky? And the land," she took a deep breath, "it's the deepest green and the way it undulates, it's just like…" She took a breath. "…like crashing emerald waves, while the pines, so damn tall and grand, stand sentry over it all. So no, I do not want this development marring all of that." She faced forward and gritted out. "Keep your opinions and shove them up your stupid damn hairy ass."

And didn't that little tirade give me a warm feeling deep down in my belly.

Roar - Katy Perry

CHAPTER 15
Cassidy

I had never wanted to commit violence more than I did at that moment. Especially as I could feel the ass wipe staring at me.

"Gunner, to quote a Clockwork Orange, I'm not going to hurt you, but I will if you make me." I turned my stare on him, and I knew it was hard because he reared back.

"What did I do?"

I blinked slowly. "Aside from breathing too close, which I have to say is off putting seeing as I'm not a lover of garlic." I shook my head and turned back to watch what was happening on stage. "Not to mention the fact that every conversation we have ends up with you disrespecting me."

Thankfully, Mayor Taylor tapped the microphone to start the meeting. "Good evening everyone, thank you for coming tonight."

The woman sitting next to him sighed and smoothed down her skirt as she looked off to the side.

"Who is she?" I whispered to Gunner.

"Are you talking to me?"

I turned to glare at him and had to clench my hands into fists to avoid physical violence. His smirk was irritating at the very least.

"Yes, I'm talking to you. Who is the woman who clearly doesn't want to be here?"

"Grace Rogers, Mayor of Sweet Maple Falls. The little round guy, that's Ron Matthews the mayor of Clementine Hills. And the other guy, on the microphone, that's—"

"I know who our Mayor is, Gunner," I snapped. "She agrees with the development then?"

"I do believe she might." Gunner cleared his throat. "I think we're ready to start." He pointed at the stage, and I gave it my full attention.

Mayor Taylor led the discussion about the development, explaining the plans that had been presented to him by the County Mayor's office. The hall fell into shocked silence as he laid everything out. The meat packing factory with its huge, refrigerated warehouse of thousands and thousands of cubic square feet. Then there were the forty, two-story houses and three two level apartment blocks with eighteen apartments in each. Not to mention the infrastructure of roads and sidewalks around it all. And that was only the beginning, there was much more coming in another three phases which would affect Clementine and Sweet Maple.

"And where do the County think all the children from those properties are going to go to school?" A woman I recognized from the bank asked. "My kids are at the high school and it's already full to busting, seeing as it's for all three towns."

She wasn't wrong, I had a friend who taught Math at the high school, and she was always telling me how big the classes were. How stretched they were for books and equipment. We were lucky that each town had their own elementary school otherwise we'd be in the same situation. Mrs. Wright was always telling us how tight the budget was, and we were just one small town. Add more kids to that and I dreaded to think how bad it would get.

"Because I'm betting there are no school extensions in those plans of yours," she continued, wrapping her arms around her waist. "Our kids' futures will look bleak if you let them do this."

"I agree, Sylvia," Mayor Taylor responded, glancing at Mayor Rogers. "And I have already raised this as a concern with the County."

The discussion continued until the mayor asked for any other questions. Gunner raised a hand and stood. "We're the tiniest damn county in the state, so why the hell have these businesses and property developers decided to build here?" He pointedly looked at Grace Rogers. "Is there some incentive they're getting that we don't know about?"

Mayor Taylor smirked and raised an eyebrow. "Grace, do you want to answer that seeing as you spoke to the County only yesterday." Grace reared back in her seat. "You did go to County Hall didn't you?"

She shifted and clutched her phone to her chest, like it could protect her. "I haven't spoken to them any more than anyone else, but I can assure you that there will be no incentive. The land speaks for itself. It's the best place for them to build."

"Well, I think I will have to disagree with that." Gunner scoffed and folded his arms over his chest, his biceps bulging against the cotton of his shirt. A white button down that looked very much like the one he'd worn on our fateful date all those years ago. One that made his golden skin look even more tanned. "Are they aware that wild weasels live along that part of the land? And they're breeding at the moment, so have the necessary environmental checks been done?" He leaned forward, expecting an answer. When Grace Rogers inhaled slowly and her shoulders lifted almost to her ears, Gunner grimaced and shook his head. "Thought not. Can I suggest that whoever has *the ear* of the County speak to them about that and get things put in place."

He didn't sit down but continued to stare at everybody on the stage. Mayor Taylor nodded at Gunner and then turned to the other two mayors up there with him.

"I think maybe we have a few questions to ask," he aimed at them before turning back to everyone else. "Thanks for that Gunner. Anyone else?"

Gunner took his seat again and growled from the back of his throat. "Fuckers."

My skin pebbled with goosebumps as his arm brushed against mine and every inch of his manliness wafted through the air. I could smell his cologne, nothing overpowering, a subtle mixture of spice and…roses. It hung in the air to the point that I felt I could touch it. And the worry about the wildlife, that I hadn't expected from him. He kept on surprising me.

I leaned in closer to him. "I didn't know you had weasels on the property."

"Yep. We also have a family of beavers living in the pond on the south boundary and Wilder said he saw a couple of Golden Eagles up near the high ground." Gunner leaned closer causing the hairs on my arms to stand on end. "Not to mention the bunnies."

I huffed out a laugh, disappointed at feeling amused by him. "Bunnies?"

"Yeah, they're all cute and fluffy and procreate like there's no tomorrow. Shane isn't so fond of them if they wander into the lavender field, but I think we've solved that issue. I won't tell you how, it might upset you."

I gasped. "You shoot them?"

"Never said that. We have other ways." He wiggled his fingers on both hands and made a sizzling noise.

"Oh, my God, you're right I don't want to know." I turned back to the stage as Mayor Taylor was talking about the next steps. How we place our objections with the County.

"Now," he said. " I know we'd all love to storm county hall and demand they reconsider their plans, but we can't do that."

"Works for me," Nash called out. "Wilder is in Denver today looking at machinery, but he'd agree with me," he slapped Gunner on the back, "and him. Right Gun?"

"Right. Let's drive down there right now," Gunner agreed.

"Boys," Mayor Taylor warned. "Let's not get too riled up just yet."

"We shouldn't be getting riled up at all." Grace Rogers stood gracefully and walked to the microphone, taking it and addressing the crowd. "The plans for this development have been finalized and they *will* be breaking ground soon. Nothing is going to change that."

"And the issues we've raised tonight?" I asked. "The environmental ones, the schools, the general overcrowding."

She pinned me with a glare that said, 'we've covered that, bitch, now shut up'. "I don't think there's much else we can say about that for now."

"Why, because you don't have the answers?" I returned. "Or are you just acting like you don't?"

Gunner laughed quietly beside me. "Keep poking with that stick, honey."

I flattened a hand against my stomach, hoping it might stop the butterflies that his words had started.

Grace Rogers didn't respond but turned and left the stage, leaving the other two mayors to field a bunch of questions that were being thrown at them.

"This is going to be so much worse than anyone thought." Nash sighed, rubbing a hand over his head. "I never thought about the high school."

"Not to mention the traffic." I looked at Gunner. "The noise is going to be bad for the horses isn't it?"

He nodded. "Not to mention the pollution for them and the kids at the camp."

"Pollution?"

Nash nodded. "Yeah, not just the energy usage emissions but the chemicals from the packaging, the waste that could end up in landfill."

"And we've already had the problems with water pollution," Gunner added. "Admittedly Dad did that, but the Public Health & Environment's water division will be making double sure it doesn't happen again. A plant that size could leak nitrates and phosphates into the water table. It'll ruin our well water and kill any fish in the creek. The runoff alone could poison the soil."

"The slightest hint of pollution and they'll shut them down, surely?" I asked.

"Them and us," Gunner replied. "Our cattle and the cattle of three other ranches drink from that creek."

"Plus, can you imagine parents wanting to send their kids to a camp with the stench of meat in the air?" Nash said.

"This could create access problems for us, too," Gunner added. "The other entrance we were thinking about will be right next to the factory entrance. And there's bound to be safety issues with having kids so close to it."

My stomach bottomed out at the idea Nash and Gunner might be reconsidering the plans. "Do you think it might mean we can't go ahead?"

"Like fuck," Gunner growled. "The kids need it. We just might have to get it up and running quicker than we'd hoped. Get it established before that monstrosity comes along."

"The wedding venue might be a no go, though," Nash replied, his tone flat. "Unless we move it to the other side of the property. No bride is going to want a meat packing plant as the backdrop to her wedding pictures. And that is going to cost us a whole load of cash." He fished his phone from his pocket. "I'm going to call Dougie and see whether he knows a good corporate attorney who might be able to help us."

"Dougie?" I asked as Nash stepped away.

"Family attorney. He's taken care of us since Mom died."

The lost look in Gunner's eyes didn't escape me at the mention of his mom. I reached out a hand, determined to comfort him, but he cleared his throat and pushed out of his seat before I had a chance.

"I'll walk you to your car."

The bottom dropped out of my stomach at the rejection, even though there really was no rejection. We didn't like each other so why would he even want my comfort?

"I walked," I said curtly.

"Then I'll drive you."

"No thanks. I've seen you drive. Walking will be much safer." It was also much easier being salty with him.

"You're not walking alone. I'll walk you and come back for Nash." He clearly wasn't taking no for an answer because he waved out a hand. "After you."

"It's a couple of blocks, Gunner. Nothing is likely to happen to me." I rolled my eyes. "It's Silver Peaks."

"It is indeed." He studied me carefully. "Sleepy little Silver Peaks where nothing happens, and we don't know how to teach our kids." He looked to the stage. "But I guess with all this it's just like the big city now with all that pollution and overcrowding. You must feel right at home."

"God damn it, Gunner, this is getting boring. How many times do we have to have this conversation?"

He held his hands up in surrender. "Okay, okay, I get it. No more talk about big city life."

"And for your information I was brought up on a farm in Trimble." When his mouth dropped open in surprise the feeling of victory it gave me was incredible. "Yes exactly, so quit with the shit about me being a city girl and I can walk home alone."

I picked up my purse and stalked out of there, wondering how one man could be so damn annoying and yet smell so delicious all at the same time.

Stay – Rihanna

CHAPTER 16
Cassidy

The rich aroma of coffee floated around my small apartment, invading every space and helping to wake me. It was much needed because I'd barely slept. Everything that had happened at the meeting was rumbling around in my head. From the issues the development was going to cause the camp, to the shock on Gunner's face when I told him I'd been brought up on a farm.

I was conflicted about that. At first his stunned face felt like a victory, but that now felt hollow. Why had I felt the need to explain myself to him? Why should I care that he had the wrong opinion of me?

Pulling my feet under me, I stared out of the window that looked onto the street. It was busy for seven-thirty on a Saturday morning. The bakery was already open with people going in and coming out with bags of bread and pastries. Next door, at the fresh fruit and vegetable store, Mrs. Sullivan was putting everything out on display while her son, Zachary, was inside laying out the ice for the fresh fish they sold. I knew that Latymer, the town's main street, would be just as industrious, especially Missy May's diner with folks going in for one of her famous breakfast sandwiches.

I sighed contentedly, glad of my life in Silver Peaks. The farmhouse I was brought up in was big, but cozy. Lots of small rooms that Mom always talked about knocking into bigger ones, to make a more open planned living space. She never got around to it, mainly because we never had the money, but also because she never had the time to while fostering kids. I loved that house, but I was just as happy here in my little apartment with its overstuffed furniture and masses of books, cushions and throws. Obviously I missed my mom, like crazy, but I knew she'd be proud of me, becoming a teacher and that made me happy and content with my home and my life.

There were nights when I felt lonely, but I could stand that. It didn't mean I didn't want to meet someone and have a great romance one day. Of course, I did. I wanted a family of my own and a nice house. I saw what Lily and Nash had and I envied them, their happiness, their deep, heart clenching love. Maybe one day I'd get myself my own Nash Miller, but for now I was content. A hook up would be appreciated now and again, but Silver Peaks was a small town, and I didn't want the parents of the kids I taught knowing all my business. Perhaps it was time to call my old college friend, Angela, and arrange a weekend visit with her in Portland.

Taking another sip of my coffee, a message on my phone startled me. It was still early for most people, except if they worked on a ranch and were up and out by five. It had to be Lily. When I picked it up and saw who it was from I almost dropped my mug. When I read it I almost spat my coffee out.

GUNNER
Morning. Thought after last night we should clear the air. And it's a good opportunity to start moving on with the camp. Get ahead of the game. Say 1030 at the ranch? I'm sorry I misjudged you.

To say I was surprised was an understatement. Gunner Miller didn't seem the sort of man who would apologize about anything. Least of all to me. I guess miracles did happen. Did I want to accept his apology, though, that was the question I was asking myself. Contemplating it for a few seconds I remembered I had nothing planned. A drive out to the ranch might be one way to spend the day. But did I want to spend a precious day off with Gunner? Arguing and backbiting and being plain mean to each other.

"Yep," I said to myself, with a grin. "That sounds like a whole lot of fun."

***

The old track to the ranch, once little more than a dirt road, was now a smooth gray block road that shimmered in the morning sun. It ran alongside sprawling green fields dotted with wildflowers and flanked by towering cottonwoods whose leaves rustled in the breeze like distant applause. The scent of lavender drifted through the air from the ranch's deep purple lavender field, its blooms swaying lazily under the weight of bees. The road curved gently past it, rising toward the main house, then stretching on toward the stables—*Gunner's stables*, proud and still beneath the wide Colorado sky. Coming to the house, I stopped and parked up. As soon as I got out of my car, laptop bag in hand, the front door was pulled open, and Lily appeared. She was wearing skinny jeans and a thick red sweater which fell almost to her knees and on her feet were cozy suede Ugg slippers. With her hair in a braid hanging over her shoulder, she looked young and happy so different to the quiet, closed off Lily that had come back to town just over two years before.

"Hey, morning." Wrapping her arms around her waist, Lily beckoned me inside. "Coffee is on, and the fire is lit."

I looked up at the sky. It was clear and still, eerily so. "I should probably go and see Gunner before the snow starts." On my way over it came over the radio that snow was coming, but I was practically at the ranch, so it seemed silly to go back.

"Come back here before you go back to town," Lily told me. "If it looks like it's coming in before you can get back you can hole yourself up here." She shivered against the cold, and I pulled my coat tighter around me.

Nearby Telluride retained snow coverage at this time of year because of its altitude and north-facing slopes, whereas in Silver Peaks the weather was getting warmer. It wasn't unusual, though, to get the odd snowstorm and it looked like today was going to be one of those days.

"I will," I replied. "But hopefully it won't take too long."

Lily grinned. "He's in a strange mood this morning. Quiet and…" She tilted her head to one side. "Thoughtful."

"Hmm. I'm not sure Gunner has ever been thoughtful about anything."

My friend chuckled. "I think you're too harsh on him and you should cut him some slack."

"You would say that he's your family."

"He is and not really as bad as you make out. Now," she pointed over to the stables, "go and see him and I'll have a hot drink and a seat by the fire waiting for you."

With a roll of my eyes, I watched her go inside and then made the short walk to the stables. When I got to Gunner's office the door was ajar, and I could hear shouting coming from inside.

"What the hell is going on with you?" Gunner yelled.

"You never think you're wrong, do you?" It sounded like Charlie, his training assistant.

"I know I don't always get it right, but on this occasion it's wrong to try and jump that horse yet."

Not sure whether to interrupt or not, I did a full three-sixty and looked around. There was someone leading a horse out of the corral and over by the stables some of the hands were cleaning stalls and brushing down horses. It was a hive of activity, and I knew the kids would love being around this place. The argument happening on the other side of the door, though, didn't augur well for a peaceful, harmonious camp where kids could relax.

"Damn it," I muttered and lifted my fisted hand to knock. "Anyone in?"

Silence fell and I heard feet shuffling with the door being pulled open a few seconds later.

"Cassidy." He breathed out my name like it was a blessing. "Come on in."

The moment I stepped inside I could feel the iciness engulfing the room.

It was like the snow had already fallen in there.

When I looked over at Charlie, her face was beet red, and her jaw was tight as she slammed her fingers on her keyboard. She didn't even look up as Gunner pulled his visitor chair around to his side of the desk.

"Coffee?" he asked.

"No, I'm good, thanks."

As he poured himself a mug, I watched his chest rise and fall, clearly anger still ebbing through his veins. It felt awkward and uncomfortable, and I had a ridiculous temptation to burst into song or crack a joke. Anything to break the tension. It was eased a few seconds later when Charlie got up from her desk and stormed out of the office. As soon as the door closed behind her there was an instant melting of ice and sighing, Gunner flopped into his chair and groaned.

"I don't want to appear unprofessional here," he said, "but she is testing my last nerve at the moment."

"I kinda got that."

He glanced at the door. "Shit. Sorry about that. I just don't know what's going on with her. She used to be so reliable, dependable, but the last few months have just been hard work with her."

"In my experience when a kid plays up in class there's usually something else going on. Parents splitting up, someone in the family is ill, or maybe there's a new baby in the house." I cleared my throat, not sure what his response would be. "Have you asked her?"

When he didn't immediately answer, I expected to see a glare full of fire. Instead, he pinched the bridge of his nose and sighed.

"I never even considered it. She lives in the apartment above the stables and her folks live in Tennessee, so have never thought she might have personal issues." He looked at the door. "Are you okay to give me a minute?"

"Yeah sure."

He jumped out of his chair and ran from the office leaving me marveling at the fact that he'd actually listened to me.

What Makes You Beautiful - One Direction

CHAPTER 17
Gunner

Charlie was watching Benny, one of the stable hands, working a horse in the indoor school seeing as the snow had started, when I caught up with her. At least she was acting like she was watching him, but I could see she was looking off into the distance.

"Charlie," my voice was low and neutral. For as angry as I was with her, Cassidy was right there might be other things going on that I didn't know about.

Her head swung in my direction. "What?"

"I think we need to talk."

"We talked. You made it clear that you're not happy with my work." Her hands clenched the top bar of the fence. "Seems like you're not happy with me full stop."

I took a breath, because she was right, I wasn't, but I needed to get to the bottom of why our relationship had changed so drastically.

"What's going on, Charlie? We used to work so well together. A well-oiled machine." I put my hand over hers holding the fence. "You've seemed distracted lately. Is everything okay back home?"

When she looked at me her eyes were full of tears, and I suddenly wished that I'd had the conversation with Cassidy earlier. I wished that I'd spoken to Charlie earlier.

"Come on Charlie." I gave her hand a squeeze. "Talk to me."

She nodded slowly, took a deep breath and then began to talk.

***

I burst back into the office, stamping snow from my boots. "I'm so sorry. I didn't mean to leave you waiting so long."

The smile she gave me hit like a physical force. Not the polite curve of lips I'd expected, but something soft and radiant that stopped me mid-stride. It reminded me of someone else—of Mom's expression when I'd read her a whole chapter without stumbling, or when I'd first cantered around the paddock without falling. A smile that said she saw something in me worth being proud of.

"Did you figure it out?" she asked, leaning forward in her chair.

The words wouldn't come as Cassidy moved to the edge of her seat, hope and maybe excitement shining in her eyes. She was the sun peeking through the clouds.

"S-she, erm, she," I blew out a breath, still floored by the effect of Cassidy's gaze on me. The memories that it evoked despite never having been gifted with it before. "She's been offered a job back home in Tennessee and didn't know how to tell me. Rightly or wrongly, she was angry with herself because she didn't know how to approach me. That anger came out in the form of playing up."

"And now?" she asked, rolling her lips in, waiting.

"She's leaving." I shrugged. "Can't deny it hurts that she doesn't want to stay and learn from the best, but she's going to be head trainer with a team of six working for her. It's a great opportunity for her."

"And she's going with your blessing?"

"Yeah, I guess so. I've told her she can call me any time for advice." I was glad we'd finally got to the bottom of things, even though it had left me with a huge headache. I needed a new assistant, but no one I already employed was ready to step up, so I'd have to recruit. "Finding someone to replace her isn't ideal, especially with the plans with the camp."

Cassidy gave a one shouldered shrug. "We'll manage. Unless you want to postpone."

"Nope. No way. Like I said with that fucking development we need to get ourselves established and the beginnings of a great reputation so, no, we forge ahead."

Cassidy nodded and reached for her notebook. "I made some notes while you were talking to Charlie. Things that we can do quickly. Things that we need to start to put in place in readiness. Give it a quick look over and if you agree with them I'll put them on a spreadsheet."

"Okay." I sat in my chair and looked down at the notes in her neat, cursive handwriting. "Funny I always thought teachers were like doctors and had awful handwriting, but yours is pretty. My mom had beautiful handwriting, too."

She smiled softly and boy it gave me a kick to see a little blush creep up her neck.

I rolled my chair closer to her, ready to change the subject from my mom. "Talk to me about what you think we need to start with."

"Well, there's a whole host of permits that we need, so I think they'd be a good start," she told me. "Because if we don't get them then there's no camp."

I looked down at the list. Each point had an email address next to it and what the permit was needed for. She was nothing if not organized.

"I'm happy to contact them all, get the ball rolling." She looked up at me, briefly sucking on her bottom lip. "Could you start contacting some of the equipment suppliers? I can send you a list, just to get an idea of costs?"

I nodded as Cassidy ploughed on. "I've also come up with some ideas for sponsors, but I guess that's something we need to talk to Nash and Wilder about."

"We can, but there's no harm in me putting out some feelers. And," I said with a shrug, "Nash made it clear this is our baby so I'm sure he'll be on board with whatever we decide."

Nash, Wilder and myself were all equal partners in the ranch. Mom left it to all three of us, which we discovered once we retrieved her will that Dad had hidden, but Nash, as the eldest, was the one we all turned to for the final decision or advice.

"Okay then," Cassidy said, her leg bouncing, "let's get started."

Her enthusiasm was not only catching but it was cute as hell. It was also another reason why I was rethinking how I felt about her.

***

"Damn," I said, stretching my back and neck. "I know now why I need Ruthie in here to do the admin for me. I am not built for sitting at a desk for hours."

Cassidy's head looked up from the spreadsheet she'd created and was updating. She'd pulled her hair up into a mess bun on top of her head and there was a pink blush to her cheeks. It might be snowing outside but it was warm in the office with the log burner roaring away in the corner. I was grateful for that in more ways than one because Cassidy had stripped off her sweat top and was down to a tight, pink t-shirt with a cartoon heart with legs and arms on the front.

"When does Ruthie start?" she asked, reaching for a mug of coffee which had to be cold by now.

"Three weeks. And it can't come too soon, especially as I now need to find a new assistant."

"I'm sure you'll find the right person."

She stretched her arms, and I couldn't help but notice how her tits pushed against the cotton. I whipped my gaze away, not wanting her to notice or think that I was some sort of creeper. The temptation was too much, though, and my eyes went back there. She'd dropped her head back, twisting it from side to side and I had a huge desire to lick up the column of her slim, smooth neck.

"We should call it a day," I croaked out, aware that my dick was suddenly feeling trapped in the confines of my jeans.

Cassidy picked up her phone and looked at the screen, blinking. "I didn't realize the time. It's getting late. We've worked through lunch."

I put a hand against my belly. "Now you mention it, I'm feeling hungry. We should go over to the house and grab some food."

When I stood up, my gaze went to the window, and I was surprised by how heavily the snow had fallen. Against a darkening sky, flakes of white confetti danced in the wind transforming the outside to a magical snow globe.

"You have snow tires on your car?" I asked, turning to look at her.

It was clear from the way she grimaced what the answer was. "Is it bad?" Getting up from her chair, she craned to look out of the window, having to stand on her tiptoes because she was so small. "Ah, shit."

"I don't think you're getting back to town tonight, sweetheart." Realization of what I'd just called her hit me, but it was too late to take it back. "Let's get to the house otherwise we may get snowed in here."

Alarm flashed in her eyes, and I couldn't help but laugh. "I'm joking, but you're definitely not going back to town."

"I could borrow a truck," she suggested.

I held my breath for a beat. "No fucking way. You'll be safer staying at the house. Now, let's go and see what leftovers Ruby left in the house for us all."

Ruby, our new cook for the ranch hands, liked to stock up the family refrigerator with whatever she'd made throughout the week. While Lily's cooking was awesome, Ruby's was on another level, and I was pretty sure we'd all gained a few pounds since she'd been working for us.

"You ready?" I asked after a couple of minutes of Cassidy gathering her things.

"Yep, all good."

When I opened the door to the swirling snowstorm, I put an arm around her, guarding her from the weather. I tried to ignore the way her small body against mine made me feel ten feet tall. Made me think I could conquer everything or everyone because it was the most alien feeling ever.

Come on Get Higher - Matt Nathanson

CHAPTER 18
Cassidy

By the time we made it to the main house I was burning up. The weight and feel of Gunner's arm around me made me hot. Not like I had a fever but a longing desire. It scared me to think he had that effect on me, but the feelings it evoked were exciting, too.

"In you go," he said, opening the front door and stamping the snow from his boots. "Honey, we're home!"

I paused to stamp my own boots and chuckled when I heard Wilder yell, "Your family don't live here any longer, you need to leave."

"He thinks he's the funny one," Gunner grumbled.

He was grinning, though, when I glanced at him, and it was clear he did think his brother was the funny one. When he moved to help me with my coat, my heart did a fly-by of my rib cage and added a loop-the-loop before landing back in my chest.

"Go into the lounge and get in front of the fire." His voice was deep and raspy, like there was something stuck in his throat.

When I looked at him his eyes were darting around the foyer. Looking anywhere but at me. Taking off his own coat, he hung them both on the rack. His broad shoulders filled out his Henley to perfection. His ass in his jeans was even better.

"Cassidy." I turned to see Lily in the doorway. "Looks like you're staying overnight."

"It does." I glanced at Gunner who was hovering by the staircase, hooking his hands into the back pockets of his jeans. "I hope you have some spare jammies for me."

"I do and if not I'm sure one of the boys has a tee you can borrow." She turned a mischievous grin on her brother-in-law. "You have one don't you, Gun?"

He narrowed his eyes. "Yeah, I'm sure I do." He moved past me for the lounge, and I heard him whisper, 'meddlesome woman'.

As he disappeared into the lounge to yells from Bertie and squeals from Billy, Lily sauntered my way.

"What's happened?" she asked, tipping her head on one side and perusing me. Just like she did with the kids in her class when they were regaling her with some fantastic tale.

"Nothing's happened." I frowned. "What are you talking about?"

When I tried to walk past her she caught my hand. "Do not lie to me Cassidy Ann Turner."

I burst out laughing. "Boy you get all country when you're being nosey."

"So?"

"We've been working on the camp. Calling about permits, getting costs for equipment. That's it."

Lily put a finger to her lips. "Hmm. You both look different. Shifty."

"Shifty! What the hell does that mean? How do we look shifty?"

"Not bickering for one. Or calling each other names like my third graders." She winked and then turned on her heels. "Come on in, get warm by the fire while I get dinner started."

Then she disappeared leaving me wondering what made her think something had changed between Gunner and me.

***

The house had finally quieted. Nash and Lily had gone to bed hours ago, and Bertie had been tucked in with a story that Gunner insisted on reading to her despite her protests that she was too old for bedtime stories. As for me, I couldn't sleep, so after what felt like hours of tossing and turning I found myself in the kitchen, standing by the window watching the relentless snowfall in the glow of the moonlight.

"Can't sleep?" Gunner's voice came from behind me, low and gravelly with tiredness.

I spun around, finding him in the doorway wearing flannel pajama pants and a worn gray t-shirt that clung to his shoulders. His hair was mussed, like he'd been running his hands through it.

"Too much on my mind," I admitted, wrapping the borrowed cardigan, Lily's, tighter around myself. "And I don't usually need coffee to function, but I think I had too much today. It's your fault for brewing such good java."

He chuckled and moved toward the refrigerator, pulling out a carton of milk. "Hot chocolate helps. My mom used to make it whenever I couldn't sleep."

The mention of his mom caught me off guard. It was the second time today he'd referenced her, and I couldn't help but feel there was something significant in that. I got the feeling he didn't talk about her much outside the family, so it felt like an honor in some ways.

I watched as his large hands worked with surprising gentleness, measuring cocoa and sugar into a small pan of milk warming on the stove. The domesticity of it made something flutter in my chest.

"Thank you for today," I said softly.

He glanced up, his eyes catching mine. "For trapping you here in a snowstorm? Or leaving you in my office alone while I dealt with my assistant?"

I smiled. "For listening to me about Charlie. For taking my suggestion seriously."

His hands stilled from stirring the pan for a moment. "It was good advice. I should have thought of it myself."

"We all have blind spots."

The silence between us felt different than our usual tense standoffs. This was something quieter, more intimate.

Gunner poured the hot chocolate into two mugs, then nodded toward the living room. "Fire's still going. It's warmer in there."

I followed him, settling onto the plush sofa while he placed the mugs on the coffee table and then kneeled to stoke the dying embers of the fire back to life. The room was cast in flickering amber light, shadows dancing across the walls.

Gunner reached for a mug and handed it to me before settling beside me, not too close, but close enough that the heat rolling off him made my skin hum.

"You still cold?" he asked, his gaze flicking to where my hands curled around the mug.

"A little," I said with a soft laugh. "I think I have issues with my circulation."

He didn't respond right away. Just reached for the throw on the armchair and, with an unexpected tenderness, draped it over my legs. His fingers grazed my knee as he tucked the blanket in, the touch fleeting but electric. Like he knew exactly what he was doing and exactly what it would do to me.

"Better?" he asked, his voice lower, rougher.

I nodded. Words didn't feel safe right now. Not when everything between us suddenly felt charged. Intimate. Like the space we shared had shrunk, holding only the two of us and something sharp-edged and inevitable.

The wind rattled against the windows. The fire crackled. I sank deeper into the couch and the blanket, my fingers tightening around the mug, but my eyes, traitorous things, kept drifting to him. To the strong curve of his jaw, the dusky stubble that shadowed his skin. The way his lashes fell like secrets when he looked down. He was entirely too beautiful for someone who drove me this insane.

"You're staring," he said without looking at me.

I didn't even try to deny it. "Just trying to figure you out."

He turned then; one brow cocked with amusement. "And what's the verdict, Miss Turner?"

"That you're not who I thought you were," I said, letting the truth show in my smile.

A slow, almost smug curve touched his mouth. "That's a good thing, right?"

"Undecided."

Gunner laughed, and the sound landed somewhere deep in my chest, warm and dangerous. When he shifted, our shoulders brushed and neither of us moved away. I could feel the shape of his presence like gravity.

"You know what," he said after a beat, his voice quieter now, "I was wrong about you, too."

"Oh?" I tilted my head, watching him over the rim of my mug.

"I had you pegged as this uptight city teacher who thought she knew better than the rest of us country folk." His eyes met mine, steady and unflinching. "But you care. About these kids. About this place."

His words slipped under my skin like silk, threading into places I hadn't even known were aching for validation.

"And now that I know you're a farm girl," he added with a crooked grin, "I have to come up with new reasons to find you irritating."

I snorted. "Irritating?"

"Okay, challenging." He corrected, with a wink. "Which is basically my kryptonite."

I groaned, followed quickly by an impossible smile. He looked unfairly good in the firelight; golden skin, strong arms folded, mug balanced on his chest like he did this every night. Like we belonged here.

I set my own mug down and leaned back, just a little. Close enough to smell him. A warm spice and cedar, and something deeper, uniquely him. Close enough that if I shifted even an inch, our legs would touch.

"You know we could be good together," he said then, so softly it didn't feel like a confession. It felt like a promise.

My breath caught. "At the camp?" I asked, even though I knew he didn't mean just that.

"That too."

He turned, placing his mug beside mine, and lifted a hand, slow, like he didn't want to startle me. He tucked a strand of hair behind my ear, his fingers warm against my skin, lingering.

His palm cupped my cheek, rough and gentle all at once. "Cassidy," he murmured, my name like it was a secret between us. "I've been trying not to want you. But I think I'm losing that fight."

I felt the pressure of longing against my ribs as I leaned into his touch without thinking, my eyes fluttering shut as his thumb traced the curve of my cheekbone.

Peace and chaos warred in my chest. Everything about this moment felt like a lullaby and a lightning strike.

When I opened my eyes again, his face was closer. His gaze flicked down to my lips. The air crackled.

"I should—" I started, unsure what I was even about to say.

"Don't overthink it," he whispered, his nose brushing mine.

His breath was warm and sweet and close. My hand moved of its own accord, settling against his chest. His heart thudded beneath my palm, strong and fast, echoing mine.

"Tell me to stop," he said, his voice low and rough.

"I can't," I breathed.

And then he kissed me.

Soft at first. Testing. Questioning. My sigh was the answer he needed. His hand slid into my hair, tilting my face just so as he deepened the kiss, his mouth warm and patient and devastating.

The tension we'd built up for weeks unspooled in a single touch. He kissed like he meant it. Like he didn't care that there were a dozen reasons why this was dangerous. He kissed me like I was the only thing tethering him to the earth.

I melted into him, my fingers curling into his shirt. I could feel him everywhere, his hands, his heat, his heartbeat crashing against mine.

When we finally broke apart, breathless and wide-eyed, he rested his forehead against mine.

"Still think I'm irritating?" he murmured, his voice husky.

I grinned, tracing the stubble along his jaw. "Completely," I said.

And then I kissed him again, just to prove how much I didn't mean it.

From the Ground Up – Dan + Shay

CHAPTER 19
Gunner

Ever wake up with excitement deep in your belly and for a moment wonder why it was there? It was a lot less than a moment before it struck me, why I had hosts of damn butterflies. It was that kiss. Both the kisses. Can't say I wasn't shocked when Cassidy pulled me in for another one, but I wasn't about to say no. As kisses went it was pretty spectacular. Hard when it needed to be, gentle when it needed to be, and her lips were as soft as the plumpest pillows.

The honker I woke up with was proof of how good it was. Not that I didn't wake up with one every day, but today's was all about Cassidy and was a full on angry bishop. It was her I'd dreamed about when I'd finally got some sleep.

It was her that I'd have loved to have dragged into my bed last night. Her who'd I'd have loved to have feasted on and to have fucked all night long. I stopped myself, though, because it would have been wrong. We'd only just stopped bitching at each other, or maybe it was a temporary ceasefire, but one day of being pleasant to each other wasn't the best basis for a night of bambam.

Besides which, we might have been hostile with each other for the last three years, but she deserved my respect. A few dates, a nice dinner first… maybe. Although, if she carried on eating her breakfast yoghurt in the way she was then I might just throw her over my shoulder and fuck the respect. The only respectful thing she would be getting would be the attention I paid to her while she lay naked on my sheets.

"Enjoying that?" I asked as she licked the spoon clean. Thank fuck I'd gotten dressed before coming down for breakfast because a steel hard dick in my pajama pants would be obvious, never mind obscene.

She frowned. "Yes, why?" She gave the spoon another lick before dropping it into the bowl. "Is it yours or something?"

"Nope. Just checking breakfast is to your satisfaction." Was it illogical to be jealous of a spoon?

"Pancakes?" Nash asked from over by the stove. Bertie was sitting on the counter next to him, slowly pouring the batter into the pan for him.

"You should say yes," I told Cassidy. "He makes the best pancakes."

"And cupcakes," Bertie chimed in. "Remember when you made them for Getting To Know You Day, Daddy." She turned to us. "They were an absolute triumph, Miss. Turner."

Cassidy smiled widely, her eyes soft on my niece. "I remember. They were the talk of the moms, if I remember."

Nash turned and grinned with a shake of his head. As a single dad he'd been very popular with the ladies of Silver Peaks. His heart had always been with Lily, though. Anyone else never had a chance. Even Bertie's mom had only been a one night thing. Thankfully, for us, and Bertie, she didn't want anything to do with the amazing little girl helping her dad with pancakes.

Her mom signed all responsibility of her to Nash and then went to work on the cruise ships. That meant we got to have her in our lives permanently, because she was our sunshine and not just on the rainy days. Raised by three men, who'd practically raised themselves, it meant her vocabulary leaned more toward a twenty-five year old rancher than a ten year old princess but Lily was working on that.

"How many pancakes do you want?" Nash asked, changing the subject.

"As many as you're willing to make," I told him and rubbed my stomach. "I'm a growing boy."

Cassidy cleared her throat and shifted in her seat, glancing at me as Lily came in with Billy toddling at her side.

"Oh babe, you're making pancakes. Thank you." She went over to Nash and reached up to kiss his cheek. "I'm starved."

I watched as Billy went over to his toys and dropped his little ass to the floor and began building a tower with plastic bricks. Lily leaned in to kiss Bertie's cheek and tickled her sides getting a loud belly laugh from her. They were the ideal picture of domesticity, and I envied them. I would love what they had, but maybe in another lifetime. For now, I had my horses and the camp to concentrate on. I looked at Cassidy as she gazed at the tableau of family perfection, too. For as good as our kisses had been we were probably best just staying as frenemies.

Breakfast continued with the usual chaos as we all tucked into the stack of pancakes Nash put on the table. They were almost gone when Wilder appeared looking a little worse for wear.

"Wow," Bertie said, a forkful of pancake halfway to her mouth. "You look icky Uncle Wilder."

He leaned down to kiss the top of her head. "I feel icky baby. I need coffee."

We watched as he walked over to the jug and poured himself a mug. All his movements were slow and deliberate, and it was clear he was suffering from the hangover from hell.

"How the hell did you get back from town?" I asked, glancing through the window at the snow still settled outside.

"I didn't go to town." He took a swig of coffee and groaned. "After getting the cattle into the storm shelter the guys had a poker game in the bunkhouse. It went on until about three this morning."

I glanced at Cassidy, aware that we had been making out on the sofa until just before three. We were lucky that Wilder hadn't caught us.

"You win?" Nash asked, reaching for his coffee.

"Just about broke even. Charlie, though, she cleaned up."

"Charlie was in the bunkhouse playing poker?" I knew all the guys we hired were decent men, but the idea of Charlie in there with almost twenty men all drinking was a little unsettling.

"Don't worry." Wilder took the seat next to me and dropped into it with a huff. "She can handle herself, but also we were all totally respectful and I walked her back to the stable apartment at the end of the night."

"That's good. But talking of Charlie, you should all know she's leaving." My eyes met Cassidy's who gave me a small smile. One that said, 'it'll be fine'.

"No way!" Nash exclaimed.

"Why?" Lily asked and then turned to Wilder. "You didn't, did you?"

"No!" He pushed his fingers against his temple and then repeated, softer, "No I didn't."

"She's got a job back home in Tennessee. Heading up a training program."

Nash slapped my shoulder. "This has to be a pain in the ass for you. You going to promote from within?"

I shook my head. "No, no one is ready. Katie might have been if she hadn't left for veterinary college. So, I'll place an ad on the usual websites, maybe talk to Deacon. He usually knows a few people on the circuit looking for something." I pointed at Wilder with my thumb. "So, he isn't why she's leaving, but that doesn't mean he didn't."

"Damm it," Wilder exclaimed. "I told you I didn't."

"What never?" I asked, surprised.

Wilder held his hands in the air. "No never I just liked you to think I did because it annoyed the shit out of you."

"You really didn't?" Nash seemed equally as shocked as I was that Wilder had never hooked up with Charlie.

"No, I didn't."

"What didn't Uncle Wilder do?" Bertie asked, pushing her finger through the syrup residue on her plate.

"He didn't do disgusting things like wipe his plate with his finger," Nash grumbled, taking Bertie's plate away from her. "You dirty little munchkin." They grinned at each other, love shining through and that twinge momentarily came back in my chest.

"Go and wash up, baby," Lily told her, giving my niece just as brilliant a smile as Nash had.

As Bertie made a song and dance about leaving the table to go to the bathroom, I looked over at Cassidy. She was staring out of the window. I wasn't sure if she was distracted by the weather outside or deliberately ignoring the goings on at the table. I often found myself doing that, since Nash had gained his own little tribe. When they were together, loving each other and family time, I felt like an outsider, even if Wilder was there, too. Someone encroaching on their private time. Although, I knew for a fact if Nash or Lily knew I felt like that they'd be devastated. Maybe that was how Cassidy was feeling.

"You okay, Cassidy? Worried you might get stranded here another night?" I asked with a chuckle.

Her gaze swung to mine. "Not worried, but I was just wondering if I could get back to town. I have stuff I need to do ready for school tomorrow."

Nash pulled out his phone and clicked on the screen. "Says the roads should be clear by noon. The plows out since dawn."

"That's good," Cassidy replied, though she didn't sound as enthusiastic as I'd have expected.

Funny because I didn't feel it about her leaving either. "Before you go," I said standing up a little too quickly, "we should finalize those camp permit applications that we started on yesterday. Make the most of being snowed in together."

Lily shot me a glance, narrowed her eyes on me and then grinned. "Good idea. Then have some lunch here before you go back to town."

"Okay, if you're sure?"

"Absolutely," Lily replied with a nod. "It's chicken with all the trimmings.

"Don't you think it's weird we live on a cattle ranch and yet eat chicken?" Wilder asked, lifting his head from where it was resting on the table.

"No, because I don't want any of you dying of a heart attack." Lily patted his back. "You boys used to eat far too much red meat."

"Well, it sounds good to me." Cassidy stood up and started to collect dishes from the table. "I'll do the dishes and then we can get started."

"No way." Lily waved her off. "You two go and work. Wilder can help me, can't you sweetie?"

My brother groaned and with his head back on the table reached out for a plate and shoved it toward Lily. "There you go."

Nash swatted him. "You are a waste of space. Just go and check on that heifer in the observation pen, the one with the septic tale. The fresh air will clear your head, and if that doesn't then the stench inside there will."

When we got to my office I slammed the door on the cold and snow outside and immediately the air felt charged. Cassidy stood by my desk, her fingers tracing the edge of it.

"So," we both said at the same time, then laughing awkwardly.

"About last night," I started.

"Yeah we should probably talk about that," she agreed, tucking her hair behind her ear-the same spot where I'd touched her in the darkness of the night before.

I took a step closer. "I'm not good at this sort of thing."

"What sort of thing?" Her eyes challenged me.

"The morning after kissing a woman I'm supposed to be professional with." I ran a hand through my hair, wishing I was wearing my Stetson because weirdly it made me feel more confident and assured. "Especially one I've spent years arguing with."

She smiled and flicked out her tongue along her bottom lip. "Is that what we were doing? I thought that maybe it was foreplay."

My jaw nearly hit the floor as heat rushed through me. Shit, she was a surprise, and I was pretty sure she might just be one of the best kind. Before I could respond, my phone rang. It flashed up as 'County Office'. Who the hell would be calling me from there on a Sunday morning?

"I should take this," I said reluctantly.

Cassidy nodded and moved over to Charlie's desk to give me some privacy, not that I needed it.

"Gunner Miller," I answered.

"Mr. Miller, this is Sandra O'Neil from the County Environmental Department. I know this is a Sunday, but I've received a concerning report about potential violations at the development site near your property."

I straightened and looked at Cassidy. "What kind of violations?"

"Construction equipment was moved in overnight, despite the snow," Sandra replied. "And they're clearing land in an area marked as protected wetland habitat. I urgently need your help."

It looked like permits for the camp would have to wait.

"Son of a—" I cursed and shook my head, my gaze on Cassidy. "Sorry. How is that possible? Don't they need permits?"

"They do," Sandra told me. "Which is why I'm calling. I need documentation of the wildlife you mentioned at the town meeting. Specifically, the weasel breeding grounds which borders your land and the area they've moved machinery to. Anything at all that you have that proves what it is and where it is."

Cassidy was staring back intently; concern etched on her face.

"Yeah, I can get that to you," I said. "I even have photos, GPS coordinates."

"That's fantastic. The sooner the better. They're moving fast." She sighed heavily. "But can you keep this between us, not everyone here sees this as a potential issue like I do."

"Basically, the County Mayor says it's a done deal but not everyone is on board. Am I right?"

"I can't comment on that, Mr. Miller, but let's just say money means more than wildlife to some people."

"I get you." I mentally thought about the details that I needed to gather. "Give me a few hours and I'll email it to you."

"I'll give you my personal email," she laughed humorlessly, "I'm sure you understand why."

"I do. Now, what's the address?"

After hanging up, I explained the situation to Cassidy.

"Sounds like they're trying to destroy the evidence before they can be stopped," she said, anger flashing in her eyes. "We need to document everything today."

"I need to show you something first." I pulled open my desk drawer and took out a folder. "These are some other camp plans I've been working on since you suggested it."

I spread out a rough but fairly detailed drawing across my desk—a larger facility than we'd discussed.

"I've been thinking," I started unfolding more of the plans across my desk. "This room here," I stabbed a finger at the blueprint, "it could be an office. Your office if you like, with built-in bookshelves. It would have full southern exposure, the view of the mountains and enough space to do, well, whatever you need to do. Then all along here," I continued, drawing an invisible line. "That would be more riding rings, a small swimming pond, cabins. Maybe even a workshop and classrooms."

"Gunner, this is... incredible," she breathed.

The awe in her eyes made me falter and wonder what it would be like to receive the gift of that expression every day. I continued, wanting more of it from her.

"I was thinking that the camp doesn't have to just be a summer thing. These kids need and can get all year-round support." I met her eyes. "I want to register a non-profit so that with the right funding, we could make this permanent."

Her eyes widened. "Why didn't you say? Have you told your brothers?"

"Nope. I wanted to be sure we could do it. That you were all in because I gotta be honest with you, Cassidy, this is bigger than I can create on my own." I hesitated. "And because I was stubborn and didn't want to admit you might be right about some things."

She stepped closer, her expression unreadable. "And now?"

"Now we need to save the land so we can build this place. Together." I reached for her hand. "About last night—"

The door burst open, and Cassidy and I pulled apart as Nash appeared. "Sorry to interrupt, but Wilder just radioed in from the storm barn. Those bulldozers are getting closer to our property line. Further down now, by the south pasture. Close to where Wilder thought about building his cabin."

"Shit. We're coming," I said, not taking my eyes off Cassidy. "We've got work to do."

She nodded, a determined look replacing the vulnerability from moments ago. "Let's go protect your ranch and our camp."

As we headed out, I knew two things with absolute certainty: we were going to fight for this land with everything we had, and whatever was happening between Cassidy and me was far from over.

Thinking Out Loud - Ed Sheeran

CHAPTER 20
Cassidy

Gunner drove us to the property line on an ATV while Nash and Wilder followed on horseback. I wasn't expecting him to ask me to go, but when he told Nash, 'we're coming', air rushed from my lungs. Trepidation was mixed with excitement at the idea of sitting behind him, wrapping my arms around him to hold on. I'd started off holding the seat bar behind me but then he'd barked out his command.

"Arms around my waist, sweetheart."

My adrenaline spiked, as heat spread through my body. He'd spent three years being salty with me and one snap of an order and I was turned to mush.

As we approached the boundary line, the ATV started to slow to a stop, and Gunner stood up in his seat.

"Fuckers." He got off the vehicle and walked closer to the fence. The machinery looked to be less than fifty feet away on the other side, with diggers poised to start work.

Nash and Wilder rode up alongside, urging their horses to a halt, dismounting and joining their brother. From my seat on the ATV, I watched the three of them. All three had the same stance, hands on hips and legs wide apart. They all wore Roper style boots as opposed to Western style, each of them filled their Wranglers and their shearling lined denim jackets to perfection and the Stetsons that Gunner and Wilder wore were the icing on the cake. Nash always preferred a ball cap, often backwards which was another level of sexy. The Miller brothers were definitely a sight to behold.

"Cassidy, you got a minute?"

Nash calling over to me woke me from my daydreams and took my attention away from one of the brothers in particular. Because Gunner's ass was just that little more perfect than the others.

"Yeah, what is it?" I jumped down and clapped my gloved hands together. It was still cold, even more so racing across the land on the back of an ATV.

"You told me once you grew up on a farm, right?" Nash asked. "Didn't you sell produce from it?"

I glanced at Gunner, who was looking down at his boots. "I did and yes, we sold eggs and vegetables."

"So, you must have encountered all sorts of regulations."

"Some," I replied. "Why, what are you thinking?"

Nash stared ahead; his brow furrowed. "I'm thinking that whatever they do might just affect the grass in this pasture and this is the grass we use for winter hay. Without it the cattle will either starve or we will because we have to pay over the odds for it from someone else." He looked at me. "And then there's the effect on the ranch and your camp."

Gunner pointed at the perimeter wire fence. "That fence is there because a long time ago, when our Grandpa ran the ranch, the County told him we couldn't be an open range ranch. For years no one understood why, well it looks like now we know."

"Took the assholes forty years to do something with it, though," Wilder grumbled, taking his hat off and running a hand through his hair. "Never thought they'd bring it this close, though."

"Well, they have," Nash replied, sounding defeated.

"Where do I come into it?" I asked. "I mean, I'm more than ready to help with the fight, but I'm not sure what I can do."

Nash held up a finger. "Ah, but that's where you're wrong. You see, as a farmer you'll know about the boundaries between cultivated areas and wild spaces. You and your mom must have known the importance of transitional ecosystems and if you look closely at that disturbed soil you can see that these shit heads are going to be destroying it."

I shrugged. "We weren't a huge farm, Nash. I mean we had regulations we had to adhere to, and we knew about crop rotation and had seasonal growing knowledge but I'm not sure how that helps."

"It helps because you have experience of the kind of things they're bound to throw at us when we dispute this," Nash replied. "And Lily tells me that you're a stickler for detail, so if we list the objections, you think you could put it into some document that they'd take notice of?"

"I'd be happy to," I told him, feeling something in my chest—pride, that they valued my help, even though I wasn't part of the family. "But you know you're all intelligent men. You don't need me."

"I'm not sure that's true." Gunner laughed. "We're the best when it comes to running a ranch. Plus, we can all argue the toss with the best of them, but I think what Nash is trying to say is that basically none of us know how to present our arguments without telling them to fuck off."

"True," Wilder replied with a humorless laugh.

"Any help you can give from yours and your mom's experience would be invaluable," Nash added.

I nodded, thinking back to when I was about fifteen. "Actually, Mom had to deal with a watershed protection regulation once. Our vegetable plots were uphill from a protected wetland area, and they wanted us to change all our drainage and runoff because of it."

"What happened?" Gunner asked, his eyes so intense on me that it felt like there was no one else around. "How the hell did you deal with that? That's huge."

"I know," I sighed, recalling how worried Mom had been about the money. "We weren't allowed to alter the natural water paths either, so it was a huge undertaking. Mom argued and got them to share the cost in the end, but the point is," I pointed toward the machinery, "if they're disturbing natural drainage patterns and from the position of the creek and pond they probably are, then that's a clear violation."

"In what way?" Gunner's gaze turned to Nash. "You know about this?"

Nash scratched at his stubbled cheek. "Yeah, now you come to mention it, the water division talked about it when they were investigating the pollution of the creek. They were worried obviously that because of the flow it would go down into the supply for the town."

Gunner moved closer to the perimeter and looked up the hill and then back down. He turned back to us. "So, you're saying if they disrupt the natural flow here it will impact downstream on the wetlands and then further along to the pond where the beavers are?"

"And maybe the creek?" I asked.

Nash shrugged. "Not sure. I guess it might."

"Well, even if it doesn't, I know they should be doing all sorts of tests to check the flow and the water levels. There's a whole host of documentation, written observations and soil samples that need to be completed. I remember helping Mom with it all, so if they haven't done that…"

Gunner exhaled while Nash and Wilder grinned. They remained silent as I looked between the three of them, waiting for one of them to say something. Watching as they looked over their land in silent understanding of what it meant to each of them. Brothers who were willing to go to battle for their home.

"Thank you," Gunner finally said, a shy smile touching his lips.

And it suddenly didn't matter what had been said between us before, because those two words meant everything.

"Okay," Nash said, clapping Wilder on the back. "Let's get back to the house and decide what to do next."

"My vote is getting some of the guys to smash up the machinery in the middle of the night," Wilder grumbled.

"It's not an awful idea," Gunner replied and then looked at his older brother. "But we're not going to, don't worry. I need to send all the proof of the breeding ground to Sandra O'Neil first anyway."

"Who?" Wilder asked.

Gunner quickly explained who she was and instantly Nash's shoulder's relaxed. "That sounds positive, a little lifeline maybe," he said, slapping his brother's shoulder.

"I still think we should smash up the machinery," Wilder scoffed.

"Maybe that's our last resort." Nash walked toward his horse which was waiting patiently with Wilder's. "See you back at the house. I'm going to check in with Ray and see what he thinks about moving the cattle down from the storm barn to the winter barn. The long range forecast suggests more snowstorms might be on the way." He sighed. "I mean I know it can change, so I want his advice."

I knew Ray was their foreman, running things when the boys weren't around, and I knew from Lily the winter barn was where the cattle were kept during bad weather. See, I was learning. Although, I wasn't really sure why it mattered.

"Okay, bro. We'll get back to the house. That's where all the stuff is I need, anyway." Gunner waved a hand toward the ATV. "Your chariot awaits, Miss. Turner."

Flashing him a smile, I moved past him and felt weird that I was looking forward to wrapping my arms around his waist again.

"Okay," Lily said as she sat back at the dining table after checking on the kids watching TV, our war table as Wilder had named it. "We now have a list of arguments against the development, ones that affect the ranch." She turned to me. "And you have enough time to document it all, Cassidy?"

"Of course. What else do I do in the evening except read or watch TV?"

Lily laughed. "She says that because she has every lesson planned from now until Summer break."

I groaned. "Now you make me sound really boring."

"She clearly doesn't know you that well," Gunner muttered, cocking an eyebrow.

Thankfully I was the only one who heard him because Nash and Wilder were arguing over the last cookie on the plate of homemade ones that Lily and Bertie had created.

Yet, Lily clearly had heard, though, because she was smirking at us both. 'Okay?" She asked.

"Good thanks, Lily." Gunner stretched his legs out and relaxed back in his seat. "Perfect in fact."

God, he was cocky, but I was beginning to like it.

"Something you need to tell me?" Lily asked, looking between us.

"No," I snapped. "Why would there be?"

"Yeah," Gunner added. "What on earth can we possibly need to tell you?"

She narrowed her eyes on us, staring us down until we heard Bertie yelling for her from the lounge. Sighing, Lily stood up and pointed at us. "I will find out."

"Meddlesome woman," Gunner muttered as she walked away and then turned to me. "Ignoring my sister-in-law, are you sure that you have time for all of this?"

"Yes, I'm sure." I swallowed back the moan of appreciation as he linked his hands behind his head, making his biceps bulge. "I want to help."

"There are some other ways you could help." His tone was suggestive as his tongue darted out to run along his lower lip.

"And what would they be?" My pulse was too fast. The butterflies in my stomach were flapping their wings too fast. My lungs were too tight.

"Well," he leaned forward, stretching his arms across the table., "I was thinking—"

"Gunner, did Deacon send that architect's number over?"

I didn't get to hear how else I could help Gunner, because his attention was taken with Nash. As the brothers continued to discuss development plans, wedding venues and kid's camps I watched them. They were a family who loved each other deeply and I could see why Lily had been heartbroken to lose them. Maybe working alongside them, with Gunner, wouldn't be the worst thing in the world.

F**kin' Perfect - P!nk

CHAPTER 21
Gunner

The last few days had been busy. We'd started calving late this year because of some bad weather in February. That meant that we still had heifers giving birth, so for the last week we'd all been up by three helping with the births. We'd lost one heifer which had been an awful experience. Thankfully, Rose, our vet, was able to save the calf and then Nash and I managed to get another heifer, who'd just had a calf two days before, to adopt it. Then there was Songbird and her foal. Songbird was doing great but the foal, Gypsy, was struggling to wean, still preferring her mother's milk. It wasn't anything we couldn't handle but it was just more to do along with getting the documents and images together as evidence against the development. One good thing was that they hadn't yet broken ground and I wondered if it was Sandra O'Neil who had managed to get us some thinking and planning time because of the details I'd sent to her.

Cassidy had been over last night. She came over after dinner to show us her first draft of the documentation. I was blown away by it, we all were. The wording, the way she'd bullet pointed each of our points of argument and then gave measured responses on how they should be addressed. It was perfect. Her visit had been fleeting, though, and as much as I wanted to make her stay so we could talk, she said she was meeting someone in Downtown Bar & Grill. And that had kept me awake most of the night.

"Who do you reckon Cassidy was meeting last night?" I asked Wilder, trying to act unaffected while I rode alongside him. The sun was just peeking over the horizon, and we were herding the cattle to the winter barn because there was worse weather on the way. I was normally tied up with the horses, but it had been a while since I'd been out working with the boys, so I'd joined in, needing the air and shit banter to help clear my head.

"Jack," Wilder yelled, "you've got a runner."

A steer had made a run for it, either spooked by the thundering feet of cattle and horses or just wanting some alone time.

As Wilder moved his horse, Alice Elcott (yep, Bertie had named the mare), to edge another possible runner back into the herd, he grinned at me. "You worried that she's got herself a boyfriend?"

"No. Hup hup," I yelled as some of the cattle started to dawdle. "Why would I care? Just interested."

His smirk said everything because he knew me. I'd never cared what Cassidy was doing before, so he had to be wondering why I did now.

"You starting to get the feels, brother?"

Yep, I was right he was wondering. "No. Why would I be?"

"Well, you've been spending a fair bit of time together recently. Working on the development stuff and the kids camp." He dropped back alongside me. "I mean I'm not surprised; you've spent the last three years having angry foreplay.

"We have not." We totally fucking had if I was being honest with myself. Years of sniping and backbiting with each other had led to kisses in the dead of night. Kisses that I could still feel and taste on my lips. "She's not what I thought she was, Wild. She's so much more than I gave her credit for."

Wilder wiggled his brows. "So, you do like her. Well, well, well."

"I didn't say that. I just said that she's different from what I thought. She lived on a farm, you know."

"I know she did. I knew before it was even mentioned the other night."

I blinked at him. "How did you know?"

He sighed. "I actually talk to people. It's a concept you should get on board with. You talk to someone, ask them questions about themselves, tell them about yourself. And then," he said, pointing a finger at me, "if you realize that you like them, and maybe they like you, you ask them on a date. How does that sound?"

"Like you're a stupid dickweed who lets his penis rule his life."

"Unlike you, big brother, whose penis has been in its hidey-hole for waaaay too long."

Peanut, my horse, moved to the side of a cow that was getting ready to run. He was such a good horse, knowing exactly what he needed to do without much guidance from me.

"My penis gets plenty of action," I yelled across to Wilder.

He waved his gloved hand. "Yeah, I've heard you cranking."

"I do not cry while I'm wanking, you fucker."

He shrugged. "Not what I hear when you're pulling on your dick, every damn night," he said with a long, exaggerated sigh. "We have another runner. Jack! Let's go get it."

As he rode off I wondered two things. Should I ask Cassidy on a date, and did I need to wank less?

***

Things between Charlie and I were better. They weren't perfect but much improved now that things were out in the open. Today she was taking a day to prepare for her move back to Tennessee. I'd also got her to make a note of her daily tasks, and I was going to ask Ruthie to type it all up when she started. That way whoever I took on as her replacement would have some sort of guide to follow.

The snow had stopped outside, but it had been replaced with wind and rain which was building up to be an apocalypse out there, random weather for the time of year. After getting the cattle to the storm barn we heard a tree had come down on the north edge of our land. It wasn't particularly dangerous, but it was in good grazing land, and we didn't want any cattle hurting themselves on it. Wilder had taken a gang of guys over to get it sawn into logs. I told him to wait until the weather calmed down, but if there was one thing my brother was, it was a doer. He didn't procrastinate like me, or way up a thousand options like Nash. He just did.

"Knock, knock."

I turned to see the door cracked open and Cassidy's head, wearing a pink wool hat with a huge gray bobble, poking around it.

"Come on in," I called, getting out of my chair. "It's hateful out there."

She pushed inside, her coat wet and her nose bright red with cold. "Hi, I thought we could do some camp stuff, but if you're busy."

I glanced at my phone, shocked that was the time, that school was out for the day. "No, come on in. I have time."

"I didn't have anything on tonight so thought…damn glasses." They were steamed up and as she wrinkled up her nose she snatched them from her face. Wiping them with her gloved fingers she gave a heavy sigh. "I forgot to take my contacts out last night so thought I should wear these today. I'm thinking of having laser treatment. What do you think?"

I didn't say anything, I couldn't because I was speechless at how damn beautiful she looked. Her hair was down, damp strands from the rain hanging over her shoulders, there was a cold pink to her cheeks and the end of her nose, and she was wearing a lipstick just a shade darker than her lips, yep, I knew exactly what color her lips were. Her whisky colored eyes framed with thick lashes studied me as her fingers gripped her glasses.

"Gunner, are you okay?" Her eyes went narrow as she leaned a little closer. "I think you look a little bit weird." She put her glasses back on. "Yep, you definitely look weird. Have you heard something about the camp or the development?"

"N-no. All good. You look frozen. Take your coat off, it's wet. I'll pour you some coffee." I didn't move, though, because I couldn't. There was something about her. Something different. It was like she was standing taller although she was a tiny little thing, barely reaching my shoulder.

Frowning, Cassidy shoved her gloves into her pockets and then shouldered out of her coat, grabbing her hat off her head. Her hair stood on end, static running through it and her plaid shirt had a few buttons undone, showing the curve of the top of her breasts. She was fucking beautiful. Exquisite. How the hell had I never noticed before? Why had I been too busy fighting with the person I *thought* she was to get to know the real Cassidy?

"Sit down and I'll get you that coffee." I held out my hand for her coat and taking it from her hung it on the hooks by the door. "I have a sweater here somewhere if you want to wear it."

"I'll be fine. Coffee will warm me up." She took the visitor seat at my desk and rubbed her hands together. "I heard on the radio that we might get more snow again soon."

"Yeah, we moved the herd to the winter barn early this morning." I cleared my throat and moved over to the coffee pot. "Creamer no sugar, right?"

"Please." She put her phone on my desk and then reached down for her purse. It was a huge thing, but I hadn't noticed it because my attention was all on her. A buff colored folder appeared from inside and was placed next to the phone.

"More camp stuff?" I asked, placing the coffee in front of her.

Glancing up at me, she sighed. "Yeah, my stupid laptop decided to die. I took it to the IT repair place in Clementine Hills, but he's not convinced he can rescue it. It is old to be fair, so I probably need to invest in a new one."

"That's shit." I took my seat opposite her. "So, what's in the folder?"

"Oh, it's some details about the camp," she pushed it toward me, "I at least managed to print it off before the laptop died. I found this app that can create images from the description that you input. So," she started to flick through the pages and pulled out some photographs.

They were clearly computer generated but depicted how the camp and stables could look. One image showed a state of the art stable block with two horses in showers, while the other was the interior of the building where the kids would sleep. There were bunks and a kitchen area, as well as a sofa and bean bags.

"They were just something I was messing around with, but it will give us some ideas when we speak to the architect for the building for the kids." She looked up at me. Her eyes tentative. "The stables obviously don't need changing."

"I don't know. I quite like the idea of those horse showers. Some of the ranch horses get really dirty when they're working. It would be great." I looked closer and made a mental note to investigate it further. As Cassidy leaned in next to me I caught the scent of her light and fresh perfume that seemed to cling to her. Her shoulder brushed mine as she pointed at the picture.

"Right here is where we could put a little classroom maybe, so the kids can learn about horse anatomy, or training programs. Basic stuff, though."

I nodded and found myself leaning toward her, not to see the picture better but simply to be closer. It was a bad idea because suddenly the ground shifted beneath me.

"What else you got?" I asked, straightening up to create distance between us.

As if she felt it, too, Cassidy quickly shuffled to the side. "A-a spreadsheet of the um, the permits and their um status," she said, stumbling over her words. "A list of things that we need to buy and the email addresses and mobile numbers of the contractors we already have on board. Then this," she searched through the papers and picked another out, "this is a list of possible investors. The ones we discussed with everyone the other night, plus some others that I looked up online who invest in similar projects."

"That's fantastic, Cassidy." I looked up to see her looking at me tentatively. "Honestly, it's great. Thank you."

"I hope I haven't overstepped."

"Not at all." It felt strange that she hadn't given me shit about it but instead was worried about upsetting me. Normally we'd be verbally battling by now. Since the kisses, though, things had changed. How I felt about her had changed. "How was your date?" No fucking idea where that thought came from, but it was too late, I'd asked the question I'd been determined not to ask.

"Date?" She picked up her coffee and took a sip, giving a satisfied moan. One that made me wonder what her other moans sounded like. "What date?"

"You went to Downtown last night. Said you were meeting someone."

"Oh, that. Yes I was meeting Lola Michaels, who works at the library. I read to a group of kids once a month and she wanted to thank me with a nice bottle of wine."

"A nice bottle of wine in Downtown Bar & Grill. Is that even possible?"

"It was actually okay. I think Delaney has upped his game."

Rubbing my hands together, I wondered why my stomach was churning even though I now knew she hadn't been on a date.

"You had a nice evening then?"

"Lovely, thanks. What did you do last night?"

"Early bedtime. We were up at three-thirty this morning."

Cassidy nodded and cleared her throat and suddenly everything felt awkward. Not awkward as such but different, like the bickering between us was easier than being friends. Like a couple of kisses has turned the world on its head, but then again wasn't that what great kisses were supposed to do. Didn't I need to do something with that knowledge? I liked discomfort, I relished being outside my comfort zone, so why the hell was this with Cassidy fucking with my head?

Because I was afraid she'd reject me. Because what if I didn't light a fire within her like the one she lit within me?

Fuck it. "Talking of nice wine, I was wondering whether maybe you'd like to go out one night. For a drink." I swallowed and licked my lips, waiting for what felt like an eternity for her to reply. "I know it's probably—"

"Yes, I'd like that."

Her hand rested on her breastbone, delicate fingers splayed out underneath the long, slim column of her neck and I thought I saw a tremble to them. As my eyes lingered on them, she instantly dropped her hand to the desk, edging it toward her phone.

"We could talk some more about the camp."

Cassidy shook her head. "We can talk about the camp any time. A date would be nice, because that is what you're suggesting, isn't it cowboy?" She smirked. "Although, I'm hoping it'll be better than the last one. That was awful."

Instantly we felt back to normal, and my shoulders sagged with relief.

"Not totally awful. A date with me could never be awful," I joked. "Plus, I never said it was going to be a date."

"Liar." There was a gleam in her eye, so bright that I could see it behind her glasses. "It is a date, and you know it. I'm thinking you might want some more of those kisses we shared."

I laughed. "And you say I'm the one with ego."

"Your ego is so big it probably needs its own zip code," she replied, her lips curved into a grin."

"And yet you don't seem to be able to stay away from my neighborhood."

Inhaling, she perused me carefully. "Where are you going to take me on this date, then?"

Shaking my head I couldn't help but chuckle. "I thought we established that I never said it was a date."

"And I thought *I* established that it was." She lifted her leg and crossed it over the other, relaxing back in her chair with her mug to her chest. "But if you're not sure you want it to be a date then I'm not sure I want to drink with a man who is too scared to be honest with himself. Besides, we weren't very successful at the dating thing last time. And that's me being honest."

"If we're all about honesty, I guess I should be, too. You want me to be?" I asked, getting out of my chair and rounding the desk. She nodded, her bottom lip caught between her teeth. "To tell you exactly what I'm thinking or feeling."

When I reached her chair, I took hold of the arms and turned her around, so she was facing me. Pulling her between my legs, I looked down. Her face was upturned, her lips pouting naturally, perfect and waiting to be kissed.

Her chest was heaving, deep and slow, matching the rhythm of my own, the air charged with anticipation.

"Although, I'm not sure you're ready to know what I'm thinking or feeling about you, Miss. Turner." Moving in closer, I gripped the arms of the chair tighter. Holding on like my sanity and my reasoning depended on it. As her lips parted slightly, I felt her soft breath on my skin. When her tits moved upward with her inhale I also felt my dick stir in my pants. She had me transfixed, caught in the deep whisky luster of her gaze. Trapped and not eager one bit to escape.

"Considering you're not supposed to like me very much, you're staring a lot," Cassidy said softly.

"Not staring Cassidy, just judging."

Her eyebrows raised. "You're judging me? What for?"

I shook my head. "Sorry, my mistake. Not judging but trying to make a judgement. Try to judge whether you can take my thoughts and feelings or whether you're a quiet, shy farm girl who might just be a little scared."

She gasped, sharp and short and when goosebumps pebbled her skin I knew she was as turned on as I was. I knew she'd be as wet as I was hard.

"No longer a city girl, now I'm a shy farm girl."

"Now I know you better."

She uncrossed her legs and planted her foot on the floor, parting them slightly. Like it was an invitation for me to move in closer. I stayed where I was. As much as I wanted to throw everything off my desk, undress her and make her yell my name, I wouldn't rush this. I wouldn't threaten to spoil this by acting like I'd never seduced a woman before. Besides which I'd promised her a date, well, pretty much.

"What if going on a date spoils us working together?" she asked, linking her fingers together over her stomach.

"It won't but maybe we should just keep it to ourselves. You know how meddlesome Lily can be."

Cassidy laughed. "Just a little, so yeah, I agree. We keep it just between us and if it's as disastrous as last time then no one needs to know."

"It won't be like last time. It won't spoil us working together."

"What if it does?"

She had a point, but at this stage I couldn't think of anything more important than spending time with her outside of work and maybe getting more of those fucking delicious kisses.

You're Still the One - Shania Twain

CHAPTER 22
Cassidy

What the hell did you wear for a date with a cowboy? I mean I'd been on with him once before, but I hadn't kissed him then. I hadn't seen him at work. Hadn't heard how he dealt with people who weren't doing their job properly. It was kind of hot.

Now, I was desperately searching through my closet for something suitable to wear. I wanted to call Lily and ask for her advice, but Gunner was right. We should keep it between us until we knew it wasn't going to be a huge mistake.

Sitting on the bed I gazed at the contents of the closet, some of which had spilled out onto the bed and floor. It struck me as I looked at the whirlwind that had hit my bedroom, aside from Lily I didn't have anyone else to call. I had a few friends, like Lola from the library and Katelynn who taught fifth grade and shared supervision of recess with me. Mrs. Wright was always there for advice but more educational than fashion. Lily had become my best friend, though, since she moved back to Silver Peaks, and it should be her I was asking. I couldn't, though, so I had to figure it out myself.

"Okay," I sighed, standing up and going to my closet. "You will not beat me."

***

"Wow," Gunner said as I stood in the doorway of my apartment. "You look incredible."

I felt my cheeks heat as I looked down at myself. "I hope I picked the right kind of outfit."

Gunner blew out a breath, his eyes looking directly into mine. "Like I said, incredible."

I'd gone for leather look pants, a cute red sweater that finished just above my waistband and some high black boots with a silver buckle at the ankle. The heel was so high and thin, I was grateful there wasn't still snow on the ground. I just had wind and rain to contend with.

"I'll get my coat." I reached behind the door for it and then grabbed my bag from the console table. "Okay, let's go."

Gunner stood back and let me walk in front of him, down the stairs and to the main door to the street. My apartment was small and cozy and above the bookstore which I loved. It was like having my own personal library. Deidre and Wallace, the owners, were always happy for me to go in and browse, sometimes for hours. They even made me cups of English tea to drink while I curled up in a chair and read the book that I always ended up buying. Hence why my own bookshelves were full to bursting.

Gunner's brand new sleek black F-150 truck was waiting and instead of parking in one of the diagonal spaces he'd parked it close to the edge of the sidewalk. He rushed around me and opened the door.

"You need help getting in?" he asked, letting his eyes drift down the length of me in a not-so-subtle once-over. "You're kind of tiny even in those boots…and those pants are…"

Tight. They were tight. Hence the choice of a tiny thong that was already riding the fine line of comfort.

"I can manage," I said, channeling all my independent woman energy.

Gunner grinned and tilted his head, all smug cowboy confidence. "Go for it."

He stood back, one hand braced on the top of the truck door, watching me with undisguised amusement as I heaved myself up as gracefully as possible. Once I was in, I smoothed my top, pretending the move hadn't winded me a little. The interior was surprisingly clean, all rich leather and still carrying that faint new-car scent. That was, until the driver's door swung open, and Gunner's scent wrapped around me like a hug I wasn't ready for, woodsy, warm, and unmistakably him.

"Okay?" he asked, buckling in beside me.

"Yep," I said, voice breathier than I meant. "You ready?"

"I am." He threw me a crooked smile.

"So, where do the family think you are tonight?"

"Boys' night with my high school buddies," he said, voice low, conspiratorial. "I was suitably sketchy about it."

I laughed. "Same when Lily asked me. I mumbled something about grading and face masks."

"It's for the best," he said, giving me a wink that flipped my stomach.

I stared at the side of his face as he pulled onto the road, his features lit in gold from the dash lights. How could a wink make me feel off-balance? I wasn't the girl who blushed at smiles and swagger. But Gunner had this way of being so casually charming that I couldn't find my footing around him.

"Where are we going?" I asked, needing something to hold on to.

"Somewhere nice." His grin grew wider. "You'll see."

As he drove, his left wrist rested over the steering wheel while his right elbow leaned against the center console. The picture of effortless control. It wasn't fair how good he looked doing absolutely nothing, just driving with calm confidence, bathed in the glow of passing headlights. I wasn't the kind of woman who fell for the strong-and-silent type. But somehow, I was starting to think I'd underestimated just how dangerous Gunner Miller could be to my resolve.

"Cassidy, you okay?"

I blinked. "Yeah. Sorry. Just thinking. Long day. We talked about Shakespeare today."

"I know. Bertie's been quoting bad sonnets since she got home," he said with a laugh. "She's very committed. Let's just say I don't think poetry's her path."

"She gives one hundred percent to everything," I said, my whole body softening at the thought of her. "She didn't stop until she made it to the top of the gym rope last week. It took forty minutes, but she wouldn't quit."

"She had a Pre-K teacher who once told Nash she was obstinate." His voice was quiet now, sincere. "So, I'm glad she's got a teacher now who appreciates her determination."

I turned to look at him, caught off guard. "Thanks."

He gave me a small smile, one that twisted something inside me. "Just saying what I feel."

"How was your day?" I asked, taking a deep breath and moving the attention from me

"Not bad. Charlie and I took in an ex-racehorse that'd been abandoned. A stable girl smuggled him out in the middle of the night. Said what they were doing to him was wrong."

I gasped. "She just… took him?"

"Yep. She was determined that he wouldn't suffer any longer. And now she has a horse full of trauma."

"That's… brave," I said, moved. "And reckless."

"I don't even want to think how she managed to get a million dollar racehorse past the security." His smile was one that told me he was proud of what she'd done.

"And she brought him to you." And I felt a sense of pride on his behalf.

"She's from Sweet Maple Falls and knew about our program. Reached out to me." He said it nonchalantly like it was no biggie, but his reputation said otherwise.

"Was she prosecuted?" I asked.

"Nope. As long as she kept quiet, the owner let it go. Which tells me he'd put that horse through some awful shit if he's willing to do that." He turned off the main road onto a narrow gravel path, his profile etched in moonlight. "She's got experience. I even wondered if maybe she could replace Charlie."

The thought made something sharp flash through me, jealousy, maybe. The idea of another woman being around him, working beside him.

"Is she young?" I asked, pretending to keep it casual. "Willing to learn?"

He glanced over, his frown telling me he heard the edge in my voice. "Probably Wilder's age. Feisty. Not my type. Why?"

"Just curious." I exhaled, tension leaving me in a rush. "Definitely Wilder's type, though."

Gunner chuckled. "Exactly. Which might just be a reason not to hire her."

I laughed with him, but my chest still buzzed.

"You don't want to lose her," I said, smoothing my palms on my thighs. "You should call her back."

His eyes flicked toward me. "I will. Tomorrow. But tonight…"

He reached over slowly, hand brushing mine where it rested on the console. His pinky grazed my knuckle, a feather-light touch that somehow made every nerve ending in my body sit up and pay attention.

"…tonight's all about you."

His voice was like velvet, low and warm, and that smile, lazy, intimate, just for me, knocked the breath clean out of my lungs.

My fingers curled instinctively toward his, craving contact.

I turned my head away before I could say something I shouldn't. But my smile lingered. And so did his touch.

Around thirty minutes later, Gunner turned the truck onto a quiet farm track, the tires crunching over gravel before easing onto a smooth stretch of blacktop. The headlights lit up the courtyard ahead, and my breath caught.

Huge terracotta pots overflowed with late summer blooms, placed like sentinels along the perimeter. It was still a working farm because I could see the tack neatly hung on a rail, a barrow overflowing with fresh hay, and a tractor halfway caked in dried mud, but every detail screamed hard work, love and intention.

We rolled to a stop in front of a stable door, where a hand-painted sign read: Apple Bloom Farm.

"We're here," Gunner said, turning off the engine. He gave a slow exhale, like this moment had weight for him, too. "I hope you like it."

I peered through the windshield, absorbing the view, the unexpected softness of it. Even in the dark, it glowed.

"It's a farm," I whispered, more to myself than to him. "A real one."

He nodded, rubbing his palms against his jeans like he was nervous. "It's family-run. They grow their own stuff, raise their own meat, even churn their own butter or some such nonsense. There's a restaurant in the back barn, kinda rustic, but…" He shrugged. "I figured, growing up on a farm, you might like it."

I turned to him slowly, heart full in my chest. It wasn't the place; it was *what it meant*. He hadn't picked somewhere fancy to impress me. He'd picked something that whispered *I see you. I know you. This matters to you, so it matters to me.*

"What are we doing here?" I asked, voice soft.

"Eating," Gunner said, his smile a little sheepish now. "You didn't eat already, did you?"

"No. You told me not to."

"Good," he said, chuckling. "I made a reservation. Apparently the pork chop changes lives."

My laugh was too breathy to sound normal. I nodded, blinking hard. He remembered where I came from. He understood that dirt and work and animals weren't beneath me, they were part of me.

"Is it okay?" he asked. And it was the way he asked it, not just casual but careful, cautious, like he *needed* it to be okay. That undid me.

"It's perfect," I whispered. My throat was tight. "Absolutely perfect."

Before I could stop myself, I leaned across the console and pressed a kiss to his cheek. His stubble was warm, rough against my lips. The scent of him, earth, soap, and that subtle spice that was just Gunner, filled my head.

"Thank you," I murmured, lingering a second longer than I meant to. "Thank you so much."

Gunner let out a breath that trembled at the edges. His eyes searched mine, and for a second, the whole world stilled. No teasing. No sarcasm. Just quiet understanding.

"Okay," he said, voice husky. "Let's get in there and see what you've been missing since you left that farm of yours."

As I stepped down from the truck, the cool air brushing my skin, I realized something with perfect clarity:

Gunner Miller hadn't just planned a date. He'd given me a piece of home.

And somehow, I knew that he was going to be the hardest thing to walk away from.

Better Days – OneRepublic

CHAPTER 23
Gunner

Watching Cassidy eat that buttermilk-roasted chicken like it was a religious experience might've been the hottest thing I'd ever witnessed.

Every slow bite was a show. The gentle scrape of her fork against the plate. A moan here, a lip lick there, her eyes fluttering shut as she savored the jus like it was the secret to happiness itself. It was intimacy in its purest form and my jeans had officially become too damn tight, and I wasn't sure if it was the food, the wine, or just her, glowing in the golden candlelight.

"You're kind of enjoying that, huh?" I murmured, leaning my forearm on the table, trying not to picture that same mouth doing things that would land us in a different kind of room entirely.

"I can't believe I didn't know about this place," she said, rubbing her stomach with this dreamy little hum that I felt straight in my spine. "It's unbelievably good."

Then she leaned in, conspiratorial and damn near lethal. "Do you mind if we have dessert?"

Mind? I'd watch her eat cake every night for the rest of my life if it meant I got to see her like this, unguarded, glowing, happy.

"They do a sharing plate," I said. "Three different desserts. Want to try that?"

She nodded enthusiastically, her eyes sparkling with wine and mischief. "Just warning you now, I'm probably going to eat more than my fair share."

"That's fine. I'll let you." I grinned, but inside I meant it. I'd let this woman have whatever she wanted from me. Anything. Everything.

When I asked about the farm she grew up on, her face softened like sunlight on water.

"Well, we weren't exactly big time," she said, wrapping her fingers around her wineglass. "We had chickens, pigs, goats… veggies. My dad had dreams of expanding, but when he died, Mom just didn't have the energy."

My heart gave a sharp twist. "I'm sorry. That must've been… hell."

She nodded, but it wasn't just grief in her eyes. It was resilience. "Dad died when I was seven. Cleaning his shotgun and the safety was off. One second he was there, the next…" She swallowed. "Mom passed away when I was eighteen. Cancer."

I reached for her hand across the table, not even thinking. Her fingers threaded through mine like they belonged there.

"Shit, Cassidy. I didn't mean to bring up anything painful."

"It's okay," she said, smiling faintly. "I like remembering them. Dad was always singing, always calling me Cassie, he was the only one allowed to."

She laughed softly, and something about it shattered me in the best way. "Mom was beautiful. Kind. She fostered kids after Dad died because they always wanted a big family. When she passed, I had three foster siblings. I took care of them until they found more permanent homes."

I stared at her, stunned. "You were eighteen."

"I was," she said, lifting her chin a little. "But we managed. It's why I became a teacher."

Jesus. She was lightning and soft rain. The strongest woman I'd ever met, wrapped in sarcasm and tight jeans. She talked about hard things like she'd already done the breaking and come back stronger. And I... I was falling for her, hard and fast. Faster than should be possible after just one kiss and one date.

The waitress appeared to take away the dishes and asked about dessert, so I ordered the sharing plate. And, if Cassidy wanted to eat it all then I'd let her.

"What about you?" she asked as we watched the waitress walk away, her hand still in mine. "Did you always want to work with horses? I know you said they helped after your mom died."

"Well, I knew I'd always end up working on the ranch. Horses specifically?" I gave a one shouldered shrug. "I've always loved them. Could ride from an early age. We only really had working horses, though. Then, when Mom was alive, she got this beautiful mare, Ariel, and she was skittish as hell. She wouldn't let anyone on her back. Dad went crazy at Mom for buying her and none of us had any clue why she did. It wasn't like she could ride her."

"What happened?"

"Mom asked me to spend time with her. You know, clean her stable and brush her, feed her apples, generally show her some love. So, I did, and I watched YouTube videos on how to get a horse to let you ride it." I grinned and shook my head at the memory, and the warmth it filled me with. "I was eight years old and thought I could miraculously get her better."

Cassidy's eyes narrowed on me. "And you did, didn't you?"

The belief she had in me, hit me like a brick in the middle of my chest. Like every angry word we'd had in the last three years hadn't existed. As if she'd always known me, always knew the man I was underneath the bravado. Always knew there was plenty of sweet beneath the sour.

"Yeah, I did. Not until after Mom died, though. My training of Ariel kinda stalled for a while, but later I made it my mission…for Mom." I drew in a breath, still feeling the ache of Mom not knowing how we'd all succeeded in life, how we'd fulfilled her dreams for our home, how I'd fixed her horse. "Ariel was my horse for a while until I got Peanut, but now that beautiful girl lives on the ranch, living out her last days grazing or running the pastures without a care in the world."

After we shared dessert and stories, she asked more about Ariel and how I trained her after Mom died.

When I told her stories about my beautiful chestnut mare, her face lit up like she could see the eight-year-old version of me. She believed in that boy. Believed in me like it wasn't even a question.

"You think maybe your mom got her for you, not her?" she asked, voice soft.

That hit something deep. A place I didn't let many people near.

"Yeah," I admitted. "She must've known I needed something to pour myself into." I gave a quiet laugh. "I was a restless kid, never had a dream to hold on to like Nash. Even at that age he knew he wanted to play in the NFL, and Wilder knew he wanted to be the boss on the ranch someday. He was this tiny, scrawny little thing who used to follow Gus, our old foreman, around. He even wore a Stetson and roper boots." I chuckled recalling him sticking his thumbs into the belt loops of his jeans and nodding his head sagely, just like Gus. "Although Mom had to stuff paper in the ends because she couldn't get a pair small enough for him. I was less focused and then Ariel came along." My smile was accompanied with a lump in my throat. "So, yeah, I guess Mom did get her for me."

"You know," Cassidy said, softly. "I've only known Nash well for the last couple of years, but I've spent a lot of time with him and Lily. Time when we've drunk a lot of wine and whisky, but never once have I heard him talk like this, about your mom or you all when you were kids."

"Losing Mom changed him," I said, brushing my thumb across the back of her hand. "Broke something in him that only now Lily's stitching back together."

The air between us shifted again. Warm. Weighty. Like we were standing at the edge of something real.

"She's a big believer in talking and talking helps."

"You're right. If only I'd known talking to you could've changed everything," I whispered. "I wouldn't have been such a dick all these years."

Her smile was small, bittersweet. "It's scary how big the change is and how fast it feels like it's happening."

She was right. It was terrifying. But for the first time in a long time, I was ready to be scared.

Later when I pulled up outside the bookstore, a crashing drumbeat pounded in my chest. It was like the crescendo to some epic film score. It was going that fast and was that loud in my ears. What I did next could change everything. One wrong move and we could go back to being enemies, or the very least professional acquaintances. That was why no matter how much I wanted to follow Cassidy up the stairs to her apartment and lavish all my attention on her for the whole night, I knew I had to leave her at the door.

"I'll walk you to your door," I told her, my voice feeling big in the darkness of my truck.

She laughed softly. "It's like two feet away, Gunner."

"It could be two inches, but I would not be a gentleman if I didn't walk you to it." I unbuckled my seat belt and opened my door. "Wait there."

"Gunner!"

"Cassidy, I'm lacking in many things, but manners isn't one of them. My Mom taught me everything I know."

When she sighed in defeat, I got out of the truck and ran around the hood to her side. She'd already unbuckled her belt by the time I opened the door, so I held out my hand.

"Be careful." I grinned. "It's a big drop for an itty bitty thing like you."

She tried to scowl but her lips lifted at the edges giving her away. "Thank you."

"This door have a bolt?" I asked after the two seconds it took us to reach her front door.

"It does, as does the one to my apartment. Why?"

"Because I want you to bolt it once you're inside." I looked up at the bookshop, considering how safe she was. Whether anyone could scale the walls somehow to get to her front window.

"Gunner," she sighed.

"What?" I turned my gaze back to the frown and the beautiful eyes narrowed on me.

"I've lived here for a long time, alone. I know how to be safe. In fact, I have a baseball bat next to my bed and a mean right hook. Just ask my ex."

"He hurt you?" My hands immediately went to fists at my side. "Was he some college prick who wore his sweater tied around his neck?"

Cassidy giggled and placed a warm palm against my chest. "No, he was an Insurance Broker from Durango who cheated on me. I went back there after college and hooked up with my old high school boyfriend who apparently hadn't matured one bit since he was fifteen. I found out he was fucking his mom's PA so socked him in the jaw."

"*His Mom's PA*? What a dick, not only did he cheat on you but not even with his own PA, but his fucking mom's!"

Laughing full out loud now, Cassidy hugged me. "God, anyone ever tell you you're funny when you're angry."

"No, but let me tell you, you're downright scary when you are."

When she kissed my cheek, my irritation drifted away, and I moved my head to look at her. Maybe I could gauge from her eyes what I should do next. Maybe I was a damn pussy even wondering. Usually if I liked a girl I said, 'I'd like to kiss you now, is that okay' and then damn well kissed her. Cassidy, though, she was different. I felt like I needed— *no, wanted*—to do everything perfectly.

Then she surprised me again. "Gunner, just kiss me honey, because it's getting damn cold on this sidewalk and it's getting late and you have to be up in like," she looked at the gold and silver watch she was wearing, "five hours."

When her lips parted and she let out the softest sigh, I didn't make her wait any longer.

Unlike our heated kisses on the sofa, this one started gently, a question, an answer, a promise. Her lips were soft against mine, tasting faintly of the chocolate dessert we'd shared. When her hand slid up to cup my jaw, her fingertips cool against my skin, something shifted between us. Not just desire, though God knows that was there, but something deeper. Something that felt like finally finding solid ground after years of treading water.

I kept it slow, savoring the way she sighed against my mouth, the way her body swayed toward mine. When we finally broke apart, her eyes fluttered open, those whisky depths soft and wondering in the dim light from the bookstore window.

"Goodnight, Cassidy," I whispered, my voice rougher than I intended.

She smiled; her cheeks flushed from our kiss. "Goodnight, cowboy."

And damn if that didn't nearly break my resolve to leave but when I heard the bolt slide across the door once she was inside, I knew it had been the most perfect goodnight I'd ever said to a girl.

High Hopes - Panic! At The Disco

CHAPTER 24
Cassidy

Stretching lazily, the excitement in my stomach rolled through me, to every inch in my body. My fingers, my toes, my everything. I felt exhilaration like I'd never felt before. Like I wanted to jump out of bed and run five miles. Hmm maybe not, my bed was lovely, warm and cozy. Looking up at the bedroom ceiling my cheeks ached with smiling.

"Oh my God." I kicked my legs up and down like an over-enthusiastic kid waiting to open their Christmas gifts. The eek that fell from my mouth was loud and high-pitched, but I couldn't help myself. Gunner had kissed me again, or I'd kissed him, but it didn't matter. We kissed and we had an amazing date. It had been a perfect date. He hadn't even let me pay my share. He'd insisted on picking up the whole check, growled at me in fact. A growl that I was beginning to like. A growl that sent a little shiver through my core. A growl that I only thought existed in romance novels.

Glancing at the clock on my nightstand, I realized that I needed to get ready for work. As much as I would have loved to have stayed in bed and relived every single moment, word and touch, I had a job to get to.

***

"Miss. Turner…Miss. Turner…hello."

I shook my head and quickly turned to the voice shouting my name. It was Elodie, one of my pupils and Bertie's best friend. Concern in her bright blue eyes.

"I'm sorry, Elodie, how can I help?" I'd been distracted with thoughts of Gunner and our date. Wondering whether he would invite me out again.

"The bell went for lunch, but you didn't say we could go."

I glanced at the clock on the wall and was startled. "Yes, of course, sorry. All of you, off to lunch now." The whole class was already lined up at the door, good well-behaved kids who always did as they were asked.

"Woah, thank goodness," Bertie groaned, rubbing her stomach. "My belly feels like my throat's been cut."

I wasn't sure who taught that child some of the things she came out with, but I'd put money on it being one of uncles.

"Off you go, guys," I said, not even trying to bite back the smile I'd had all morning.

They all trouped out chatting animatedly and not for the first time I was grateful for my career choice.

Once everyone had disappeared, I pulled out my lunchbox and popped it open. I usually ate in the staffroom or outside at the picnic tables with the other teachers, or with Lily, especially when there was gossip worth dissecting. But today, she was locked in a meeting about prom logistics, and honestly… I wanted the quiet. I wanted to replay every second of last night's kiss like it was my favorite scene in a movie.

I hadn't felt giddy like this since I was a teenager. Maybe not even then.

"Do not open that lunchbox."

I looked up, startled, my stomach flipping at the sight of Gunner filling my doorway like a fantasy I hadn't dared let myself wish for.

Wranglers. Shearling-lined denim jacket. Hat in hand. Hair slightly mussed like he'd been running his fingers through it in the truck.

He looked every inch the cowboy romance cover that had come to life.

"Gunner, what are you doing here?" I asked, my voice catching as I dropped the lunchbox to my desk.

"I brought you lunch," he said, holding up a brown bag with a boyish, almost bashful smile that made my chest twist. "Is that okay?"

That glint in his eyes, half mischief, half something softer, lit a flame low in my belly.

"It's more than okay," I said. "Come sit with me."

He crossed the room with that lazy, confident stride that made my knees weak and my stomach flutter. As he passed me, our arms brushed, and a thrill shot through me when he hooked his pinky with mine in a secret little tether.

"Hey," he murmured, leaning in, lips brushing mine in a kiss so gentle it melted me from the inside out. "It's good to see you."

When he pulled back, his gaze dropped to my mouth. His thumb swept across my bottom lip like it was instinct.

"Look how fucking plump those lips are," he whispered. "Just right for kissing."

I couldn't breathe. I couldn't think.

"I think maybe it's your fault," I managed, barely. "You kissed them pretty stupid last night."

"Nothing stupid about those kisses, Cassidy," he said, low and rough, adjusting his belt like it might tame what I'd just stirred up.

"Maybe we should eat," I suggested, because if we didn't, I was going to climb into his lap and forget we were in an elementary school classroom.

"Good call." He flashed me a grin that turned my insides to syrup.

He stripped off his jacket, every move somehow sensual, and slung it over the back of my chair. His red plaid shirt clung to his chest and arms in all the right ways, sleeves rolled up to reveal forearms like sin and golden skin that practically dared me to touch it.

Sitting down far too gracefully for a man his size, Gunner opened the bag and laid out our lunch—two sandwiches, two apples, and two juice boxes.

"Miller beef with mustard mayo. Homemade. It's good." He slid one packet toward me with a wink. "And the apple? Thought it might earn me some extra credit."

I laughed, full and bright. "You brought me a juice box too. You're really pulling out all the stops."

"I like to impress my teachers. Especially the pretty ones."

He pushed the straw into my juice box and handed it to me like it was a love potion. I suddenly wanted to sip it just to keep his attention on my mouth.

As we ate, the energy between us, effortless and electric.

"I should be doing paperwork," he said with a groan. "But I couldn't stay away."

"You drove all this way just to bring me lunch?"

He gave me a look so sincere it made my chest ache. "I missed you. I know it's only been a few hours but…it felt too long. Too lonely. Which is ridiculous because I've got ten stable hands who think I'm God's gift to horse training, but apparently none of them have your smart mouth or that thing you do with your eyebrow when I'm being an idiot."

"You are an idiot." I could feel my blush spread from my neck to my ears. "But you're dangerously good at this."

"Only with you," he said simply. And I believed him.

He reached across the desk and took my hand, thumb brushing back and forth. "I think we should tell people about the date."

"It was one date," I teased, even as my heart galloped behind my ribs.

He leaned in, eyes locked on mine. "You want there to only be one?"

I shook my head, no voice left.

"You think there's something happening here?"

I nodded.

"You want to cool it?"

This time I found the words. "No."

"Didn't think so." His smile softened. "You tell Lily. I'll tell my brothers. We're dating now."

My teenage crushes had nothing on this man and the way he was making me feel. The way his eyes on me made my blood heat, made my panties wet. This was the man I couldn't bear to talk to only a couple of weeks ago. Now I didn't want this lunch break to end.

I let out a breathless laugh. "Okay. We're dating."

"Excellent," he said, voice gravel and warmth. "Now drink your juice, sweetheart."

I nearly choked on the straw. His eyes tracked every movement of my lips, and damn it, I needed to change my underwear.

When we finished eating, the tension between us settled into something deeper. Something quietly building.

It was more than chemistry now. It was…possibility.

"So," I said, needing a subject change before I launched across the desk, "any word on the permits?"

"Not yet. But…" He reached into his jacket pocket and handed me a letter. "This came today."

I scanned it. "Jenkins Industries? They want to talk about sponsoring the camp?"

"That's what it says," he said carefully. "But Nash did some digging. The owner is a guy called Nate Jenkins."

I looked up sharply.

"He's behind the development," Gunner finished.

"What do you all think about talking to them?" I looked over the letter again.

"Depends on you," he said, his voice low and deep.

"Me?"

"Yeah, you, sweetheart. What do you think we should do?" He brushed my hair from my face. "Your opinion is important to me."

My heart stalled and our eyes met.

His hand remained wrapped around mine, warm and steady, while everything else blurred at the edges. Two certainties crystallized in that moment: whatever was beginning between us would demand everything I had to give. And somehow, I already knew that this man would break me apart and rebuild me, piece by piece, in ways I'd never imagined wanting.

Sucker – Jonas Brothers

CHAPTER 25
Gunner

I hated leaving Cassidy at school. Lunch had been great, even with the shadow of Jenkins Industries looming over us. It had been good to spend time just chatting and enjoying being together. When I got back to the ranch Nash and Wilder were walking toward the house. When they saw my truck they both waved a hand.

"Hey," I said as I jumped out. "What's got you two looking so pissed?"

"This Nate Jenkins thing," Nash said with a sigh. "I'm puzzled as to why he'd want to sponsor the kids camp while building that fucking monstrosity."

"Let's get inside and talk about it," I told them. "We need to decide what to do about it."

Wilder looked at his phone. "I have an hour before Rose gets here to wank Gideon Pontipee off."

"Wilder," Nash groaned. "She's coming to extract our bull's semen to check if he's still fertile, not to wank him off."

Wilder shrugged as I chuckled. "Same thing." He jogged up the steps of the porch and into the house, leaving Nash and I staring after him.

"You think maybe Mom found him in a dumpster somewhere?" Nash asked.

I nodded. "Yep, most definitely. Covered in bean juice and used condoms would be my guess."

Laughing we both followed him inside, finding him in the kitchen already pouring out three mugs of coffee.

"Felicia is upstairs with Billy," Wilder said as we walked in. "She took him up for a bath seeing as he's covered in paint."

Felicia ran the lavender farm on our land. It used to be Mom's before she gifted it to Felicia and her husband, Shane. On the days Lily was teaching, Felicia looked after Billy, along with her grandson, Sarah's little boy, who was just a bit older. She'd done the same for Bertie as a baby. Thank God for her. She made life easier for all of us.

Hearing squeals of laughter upstairs, I smiled and sat at the table with Nash while Wild brought the mugs over, placing one in front of each of us.

"Okay, what are we going to do?" I asked, feeling deflated but having an idea of what I wanted to happen. "Do we talk to this company, this Nate Jenkins, or just throw his letter in the trash?"

Nash shrugged. "I don't know. What do you both think?"

"It would help start the camp," Wilder offered. "We wouldn't have to get other sponsors involved or do any crowd funding."

"We'd probably still need other funding, though." I picked up my mug and took a drink, considering whether to try it with creamer the way Cassidy took it. "If we want to make it non-profit. And, if we don't, then we'll need financial help until it starts to make money."

"You think it should be non-profit?" Nash asked.

Cassidy and I had talked about this, and it was something we were undecided on. Maybe even at odds about. "Depends what our priorities are as a ranch. As a family. Besides he may tell us to fuck off once we tell him how against the development we are. Or do we go with the trash can option?"

"Not necessarily." Wilder tapped the table. "We talk to this guy face to face and then maybe we can get him to see sense."

Nash gave a slow head nod. "Maybe. What do you think, Gun?"

"Is a guy like that going to actually listen?" I didn't want to appear obstructive, but we needed to be sure we covered every scenario.

"Well," Nash said, fishing his phone from his pocket and tapping on the screen. "I did a bit more digging and found out he's quite the philanthropist." He put his phone on the table and turned it to face Wilder and I. "He sponsors a kid's charity in Florida, a school in an African village and runs an apprenticeship program at his firm for under privileged kids who can't afford to go to college."

"Wow, quite the Saint." Wilder peered down at the screen. "He's a good-looking bastard, I'll give him that."

"Handsome *and* generous," I said. "Not unlike myself."

"Yeah," Wilder cocked an eyebrow. "Just like yourself."

"He is both those things it seems," Nash added. "But he's also responsible for a few housing developments in rural areas. Building an industrial unit alongside one of them is a new thing for him. He's never done that before."

"The housing wouldn't be so bad if it was sympathetic in style." Wilder sighed and pinched the bridge of his nose.

"Actually," Nash picked up his phone and flicked at the screen again. "His developments are pretty nice. The houses are high end rustic ranch and craftsmen bungalows. All the landscaping is sympathetic with the area, with appropriate planting and water features like ponds. And," he said pointing at the sale price on the website, "they're not cheap."

"Maybe we should ask the County if we can get some images of this development. They must have some mockups," I suggested.

"Yeah," Nash agreed. "I'll get on to Cal and see what he can organize. In the meantime, what do we do about Mr. Jenkins' offer?"

"I think we should meet him." I banged my palms on the table, my mind made up a couple of hours ago to be honest. "Listen to what he's got to say, but I don't think we agree to anything without thinking about it further."

"Absolutely agree." Nash nodded. "Wilder?"

"Seems like a plan. Do we need to ask Cassidy?" my youngest brother asked. "It was her idea."

I cleared my throat. "No need. She agrees with me, we talk to him, see what he has to offer and then discuss it further."

Both my brothers looked at me, their mouths dropping open in unison. Surprise didn't seem to cover it, because as far as they knew Cassidy and I didn't converse unless necessary.

"And how would you know that?" Nash asked. "How would Cassidy know about the letter? Did you call her?"

"Of your own volition?" Wilder's eyes were wide with astonishment.

I shook my head. "Nope. I took the letter when I went to have lunch with her and showed it to her. We talked about it and agreed we should speak to this Jenkins guy and then think about it. I just wanted us to consider all the options before I said anything."

"You had lunch with her?" Wilder looked at Nash and then back to me. "Without throwing plates at each other?"

"Yep. I had lunch with Cassidy because we are dating. We went out for dinner last night and had lunch today. I know it's a bit of a turnaround seeing as we hated each other only a short time ago, but it is what it is. Life is too fucking short." I looked between them both. "Any other questions?"

They both shook their heads, surprising me. I'd expected Wilder at least to ask some sort of stupid bullshit question but he stayed silently shocked.

"Great, now who's going to contact him to arrange the meeting?"

Sitting in my office later that night, I scrolled through everything that I could find about Jenkins Industries. The only light was that of my screen and the dying embers of the wood burner. Everyone had finished up about an hour ago, all the horses were in their stables and Charlie had gone up to her apartment, probably packing the last of her things. She was leaving in a couple of days, and I still didn't have a replacement for her, although I had made a mental note to speak to Tally, the girl with the horse, when she came to check on him tomorrow.

As for Charlie, I could have made her stay on, see out the month her contract said. However, because she'd delayed in telling me about the job she only had two weeks before she needed to start. Being the nice, kind boss that I was, I'd given her an early leaving date so she could have time to settle into her new apartment and spend some time with her family.

Pushing my problems with an assistant to one side, I continued reading the screen. It appeared that Nate Jenkins was a self-made millionaire and was still only thirty-four. Seemingly, he'd made his first million by the age of twenty-seven when he bought an old run down warehouse, three years before, and turned it into apartments. They were sold for millions because of where they were. Every single picture there was of him he was dressed in a suit; I hadn't found one with him in anything casual. Even those of him doing his grocery shopping he was wearing one.

With all the charity work he did and sponsorship he seemed like an okay sort of guy, but then anyone could throw money around and come across as decent. I guess we'd soon find out seeing as we had a meeting with him in a week's time.

Sitting back in my chair, I stretched out my arms and groaned as each of my muscles ached. The deep ache you got after a long day at work. I was ready for my bed, but I needed a long soak first. A shower just wouldn't cut it.

I had turned off my computer when my phone rang. It was almost nine, so I wasn't sure who'd be calling but when I turned it over and saw it was Cassidy, the ache in my muscles immediately disappeared.

I stared at her name on the screen for a beat longer than I should've. Not long ago, I wouldn't have answered. Would've let it ring out just to prove a point I didn't even believe in anymore. But now? Now it was different. Cassidy wasn't just someone I worked with. Or argued with. Or tried not to think about every damn night. She was becoming the person I wanted to tell when things went wrong. The voice I wanted to hear when the day finally stopped spinning. She was steady in a way that caught me off guard, not quiet, not soft, but unshakable. And somewhere along the line, I'd stopped resisting it. Maybe I never really had.

"Hey, sweetheart, you okay?" My smile made my cheeks ache as I got myself comfortable in my chair.

"I'm good. What about you?" I knew from her voice that she was smiling, too, and was surprised how much damn joy that gave me.

"Better now." I liked how my stomach flipped.

"That's good." It was said on a breathy exhale and instantly I wondered whether she was on her bed. Whether she was naked or wearing those cute silky PJ shorts I'd seen her wearing in our kitchen.

"Where are you?" I asked.

"Home, on the sofa under a blanket."

I sat up straight, concerned. "Do you not have heating, sweetheart?"

"I do, but I like to be cozy. And that's new, I like it."

I frowned. "What is?"

"Sweetheart," she replied softly. "I like it very much."

"Good." Swallowing, I rubbed my chest. Mom used to have cute names for each of us. Nash was honey, Wilder baby and I was sweetheart. 'You'll always be my number one sweetheart' she'd say as she ran a hand down my hair. "Sweetheart it is. So, what can I do for you? Or did you just want to hear my voice?"

"As lovely as your voice is, I was wondering what the guys and Lily said about Jenkins Industry."

"We're all on the same page. Everyone agrees we meet and then discuss his offer further. We've set one up for next week. Friday afternoon at four. Think you can make it?"

"Me?" She sounded shocked.

"Yes, you. It's your camp, too. It was your idea and you're going to be a big part of it." My heart stalled. "You are, aren't you?"

"I-I guess. I suppose I thought maybe I'd help to set it up but hadn't thought much after that."

Her hesitation made me feel disappointed in myself. Had I not made it clear to her that she should be involved?

"Cassidy, if this becomes as big as we want it to be we're going to need as much help as possible. I know you love teaching but maybe one day you could teach here." Blood rushed to my head, and I realized I'd probably jumped the gun. Who knew what would happen with the camp. Who knew what would happen between us. Maybe we'd last, maybe we wouldn't, it was far too soon to know. Far too soon to be suggesting she come and work on the ranch with us. We'd only just started dating for pity's sake. "Listen, I'm moving too far ahead, I know, but the main thing is you're a part of this, so yeah, we'd like you to come to the meeting." In the spirit of honesty, I continued. "I like you Cassidy, more than I ever thought possible. Quicker than I thought possible, so I know this could turn to shit quite easily but in the meantime let's just go with it, work together on this and see what happens. Okay, sweetheart?"

There was no sound except for soft breathing on the other end of the line and I wondered if I'd scared her off.

"Cassidy?"

"I'm here. Thank you, Gunner," she whispered, softly. "For wanting to involve me, for believing in this and…" she paused and cleared her throat. "For believing in me and I'm glad that we made friends."

I got a weird sensation in my chest, wondering when hate turned to like and like turned to…fuck I wasn't going there, not after a handful of kisses, a date and a lunch in a classroom that smelled of ten year old boys.

"I'm glad, too, sweetheart. Now, tell me what are you doing tomorrow night? I need to see you, it's been too long."

Her laugh tinkled down the line, stealing my breath and putting a huge smile on my face. "I saw you at lunch, Gunner."

"Like I said," my voice a deep, needy, growl. "It's been too long."

Lover – Taylor Swift

CHAPTER 26
Cassidy

Sweetheart. One word but it meant so much to me. I mean I was an independent woman who believed in girl power, but if a man wanted to treat me like a princess and give me a cute nickname then I was up for both. Funny how that man appeared to be Gunner Miller. The man I'd hated for so long. Maybe it was true that the line between love and hate was dangerously thin, because it certainly seemed so between Gunner and me. I could feel myself falling. Not quickly. Not dramatically. Just deeper than I meant to, with every word he didn't say.

And now. The things he was suggesting. The plans he had. They all included me, and it felt right.

The idea of working on the ranch, teaching on the ranch, had never been on my radar. Now he'd mentioned the possibility of it, though, it kind of felt exciting. Imagine teaching kids in that environment. I'm guessing it wouldn't be a full curriculum, but Math was my major, where History was Lily's. If Gunner's idea of having kids there long-term worked out, between us she and I could keep them on track with their schoolwork. It would mean we wouldn't have to limit camp to school break periods. But that was all pie in the sky for now, especially if the meeting with Jenkins Industries didn't go well. Yep, it was a long, long way off.

Trying to put it from my mind, I watched Lucas pick up his workbook and bring it to my desk.

"Hey, Lucas. Have you finished?"

"Yep." He grinned at me and put his book in front of me so I could check his answers.

Every single one of them was right, including all his workings out of each math problem. When I handed his book back and he saw all the ticks and 'Good work' written at the bottom, his cheeks went red. In fact, he blushed right up to his ears.

"Well, done. That's excellent." He was doing so much better now that Ruthie was getting help. Gunner had even bought her a new clothes washer, stating he would take ten dollars a month from her salary to pay it back. Then he'd upped her salary by fifteen dollars saying he'd miscalculated it. He certainly was not the man I'd thought he was.

"Miss. Turner, am I coming to the ranch with you after school?"

I gave him a soft smile, trying to hide my own excitement that clearly mirrored his. "You certainly are. I believe Gunner is going to give you and Bertie some riding lessons."

Lucas clutched his hands into small fists and grinned. "I can't wait. It's going to be awesome."

It certainly was because I was going to spend the evening with Gunner. Nash and Lily were going to take the kids to the funfair in Sweet Maple Falls once they'd had their riding lesson and Wilder was off to a poker night in the bunkhouse, so we'd have an evening to ourselves.

I had to be honest it was a mixture of excitement and nerves in my belly, because being alone with Gunner I wasn't sure I could be happy sticking to kisses on the sofa. I also wasn't sure, though, whether two dinner dates, a lunch date and several phone calls over the last week were sufficient for me to move onto the next phase. I wasn't a prude, but I was cautious and maybe I was throwing myself too wholeheartedly into this thing with Gunner.

"Are you going to learn to ride, Miss. Turner?"

"Actually," I said. "I can already ride a horse. I learned how to ride when I was your age. I mean I haven't ridden for a long time, but I'm sure I could remember if I had to."

"You should come with us. I'm sure Bertie's uncle Gunner will teach you."

My lips tickled with a brief smile as I thought about all the other things I'd love for Gunner to teach me.

"Maybe I will come along for a ride this evening," I told him. "It might be fun."

***

In the late afternoon pale sunlight, Gunner stood in the center of the paddock guiding the kids on their ponies. "That's it, short stuff, nice and gentle with the reins," Gunner called, his voice steady as he watched his niece guide her pony in a slow circle. I was leaning against the white wooden fence, smiling at the way his entire demeanor had softened around the children. The sharp-tongued, sarcastic rancher had transformed into someone patient and encouraging, his instructions kind and clear. "Lucas, sit up straight, buddy. Remember what I told you about your posture?" Gunner moved up to walk alongside him and the gentle palomino pony and adjusted Lucas' shoulders.

The crisp air smelled faintly of pine and damp earth, the last traces of snowmelt making the dirt rich and dark beneath the ponies' hooves. The late sun slanted low across the paddock, turning the wooden rails to gold and casting long shadows that made everything feel just a little more magical, like we were standing at the edge of a story only just beginning.

"There you go. Christine can feel everything you do up there now." Lucas beamed with pride, his small hands gripping the reins the way Gunner had taught him. "Like this, Mr. Miller?"

"Perfect," Gunner affirmed with a nod. "You're a natural and what did I say about calling me Mr. Miller?"

"Not to." Lucas gave him a shy smile. "Okay, Gunner." Grinning, Gunner removed his Stetson and wiped his brow. The day was warming, but a lingering chill still clung to the air, hinting at the stubbornness of winter even as spring fought its way in. I turned my attention to Gunner, watching the broad span of his shoulders, the way they stretched the worn chambray shirt across his back as he reached up to help Bertie with her stirrups.

"Miss. Turner!" Lucas called excitedly, waving. "Look at me! I'm riding." His enthusiasm made me giggle and filled my chest with heat. "You're doing great, Lucas. Really great."

Gunner turned to face me, and a slow smile spread across his face, making my breath catch. He said something quietly to Bertie, then made his way over to where I stood.

"Enjoying the show?" he asked, resting his forearms on the fence between my hands. He was close enough that I could smell him. His scent, spice and roses mingled with leather and that something which was uniquely him.

"They're doing so well," I said, nodding toward the children. "You're good with them."

Gunner shrugged, but I caught the pleased look in his eyes. "Kids are easier than adults sometimes. They just say what they mean and mean what they say. And they try harder."

Our eyes met and something unspoken passed between us, an acknowledgment of how we'd changed together.

"So," he said, his voice dropping to the low, intimate register that sent a shiver down my spine. "Lucas tells me that you used to ride. Care to show me what you remember?"

I braced my arms on the face and shook my head. "Oh, I don't know about that," I hedged, suddenly nervous. "It's been years."

"Scared, Miss. Turner?" The challenge in his voice was playful, teasing."

"In your dreams, cowboy."

His grin widened. "Come on, then. I've got just the horse for you."

Before I could protest further, he climbed over the fence and held out his hand. I took it, trying to ignore the warmth that spread from where our fingers connected, up my arm and straight to my chest.

"Bertie, Lucas, take your ponies to the rail and hold it there," Gunner instructed. "Miss. Turner's going to join us for a ride."

The children's excited chatter only served to heighten my nerves as Gunner led me to a chestnut mare waiting patiently at the other end of the paddock.

"This is Stevie," he said, stroking the horse's neck. "She's gentle but responsive. Perfect for someone who just needs to remember what they already know."

I reached out a hand to let the mare sniff it. "She's beautiful." I looked up to find Gunner watching me and my stomach flipped. It felt good to be under his gaze. Like the Summer sun was beating down on me. "Who's the Fleetwood Mac fan?"

He chuckled. "You got that, did you?"

"I did. Songbird, Gypsy, Stevie and Christine."

"My mom loved them." Something vulnerable flickered across his face, quickly turning into a full on grin. "I managed to name them all before Bertie got her Seven Brides obsession and I told her a little white lie that Gypsy's name had to be linked to her mom's for her breeding papers."

"That girl," I chuckled. "I admit I like your choice better, but I'm glad she's not called Tusk, or I might be a little scared to get on her."

"She's particular who rides her which is why I know she'll take real good care of you." The trust implicit in his words wasn't lost on me. "Ready?" he asked.

I nodded as he interlaced his fingers to create a step for my foot. As I placed my boot in his hands, I felt the solid strength of him, unwavering as he boosted me up into the saddle.

The world shifted as I found myself looking down at him, the familiar feel of a horse beneath me bringing back memories I'd forgotten I had—of my dad leading me around in a circle, encouraging me to sit up straight, just like Gunner had with Lucas. There was muscle memory there, too.

"Feel good?" Gunner asked, his hand resting lightly on my calf as I adjusted.

"Better than I remembered," I admitted, warmth spreading through me at his touch.

He reminded me how to hold the reins, his hands covering mine, adjusting my grip with gentle precision. Each brush of his fingers leaving trails of heat.

"Posture," he murmured, a smirk at his lips as his hand found the small of my back to guide my posture. "Shoulders relaxed."

He led me to the gate, opening it so that Stevie could walk us into the paddock. As his palm pressed against my spine, everything around me disappeared. His touch steadying and unsettling all at once.

"What did I say about posture?" he reminded me. "Unless you want to fall off and have me rescue you."

"Don't flatter yourself, cowboy. I might just prefer the company of the horse."

"Now I know that's not true, Miss. Turner." He flashed me a smile, followed by a wink which sent a signal straight between my legs. His concentration went back to the lesson. "Now, light pressure with your legs," he instructed, his voice a deep rasp that made my nipples hard. "Let her know you're ready."

I did it as he directed, and the mare moved forward in a smooth walk. Gunner stayed beside us, one hand resting lightly on Stevie's neck, the other hovering near my leg. Not quite touching but close enough that I could feel the promise of it.

"See," he said with a smile in his voice. "Your body remembers."

And it did, the rhythm, the subtle shifts needed to communicate with the horse. When I looked at him, though, I knew that there were other things that would stay with me, more than how to ride a horse. The way Gunner's eyes crinkled at the corners when he was pleased, how his hand felt against my spine, but most of all the timbre of his voice when his words were for my ears only.

"I think I've got it," I said, growing more confident as the three of us completed another circle of the paddock.

"You definitely do," he agreed, stepping back to watch me. "Try a figure eight, gentle on the turns."

Bertie, who was leading our line, turned around in her saddle. "Can I try that Uncle Gunner?"

"Nuh uh, short stuff," he chuckled. "You need more practice first. Miss. Turner has a lot more experience than you."

"Hardly." I made a grimacing face, making Bertie give out a loud belly laugh.

Lucas, clearly not as comfortable in the saddle, sat upright and stiff. "What's funny?" he asked, still looking dead ahead.

"Miss. Turner made a funny face," Bertie told him. "She's going to do figure eights now."

"I want to see," Lucas pleaded.

"Hey," I called. "I'm no barrel racer. This could go horribly wrong."

Gunner laughed deep in his chest and moved over to Lucas. "Give Christine a little squeeze with your right leg, just there behind her girth," he told him. "Gently, and she'll turn around."

Lucas completed the maneuver, with a lot of help from Christine, and raised his fist in victory. "I did it, Bertie. I got her to turn."

Bertie, who had already turned her pony, Caleb Pontipee, grinned at him. "That was so good, Lucas."

"Okay, guys," Gunner said, placing his hands loosely on his hips. "Let's watch Miss. Turner do a figure eight."

Feeling absurdly nervous, I guided Stevie through the pattern. On my third go around I caught Gunner watching me, pride evident in his expression. Not the smug satisfaction I would have once expected from him, but something warmer, more genuine.

"Uncle Gunner, is Miss. Turner going to jump the fence next?" Bertie called from where she and Lucas watched me, wide-eyed like I'd just done something spectacular.

Gunner laughed. "Not today, short stuff. Baby steps."

"I don't know," I teased, feeling bold as I circled back toward him. "I'm a quick study."

"That you are," he agreed, reaching up to take the reins as I brought Stevie to a stop in front of him. "But some things are worth taking slow."

The double meaning in his words hung between us as his hands came to my waist, strong and sure as he helped me to dismount. As my feet touched the ground, I found myself pressed against him, his hands lingering at my sides as I tilted my face up to his. His body warm from the sun and an afternoon's work.

Time seemed suspended in the golden light, the soft nickering of horses and the distant laughter of Bertie and Lucas fading as I became acutely aware of his heartbeat. It was strong and fast against my palm where it rested on his chest, shifting when my gaze rested on his lips.

"Thank you for the lesson," I whispered, my feet rooted to the ground despite every instinct telling me to step away.

Sunset burnished his face in gold, softening the hard edges. His gaze dropped to my lips just for a heartbeat, but long enough.

"Anytime, sweetheart." The word hung between us, heavy with something that hadn't been there before. "You're a natural. Most people fight the horse, trying to force control." He paused, something shifting in his expression. "But you... you moved together. Trusted each other."

The way he said it made me wonder if we were still talking about riding.

I felt like I understood the words he wasn't saying—that we'd been on the same journey—that we'd started to trust each other as we worked together.

I swallowed and admitted, "Maybe I'm learning to trust more than I used to."

Gunner scratched the back of my neck and gave me a crooked smile. "Guess we're both getting better at this whole trusting-people thing. Weird, huh?"

I smirked, but my voice was soft. "Weird is one word for it. Terrifying is another, but also... kind of nice." "Yeah, well... I was definitely supposed to play it cool. Keep things casual. But instead, I'm over here knowing the rhythm of your breathing better than my own playlist." He shook his head, grinning. "And there you go; you've somehow got me saying stuff I didn't even know was in me. So...nice ambush, sweetheart."

I tried to act like my heart wasn't doing cartwheels. "You really suck at casual, you know, and for the record I love the stuff you say?"

Gunner's smile was slow and sweet and worth every moment of our rocky past. Every argument, every misunderstanding had led us here.

I felt the warmth of his palm still lingering at my waist. "Seriously though, sweetheart, you did good out there," he murmured, his voice lower than before. When our eyes met his expression changed, something that made my breath catch. Something that promised so much.

"Uncle Gunner!" Bertie's yell broke the spell. "Lucas wants to know if he can trot."

For a moment our gazes were locked, his eyes holding mine for more than one more charged moment before he sighed and stepped back.

"Duty calls," he said with a rueful smile.

As he turned to rejoin the kids, his hand brushed mine, brief, deliberate, a promise of later when we were going to be alone.

I watched him go, his large body blocking the pale sun casting him in shadow and I felt something settle within me. When he turned and caught me staring, his smile softened and I knew then that it was this ranch, these people—him. Somehow, when I wasn't expecting it, it felt like I'd found family again.

Speechless – Dan + Shay

CHAPTER 27
Cassidy

"Damn those kids were excitable," Gunner said as he passed me a jar of pesto. "I could have cooked, you know?"

I grinned at him over my shoulder. "I know, but I wanted to do it as a thank you for the riding lesson. And yes the kids were excited about the funfair. Even Billy and he probably had no idea where he was going."

"I think he could sense Bertie and Lucas were about to pop." Gunner propped his chin on my shoulder. "That looks good. I'm starving.'

"It's only chicken and pasta."

"Still looks good." He gave me a quick kiss on my cheek. "I'll get the dishes."

As I emptied some sour cream in, I watched him take two plain white pasta bowls from the cabinet. As he reached up his t-shirt rose giving a hint of tanned back. A thin slither just above the waistband of his briefs. It was also an opportunity to look at his ass, which was incredible in the soft, worn jeans he was wearing. When we finished the riding lesson and came inside he nipped upstairs to shower, appearing a little later, barefoot and in an old gray t-shirt, and the ends of his hair damp. As he came into the kitchen where I was talking with Lily it had to have been obvious the effect he had on me. I could barely breathe for one.

Continuing to set the table for dinner, his movements were confident and fluid, strong and masculine. He was all man. Deep veined hands that gripped two glasses and placed them on the table. When he filled a water jug from the faucet I couldn't stop looking at his tanned forearms and the strength in them borne from years working on the ranch.

"I can feel your eyes on me, sweetheart," he said, his attention still on the water jug.

"Am not," I lied, warmth filling my belly.

"Yes you are." He chuckled. "Can't keep them off me, in fact."

I turned off the stove and spooned some pasta into each of the bowls, an extra serving for Gunner. Placing them on the table, I went to the oven and pulled out the bread rolls that I was keeping warm.

"Food's up."

Gunner pulled out a chair and waved for me to sit down. "After you."

As I sat, he helped to push my chair closer to the table and then moved around to the other side to take his own seat. When he sat, he gazed down at the bowl of food, inhaling the steam.

"Smells incredible."

I shook my head. "Seriously, it's pasta."

His gaze lifted to mine from beneath dark lashes and my blood heated. My feelings for him had gone from zero to, 'I need you naked', in a short time. He had gone from an overbearing idiot to sweet honey.

As we both tucked in, Gunner moaned around his fork. "This 'seriously, it's pasta' is seriously good."

It was ridiculous how much pride I felt. Ridiculous at how gooey he made me feel inside. It was also scary how much I wanted him.

"What's for dessert?" he asked, spearing a piece of chicken. "Something sweet?" The way his eyes grazed over me, I was almost certain that I would offer myself up with cream.

"I think all that teaching us to ride has built up your appetite."

"Did you enjoy it?" he asked, pouring us both a glass of water. "Getting back on a horse."

I didn't have to think about it. "I did. It reminded me of Dad."

Gunner's brows raised. "Really? Tell me about it."

"I had a sudden memory of him leading me around on my pony and getting me to sit up, just like you did." I felt a little pain in my chest, one I hadn't felt about Dad in a long time. My grief was always for Mom and the pain she'd gone through before she died and the years that we'd missed out on. "I was so young when Dad went," I continued. "I barely knew him to miss him. Sometimes, though, like today I remember little things that make me sad that we didn't have him around for longer. Mom always told me stories about him and the kind of man he was, and I think I'd have liked him. I think I'd have driven him nuts, too."

Gunner smirked. "You mean all the boys hanging around you would have."

"I didn't have that many boys hanging around," I argued. "Probably a fraction of the girls that you had."

He shrugged. "A few." When I smirked, he threw his hands in the air. "Look, there were three of us boys living here. All of us handsome and strong so no wonder they came here in bus loads."

The laugh burst from my stomach and barked out loudly. "Bus loads?"

He relaxed back in his chair and contemplated me as he chewed. "You have the dirtiest laugh I've ever heard. Who do you get that from?"

"My mom. She laughed a lot. Even when she was ill. You know she had Queen's Another One Bites the Dust played at her funeral, and we all had to wear yellow."

Gunner laughed and shook his head. "You're joking about the song?"

"No, I'm not. And we had party poppers at the wake afterwards." I sighed at the weirdly happy memory.

"A bit different from my mom's. That was a real sad affair. Dad sat in the corner wailing, which turned out to be a big fat lie." His jaw went tight, and his nostrils flared. "Stupid, lying bastard. He was having an affair," he explained. "We also couldn't stop Wilder from crying. Poor kid was devastated. And," he sighed, "life didn't get much better until Nash and Lily started dating and Lily brought some much needed laughter to the house. She also spoiled Wilder."

"Like she does now," I joked.

"Just like she does now. Of course, when she left Nash left for college and Wild and I were left here with Dad. Not that he was around much. We tried to make it feel like home, but we were two young kids. You don't really think about warm dinners, comfy cushions and filling a house with laughter when you're that age."

My throat itched as tears ebbed at my lashes. The pain of losing their mom must have still been fresh. "So, your dad basically left a sixteen year old and a thirteen year old alone?"

"That's about the size of it. Felicia kept an eye on us and made sure we were fed, but most of the time it was just me and Wilder, until Nash came home." He laughed emptily. "His college career was short to say the least."

I knew from Lily that Nash had been destined for professional football, but a bad injury during practice a few months into college had put paid to that.

"Did it feel better when he came home?" I asked, a forkful of pasta paused mid-air.

"Some. It was good to have him back, but he was so fucking sad it was unbearable." He took a sip of water and shook his head, like he was trying to dismiss the memories in there. "I didn't think he'd ever get over losing Lily and his career but then there was Bertie." His smile was blinding and more feelings wound their way around my heart, like a vine. "Then the laughter came back and even more when Lily came home. Nash is like our barometer, you know. He's happy the rest of the house is happy."

"Because he's the eldest?"

"Maybe, or maybe because he's the boss." He laughed heartily and went back to his food.

As I watched him eat it struck me that I liked being there with him. Just sitting there eating and chatting like it was the most normal thing in the world.

***

The living room fire had burned low, casting the room in amber shadows. What had begun as lingering kisses on the sofa were starting to deepen as our bodies shifted closer to each other with each passing moment.

I felt Gunner's hands at my waist, purposefully sliding beneath my sweater, tracing the curve of my spine. The warmth of his palms against my bare skin sent a shiver through me that had nothing to do with cold.

"How long do we have?" I whispered, stretching my neck, silently urging him to put his mouth on the sensitive skin.

"Hmm?"

"How long until they're back from the funfair?"

"There's the bonfire and fireworks at eight, they…" He kissed below my ear. "Go on for about an hour…" Another kiss. "And then they'll have to take Lucas home…" And another kiss. "And then come home, so that's another hour at least. Fuck you smell so good. Taste so good."

"You kiss so good." Heat pulsed in the pit of my stomach, creating a throb in my panties, and I instantly parted my thighs for him to lie between them. "What can we do in two and a half hours?"

"This," he murmured against my mouth, as he gave his hips a gentle thrust.

It didn't matter that we were both in our clothes, the friction was exactly what I needed, yet it wasn't enough. I reached under his t-shirt, my fingers working inch by inch along his smooth skin as his hard on strained against his jeans.

"That's so good," I groaned, lifting my hips to meet his.

His breath caught as I slipped my hand inside his shirt, palm flat against his chest, feeling the steady thunder of his heartbeat. The tenderness in his eyes as he watched me explore made me feel bolder. I moved my hand further south.

When my fingers brushed against his stomach, tracing the defined muscles there, Gunner groaned softly. He caught my wrist, placing a kiss against my pulse point before guiding my hand back to his chest.

"As much as I want to feast on you, two and half hours isn't enough." His voice was strained with restraint. "We should probably slow down."

"Maybe I don't like slow," I whispered, reaching up to pull him down for another kiss.

This one was different, hungrier, with an urgency that had been building since that first night on the sofa. His tongue traced the seam of my lips, seeking entrance that I readily granted. His hands, rough with calluses, skimmed my ribs, his thumbs brushing the underside of my breasts through the thin lace of my bra.

I arched into his touch, wanting more. When his mouth trailed down my neck, I tilted my head back, giving him better access. It was my favorite spot to be kissed. At least I thought it was until his teeth grazed my collarbone, followed by the soothing warmth of his tongue, drawing a soft moan that felt like it came from the pit of my stomach.

"Cassidy," Gunner breathed my name like a secret wish. "Come with me."

He stood, extending his hand to me. It was an invitation, not a demand so I took it without hesitation and let him lead me up the stairs. We passed a gallery of pictures on the walls. Happy family memories, including Lily and Nash's small family wedding in their back yard. I remembered avoiding Gunner as best I could the whole day, even if I did appreciate how good he looked in a tux. The memory made me wonder about being part of the gallery one day. However, it was brief, as I quickly pushed it away.

"This is me." Gunner looked at me over his shoulder and gave me a brilliant smile. He then pushed the door open with his hand.

As we walked inside, I noticed the personal touches—books, a photograph of him, his brothers and Bertie when she was smaller. A huge bed dominated the room with covers of the deepest red, plump pillows piled haphazardly and wooden shutters, half-closed, at the window onto the acres of rolling emerald land at the back of the house. Then there was the scent of his cologne. Intoxicating and manly. The scent of him.

Before I could take in anything else his hands were on me again, this time pushing my sweater up and over my head. The cool air against my skin was quickly replaced by the heat of his gaze, appreciative and reverent as he took in the sight of me in my simple white lace bra. The rough calluses of his fingertips caught slightly against my skin, each drag leaving trails of heat that seemed to sink beneath the surface. His scent clung to his skin, earthy and masculine in a way that made me want to bury my face in his neck and just breathe him in.

"Beautiful," he murmured, bending to press a kiss to the hollow between my collarbones. His fingers traced the strap of my bra, following it down to where it met the cup, then along the edge where fabric met skin. "I've thought about this since the first time I saw you in that classroom, all prim and proper. Wondered what you'd look like coming undone for me."

His words sent a shiver down my spine, the low rasp of his voice almost as arousing as his touch. "And how am I measuring up to your fantasies?" I asked, my voice breathy with anticipation.

"Better," he growled, pressing his lips to the swell of my breast. "So much better."

I worked my fingers up his shirt, pushing it up and over his head to reveal the body I'd only imagined he had. The reality was so much better than envisaging. Broad shoulders tapering to a narrow waist, skin bronzed from working outdoors, scattered with freckles that I was desperate to trace with my tongue.

"God, look at you," I whispered, running my palms over the hard planes of his chest. "All due to the work I watched you do on the ranch whenever I visited Lily."

"You were watching?" His eyes darkened with desire as his hands found my waist, thumbs stroking the sensitive skin just below my ribs.

"Every chance I got," I admitted, leaning in to place a kiss on his collarbone, then another lower on his chest. "Even when I thought I hated you."

When my hands reached for the button of his jeans, he stilled them, bringing them to his lips instead.

"Not tonight," he said, his voice husky. "We don't have time. Tonight is about you." His eyes locked with mine. "I want to taste you, Cassidy. I've been thinking about how you'd feel against my tongue since that first kiss."

The bluntness of his words made heat pool between my thighs. "Yes," was all I could manage.

Before I could protest, he was kissing me again, walking me backward until my legs hit the edge of the bed. As I sat on the deep, soft mattress, he knelt in front of me, his hands on my knees, gently parting them so he could position himself right at my core.

The sight of Gunner Miller on his knees, looking up at me with such desire, made my breath catch. He reached behind me, finding the clasp of my bra with practiced ease, his eyes never leaving mine as he waited for permission.

I nodded, and the garment joined my sweater on the floor. His sharp intake of breath was gratifying, as was the gentle reverence with which his hands cupped my breasts, thumbs circling my nipples until they hardened into tight peaks.

"Perfect," he murmured, lowering his head to capture one sensitive peak between his lips. "Fucking perfect."

When his mouth replaced his hand, the wet heat of his tongue against sensitive skin sent a jolt of pleasure straight to my core. I threaded my fingers through his hair, holding him to me as he lavished attention on first one breast, then the other.

"You like that, sweetheart?" His breath was hot against my damp skin, sending another rush of arousal through me.

"God, yes," I gasped, arching into his touch. "Don't stop."

My hips shifted restlessly, seeking friction that wasn't there. Understanding my need, Gunner's hand slid up my thigh to the waistband of my jeans, his fingers working at the button.

"Okay?" he asked, his voice rough with desire but his eyes still seeking confirmation.

"Please," I whispered, lifting my hips to help as he tugged the denim down my legs.

His hands returned to my thighs, tracing patterns on sensitive skin as they moved higher, the pressure building within me with each inch they covered. When his thumb finally pressed against the tiny bud of nerves through the thin cotton of my underwear, I gasped at the contact.

"Fuck," he murmured, his eyes locked on my face as he repeated the motion, applying more pressure this time. "You're soaked through. Is that all for me, sweetheart?" The pride in his voice was unmistakable.

"Yes," I breathed, beyond embarrassment as his fingers teased me through the damp fabric. "Only you."

The teasing touches through fabric quickly became frustrating and I reached for his hand. I guided it beneath the elastic, eliciting a groan from both of us as his fingers finally met slick heat.

"Christ, Cassidy," he breathed, his forehead resting against mine as his fingers explored, learning what I liked, what pulled soft moans from my throat. "You feel incredible. So wet, so ready." His fingers found my entrance, circling before slowly sliding inside. "You're going to feel so good wrapped around me when I finally get inside you."

The combination of his words and the pressure of his palm against my clit had me writhing against his hand. "More," I pleaded, beyond pride.

He built me up slowly, methodically, watching my reactions with an intensity that made me feel both exposed and cherished. His thumb circled my tiny bundle of nerves as his fingers curled inside me, finding that perfect spot that had me gasping his name.

"That's it," he encouraged, eyes dark with desire. "Let me hear you. I want to know exactly how good I'm making you feel."

When I was close, trembling on the edge, he slowed his movements, drawing out my pleasure until I was begging.

"Gunner, please," I whispered, my hands clutching at his shoulders.

"Tell me what you need," he demanded softly, his rhythm maddeningly steady but not quite enough.

"I need to come," I gasped, beyond shyness. "Make me come, Gunner."

"Sweetheart, look at me," he commanded softly. When I did, the connection in that moment, his eyes holding mine as his fingers finally pushed me over the edge, was more intimate than anything I'd experienced before. "That's it, let go for me."

My release crashed through me in waves as his fingers continued their relentless rhythm, drawing out my pleasure until I was gasping his name, clutching at his shoulders as my body convulsed around his fingers. My chest heaving as I gripped the comforter and continued to thrust against his hand. It was too much, but not enough, as my clit continued to throb its own beat.

Before I could catch my breath, he lowered his head between my thighs, trading his fingers for the heat of his mouth. The first stroke of his tongue against my oversensitive flesh had me crying out, my hands tangling desperately in his hair.

"Too much?" he teased, his breath scorching against my core.

"No…" The word scraped from my throat, barely a voice at all. "Don't stop."

His answering hum vibrated through me, sending a shockwave of pleasure spiraling straight to my core. He devoured me with the same relentless focus he gave everything else, tongue circling my clit before dipping lower to taste me like I was his only salvation. His hands pinned my thighs wide, powerful and unyielding, keeping me open for him.

"You taste even better than I imagined," he murmured against me, every word a sinful vibration against my raw flesh. "I could do this for hours."

The sight of him between my legs, broad shoulders anchoring me in place, eyes dark with hunger, nearly undid me. Then his fingers slid back inside me, curling deep while his tongue worked its magic, and I shattered.

"Gunner, I'm going to—" The words dissolved into a broken cry as release ripped through me, harder and hotter than before. My back arched, my body trembling violently as wave after wave of ecstasy left me breathless.

When the aftershocks finally released me, he moved up to gather me against his chest, fingers drawing lazy, possessive patterns along my spine. I melted into him, boneless, yet acutely aware of the thick, insistent press of his arousal straining beneath his jeans.

"What about you?" I whispered, sliding my hand lower with intent. "I want to taste you. To feel you."

He caught my wrist, bringing it to his lips instead. "I told you, sweetheart, I don't have enough fucking hours to do everything I want. Tonight was about you and that was just a taster of what is to come. You touch me and I might just explode like one of those fireworks at the funfair." He kissed me gently, cupping my face. "When we have sex, sweetheart, I'm going to fuck you so hard you'll think you're still straddling that horse."

I burst out laughing, not one bit disappointed that he'd gone from tender to coarse in a split second. "Promise?" I teased, rolling my hips against his evident arousal.

He groaned, his hands tightening on my waist. "You're playing with fire, Cassidy."

"Maybe I like getting burned," I whispered, pressing another kiss to the corner of his mouth.

"I know you're an independent woman, Cassidy," he said, kissing away the remnants of my laughter, "but when we get a night together I'll be in charge. You okay with that?"

Tracing his eyebrow with my fingertip, I nodded. "I am a strong, independent woman, Gunner, but if that night you demand I get down on my knees and suck your dick, then it'd be my pleasure." I leaned closer to whisper in his ear. "I've thought about that too, you know. How you'd taste, the sounds you'd make as I took you into my mouth."

Gunner's laugh rumbled from his chest, though I felt his cock twitch against my hip. "Why the hell did I act like a dick for the last three years?"

I shrugged, dropping a kiss to his sharp jaw. "I wasn't exactly innocent was I?"

His eyes grazed over my face, going softer than I'd ever seen them before. Deep chocolate pools of honesty.

"That was then and this is now, sweetheart. We realized in the end."

The tenderness in his voice, the restraint that he'd shown, made me understand so much. This wasn't just physical, this was Gunner showing me that my pleasure mattered, that we weren't rushing into something that deserved time.

"I think I quite like you, Gunner Miller."

His fingers trailed lazy patterns on my bare shoulder, and I realized how far we'd come from that disastrous first date. The man who held me now, who had put my needs before his own, was someone worth taking time to know properly.

"Want to stay the night?" he murmured into my hair.

I could sense he was already half-asleep. No wonder how early he started work every day.

"What about Lily and Nash and the children?" I asked, half-heartedly. "What do we say to them?"

He sighed contentedly. "We say that my girlfriend stayed the night." He pulled me closer. "Unless you want to go home, and I'll follow you back to town."

I pressed a kiss to his chest, right over his heart. "I'm not going anywhere," I told him and tapped his shoulder. "You should get undressed, babe. Get undressed and under the covers."

Another sigh was followed by a nod. He unwrapped himself from me and quickly undressed, leaving his clothes where they fell before getting under the covers with me.

"Okay, sweetheart." I was immediately enfolded in his strong arms again. "Let's get some sleep."

And within minutes we were fast asleep, wrapped around each other while I dreamed about life on a ranch with a man who took my breath away, caused a fluttering in my stomach and made my pulse race, all while letting me be me.

10,000 Hours – Dan + Shay & Justin Bieber

CHAPTER 28
Gunner

After the night before, waking up with a honker was totally expected. Waking up alone *wasn't*. I thought that maybe I could give Cassidy another taster of the mind blowing orgasms that I offered. She, however, was nowhere to be seen. I waited a couple of minutes wondering if maybe she was in the bathroom, but when she didn't return I knew she'd left my bed. Who knew how long she'd been gone because her side of the bed was cold.

Turning on my side, I picked up my phone where it was charging on the nightstand. It was a little after seven-thirty. Saturday was the day me and my brother's took off, but we were still usually up and about by seven.

I quickly dressed in last night's clothes, which I noted had been folded neatly on the armchair by my window and left my room. When I checked the kid's rooms all I found were empty beds and a chaos of toys and books, the remnants of two happy, well-loved tiny humans. The bathroom was empty, only a couple of damp towels hanging over the side of Lily's beloved free standing claw foot bath that Nash had installed for her. Still no sign of Cassidy, my blood went cold. Had she thought that last night was a mistake? Would she really have taken the time to fold my clothes if she'd been desperate to get out of there?

Running down the stairs, I felt a nervous sickness in my stomach, the like I'd only felt once before. It was the day Mom died and Sheriff Donnelly, Sheriff Jackson's predecessor, knocked on the door and said he needed to speak to Dad. It was only when I reached the bottom step that my heartbeat righted itself. I could hear Cassidy talking to Lily in hushed tones followed by Lily's laughter.

"What's so funny?" I asked, standing in the doorway and drinking in the sight.

Cassidy turned her sparkling eyes on me and clutched her mug of coffee to her chest. A chest covered in one of my t-shirts. It was way too big, falling past her knees and off one shoulder but I didn't think I'd ever seen a more gorgeous outfit on a woman.

"Morning," she said, her voice all breathy.

"Morning, sweetheart." I pointed a finger up and down her body. "I see you borrowed my tee."

"Yeah, is that okay? Lily told me to grab it out of your pile in the laundry. I spilled milk down my sweater."

"Rather Billy did," Lily chipped in, drying her hands on a towel. "Cassidy brought the kids down for breakfast at six to give us some more sleep." A smirk licked at my sister-in-law's lips. "Wasn't that kind of her?"

"Hmm," I mumbled walking toward Cassidy, the smell of coffee and laundry settling around me. "She shouldn't have." I took the mug from her hand, placed it on the island counter and then wrapped an arm around her waist, pulling her hard against me. "I missed you." Before she could reply, I dropped my mouth to her and kissed her hard, making it clear just why she shouldn't have got up with the kids.

After what could have been seconds, minutes or hours, I wasn't sure, Lily cleared her throat. "Just so you know, Bertie is already asking questions about why Miss. Turner was here for breakfast."

Slowly removing my mouth from Cassidy's I looked at Lily, my arms still wrapped around my prize. "What did you say?"

"*I* told her that you and I were friends and so I'd had a sleepover," Cassidy answered the question.

I turned back to her. "I thought we agreed we would say you were my girlfriend, and you stayed the night."

Lily made a funny little noise, a cross between a gasp and a snort of laughter, and I wondered whether she was about to choke.

"You okay, Lil?" I asked, giving her a raised eyebrow.

"Ah ha. All good," she replied through a cough. "I'm just going to find Nash and Wilder, they're outside playing football with Bertie and Billy. They both owe me fifty bucks."

I frowned. "Did you all have a wager on us getting together?" I asked, pulling Cassidy closer.

"Lily!" Cassidy sighed. "You're my friend."

"Exactly." Lily patted Cassidy's arm. "Which is why I won the bet and they didn't. They had Summer break and Thanksgiving." She threw the towel on the side and then went out the back door leading to the small pasture where Nash had made a jungle gym for the kids. Before she closed the door I heard her yell. "Hey guys, guess who won the bet, that's right, not you losers."

Cassidy and I started to laugh and my hold on her grew tighter as we watched each other.

"I thought you'd gone," I told her, feeling unnecessary anxiety.

"I had to get out of bed, you my friend are like a furnace." She patted my chest. "I thought I was going to melt into the mattress."

"You should have woken me."

She shook her head. "No, you needed your sleep. I know Saturday is your day off. Besides, it was nice to get some sleepy squidges from Billy.

And then of course Bertie woke and came down and found us, so I just gave them their breakfast." She inhaled. "I'm sorry if I worried you."

"It's okay, but next time wake me."

Hesitancy flashed through her eyes. "So, there will be a next time?"

"Of course there will." I dropped a kiss on her lips. "How the hell else do I show you my full repertoire of orgasms if I don't get to have you all night? And to be honest when you have a dick as beautiful as mine, it'll be hard for you to say no once you get a look at it."

She smirked and rolled her eyes. "Is that so?"

"Absolutely." I was about to kiss her again when the back door burst open and Nash barreled in.

"Sorry to interrupt guys but I've just had a call from Nate Jenkins. He's in town and wondered if we could meet him in a couple of hours." He looked at Cassidy. "You think we're ready with the documentation?"

"I do, but I'll need to go home and get the printouts I did on the school computer and the pen drive of some other stuff it's saved on. My laptop is still being repaired, can we take yours, Gunner?"

"Sure sweetheart."

She chewed on her bottom lip. "I'll need to shower and change if you want me to come."

"Of course we do," Nash and I both said at the same time.

"If I go now I think I can be back here in an hour and a half. Or I can try." She looked at me with a little trepidation in her eyes. "I feel like we need to have one last check-in to make sure we're all prepared, because this could be important."

Blowing out a breath, I nodded and turned to Nash. "She has a point."

"Okay, I'll call him back," Nash's reply was immediate. "I'll ask if he can make it after lunch instead. He pulled out his phone and then looked at us both. "Let's hope he's a good man underneath the suits and the money."

I hoped so, too, but something told me the fight for our town's land wasn't going to be that easy.

***

When Nate Jenkins asked us to meet him at Rafferty's bar in Clementine Hill I thought he was joking. The man was a multi-millionaire. I expected to at least be seated in the library of his huge mansion, assuming he had a huge mansion. As we were meeting him in a bar I was surprised to see him walk in wearing a suit, albeit without the tie at the neck of his crisp white shirt.

"He looks very serious," Cassidy whispered next to me.

He was also a good looking bastard and instinctively I placed a hand on her thigh. As he approached our table we all stood to greet him. Nash was first to hold out his hand.

"Nash Miller, good to meet you."

"Hey, Nash, great to meet you, too." Jenkins flashed us all a smile and then held his hand out to Cassidy. "You must be Miss. Turner, the one who provided such an impassioned and well-thought out argument as to why I shouldn't develop the land."

Pride for my girl had me grinning until my cheeks ached. He was right it had been well-thought out and impassioned.

"Wilder Miller." My youngest brother hung one hang from his hip while Jenkins shook his other.

"And so, you must Gunner. The middle brother."

"You've done your homework." His handshake was strong and his palm cool. They were two positives at least.

"I'm a great believer in knowing who your opposition is." He smiled but it was flat and that was a negative.

"Keep your friends close and your enemies closer," Nash said in a low voice.

"Exactly," Jenkins agreed. "Now, shall we sit. I asked Milo, the owner, to reserve us a table out the back where it's quieter."

I looked around the bar, with that familiar odor of beer and cleaning products, to see there were only two other people in there. One of them was the barman counting bottles of beer. It couldn't be any quieter unless it was closed.

Jenkins moved past us, and as he did Cassidy shrugged her shoulders as if she was asking me what I thought. I held out my hands, palms up, silently telling her I didn't know what to think.

"Let's keep our powder dry folks," Nash said quietly as we followed to the back of the bar. "Only discuss what we've documented and don't be drawn into any other conversation about any other part of the land. And *do not* lose your tempers."

Wilder smirked and saluted him. "Sir, yes sir."

Shaking his head in disbelief, Nash followed our host to a room with a pool table and three or four other tables dotted around. One of them had a jug of water on it and five glasses. There were also five glossy booklets.

"Looks like he's come prepared, too," Cassidy whispered.

"Yep, sure does." I took her hand in mine and gave it a squeeze. "We're ready for him, though, sweetheart."

A little while later my personal impression of Nate Jenkins had changed somewhat. The man was passionate about his work. More importantly he was passionate about the environment. Which begged the question why he was building a damn meat packing factory. A question that I was about to ask.

"You strike me as a man with principles, Nate." He'd insisted we call him that just as Cassidy started to discuss our report that she'd written. "Which is why I'm amazed that you're building an industrial unit so close to the wildlife."

His expression darkened, his jaw going tight. "Yes, I did receive the report from Ms. O'Neil from the County Environment Department." He cleared his throat. "And as you say I am a man of principles, but I'm also a businessman. If you read the booklet that I've provided then you'd see it's going to be environmentally friendly. From the power to the packaging."

"There'll still be pollution of some kind," Wilder stated. "Why should we have to deal with that?"

"You'd rather it be built in a town. Let them deal with it.?"

"Call me selfish, *Mr.* Jenkins but yes, I would." Wilder leaned his forearms on the table. "I don't believe anything can be totally safe for the environment. Is the meat organic?"

Nash cleared his throat and stared at our brother, silently warning him not to lose his cool.

"Is your meat organic?" Nate asked.

Wilder ignored the scuff of Nash's boot against his own. "Our cattle's primary food source is grass and hay when pasture isn't available with grain as supplementary food if needed. You can test any of our cattle and will not find any shit pumped into them." Wilder's nostrils were flared and his arms folded across his broad chest. He was pissed and when Wilder got pissed he either laid people out cold with his words or laid people out cold with his fist. Thank fuck the fists hadn't seen much action for a while since Lily had made him realize that words often packed a stronger punch. I was pretty sure that neither would be welcomed by Nash.

"I think what Wilder is trying to say," I interjected. "Is that we're still concerned about the effect on the local environment and land. As much as we believe your assurances that you're doing what you can to protect our land and people, you can't possibly give us one hundred percent assurance."

"Gunner is right," Cassidy added. "The land and the area is important to everyone, not just the family. I mean have you seen how spectacular the mountains are, how green the pastures are, how blue the sky is." She took a deep breath. "No one wants that beauty marred, not to mention the effects that you don't see."

I must have had some kind of soppy look on my face, because Wilder was staring at me, one eyebrow cocked as he mimicked wiping drool from the corner of his mouth. While Nate's concentration was on my girl, I gave Wilder the finger and earned myself a kick under the table from Nash.

"I take on board your concerns," Nate said, garnering all our attention again, "but I promise we will do our utmost to ensure everything is done to have the least impact on the town and your ranch. We're implementing closed-loop water recycling systems and carbon capture technology that exceeds federal standards by forty percent. The entire facility will run on renewable energy from our solar farm just outside Clementine Hill."

"A closed-loop water recycling system, hey." I nodded sagely, because I'd read about this a few nights before. "Sounds impressive, but how will you prevent contamination of the groundwater that feeds our creek and the wetlands during construction?"

Nate steepled his fingers under his chin, giving me his full attention. "We're implementing a dual containment system for all construction run off. Primary barriers include silt fencing and retention ponds with specialized filtration. Secondary measures involve continuous groundwater monitoring at twenty points surrounding the site, with automatic alerts if contamination is detected. We're working with Freshwater Environmental. They specialize in watershed protection during industrial construction."

"No expense spared," Wilder said, rolling his eyes.

"What you'll discover about me is that I don't skimp on anything." Nate gave him a flat smile. "Look, I understand your concern. My grandfather's farm was ruined by chemical run off from a nearby factory years ago. I wouldn't build something that creates the same problems I've fought against elsewhere. My pops is why I do what I do in the way that I do it."

Cassidy crossed her legs and shifted in her seat, and I suspected that Nate's tale of Grandfather's farm brought back some memories. I linked my pinky with hers and gave it a gentle tug so that she looked at me.

"Okay?" I mouthed. She gave me a beautiful smile and nodded.

"With respect to your grandfather and your reverence to his memory, Nate," Nash finally said, "we don't know whether we can trust you. We don't know you other than the fact that you want to build houses and a factory close to our land, close to wildlife. You've told us it'll be environmentally friendly," he picked up one of the brochures and flicked through it, "but aside from those figures you've just quoted there's nothing in here on how much landfill it's going to create, or by how much other energy and emissions will be reduced. I think we need some positive assurances, with facts and figures."

Nate's exhale was a little ragged as he placed a hand on the table, spreading his long fingers. He slowly tapped them as he watched Nash put the brochure back on the table. He was quiet for a little too long, clearly contemplating his words.

"Maybe we could arrange another meeting," Cassidy suggested. "When you have some figures to fact up your promises." She gathered all her papers and placed them on top of her copy of the glossy brochure. "Can we also suggest that you come out to the development site and look at the weasels and the other wildlife in the area. Sending someone else out can't possibly replace the actual experience of seeing it for yourself."

God she was good.

"I'd like this project to get off the ground as soon as possible." He raised a brow. "Seeing as your town's mayor has had it delayed."

Nash and I exchanged a look. We owed Cal a beer or two for that.

Sitting back in his chair, Nate linked his fingers and rested them on his stomach. "I'll up the sponsorship for the children's camp by fifty percent." He looked between me and Cassidy and then turned his penetrative gaze on Nash. "I'll invest in your wedding venue."

If Nash was surprised he didn't show it. Wilder had his best poker face, and I had no idea what he was thinking either. Cassidy's mouth was open as her eyes flicked between me and Nate. Another fifty percent sponsorship into the camp was huge. On top of what he was already offering that made it enough to start us off and keep us going for a year. Could we accept that, though, knowing the effect it might have on the land? Could we afford to turn it down, though.

"I think we need to discuss a few things," Nash said. "Like Cassidy said, we should have another meeting when you've got some facts and figures for us." My brother looked around at us. "I think we're ready to go guys, okay?"

"I've certainly heard enough," Wilder muttered, pushing up from his chair. He held out his hand to Nate. "It's been a pleasure."

Jenkins stood as did the rest of us and each of us shook his hand, Nash last of all holding on to it for a little longer than the rest of us.

"I'm out of the country for the next six days, but as soon as I get back I'll arrange to come and visit the site. In the meantime. I'll get my numbers person to come up with those figures you're all so anxious to see."

Wilder opened his mouth but quickly closed it when Nash shot him a glare. Our eldest brother's jaw had a tick in it. He was mad but to be fair it was a toss-up between him and Wilder as to who was most pissed.

After saying goodbye to us, the four of us stepped out into the pale sunshine. There was a cool breeze, and I was glad of my coat. Cassidy was only wearing a blazer that matched the trousers she was wearing, so I wrapped my arm around her, feeling her tremble against the chill.

"Want my coat, sweetheart?"

"No, I'm fine your truck is just there."

Nash and I had both driven our trucks over to Clementine Hill and I was more than ready to spend the next forty minutes alone with Cassidy.

"We're going to get back to the ranch," I told Nash. "You want to catch up when we get back home?"

"Nothing to talk about as far as I can see," Wilder grumbled. "He's not checked his facts and thinks he can buy us with the promise of sponsorship and investment. He seemed like a nice guy and everything but like he said he's a businessman. He's got one goal in life and that's to make himself a boat load of cash."

Nash went quiet, his gaze distant.

"You okay, Nash?" I asked.

"Hmm, just a lot to think about."

Wilder looked doubtful. "Like what?"

"It's a lot of money he's offering guys," Nash said, his lips turning into a taut smile as he pulled the collar up on his coat and fished his keys from his pocket. "But like you said, let's talk when we get home."

"Nash!" I protested. "You can't seriously be thinking about it?"

"He's not," Wilder replied. "You're not, are you, Nash?"

He'd started to walk toward his truck as Cassidy grabbed my arm. "Is he really serious?"

I shrugged. "No idea, sweetheart."

"He better fucking not be," Wilder hissed, following Nash.

"Shit, I'm glad I'm not travelling back with them." I took Cassidy's hand and lifted it to my mouth, kissing the back of it. "Come on, let's follow them back just in case a fight breaks out."

"What do you think?" Cassidy asked, skipping along beside me to keep up with my long strides. "About Jenkins' offer. Do *you* think we should take it?"

Beeping the key fob, I opened the door for Cassidy and helped her in. Her trousers weren't as tight as those she'd worn on our date, but she was still just as tiny. Once I was sitting beside her and made sure she was buckled in, I started the engine. Pulling out into the traffic behind Nash, I tried to determine if they were arguing in the truck in front of us. I leaned closer to the windshield and peered out.

"Honey, you won't be able to see from here whether they're fighting or not."

Cassidy's hand on my thigh was warm and comforting and high up, right near my dick. However, driving down Clementine Hill's main street getting a road rocket from my girlfriend didn't seem right somehow. I mean, the traffic was slow, and people could see inside the truck from the sidewalk.

"I know, sweetheart." I sighed, trying to stop thinking about Cassidy's mouth around my dick. "I know. I just hope this damn development isn't going to cause more problems than those with the land."

When I glanced at Cassidy, the look in her eyes told me she was as worried as I was, and that petrified me.

The Middle - Zedd, Maren Morris & Grey

CHAPTER 29
Cassidy

The only sound in the truck was Gunner's agitated breathing, clearly worried about his brothers arguing in the truck in front of us. He was gripping the steering wheel so hard I was worried his knuckles were going to pop through his skin. When the truck engine silenced outside the ranch house, he quickly unbuckled and threw open his door.

"I need to check on them, sweetheart."

"Gunner, I can get out of the truck on my own." I pointed to the house. "Go."

He gave me a quick kiss to the lips and then followed his brothers into the house. I followed but hesitated as I stepped through the front door. I couldn't hear any argument, but I was also aware I wasn't family. If there was going to be a heated discussion I wasn't sure they'd want me there.

"Cassidy," Gunner's head appeared around the door of the lounge. "We're in here, sweetheart."

When I entered the room, smelling of lavender and burning wood from the fire, everyone was sitting, including Lily who had Billy sleeping in her arms. Wilder moved up the sofa to make room for me, patting the seat.

"Take a seat, Cassidy. Join in the fun."

"I didn't say we should take the offer, Wild," Nash said, reaching for Billy. "Give him to me, baby, I know how heavy he is."

Lily handed their son over and shook out her arm. "Tell me again what his offer was."

"A fifty percent increase on the camp sponsorship and an investment in the wedding barn."

Lily blinked. "I can understand why you would consider it, *if* you did."

"Which is all I'm saying," Nash replied. "We should consider our options."

"There is no option." Wilder shook his head and gave out a frustrated sigh. "He's trying to buy us."

"He seemed quite open about everything. However, I'm aware that he's a businessman and could be hiding something." Billy stirred and Nash shifted him to his shoulder, his big hand cradling his son's back. "So, I'm aware that his offer could be a way of buying us. What do you think, Gun?"

Gunner, who was standing, glanced out of the window, taking a moment before answering. He sighed and shoved his hands into the pockets of his pants before turning to us.

"His offer is incredible," he replied. "It would keep the camp going for a year and as for the offer of investment in the wedding barn," he looked directly at Nash, "that would *also* be incredible. Imagine what you could do with that."

"So, you do think we should take his offer then?" Wilder asked him.

"Not saying that, Wild. What I'm saying is let's see what the numbers are like when we next meet him."

"And then take his fucking money?" He pinched the bridge of his nose. "Are you not worried about our property value on top of the problems for the camp and the wedding venue? Even for people closer to town. How are they going to sell on when buyers realize they're living in a town with a meat processing plant, no matter how 'green' Jenkins claims it is? I vote we just tell him to fuck off."

"Of course I am, Wild." Nash was doing his Dad voice, soothing and understanding. "But I think we have to accept that this development is going to go ahead in some form or other at some point."

"Nash is right," Gunner added. "Jenkins has many more millions than us to fight this and so let's be smart about it and not make an enemy of him." He sighed. "Let's not tell him to fuck off just yet."

I was acutely aware that Wilder was getting uptight beside me. His whole body was tight as he wrung his hands together. It looked like he was gearing himself up to jump out of his seat. Maybe it was time to try and diffuse the situation. "How about I go and get us some coffee and a plate of cookies?"

Wilder patted my knee. "I'm fine, Cassidy, I'm not about to lose my shit. This is how our family discussions usually go. Nash and I disagree, and Gunner sits his ass on the fence until Nash and I arm wrestle for it. Which, I might add, I usually win."

"I think you'll find that I don't sit my ass on the fence. I think you'll find I'm the voice of reason." Gunner rolled his eyes. "Dick. Making me sound like a pussy."

Laughter was inevitable because he looked so damn annoyed it was cute. Once I started, Lily soon joined in quickly followed by the three brothers and all the while the youngest Miller man continued sleeping.

"Okay," Nash finally said, "what do we do about Jenkins and his offer?"

"Can I make a suggestion?" I offered.

"Go ahead sweetheart." Gunner gave me a perfect smile as he finally sat down in an armchair.

"How about instead of simply accepting or rejecting Jenkins' offer, why don't we ask for some binding conditions?"

"Such as?" Lily asked.

"Well, like he has to have, and document, a quarterly environmental test. Call it a performance bond that means he'd have to pay for remediation if standards aren't met or are a direct oversight." I glanced at Gunner who was studying me carefully. His gaze was soft as his hands rested on the arms of the chair. "If he's not willing to do that then maybe he's not as worried about the environment as he says he is."

"That's a good idea." Wilder moved to the edge of his seat, clearly buying the idea because his body was no longer stiff and unyielding.

"You could also make some other demands," Lily suggested, brushing a hand over Billy's head. "You want the camp to be more educational so ask him to incorporate a nature trail in the development. One with educational stations that connect to the camp."

Nash's eyes lit up. "I like that idea, baby. If it's part of his land he's more likely to protect it. Make sure it's of a good standard in the first place."

I looked at Wilder whose shoulders were much more relaxed now. "You and all the townsfolk could also petition for a state environmental review," I offered. "That way when his report comes back if it doesn't match the review then you have your answer about accepting his offer."

Wilder grinned at me. "That's a fantastic idea. I think that's exactly what we should do. Nash, Gun?"

The two brothers looked at each other and nodded.

"I agree it's a good strategy." Nash pushed up from the sofa. "I'm going to put Billy down in his playpen and then start dinner. You staying Cassidy?"

"Yep, she is." Gunner got up, too, walked to me and held out his hand. "Come with me sweetheart. Message me when dinner is ready."

He pulled me up and then dragged me out of the room.

"Gunner, where are we going?" I asked, running behind him to keep up. When he reached the stairs and started to climb them I tugged on his hand. "We can't, everyone is downstairs. Where's Bertie, is she in her room?"

Gunner chuckled and paused on the landing. "I told you last night, that will only happen when I have time to enjoy devouring you without interruption."

Damn it. I now had wet panties. I nodded and let him lead me to his room. As soon as we were inside he pushed me against the cool wall and kicked the heavy oak door shut behind him. Instantly his mouth was on mine and his hand was pulling my shirt from the waistband of my suit pants. His callused hand snaked up along my ribs until his thumb found my nipple.

"Gunner," his name from my lips was breathy.

"Ssh, less talking, more kissing."

And God did he kiss me. It was hot and sultry as he pressed his erection against my core. His tongue pushing in and out in time with the slow strokes over my nipples. As he pushed against me I thrust my hips forward, aching for any connection that might help to detonate the orgasm building inside of me.

As my fingers tugged at the ends of Gunner's hair, I nipped on his bottom lip. He groaned and I was sure I'd felt him go hard in his pants. Nice dress pants that he'd changed into for the meeting. Dress pants that were thinner than his jeans so I could feel every inch of him.

Gunner's fingers cupped my breast as his thumb and forefinger replaced the stroking with a delicious pinch.

"You think maybe you can come back to my house after dinner?" I asked as his mouth went to my neck.

"Yeah, I reckon so. Let's hope Nash doesn't take too much longer because I'm starved." He pushed his hips harder against me and I wondered whether I could wait that long. Maybe we should skip dinner and just go back to my place now.

Gunner took the decision from me, though, and pulled away, adjusting himself as he breathed deeply. "We should stop before I do something I might regret."

"You'd regret railing me against this wall?" I asked, touching a fingertip to my swollen lips.

"Never, but it would have to be quick and that I would regret. Plus, I need to change out of these damn pants back into my jeans."

"What was that incredible kiss in aid of anyway? Why pull me from the room like your life depended on kissing me."

His deep brown eyes became hooded as he stared at me, gently brushing my hair from my eyes. "Because I needed to kiss you. You were incredible today, both in the meeting and downstairs. Especially downstairs, getting us to see another option regarding Jenkins' offer. Besides which," he said, his eyes grazing lazily over my body, "you look fucking hot in that pants suit."

"I'm glad I could help." Looking down at the ground, feeling embarrassed, I said, "I liked being a part of the team."

"I like that, too. A hell of a lot."

When he dropped another kiss to my already puffy lips, I missed a breath as it struck me how great it would be being a full time member of Team Miller.

Adore You – Harry Styles

CHAPTER 30
Gunner

I'd been to Cassidy's apartment once before when I'd picked her up for our date, but I hadn't been past the doorway. The small living room was exactly what I'd imagined, comfortable and lived-in with overflowing bookshelves lining one wall. An overstuffed armchair sat by the window with a reading lamp and a small table that held a stack of books with colorful bookmarks poking out from various pages.

"Make yourself comfortable," she said, slipping off her shoes by the door. "Can I get you something to drink?"

"I'm good." I watched her move through the space, noting how she belonged there among the walls filled with the stories she loved.

She caught me staring and tucked a strand of hair behind her ear. "What?"

"Just looking," I said, stepping closer. "Your place suits you."

"Small and cluttered?" she laughed and looked up at me. "And you're entirely too big for it"

"I don't know, I think I kind of fit in perfectly." I cupped her face and ran my thumb over the apple of her cheek. "I meant that it's warm," I corrected, dropping my hand to link our fingers together. "Intelligent. Inviting."

The soft light from the table lamp caught the gold flecks in her eyes as she looked up at me. Something about being here, in her personal space, made everything feel more significant. This wasn't some hookup in a bar or even the heated moments we'd stolen at the ranch. This was something else entirely.

"I like you being here," she whispered. "Even if you make it look doll house size."

"Well, I hope the bed is big enough because I have plans." I pulled her closer and dropped a kiss to the corner of her lips. She smiled against my mouth. "Do I get to devour you for hours now?"

"Absolutely." And then she turned and led me out of the lounge.

Her bedroom continued the theme of the lounge—bookshelves, soft fabrics, and a large bed covered in a quilt that looked handmade. Photos lined her dresser, Cassidy with groups of kids, an older woman who had to be her mother based on the matching smile, and one of Cassidy as a child on a farm, a small goat standing beside her. There was also a guy wearing jeans and a denim shirt standing behind her, his hands on her shoulders. They were both grinning for whoever was taking the picture, probably her mom.

"Your parents?" I asked, nodding toward the photos.

She nodded, something soft crossing her face. The way she looked at the photo, there was so much love there. Loss too. It made me think of my own mom and the fact that we didn't talk about her enough at home. Didn't celebrate her enough, well maybe that should change.

"Strange," Cassidy said with a sigh, "even though both pictures were taken years apart, both were a year before they passed away."

When she inhaled, I moved behind her, wrapping my arms around her waist and resting my chin on her shoulder as we both looked at the photos. "You have your mom's smile and the same eyes as your dad."

"Everyone said that about me and Mom." She turned in my arms, her hands sliding up my chest. "And she always said that me and Dad were the only two people she knew whose eyes were the same color as Macallan."

"Has always been my favorite whisky," I replied. "Your mom was right."

Cassidy narrowed those Macallan colored eyes on me. "You really want to talk about my mom right now?"

"No," I admitted, dipping my head to brush my lips against hers. "But I want to know everything about you, Cassidy Turner. All the parts that make you who you are."

She made a small sound, somewhere between a sigh and a moan, as her fingers tangled in my hair. "Later," she whispered against my mouth. "Right now, I want you to stop talking."

When our lips met this time, there was nothing cautious about it. No worry that someone would walk in on us. This was a kiss with intent, with promise. Her tongue slid against mine as her body pressed closer, seeking contact. My hands found her hips, pulling her against me so she could feel exactly what she was doing to me.

"I've been thinking about this all night," I said against her neck, my teeth grazing the sensitive spot below her ear. The spot that made her squirm in the best possible way.

Her head fell back, giving me better access. "Me too. Ever since you pushed me against your bedroom wall and gave me a hint of what was to come."

Slowly, I walked her backward until we reached the bed and immediately my fingers found the buttons of her blouse, undoing them one by one. Every one revealed inch after inch of soft skin and when I pushed the fabric from her shoulders, she shivered, but not from cold.

"Your turn," she murmured, her hands already working at the buttons of my shirt.

There was something so damn sexy about the way she bit her lip in concentration as her fingers brushed against my chest with each button she released. When she pushed my shirt off, her hands splayed across my chest, tracing the muscles there with appreciation.

"You know all those times I saw you working around the ranch," she confessed, her fingertips trailing down to my stomach, "I wondered what you'd look like without your shirt."

"You didn't even like me most of those times."

"Still imagined it."

"And?" I couldn't help the smirk.

"Better," she admitted, her hands moving to my belt. "And I have a pretty good imagination."

The sound of my belt buckle releasing sent a jolt of anticipation through me. But instead of rushing, I caught her hands, bringing them to my lips.

"Slow down, sweetheart," I whispered. "We've got all night." I'd never cared about going slow before. It was always about the finish line. But, with her, I wanted to memorize every second, every sound, every expression.

Just like the smile she was giving me; it was both shy and wicked. "Promise?"

"Promise."

I lowered her onto the bed, following her down until I was hovering above her, supported on my forearms. This close, I could see every detail of her face, the light freckles across her nose, the flecks of amber in her eyes, the soft curve of her lips. I wanted to memorize all of it. Her eyes drifted shut and something moved in my chest. This wasn't just about release anymore. Every touch, every kiss felt like a confession that I wasn't brave enough to make with words.

When I kissed her again, it was slower, deeper. My hand traced down her side to her hip, then back up to cup her breast through the lace of her bra. She arched into my touch, a soft moan escaping her lips.

"You're so beautiful," I whispered, meaning it more than I'd ever meant anything.

Her hands explored my back, my shoulders, everywhere she could reach. "You're not so bad yourself, cowboy."

The nickname made me smile against her skin as I traced kisses down her neck to her collarbone. When I reached the swell of her breast, I paused, looking up to meet her eyes, seeking permission. The heat in her gaze was all the answer I needed.

Reaching beneath her, I unhooked her bra, sliding the straps down her arms. The first sight of her breasts, perfect and flushed with desire, nearly undid me. I lowered my head, taking one nipple into my mouth, swirling my tongue around the sensitive peak while my thumb circled the other.

The sounds she made, soft gasps and breathless moans, drove me wild. Her hands were in my hair, holding me to her as if afraid I might stop. As if I could ever want to be anywhere else.

"Gunner," she breathed, her body arching beneath mine.

I loved hearing my name on her lips like that, halfway between a plea and a prayer. I switched my attention to her other breast, giving it the same thorough appreciation while my hand slid down her stomach to the waistband of her pants.

When my fingers undid the button and slipped beneath the fabric, finding her wet and ready for me, we both groaned. Her hips lifted instinctively, seeking more contact as I touched her with deliberate, gentle strokes.

"Is this okay?" I asked, needing to hear her say it.

"Yes," she gasped, nails scoring half-moons into my shoulders, anchoring me to her. "Don't stop."

I eased her pants down her legs, underwear following, until she lay before me, skin painted gold in the lamplight. I couldn't look away, didn't want to as I memorized the dip of her waist, the curve of her hip, the constellation of freckles across her ribs.

"You're staring," she whispered, a flicker of something uncertain crossing her face.

"Can't help it." The confession left me raw, more vulnerable than her nakedness. "Never seen anything so beautiful."

The blush that spread across her cheeks and down her neck was almost as beautiful as her smile. She reached for me, pulling me back down to her, her mouth finding mine in a kiss that communicated everything words couldn't.

Her hands went to my jeans, pushing them down along with my boxers until there was nothing between us. The first sensation of skin against skin was electric, drawing a deep groan from my chest.

I reached for my jeans, fumbling in the pocket for the condoms I'd grabbed from home, just in case. Her eyes followed my movements, darkening with anticipation as I tore open the packet.

"Let me," she said, taking it from my hands.

The feeling of her fingers rolling it onto me was almost too much. I closed my eyes, focusing on my breathing, determined to make this last.

When I opened them again, she was watching me with such tenderness it made my chest ache. I positioned myself between her thighs, the tip of me just brushing against her entrance.

"You sure?" I asked one more time, needing to know this was what she wanted.

Her answer was to wrap her legs around my waist, drawing me closer. "I've never been surer. Of anything."

I pushed forward, entering her slowly, giving her time to adjust. The sensation was overwhelming. Tight, wet heat surrounding me, her soft gasps in my ear, her nails digging into my back. When I was fully seated inside her, I paused, resting my forehead against hers.

"Okay?" I whispered.

She nodded, her hands framing my face. "More than okay."

I began to move, slow at first, savoring each thrust, watching her face for signs of what she liked. When I shifted slightly, hitting a spot that made her cry out, I kept that angle, driving into her with increasing intensity.

How had I ignored this beautiful woman? Fought with her. Fought against letting myself even think about her. She was everything. She made me want to do better. Her beauty, her intelligence, her humor. She was… perfection.

Her legs tightened around me, urging me on, her hips rising to meet each thrust. The sounds she made, my name mixed with breathless pleas, drove me to the edge of control. This was more than just sex. I'd had plenty of that. This was something else entirely, like I was coming home to a place I never knew I was missing.

"Cassidy," I groaned, feeling my release building. "Sweetheart, I'm close."

"Me too," she gasped, her body tensing beneath mine. "Don't stop."

I slipped a hand between us, my thumb finding her most sensitive spot, circling in time with my thrusts. Her back arched, her eyes flying open as she came apart, my name on her lips like a revelation. The way she let go, trusted me completely with her body, it was the most incredible thing I'd ever experienced, and I'd forever remember it.

The sight of her pleasure, the feeling of her tightening around me, pushed me over the edge. My release hit me like a thunderstorm, intense and all-consuming, leaving me trembling above her.

For several long moments, we stayed like that, connected, breathing hard, my forehead resting against hers. Then slowly, carefully, I withdrew, disposing of the condom before gathering her into my arms.

She curled against my chest, her body fitting perfectly against mine as if we'd been designed for this very moment. Her palm flat against my still heaving chest.

"That was worth waiting for," she murmured, pressing a kiss to my chest.

I laughed softly, stroking her hair. "If I'd known what I was missing, I wouldn't have wasted years fighting with you."

"Yes, you would have," she said, looking up at me with a smirk. "You're too stubborn not to."

"Look who's talking." I kissed her forehead, then her nose, then her lips. "But you might be right."

She settled back against my chest, her body relaxing into sleep. As her breathing evened out, I found myself thinking about how perfectly she fit in my arms, how right it felt to be here with her.

It scared me, this feeling. It was bigger than anything I'd felt before, intense in a way that had nothing to do with physical release and everything to do with the woman in my arms.

But as scary as it was, I couldn't imagine being anywhere else. For the first time in my life, I understood what Nash had been talking about all those years—that feeling of finding your person, the one who makes everything else make sense.

As I drifted toward sleep, Cassidy's warmth against me, I realized with startling clarity that I was falling in love with her. And maybe, just maybe, that wasn't such a terrifying thought after all.

Watermelon Sugar – Harry Styles

CHAPTER 31
Cassidy

Waking up to Gunner's mouth between my legs as the pale morning light peaked through the drapes was the best Sunday morning I'd ever had. My muscles ached from the night before because Gunner had been as good as his word. He'd spent hours giving me his undivided attention until we'd fallen asleep for the final time, just before four.

"Gunner," I gasped, gripping his hair, making sure he didn't move his mouth from where I needed it the most. I needed him there because I needed him. When we'd stopped fighting I'd realized he was a decent man, but now, after only a short time of dating I knew so much more. Like this was different from any other relationship I'd had. That he was different from any other man I'd been with. His passion for his family, his home, his job, it made him so much more than the handsome cowboy with the incredible body. It made him the man I knew it would be impossible to forget.

"Morning, sweetheart," he murmured. "You feel like you're still riding that horse?"

"Yes," I said on a long breath. "God, yes."

He'd fucked me hard, every position he could think of. His big body between my legs as he created magic with his incredible dick. His gorgeously smooth, heavenly big dick.

"You're so good at this," I told him as his tongue continued to push in and out of me. "Really good, honey."

My grip on his hair got tighter when he hummed against my clit. The vibration waved through my body, lighting up every nerve ending and practically shooting sparks through my nipples. At least that was how it felt.

As my orgasm grew I felt like I was floating, looking down on the hottest man alive giving the most turned on woman alive the best oral she'd ever had. Gunner Miller most definitely had a silver tongue.

When I went off the edge of that cliff I went screaming, thrusting against Gunner's face so hard that he was probably struggling to breathe.

"Amazing," I gasped, looking down at Gunner who was still between my legs. "You are amazing."

He grinned at me, his face shiny from my release. "It's all in the muscle action. In fact, did you know that the tongue is a marvel of human nature."

"Really?" I lifted onto my elbows and laughed. "In what way?"

"It's composed of eight muscles, all with a wide range of movement. So, the fact that I'm that good with eight muscles all at the same time says something about the man that I am, don't you think?" He wiggled his eyebrows. "And who says men can't multi-task?"

He moved from the bed and padded naked across the bedroom, through a dancing cloud of tiny dust specs in a shaft of light, as I got a perfect view of perfect ass. It was well-defined and muscular and tanned, which gave me pause.

"How come you have a tanned ass?" I called.

"What?" Water started to run in the bathroom, and I giggled at the idea of him washing his face. After a few seconds I heard his bare feet against the tile and he appeared in the bedroom doorway, gloriously naked. "Say that again."

"I asked how come your ass is tanned?" I licked my lips, thirsty for more of him.

With his hands on his slim hips, he strolled toward me, confident and totally unabashed that his dick was still half-mast.

"How do you think?" Kneeling on the bed he crawled toward me.

"Naked sunbathing?" I asked, my eyes wide with shock. "On the ranch?"

"We have thousands of acres, sweetheart, there are plenty of secret little spots. In fact," he ran a finger down over my boob, circling my nipple, "remind me to show you sometime."

"I'd like that." My hips instinctively moved toward him, like we were magnetized.

Gunner's eyes fluttered closed as I rubbed up against him. "Something else you'd like?" he asked, his voice low and gravelly. "Greedy girl."

"So greedy," I whispered as his hand moved to cup my ass.

He pushed me onto my back and dropped his mouth to my nipple, circling it with his tongue and then sucking hard.

"I was going to suggest breakfast in bed," I told him, arching my back, desperate for more.

Gunner chuckled. "And that's exactly what I'm going to have."

And he did for another half hour before I had mine on my knees in the shower.

***

"You sure about this?" Gunner asked, holding our hands up and kissing my knuckles. "Being seen in public with me."

We were walking down Latymer, on our way to Missy May's Diner for breakfast, seeing as we hadn't managed to get any back home. Well, it was more like brunch as it was almost eleven-thirty.

"Of course I'm sure." I wrapped an arm around his bicep and leaned into him. "I'm proud to be seen with you. What about you?"

He looked down on me and frowned. "How could you think any different?" He looked genuinely concerned.

"I was joking." I ran a finger over the two lines between his eyes. "I'm delighted to be seen with you." I stood on my tiptoes to kiss him. "Do you know how many women will be spitting green fire of jealousy once they find out?"

"Does that mean you're only with me for my body?" Thankfully his signature grin was back. "Because I feel objectified now."

"Your body and your introverted nature."

He pulled me closer, squeezing my side as he dropped a kiss to the top of my head. "And I like you for your body and your meekness."

We both burst out laughing and continued toward our destination. As we reached the liquor store, we were almost bowled over by someone. It was Peggy, Lily's grandma carrying a brown bag that she could barely see over.

"Woah there." Gunner put his hands out to steady her before she and her bag fell to the floor. "On the booze already, Peggy?"

She lowered the bag and rolled her eyes. "I'm having a soiree this evening and my daughter thinks two bottles of wine is sufficient."

"For how many?" I asked, peeking into the bag where I could see the tops of four more bottles.

"Four of us," Peggy told me and then gave me a hard stare, daring me to agree with Ella.

"One hell of a party is planned I see." Gunner gave her a beautiful smile resulting in a fluttering of eyelashes. It seemed he had a similar effect on the pensioners of Silver Peaks as he did the younger generation of women.

"Want to come?" she asked, patting the back of her hair.

Gunner snickered and shook his head. "I'm going to be busy with my girl, sorry, Peggy."

Peggy's eyes went wide as she looked down at our hands. "When did this happen? Lily didn't mention it."

Lily probably hadn't because she knew her grandma would tell anyone who would listen to her. Well now the cat was out of the bag so the whole town would soon know.

"It's quite new," Gunner told her, doing some fancy armography so that his arm was wrapped around me while still holding my hand. He pulled me close so that he could rest his chin on the top of my head. "But it's going well so far." He tickled my side. "A lot of horse riding, isn't that right, sweetheart?"

Biting my bottom lip, I nodded and gave him a sneaky elbow to the stomach. He gave a quiet 'oof' and held me tighter.

"I'm pleased for you both," Peggy offered. "Down to one available Miller brother, then. Disappointing."

I felt Gunner's chest shake behind me as we both looked at Peggy's disappointed face.

"Sorry about that, Peggy," I told her.

She shrugged. "That's life. Now I need to get home and get ready for tonight."

"Let me help you." Gunner let me go and reached out for Peggy's bag of booze. "Where are you parked?"

"Just outside Missy May's."

"Oh great, we're going that way." Gunner wrapped an arm around the bag while he held his other one out for Peggy to link.

I practically swooned as the old lady looked up at him with wonder in her eyes. If that wasn't bad enough he went and patted her hand resting on his arm and then winked at her.

I was pretty sure it wasn't just me who was halfway in love with him.

Blinding Lights – The Weeknd

CHAPTER 32
Gunner

I couldn't remember the time I'd last had a whole weekend off, unless I was on vacation. I'd always start with good intentions, but after a couple of hours I'd been restless and more than ready to get back to work. This weekend, though, the first with Cassidy, I'd barely thought about work. Apart from the meeting with Nate Jenkins, but that was more of a necessity than a desire.

No, all my desire was purely for Cassidy. Especially as our relationship had moved on a stage. I had no idea that sex could be like that. Something more than gratification. Something that made me feel like I was burning from the inside with the level of need that I had for her.

"Where's your girlfriend?" Wilder asked as I closed the stable door on the rescued racehorse.

I turned to see my little brother wandering toward me, his usual confident swagger with his ball cap on instead of his Stetson. He wasn't dressed for work, so I assumed he'd come from the house after showering.

"I'm guessing she's at home getting ready for school tomorrow." That was where I'd left her, anyway. In her bed, sated, after another round of sex before I'd had to leave her. I hadn't wanted to, but she had chores to do and me staying would have meant being up at three to get back to the ranch for work. I mean, I wasn't averse to it, but I knew we wouldn't get much sleep if I stayed over.

"So, she is your girlfriend then? Not just a fling?"

"No, she is not a damn fling," I snapped, as I checked the bolts on the stable doors. "What are you doing out here, anyway?"

"Came to tell you that dinner is ready, and Bertie has questions for you."

"What sort of questions?" As I walked past the other stables, I looked at all the bolts making sure everything was secure.

"About your and Cassidy's sleepover. Whether Miss. Turner is going to be her aunt and why didn't you come home last night?"

I groaned and pinched the bridge of my nose. I didn't want to answer all the questions because I didn't want my answers to jinx anything.

"Maybe I'll eat dinner in the bunkhouse."

"Don't be a grump," Wilder said with a laugh. "She's just excited is all." He nodded at the office. "How you feeling about tomorrow being Charlie's last day?"

"Okay, I guess. I'm happy for her if it's what she wants."

"She'll be a loss, though."

"She will," I sighed, because he was right. "I'm sure I'll find someone."

We started to walk in step with each other, our shoulders brushing as we slowly made our way back to the house. As the sun dipped below the horizon, and I looked out toward the mountains, I felt content, happy. A real bone deep happiness that I hadn't felt in a long time. Maybe not since Mom died. Not the surface happiness that I got daily because I'd made progress with a difficult horse, or because Billy had said my name with a huge smile on his face, or because one of my brothers had made me laugh. *This* happiness made me feel like I had everything I could want or need. Like my heart was full and just getting fuller with every touch, every word, every kiss that I shared with Cassidy.

"You ever wonder where we'd be if Lily hadn't come back to Silver Peaks, or if we hadn't figured out what Dad was up to?" Wilder asked, moving my thoughts from goodness to bad.

"All the damn time," I replied truthfully, painfully aware of how different things could have been. "Lily coming back was what fired Nash back to life. He may not have wanted to fight Dad so hard if he hadn't found out what he did to Lily."

"You ever thought of visiting him in prison?"

"Do you?" I asked in disbelief.

"God no," he scoffed a little too quickly.

I placed a hand on his arm. "It's okay if you do, Wild. He's a rat bastard but he's still our dad. It's hard to let those kinds of feelings go."

"It's only because I want answers, you know." He looked at me with a pleading expression, desperate for me to understand.

"Wild he's been your only parent for most of your life. Of course, you want answers."

"The biggest being why? How could he do that to his own kids?" He scratched the back of his neck and groaned quietly. "Like if I was a better kid would he have been different?"

The word I had for my father at that moment would not have been welcomed in church that was for sure. How could he make this man, this kid, think him being a cheating, lying, thieving, son-of-a-bitch was his fault? This generous, funny, often annoying little brother of mine should not be shouldering that responsibility.

"If you want to know why then maybe you should go and see him," I said, placing a hand on Wilder's shoulder. "I bet he'd welcome it because I doubt he's getting many other visitors. But," I sighed, "do not go there asking if you could have done something to change him. I've thought about this, and I'm damn sure Nash has, and the answer will always be no, Wild.

That man had everything including a beautiful wife and three boys who would have adored him had he been different, yet he was still trash, so do not ever think you were the reason for that man's actions." As things were getting deep, a change of subject felt necessary and seeing Charlie through the window of the office gave me the perfect opportunity. "On another note, you know the girl who brought the racehorse in?"

"The one you told me pretty much stole it?"

"That's the one." I chuckled, still admiring the girl's balls. "Well, I'm thinking of asking her to take Charlie's job."

"Yeah? How do you know she'd be any good?"

"She's been over a couple of times to see Dream Maker, the racehorse, so I used it as an opportunity to give her an impromptu, informal interview."

"Does she know?" Wilder asked, laughing.

"No way. I can be subtle," I joked. "But in all seriousness I think she'd be a good fit. Whenever she's been here she asks a lot of questions. Ones that are pertinent and in depth, like she really knows what we're trying to do here."

"Sounds like she's the one then. What's her name again?"

"Tallulah Brown. Goes by Tally. She's from Sweet Maple Falls originally but has been living and working for a couple of different race trainers in Kentucky for the last six years."

"Kentucky! Wow, you sure she'll want to come back to little Sundance County?"

"Says she's ready because she misses home and her family." I shrugged. "We'll find out I guess if I offer her the job."

"And Ruthie starts soon. Seems like you're getting all the ladies." He laughed and slapped my back. "You always were a lucky bastard."

We'd reached the house, the warm glow of the porch light shining on the footpath leading up to the steps. It was home. This house. This land and I didn't want to be anywhere else, especially if I could have Cassidy with me.

Before we could walk up the steps, my phone buzzed in my pocket and instinct told me it was Cassidy.

"I'll be there in a few," I told my brother. He saluted me and jogged up the steps leaving me to talk to my girl. "Hey, sweetheart, you okay?"

"Hi. I'm just calling to say goodnight. I'm going to have an early night with a book, so I wanted to call you now in case I fall asleep." She chuckled. "Who am I kidding, of course I'll fall asleep; you've worn me out."

Smiling, I took a few paces from the house. "I did warn you that I was going to fuck you stupid." I adjusted my dick as I recalled all the sex we'd had over the last twenty four hours. Hot, dirty sex, slow erotic sex, her on top, me on top, me behind. We'd even thrown a reverse cowgirl in there just to keep the riding theme going. "How's that horse feeling between your legs?"

"Big and beautiful," she said almost on a moan before clearing her throat. "No, you're not doing that to me."

"What?" The laughter in my chest burst out, because I knew exactly how frustrated she was. I felt it, too.

"You know. Now, let me say goodnight and I'll speak to you tomorrow."

"Want me to come over and we can have dinner together?" *Please say yes.*

"I'd love that. I can make my famous Mac n Cheese with bacon, and if you're lucky my cinnamon rolls."

"Sounds perfect." And it did. "Seven okay?"

"Great. See you then."

"Goodnight, sweetheart. Sleep well."

"You, too, honey."

As she ended the call I thought about hopping in my truck and going over there, but she was right she needed sleep. Plus, I had some questions to answer for my niece. There really was no damn place like home that was for sure.

Somebody Like You – Keith Urban

CHAPTER 33
Gunner

My day was not going well. A night spent away from Cassidy had led to me tossing and turning. I was missing her and wished I'd gone to her place and had that early night with her. So, the morning had begun with me being grouchy and it just got worse.

It was Charlie's last day, and I'd wanted to spend some time with her, checking she'd got everything documented. Unfortunately, I hadn't banked on being three hands down because the shits were going through the place. Thank God my guys slept in a separate bunkhouse to the ranch hands because

Wilder and Nash were busy with late calving and branding and could do without the hassle. It meant that we'd been maxed out all morning. We'd had two new horses to assess, the stables to muck out, as well as feed and groom the ranch horses that were on rest. There was also the pain in my ass Dick Hazel. He was bringing Momma's Pride back having finally got pissed at having to trailer him in every day. I'd left Charlie to assess the horses while I dealt with Dickie.

"I did say he should have stayed here," I told him as I checked the horse had enough water.

"And I told you that your prices are too high."

I scoffed. "Like you can't afford it," I muttered under my breath, "Dick." And that was an adjective for him and not his damn name.

"You know there's a guy called Jimmy Destry near Grand Junction who is half your price."

"Yep and he has half my ability and success rate, so it's up to you." I moved past him and made my way out of the stables. "If you want to follow me to the office, Dick, so you can sign the papers."

"I signed them," his deep voice boomed, far too loud. "Why do I need to sign them again?"

"Because he's now being stabled here."

"Doesn't it still apply from last time?" He stopped in front of me, his huge Stetson shadowing his face.

"Nope. Besides, my rates went up last week."

"What? You actual mother fu—"

"I'd be careful Mr. Hazel." My jaw went tight as I stared at him. "You finish that, and you may be giving Jimmy Destry a call."

As he considered his options for a moment, I saw Tally approaching. She was wearing Western style boots, jeans and a shearling lined denim, walking with confidence across the yard.

"Oh hi, Mr. Miller, sorry I can come back."

"It's fine, Tally. Dream Maker is out in the paddock with Songbird and her foal if you want to go and see him."

Her eyes brightened. "He is? That's incredible. I was going to ask if we could try and integrate him with some other horses and see how he goes."

If this girl didn't want to come and work for me then I'd be pissed. "Tally, can I ask you something?" I asked, suddenly having an idea.

"Sure." She looked between me and Dick, unsure.

"If you had a horse that was spooked, even if you just showed him a set of reins what would you do?"

"You're asking me?" she pointed her thumb at her chest.

"Yep."

"What the hell is this?" Dick asked. "Am I paying for the advice of some itty bitty girl who is just here to visit her own damn pony."

My eyes widened at the rudeness of the man. He was a piece of shit and if it wasn't for the fact that I loved his horse and it needed my help, I'd have thrown him off my land.

"I'm just asking Tally a question if that's okay with you, *Dick*." I turned back to her. "Go ahead tell me what you'd do."

"I'd introduce him to things slowly. Maybe walk him around a paddock with reins hanging off it, or a saddle placed on it and then eventually take him to each in turn."

"Anything else?" I asked, giving Dick a quick glance and seeing him roll his eyes.

"Obviously I'd check him with other horses, too, and by process of elimination anything that he came in contact with on a daily basis."

She knew her stuff. "Once you've seen Dream Maker you think you could hang around, I'd like to have a chat with you."

She frowned and shoved her hands into her pockets. "Sure. Shall I come to the office?"

"That would be great." As she walked away, I turned to Dick. "Right, let's get those papers signed and you ever question mine or my staff's judgement again about your horse, I'll get you black-balled by every damn horse trainer in this country. Is that clear?"

"You can't do that," he protested.

"Yes I can, and I will. Everything I do is for the horse's benefit, not yours, so let me do my damn job." I turned for the office. "Now, are you willing to sign under those rules or not?"

He grumbled and started to walk past me. "Just give me the damn papers."

At least one positive had come from the morning. Maybe two if Tally agreed to take the job.

***

Charlie nodded and grinned at me from her seat behind Tally. She then held up a note pad with the words, 'hire her', written on it.

"You really want me to work for you?" Tally asked, sitting back in her chair and blowing out her cheeks. "I'm shocked. I mean thrilled, too, but I wasn't angling for a job when I kept coming around."

"I know that. You got me interested the moment you said you'd rescued Dream Maker from that piece of shit owner."

She glanced over at Charlie. "You leave today, right?"

"I do and honestly Gunner is the best person to work with if you want to learn everything about horse training."

I appreciated that from her seeing as we'd not exactly seen eye to eye over the last month or so. "Charlie will tell you that if there are any courses you want to sign up for, I'm happy to fund those for you. This is the salary." I pointed out the section on the contract. "That's a starting salary and after six months we'll review."

She looked down at it and I noticed her eyebrows raise. I knew it was a good surprise because I was a believer in paying people well. If you didn't, well, you know what they said about peanuts and monkeys.

"Take that home, speak to your family. You live with your brothers, right?"

She gave me a warm smile. "Cole and Liam, yeah. Our parents have moved to Florida for Dad's health."

The name Cole Brown rang a bell, but I couldn't think where. It didn't matter, though, because it wasn't him I was trying to hire.

"You didn't want to go there instead?" I looked over at Charlie, not wanting the same scenario in a year's time.

"God no, California is not the place for me." She gave a little shudder. "No, I love it here but I was convinced I'd have to get employment doing something I didn't love so I could stay. Either that or move away again."

"Well, hopefully, I've answered your prayers."

"I have a spare hour now," Charlie said, getting up from her chair. "Want me to show you a little more of what we do?"

And that was why I'd asked Charlie to step up in the first place. "That's a great idea." I reached out my hand to Tally. "I'll leave you with Charlie, but hopefully next time we speak it'll be because you're accepting my offer."

As I left them to go and work with an ex rodeo horse who'd been sent to me by my friend Deacon, I was grateful that a shit day had turned out okay. Maybe it was the shape of things to come—good things, but when I looked over toward the development site, I couldn't be so sure.

Best Day Of My Life – American Authors

CHAPTER 34
Cassidy

The kids were all occupied writing stories about their life as if they'd lived a hundred years ago. Looking across the classroom filled me with pride for what I did as a profession. Each of them was engrossed in their task, with tongues poking between teeth, noses scrunched up, and furrowed brows as they concentrated.

Lucas, though, was sitting back in his seat, tapping his pencil against his teeth in thought. It amused me to see these little mannerisms, some inherited from parents or grandparents, others seemingly appearing from nowhere.

Mom always said I pinched the end of my nose when I didn't like someone, a quirk no one else in the family shared. It was a weird trait, but it was mine.

"Okay, Lucas?" I asked. His desk was right in front of mine and I could see that he'd stalled a little.

His gaze met mine, big eyes questioning. "Does my life a hundred years ago have to be like it is now, Miss. Turner, but like a hundred years ago?"

"That was the assignment. Why? What are you thinking?"

"If I could write about the life I'd have liked to have had." He stretched his arms out across his desk, dangling his pencil off the end of it.

"You can do that, too. How would you have liked to have lived?"

"On the ranch," he replied, full of excitement and wonder. "Like Bertie does, but a hundred years ago."

"So?" I asked moving around my desk to sit on the edge of it. "What's your problem?"

He looked down at the three lines he'd written. "I don't know what sort of things they do on the ranch or what they did."

"You know what they do with the horses. How do you help Gunner?"

"I just ride the pony around in a circle." He shrugged.

My stomach somersaulted as I thought about the camp because that was exactly what it was all about; teaching kids how to work on a ranch. Lucas' wanting to write a story about the ranch a hundred years ago had given me an idea.

"Why don't you go and ask Bertie what happens on the ranch." I pointed to Bertie who was scribbling away. "In fact," I clapped my hands, "everyone can you stop for a moment." Twenty two sets of eyes looked up at me. "I'd like you to get into pairs and one of you be the storyteller and one the story writer. I want the teller to explain to the writer what their life is like now and then the other person write about it as if it was a hundred years ago. Bertie, can you partner with Lucas because he has a particular life he'd like to write about. Everyone else, pick your partner carefully."

"Sure thing, Miss. Turner." She saluted me and skipped over to Lucas' desk.

There was a little noise as people partnered up, but the incredible kids they were, none of them complained or made a fuss. Apart from Amber and

Macey, two girls who could be mean, they were insistent on being a pair, even though one of the boys, Gregory, was desperate to write about Amber's life.

Once everyone was settled, I heard them all discuss which roles they were going to take and animated chatter about their lives began. Satisfied they were working okay I slipped my phone out of my desk drawer and messaged Gunner.

> **ME**
> Hey gorgeous. How's your day going? How's Charlie's last day? xx

Within seconds he replied, making me breathless.

> **GUNNER**
> Hi sweetheart. Better now I've heard from you. Which is pathetic because I'm a grown man who can break a wild horse. A man who apparently is a lovesick idiot when my girlfriend doesn't message him back within seconds xx

> **ME**
> But what about Charlie? Is she also happier now I've messaged? Xx

> **GUNNER**
> Infinitely! Although she is having a weep at this very moment because everyone got her a goodbye gift. Good news on Tally, too, she's going to think about joining us but I'm feeling positive. How about your day? Xx

> **ME**
> Good so far, although I'll be better when I see you. I've had an idea actually xx

> **GUNNER**
> Sexual? I mean I'm not really into ass play but if it's a deal breaker we can discuss it over dinner! Xx

God, he made me smile so much I thought my cheeks might break.

THE EMERALD WAVES 237

ME
No! AND NO! About the camp. I'll tell you more tonight, but I was thinking maybe we teach the kids old ranch ways as well as new. Think the Yellowstone spin off, 1923 with Harrison Ford and Helen Mirren versus Yellowstone now, you know with Beth and Rip – actually scrap the Beth and Rip reference. She's far too angry and drinks too much. I mean I love her but maybe not for school kids xx

GUNNER
I don't know, I quite like the reference. Aren't they the ones that have a lot of energetic, angry sex?? Xx

ME
Not angry, just very hot sex. I would imagine he throws her around a great deal, and she loves it xx

GUNNER
Want to discuss that over dinner instead of ass play?

I almost burst out laughing, but just about caught it at the back of my throat. How would I explain that to the kids, 'don't mind me kids, but my boyfriend is messaging me about anal sex.'. Nope it wouldn't sound good.

ME
Maybe but what do you think about the then and now idea? xx

GUNNER
I love it. We could have little learning areas around the ranch and some displays set up. Lily would love that she'd be in her historical element. Xx

ME
Okay let's talk more later over dinner. Come over whenever you're ready xx

GUNNER
On my way now 😉

ME
See you later, cowboy xxx

God, why the hell had I fought with him when I could have been having all this goodness.

***

"I think it's a great idea," Gunner said, as he grated cheese for me. "And maybe we could get some old films to show. I'm pretty sure we've got some old family ones in the attic. My grandparents took them, of the hands herding the cattle up the mountain, branding, calving, that kind of stuff. You think they would be useful?"

"God, yes," I agreed, reaching for some of the cheese and taking a pinch of it.

"Hey, don't steal all my hard work." Gunner narrowed a playful gaze on me.

"Something you'll learn about me is I love cheese. But, on the subject of the video films, then yes they'll be perfect."

Gunner paused his grating, looking thoughtful. "You know what's funny? Three years of fighting, and it turns out we make a pretty incredible team."

"I was just thinking the same thing earlier today," I admitted, leaning against the counter. "Why did we waste so much time arguing when we could have been doing this?"

"Stubborn, I guess. Both of us." He smiled, the kind that made his eyes crinkle at the corners. "Though I have to say, making up has been worth the wait."

I felt the heat rise to my cheeks. Even after everything we'd done together, a simple comment from him could still make me blush.

"You know Cal's dad is still alive," Gunner continued, returning to grating. "He's in his late eighties and it was his ranch before it was Cal's." He cut a piece of cheese from the block and fed it to me. "I bet he'd be happy to come and do a talk. I'm sure he has a couple of his old ranch hands still alive, too. Mitch, one of our old ranch hands, I bet he'd be happy to provide some insight for the last thirty years. He runs the post office now with his wife and I think he's a little bored."

"That would be brilliant," I said excitedly as I took the milk from the refrigerator. "But I have an idea, how about we record them and show that as a film or just play the audio to save them coming over to the ranch all the time."

Gunner nodded enthusiastically. "I love that idea. Like you get in a museum."

"Exactly that. We could set up little listening stations where the kids could hear about what branding was like back then, or how they managed cattle drives without modern equipment."

"Nash mentioned once that Grandpa kept journals about ranch life. I bet there are descriptions in there we could use too." He leaned over and kissed my cheek. "How great a team do we make, hey, sweetheart?"

"Brilliant." I pursed my lips, begging for more.

"Nuh uh," he said, shaking his head. "Food first and then kisses, well maybe sex but kisses will be involved."

You couldn't argue with that, and I didn't want to. Food, kisses and sex, all with Gunner. What a perfect evening.

Death by a Thousand Cuts - Taylor Swift

CHAPTER 35
Cassidy

It had been a busy week, what with school, planning for the camp and sex with Gunner. The latter being my total favorite part. Nate Jenkins had messaged Nash to say he'd been delayed on his trip, which gave us a little more time to consider the stipulations to agreeing to not objecting to the development. If we got the rest of the town onside. Which was why there was another town meeting about to start.

Cal, Mayor Taylor, was running it, but Nash, Gunner and I were on the stage ready to put forward our suggestions. Lily was home with the kids while Wilder had gone to Bozeman for a couple of days to see another bull, because according to him, since the herd had grown poor old Gideon Pontipee's huge balls were running on fumes. Gunner had also told me that the bull was coming up for seven and so his fertility would soon start to decline.

"What will happen to him then?" I'd asked, a little alarmed.

He smirked at me and asked, "Do you really think Bertie would let us sell him for meat or euthanize him?" When I shook my head with a sigh of relief, he'd kissed my forehead. "He'll be put out to pasture, just like we did with Digby, our last bull. He died fat and happy about eight years ago."

"Well, that's a relief," I replied.

Gunner chuckled and said, "Sweetheart, if you're going to spend more time on the ranch you'll need to get used to the idea that we are a beef herd and we sell our cattle for meat. In the future that may include some of those calves you currently think are so cute."

The thing that struck me about that comment was 'in the future' and butterflies swarmed my stomach at the idea that he was thinking of me in that way.

"There's a good crowd," Nash said, bringing me back to the present.

And there was. Maybe not quite as many as the first town meeting we'd had, but probably because we were without those in favor of the development.

"Let's get going then," Cal said, looking at each of us in turn. "You all ready?"

We each nodded and our mayor started everything off.

Everyone seemed to be happy with the stipulations we'd suggested that we put forward to Nate Jenkins. They particularly liked Lily's idea of a nature trail, especially if it meant that they could use it, too. Nash was a little nervous about that because of people wandering onto ranch land and the dangers it would present if they came across the herd and spooked them. He said he'd consider ways to make it secure so it could happen, though. As for the state environmental review, everyone was behind it, so Cal said he'd start the process first thing in the morning.

"And you're sure that if he agrees to regular environmental reports he'll keep to it?" Willem Price, a local farmer, asked.

"We have to take him at his word," Nash replied. "But it will be a legally binding document that we have drawn up."

"A breach of any environmental regulation will bring penalties," Cal added. "Fines, higher insurance premiums and so on, but as Nash said it will be a legally binding document that we present Jenkins Industries with, which in turn means prosecution could be an option."

"What I've seen of Nate Jenkins, though," Nash said, "is that firstly he's a businessman who wants to succeed with a good reputation. And, while I don't know him well, at all, he strikes me as a decent man. He listened to our concerns about the environment and already has processes to put in place, so I believe that he'll keep to his word."

Willem nodded sagely. "Your faith in him is good enough for me, Nash." He took his seat again and said something in the ear of Davy, his son.

"Can I ask a question please?" It was Margie Anderson, the mom of Bella, a girl in my class, with her hand in the air.

"Yes, Margie, please ask away." Cal gave her a warm smile as she got to her feet.

"It's for Miss. Turner."

I blinked, surprised because I hadn't been asked anything. Neither Gunner nor I had needed to because it was Nash who'd fielded most of the questions.

"Sure, Mrs. Anderson, how can I help?"

"Can you assure us that you'll be staying at the school because it sounds like this camp is going to be a lot more than a summer camp." She looked around the room. "I mean I'm all for it but if we're going to lose a good teacher because of it then I'm afraid I don't want it. You'll be teaching my boy Drew next year and he's excited because he's good at math."

Math had been my major and I ran all the math camps and organized a yearly math contest, so I could understand why her boy might be looking forward to me teaching him.

"I have no intention of leaving the school," I told her. "Yes, the camp will be educational, but it won't warrant me being there full-time. The school is my priority."

A chair scraped on the stage and when I looked to my left, I could see it was Gunner's. He'd shifted it forward a little and was sitting on the edge of it, leaning forward with his elbows on his knees. He was staring out into the crowd, but from his profile I watched his Adam's apple bob on a big swallow.

Margie's smile told me she was appeased by my answer. "Thank you, that's a big relief, Miss. Turner."

As she sat back down, Cal closed the meeting and thanked everyone for coming and I heard Nash exhale.

"Not as bad as I expected," he said, running a hand through his hair.

"Pretty enlightening," Gunner added, his voice tight.

"Are you okay?" I murmured, leaning into him as Nash left to speak with someone at the edge of the stage.

"All good."

The muscle pulsing along his jawline told a different story. His shoulders had gone rigid, spine straight as a fence post.

"I'll walk you home," he said abruptly, standing before I could press further. The conversation was over, at least for now.

My stomach turned because something was off with him, and I had no idea what.

"Nash, I'm walking Cassidy home. You okay waiting for a few?"

"Sure." Nash waved a hand. "I need to talk to Cal about some water tanks, anyway. If they need to lock up here I'll wait in my truck."

Without saying anything else, Gunner took my hand and led me out of the hall. Once we were on the sidewalk I expected him to tell me what was troubling him, but he didn't open his mouth.

We'd only gone half a block when I pulled him to a halt. "What's wrong?"

His back was poker straight as he slowly turned his head. "Nothing. Not sure why you think there would be."

His tone said otherwise. "I'm not stupid, Gunner."

"I know that." He started to walk again. "Maybe it's just me."

"What?" I tried to get him to stop again but he was too strong and too determined. "Gunner, what the hell is wrong."

"I need to get back to Nash, we have an early start in the morning."

It didn't take us long to get to my apartment and when we did I expected him to leave me at the door. He didn't but followed me up the stairs and inside.

"Are you going to tell me now why you're being so frosty?" As I crossed my arms and leaned against the back of my sofa, something hit me, and nausea rolled through me. "Are you breaking up with me?"

"What? No." He breathed out slowly through his nose, shoving his hands to his hips.

"Well, your body language says different." I straightened ready for a fight, whatever that damn fight was going to be about.

He stared at me for a moment, tipping his chin up and taking a deep breath. "I thought we were on the same page here."

I was confused. "About?"

"Us, Cassidy, about us." His whole demeanor was cold, inflexible steel. Even his usually warm, soft eyes were hard, full of one emotion, anger.

Tilting my head to one side, I pursed my lips and tried to see something in his expression that would give me a clue.

After a few moments of silence, I shook my head. "I'm sorry, Gunner, but I'm lost here."

He scrubbed a hand over his face, clearly frustrated. "You told everyone at that meeting that the school was your priority."

"And it is," I responded. "It's my job. I'm paid to work there, so it has to be. I don't see your point."

"I thought the camp was something we were both committed to. The school being your priority doesn't scream that to me." He paced toward the door, and I thought he was going to leave, but as soon as he reached it he turned back to face me. "I thought you were going to teach at the camp. We discussed it."

I desperately tried to think about a conversation where I'd agreed to teach at the camp and remembered what he'd said: *"Cassidy, if this becomes as big as we want it to be we're going to need as much help as possible. I know you love teaching but maybe one day you could teach here."*

"You mentioned it would be an option maybe one day, but it was never agreed. I thought it was just an idea."

"You thanked me, Cassidy. For involving you and believing in you."

My lungs felt tight as I took a step to him. "And I am grateful, but that doesn't mean I'm just going to end my career to teach full-time at the camp."

"And why not?" he cried, throwing his hands into the air. "And in any case it wouldn't be ending your career, you'd be just taking a different path."

"But what if the camp doesn't work?" A lump rose in my throat, making it difficult to speak.

"Who the hell said it wouldn't work?" he yelled.

"No one, but what with the development and—"

"So, you're surrendering to Jenkins now are you?"

I threw my hands in the air. "This is ridiculous. You won't listen to a word I'm saying."

"Really," he scoffed. "Maybe my ears are blocked with bullshit."

"God," I muttered. "You're such a pain in the ass."

He rolled his eyes. "Welcome to my world."

"If I'm such a pain in the ass then maybe the camp is the least of your worries."

"What?" he leaned his body closer, cupping his ear.

"I think you know what I'm getting at."

His nostrils flared. "Not sure that I do."

"What if I give up my job at the school and the camp doesn't work? W-what if we don't work?"

Silence fell with a thud, like a concrete block falling to the floor and I instantly saw the hurt in Gunner's eyes.

"Gunner, I—"

"And there it is," he snapped. "Well, thanks for the belief in the camp and in me, Cassidy." He turned away and pulled the door open. "Enjoy the rest of your night."

Then he was gone, and I immediately felt sick because what if I'd just rushed us to the ending that we might never have had.

Say Something – A Great Big World, Christina Aguilera

CHAPTER 36
Gunner

The thing about being angry with someone you care about is that it fucks with your head. When that person is someone you know you're falling for it fucks with your stomach, too. Mine felt like it had a tornado inside it, whipping everything around making me feel constantly nauseous. The problem was the anger was still boiling in my blood, too. It was a maelstrom of feelings and emotions, good, bad and everything in between all because of that tiny damn brunette.

"You're such a jealous girl, aren't you?" I pulled an apple from my pocket and held it out, palm open, to Ariel, who had just nudged her way past Rocket, the horse I was working with, to steal his treat.

I often brought her into the training paddock with the skittish ones. There was something about her—so steady, so quietly sure of herself. Her inner calm had a way of settling them. Just like she did me. Just like she had every day since Mom had passed. Always there. Never leaving.

She took the apple without hesitation and ambled off, leaving Rocket to reclaim his spot at the fence. I fished out another apple and offered it up to him, just like I had my heart to Cassidy.

At least Rocket was grateful, his whiskers tickling my palm as he took the treat.

"Take my advice, Rocket boy," I muttered. "Don't let a woman in. It's not worth it."

"Oh dear, that doesn't sound good."

I turned to see Nash strolling toward me, he was still wearing his gloves and his chaps and had dirt streaked across his face.

"You look like you've had a morning."

"Yeah." He took his ball cap off and scrubbed a hand through his hair. "We lost a cow. Almost lost the calf, too, but luckily I was with a couple of the guys checking the water tanks over there."

"What the hell happened?" It might have only been one cow, but they were our livelihood. If it was illness it would not be good, especially if it was something that could spread through the herd.

"Wolf." He pinched the bridge of his nose. "I'm worried that if he's hungry enough to attack in the daytime that it's because he's got a family of more hungry wolves."

"Shit. Did you see it?" I asked, looking him up and down to check he was okay. "You sure the Mountain Lion isn't back?"

"No, it was a wolf. Managed to get a shot in. Think I caught it."

"I told you to get Wilder to teach you how to shoot." I slapped a hand on his shoulder. "You sure you're okay?"

"Yeah, I'm fine. Although, the day could have started better." He stretched his back and groaned. "The trip to Bozeman was a failure."

"Wilder called?"

"Yeah, he reckons they must have photoshopped the images they sent us because he had no muscle, looked like he might be nearer to ten than three and in our brother's words, 'his balls were like shriveled grapes'."

"Sounds like a shit twenty-four hours all round." I turned back to Rocket who was strolling across the paddock to Ariel. "I can't get him into a stable without him kicking and bucking, then someone has to stay with him for at least thirty minutes."

"Is that what he's here for?" Nash wandered to the fence and propped one foot on the bottom rail. "Because he can't be stabled."

"That and the fact they can't get him into a starting gate, which for a racehorse is pretty shitty." We seemed to be getting more and more horses with that problem. Maybe the damn jockey needed training, not the horses.

"Hmm I get that." My brother braced his arms and gave me his Dad expression. "And what's wrong with you? Why look so glum chum?"

"Told you the horse." I avoided his gaze, looking out to the green pastures in the distance. Emerald waves Cassidy had called them, and she was right, they did look like the swell of the ocean lapping against the grey of the mountains. I wanted to crumple to the floor thinking about her and what might be lost.

"Truth now. What's eating you up?" Nash grabbed my forearm and pulled me to face him. "Come on Gun, tell me."

I groaned. A deep one right from the bottom of my gut. "I think maybe me and Cassidy have kind of ended things."

He blinked slowly. "Fuck off. Really?"

"Yep. Well, I think so." We both rested our arms on the top rail and watched Rocket. Maybe it was because we were men, or maybe because we were brought up by a dickweed of a dad, but we often had our most meaningful conversations not looking at each other. "I thought she wanted the same as me, you know. With the camp."

"I thought she was all in. Last night at the meeting she was supporting it and us." He sighed and I wondered what was going through his head. Whether he was wondering what I'd done to mess it up, because let's face it I wasn't known for my relationship success. "What did she say?"

Thinking about it, her words, it didn't seem quite as negative or as world crushing as it had at the time.

"It was when she told Margie that the school was her priority," I told him.

"And?"

I turned to see him looking like I'd just told him that Unicorns really did exist. "What's that look for?"

"Of course, the school is her priority over the camp. That's her job, her profession."

"But we talked about her teaching at the camp full time?" The words rolled off my tongue with a hint of bitterness.

"Talked or agreed?" Nash asked. "Did you draw up a contract?"

I sighed. "No, of course, we didn't. We talked about it, and she thanked me for believing in her."

Nash rolled his eyes, and I knew who the bad influence was on Bertie for that habit.

"Quit with the damn eye roll, Nash."

"Well, you quit being a pussy then," he cried. Rocket's head shot up, his cautious eyes on us. "Sorry," he whispered and ducked his head in regret before putting his eyes back on me. "You need to man up and realize that her putting her job first, the kids she teaches first, is an admirable quality."

"But we were going to do this together." I waved my hand in the direction of the camp. "It was her idea; it's become something that I can't imagine not happening."

"Who says it won't happen?" He threw his hands in the air. "I heard what she said at that meeting, and she was reassuring a worried parent. Gun," he said, placing a hand on my shoulder, "what's this all about? Really?"

"I told you. It was my understanding that she was going to teach at the camp." My words were firm. The bitterness had gone but the anger was still there.

"We don't even know if the camp will work yet." He was quiet and controlled. Just like he always was. The voice of reason. "What if it doesn't go ahead because of the development?"

"So, you're doubting it now as well."

He shook his head. "For fuck's sake, Gunner. No, I'm not doubting it, but why ruin everything with the woman you love over something that we're in the first stages of or because she's good at her damn job."

"I never said I loved her," I bit back.

Nash's lips quivered into a smirk. "Whatever little bro. The point is don't push her away for something that might not even be an issue."

"Says the man who wouldn't even look at Lily when she came back."

He shrugged. "And look how miserable I was until I saw what a dick I was. Now I'm the happiest fucker on earth."

"Most annoying fucker on earth." I pushed off the fence. "I have work to do."

Nash put a flat palm against my chest. "Gun, don't ruin this because you're too pig-headed to talk to her. Whether you believe it or not you love her, or you're well on the way to it at least. That my friend," he tapped my pec with his pointer finger, "is fact and whether she teaches at the camp or not won't change that. It won't change how she feels about you, unless you carry on being a fucking turnip."

"You don't know how she feels about me," I spat back like a spoiled toddler.

Nash simply laughed, from deep in his belly, waved a hand at me and then strolled off pulling his ball cap back on.

Maybe he was right. Maybe I was being petulant about the whole thing. Damn it there was no maybe about it. Of course, Cassidy's work should be her priority. If it had been another teacher and I'd thought she was quitting on the school, on the kids, I'd be pissed. If they'd even considered it I'd have questioned their suitability as a teacher. I should be proud of Cassidy and help her to achieve whatever dream she had, not force her to fulfil mine. It still smarted, though, and I knew if I spoke to her now I'd say the wrong thing. It would all come out wrong and I knew she wasn't a woman who'd keep allowing me to fuck up. Damn it, that was what I liked about her.

I looked back out to those emerald waves she loved so much and sighed.

"I'll give you today Miss. Turner," I whispered against the wind, "but then I'm coming for you."

Irreplaceable – Beyoncé

CHAPTER 37
Cassidy

"Okay," Lily said, her sigh heavy as she flopped down onto a chair next to my desk. "What's going on?"

She'd been in my class earlier, collecting some paints and had seen straight away that I wasn't my usual self. I wasn't wearing makeup for starters and I never went anywhere without wearing my mascara. I was also wearing a blouse which in no way went with the stripe trousers that I was wearing.

"Nothing," I lied.

"Don't believe you." She looked me up and down, her eyebrows drawn in disgust. "Look at that outfit for starters."

"I know, I know. It was dark when I got dressed."

"Clearly." Linking her fingers and placing them on my desk, she leaned forward. "Is your lack of dress sense anything to do with Gunner's black mood?"

"Well, he didn't like the yellow bib overalls I wore a few months back and got covered in strawberry milkshake for his troubles, but I doubt he'd still be moody because of my clothes choice." I shrugged like it didn't matter but it did. It hurt. He'd hurt me by jumping to the conclusion that I didn't care about him or the camp. It hurt that he hadn't called to see if we could talk about it.

"What is the reason for his mood then, because I know you know." Lily's blue eyes stared at me, uncompromising yet understanding.

"We had an argument."

"Is that all? Nash and I argue all the time." She squinted at me through one eye. "Well, bicker really and I'm pretty sure he does it for make-up sex. He says I'm wild when I'm mad at him."

I loved Lily dearly, but sometimes I didn't want to hear about all the sweet that she had at home with Nash. I was plain and simple jealous, or I had been until Gunner. Now, though, it felt like I'd be going back to that place again. The one where I was an onlooker to happiness.

"I'm sure it'll be fine, Lily. Don't worry about it."

She schooled her expression into something akin to concern. "Tell me why some make-up sex isn't going to fix things."

I shrugged. "It might."

"When was the last time you spoke to each other?"

Thirty-nine hours and forty minutes ago. "Monday night at the meeting. I was asked if I was leaving here to work full-time on the camp and Gunner didn't like my answer."

"Which was?"

"That I was committed to my work here."

"Which is right." A tiny line appeared between her eyes. "But Gunner didn't agree?"

"He thought I was going to teach at the camp eventually. And by saying

I was committed to the school meant I wasn't committed to the camp."

"Okay," she replied.

I swallowed the scratch at the back of my throat, wondering when the heaviness in my chest would eventually disappear. Or would it always be there, like it was for my mom.

"Cassidy, you should talk to him," Lily urged. "It sounds like a misunderstanding that you can both work through."

"I won't be controlled, Lily. Forced to work at the camp because that's what Gunner wants me to do. I have my job, my profession." The hurt was mixing with anger and creating bitterness. Not a feeling I was used to. Not even losing my parents had made me bitter, sad and angry but not bitter because it was the circle of life as ugly as it was.

Lily's smile was soft and gentle. "Does that really sound like Gunner to you, honey? You really think he wouldn't want you to be in charge of your own life, your own destiny?"

Now she came to mention it.

"No," I said with a pout. "He wouldn't."

"So why do you really think he was upset? Hmm." She was giving me her Teacher look, the one she gave the kids when she was trying to coax an answer from them.

"I'm so glad you don't teach me. I hate that look, it's worse than your, 'I'm not mad I'm just disappointed' look."

She gave a quiet chuckle. "Have you thought about it?"

"I don't know. That he doesn't think the camp will work without me?"

Lily rolled her eyes. "Do I have to point it out to you?"

"Seems so." I scoffed and picked up my phone, checking again whether I had any messages.

"He's scared that if you're not committed to the camp then you're not committed to him either, you idiot."

My heart stopped for a beat before picking back up at double speed. "Really? You think, because I'm not so sure." Then I remembered the conversation we'd had.

"What if I give up my job at the school and the camp doesn't work? W-what if we don't work?"

"And there it is," he snapped. "Well, thanks for the belief in the camp and in me, Cassidy."

"He doesn't think I believe in him," I whispered. "In us."

Lily reached across the desk and took my hand in hers. As her thumb stroked the back of it she met my gaze. "The Miller men are complicated, Cassidy. They have a complicated relationship with the man who was supposed to teach them how to be men. He wasn't a good father even less so after their mom died, so everything they know they've taught themselves because only so much of the good came from their mom. They were so young when she passed."

"I know, it must have been so hard on all of them, Gunner talks about her so fondly."

"Unlike Nash," she gave a little laugh, but it was sad. "He barely ever talks about her. Never did when we were teenagers either. He finds it too sad." Lily exhaled slowly like she was expelling all the unhappiness she felt on behalf of her husband. "Nash broods, Gunner shoots from the hip and Wilder jokes through his worries, it's how each of them deals, Cassidy."

"Shooting from the hip is true. Then he thinks about it later, three years later in some cases."

"Exactly." Her smile was tender. "The point I'm making, Cass, is that he's probably scared of losing someone else and totally overreacted. You don't want to commit to the camp, so you don't want to commit to him. But you know maybe that's why you won't commit to the camp either."

I frowned. "Because I don't want to commit to him?"

"No, because you're scared of it. In case you lose someone or something else you love, too."

I let out a harsh breath. "How has this suddenly become my fault? He's the one who stalked away like a spoiled toddler."

Lily then gave me her Mom expression. "Not what I said but think about it, why didn't you put him straight? Explain it differently. Why didn't you say, 'I can't commit to the camp because it's not even started yet, but I love you and if there is a need for me to teach at the camp then I'll consider it.'."

"Why? Because I don't love him."

Lily snorted. "You so do. You need to wise up to that and the fact that while the Miller brothers are totally adorable, extremely hot and incredibly good with animals and children they are a little bit stupid in the ways of love and romance. Nash is getting there because I'm a great teacher, but Gunner needs a little help. We'll leave Wilder for now, but he will need assistance eventually."

I couldn't help laughing because she was exactly right about them. She wasn't right about me being in love and unable to commit, though. Was she?

Whether she was or not, I knew I had to speak to Gunner. We needed to talk and be honest with each other about what we wanted for our futures. If they didn't match up then I'd have to deal. I had to make him see, though, that the camp and us weren't mutually exclusive.

A Thousand Years – Christina Perri

CHAPTER 38
Gunner

Dawn was breaking through the mountains, and it was a breathtaking spectacle. The sky was ablaze with vibrant hues of pink, purple and orange as the sun climbed over the silver peaks of the majestic mountains and I understood why this was Nash's favorite time of the day. His favorite place to watch it, on Mom's old rocker on the porch with a cup of coffee in his hand.

Yet this morning, it didn't have that same appeal. Probably because I'd barely slept all night and felt like shit. I'd thought about calling Cassidy, but there were still some vestiges of anger in my chest. Who that anger was aimed at, I wasn't sure.

That was the thing about anger, it was often an irrational emotion, one borne because you didn't know how else to feel. You were happy but didn't think you should be so you got angry. You were grieving and you got angry because of your loss. You were in love, but the other person didn't feel the same, you got angry. You didn't listen to your girlfriend, fucked up and got angry.

Dropping my feet from the balustrade of the porch to the floor, I let out a huge sigh. Expelling all the negativity I'd stored up over the last fifty or so hours. When I'd realized I was being mad at the wrong person, I'd used work as an excuse not to call Cassidy. Songbird's foal was running a temperature, so I'd been with her until it had broken just after nine. I'd told myself it was too late at night to have a conversation of the kind we needed, so had fallen into bed and attempted to sleep. Hours of tossing and turning and I'd given up and come outside to contemplate the great pile of shit I'd dropped myself into.

Top and bottom of it was, I needed to apologize and listen to what she had to say. I'd go over to her apartment after she finished work, talk to her, ask her to forgive me and then ask her what she wanted for her future.

Firstly, I had a job to do and some planning on how I was going to get her to absolve me of being a dick.

***

"Ruthie," I cried, waving across the yard. "Good to see you." I glanced down at my phone; it was only just four. The day had screamed by since I'd started working at five that morning. "What are you doing here?"

"I took a day off to catch up on chores," she told me with a small grimace. "Said I had strep."

"Naughty, naughty," I said with a laugh as I reached her at the door of my office.

"I won't ever do that when I'm working for you." She bit down on her lip and closed her eyes. "Oh, God, have I messed up?"

"Ruthie, don't sweat it." Amused, I opened the door and stood aside to let her in. "I don't blame you. That manager of yours hasn't been wholly fair with you. What can I do for you anyway?"

Following her in, I went to my desk while she took a place in front of it her hands clasped in front of her.

"Lucas is having a play date with some friends, so I thought it might be a good opportunity for me to get started on some work before next week." She smiled hopefully. "I don't want any pay."

"No, you do the work you get the reward, Ruthie."

"You giving Lucas riding lessons is payment enough."

I waved her away. "It's my pleasure. Honestly." And it was, especially when a certain brunette joined. The thought of Cassidy maybe never coming back to the ranch made my chest tight and I swallowed thickly. "So, what do you plan on doing?"

"Entering some of those invoices on the system?"

"Sounds good to me." It was one of the tasks I'd given myself to do over the week, so I was more than happy. Plus, I was desperate to go and see Cassidy and put things right…if she'd let me. "You okay to lock up when you've finished?"

She held up the keys I'd given to her a few days before. "Absolutely. Go and do whatever you need to do. I'll be here for a couple of hours."

"Coffee should still be warm, if you want some."

She held up a water bottle. "I'm fine. You go." Ruthie turned away from me and grabbed a bunch of papers and started sifting through them.

With the knowledge that my office would soon be a well-organized hub of administration, I left to go and sort my life out. First I need to go and get something from the box I kept at the bottom of my closet.

The drive to town gave me too much time to think. Too much time to rehearse words that sounded hollow and inadequate. That was the problem with apologies; they never seemed to capture the depth of what you were really trying to say. Especially for a man like me who wasn't great at words. Which was why I hoped the little box on my passenger seat would be able to speak for me if I was lacking.

As I pulled off Latymer, I spotted her car parked outside the school. Good, she was still there. Cassidy often worked late, especially when she had math competitions to organize. Her dedication to those kids went beyond the classroom and it was one of the things I'd grown to admire about her, once I'd got my head out of my ass and realized the truth of who she really was.

I parked beside her car and sat for a moment, gathering my courage. The last time I'd been this nervous around a woman...hell, I'd never been this nervous. The thought of losing her over my own stubbornness made my stomach twist into knots.

Grabbing the small box, I headed into the school. The hallways were quiet, most of the classrooms empty, bar the odd teacher who stayed behind as I made my way toward Cassidy's room. Through the small window in her door, I could see her at her desk, head bent over papers, a red pen in hand. The sight of her made me pull up short, just to watch her, drink her in. Her hair was falling from its ponytail, and she kept pushing stray strands behind her ear as she worked.

I knocked softly, startling her. When she looked up and saw me, her expression shifted from surprise to wariness. Without waiting for any further response, I opened the door.

"Gunner." She set down her pen, straightening in her chair. "What are you doing here?"

I stepped inside, closing the door behind me. "I needed to see you."

"I'm working." Her voice was measured, careful. She was protecting herself from me and that knowledge cut deeper than any anger I'd had.

"I know. I just..." I held up the box. "I brought you something."

Curiosity flickered across her face despite her obvious attempt to remain detached. "You brought me a gift?"

"Not exactly a gift." I moved closer, setting the box on her desk. "More like a peace offering. Or maybe a promise."

She eyed the box suspiciously. "A promise of what?" Her fingertips whispered over the top of it as his gaze slowly lifted to mine.

"That I'm listening. That I hear you." I pushed it closer toward her. "Open it." I swallowed. "Please."

Her fingers hesitated over the lid before she finally lifted it. Inside was a small silver pin in the shape of a horseshoe with tiny emeralds set in it.

"It was my mom's," I explained. "She gave it to me when I first started riding. Said it was my good luck charm to make sure I never fell off."

Cassidy's eyes widened. "Gunner, I can't take this—"

"Oh, I'm not giving it to you." I smirked. "And that's a bit forward of you thinking that Miss. Turner."

Cassidy's lips twitched with a hint of a smile, and I felt my chest release, like the strap binding my heart had been loosened.

"Can I explain?" When she nodded, I crouched down in front of her. "The camp was your idea, Cassidy. And somehow I turned it into this test of your commitment to me, which was unfair and stupid." I ran a hand through my hair, frustrated with myself. "I've been thinking about what you said, about the camp not working and us not working…"

She flinched slightly, and my own heart stalled for a beat.

"The thing is," I continued, "the camp might not work. Hell, *we* might not work. But I want to try both things. And if only one works out, we'll deal with that then. And if neither works…" I swallowed hard, hating the idea. "Well, then at least we gave it our best shot."

Cassidy looked down at the pin, her fingers tracing its outline. "I never meant that I didn't believe in us. I just…I've lost a lot of people I cared about, Gunner. Not just my parents but the foster kids, too. I knew it was temporary, yet it still hurt like hell when they had to go. It felt like I wasn't seen to be good enough to see them through the next stage of their life."

She'd seemed at peace with what had happened with the foster kids. I hadn't even considered that she might feel like that. I had a lot to learn about being in a relationship, maybe we both did.

"I know." I reached out, not quite touching her but letting my hand rest near hers. "I've been there too. I know how damn hard it is even though I tried to be the positive one." I thought about my conversation with Wilder about our father. "God, Cassidy, me and my brothers have all probably had thoughts about Dad being a different parent if maybe we'd been different kids, but it's not on us and those kids being found homes isn't because you weren't good enough, it's because you were eighteen."

"I know that deep down." She blinked rapidly, voice fraying at the edges. "But when everyone leaves eventually…maybe the common denominator is me."

Something fierce and protective surged through my chest. "No." I cupped her face, thumbs brushing the soft skin beneath her eyes. "Listen to me. You're not someone people leave, Cassidy. You're someone people come home to."

"So where does that leave us?" she asked, finally meeting my eyes.

"That depends on whether you're willing to forgive a stubborn, shoot-his-mouth off-think later cowboy who's falling in love with his teacher girlfriend."

The words slipped out before I could stop them. But seeing the surprise bloom across her face, I didn't regret them.

"You're falling in love with me?" she whispered.

I nodded and blew out a slow breath. "Yeah, sweetheart I am. I hope that's enough for you and if all else fails we've got the lucky horseshoe."

Falling - Harry Styles

CHAPTER 39

Cassidy

He was falling in love with me.

Gunner Miller was falling in love with me.

"Are you okay?" he asked, his hand cupping the back of his neck. "Shit. Do you want me to go? Give you some time to think? Have I said too much?"

I shook my head and looked back down at the horseshoe pin. It was so pretty, silver with tiny emeralds embedded in it.

"Why have you brought this to me? If you're not giving it to me." My teeth caught my bottom lip as I watched him take a deep breath.

"I guess it's, what's the word…" He looked out of the window to the school yard where Edward our janitor was cleaning up stray bits of litter. "Symbolic," he suddenly announced. "It's symbolic of my belief in you. In the good luck that I want you to have no matter what your choice is. It's a loan because one day I hope that *we* can pay it forward to someone else. And," he sighed, "if there is no we, then you can."

It was then that I noticed a piece of paper folded and pressed into the lid. My name was written on in his unmistakable scrawl.

"What's this?" I asked, pulling it free.

He squinted with a groan. "A back up plan in case you wouldn't talk to me."

"Can I read it?"

He shrugged. "I guess so, I can't embarrass myself any more than I already have."

Taking a deep breath, I unfolded the single piece of lined notebook paper, the creases still fresh from where he'd hesitated and then I read.

> Cass,
>
> If you're reading this, I guess you're still not ready to talk to me. And I get that. I do.
>
> I've gone over what happened more times than I can count, trying to figure out what I could've said differently, done better, or undone altogether. But it always ends the same, with me messing up, and you walking away. And the thing is, I deserved that. I made a huge mountain out of a tiny mole hill.
>
> I told myself I was right to be angry but truth? I was just scared. Scared of you walking away. Scared of needing someone as badly as I need you.
>
> You see me, really see me, in a way no one else ever has. And that scares the hell out of me, too.
>
> I'm not writing this to beg for forgiveness or ask you to come back. I just wanted you to know that I'm sorry. For all of it. For not showing up the way I should have. For not understanding your worries. For pushing you away when you were the only good thing I had going.
>
> If you never speak to me again, I'll understand. But I hope, someday, you'll remember me as more than the guy who broke your heart.
>
> Yours always
>
> Gunner x

My eyes were burning by the end of it. Not just because of what he'd written – but because he hadn't even known if I'd let him explain in person. He'd come anyway and that was the measure of the man he was, the man I hadn't really known three years ago. He wasn't afraid to risk everything for me.

Folding the letter I put it back into the box and closed the lid, wrapping my fingers around it and pressing it against my chest. "I am committed to the camp, Gunner," I whispered. "Please don't think I'm not. It's just that this is my job, my career, my passion."

"I know, Cassidy, believe me I do. I was wrong for losing my shit like I did. I should have listened and let you explain. God," he threw his hands in the air, "you didn't need to explain. I should have just understood."

"No, you're right I should have clarified what I was thinking." I reached down to cup his cheek. "In fact, I think we both need to improve our communication skills."

Gunner rose slowly, taking my hand from his cheek and moving it to his chest, pressing his own over the top. It was warm and comforting along with his heartbeat that I could feel under my fingertips. Along with the soft cotton of his shirt. His white one that enhanced his deep ranchman's tan.

"Did you wear this shirt on purpose because you know it does things to me?" I asked.

"Maybe." He grinned. "But can you let me say what I want to say before you objectify me please."

I rolled my eyes. "I'm so sorry, please go ahead."

He pulled me to standing and I looked up at him, one hand still against his chest while my other went to his waist, anchoring myself to him.

His heart beneath my fingers picked up pace as he slowly inhaled. "I would love it if we could see the camp through together. Your incredible idea has become my dream. Your vision has brought excitement to all of us, and I got carried away. I panicked because I don't want to do it without you. I mean I would, but it wouldn't be the same." His eyelashes fluttered as his brown pools screamed panic.

"I want it, too." I protested. "I want it with you."

"But I don't want you to give up your own dream."

"Don't you see, honey, I can have more than one dream." I stood on tiptoe, so my lips were closer to his and whispered, "Teaching is a dream as are you and the camp. In fact, you're my dreamy cowboy."

Gunner groaned. "For the love of God woman, please don't ever call me that again." His lips landed on mine amidst laughter from both of us and instantly I felt my whole body relax.

"Look at us," I said as Gunner pulled away slowly. "We sorted out our differences without being mean to each other."

"Told you, we're a great team." He pulled me closer. "I can't promise I won't be stubborn again," he said, his thumb tracing circles on my palm. "But I can promise I'll always find my way back to you. Understand you." The sincerity in his eyes made my throat tight.

"Even when we fight?" I asked.

"Especially then," he answered, as he dropped his mouth to mine again, this time taking more time. Pressing his tongue against the seam of my lips, urging me to open for him. I was more than happy to, welcoming the kiss.

"We should leave," I said after what might have been hours, but was probably minutes. "I think Mrs. Wright is still here and she might walk in on us."

Gunner cleared his throat and smirked. "Yep, I think so. Missy May's for dinner?"

I thought about it for an instant. "Let's go to my place."

"You don't have to cook dinner, let's eat out."

Giving him a quick kiss to his cheek, I winked. "Oh no, honey, what I have in mind would be illegal in Missy May's."

With a raised brow Gunner grabbed my hand and had me out of there quicker than I could blink.

Earned It – The Weeknd

CHAPTER 40
Gunner

The moment that I walked back into Cassidy's apartment I felt at peace. Happy because for a moment there I thought I'd seen the last of it. My eyes followed her as she moved around the room, hanging her jacket on the back of one of the dining chairs at the small square table. She kicked off the ankle boots she was wearing and pulled her blouse from the waistband of her pants. There was an open book on the armchair by the window, her black glasses on top of it, and a pair of slippers on the floor kicked off haphazardly. On the sofa was a dressing gown and there was a half full glass of milk on the mantle over the fire. Life had continued in this little apartment for the last forty-eight hours and I had missed out on it through stubbornness.

Cassidy turned to me and grimaced. "I'm sorry about the mess. I've been a little distracted for the last couple of days." She dropped her head, a red blush covering her cheeks. "How have you been?"

I shrugged, shoving my hands into my jeans' pockets. "Miserable." I snickered. "Shit, two days and we're both falling apart."

"I know." Cassidy beamed at me. "Years of hating each other and then forty-eight hours of frosty relations and I'm a complete mess."

Taking a step closer to her, I linked my pinky with hers. "Same," I whispered. "Worse than I imagined."

We were caught in each other's gaze for a beat and the atmosphere instantly turned sinful.

As our lips met, the last threads of doubt unraveled between us. My hands cradled Cassidy's face with a reverence that I felt through to my fingertips, because she was something precious that I feared might disappear. I pressed closer, wanting to erase any remaining distance.

"I've missed you," I whispered against her mouth, the words vibrating between us. "Even though it's only been a couple of days."

"I know," she agreed, her fingers finding the buttons of my shirt. "I didn't know whether to call you or not."

I shook my head. "It doesn't matter anymore."

Cassidy's eyes fluttered close as she leaned closer and breathed in. "Can we go to my room now?"

It was what I wanted but almost died inside when I realized I hadn't brought any condoms with me.

"Hate to break the moment, sweetheart, but do you have any condoms?" I asked with a wince.

She opened her eyes, long lashes fluttering as she took a deep breath. "I do but I don't want to use them, unless you do. I'm clean, I have birth control covered. But I get it if—"

"Sounds like fucking heaven to me." I caught her hands, bringing them to my lips to kiss her fingertips one by one. "But the first one tonight will be slow," I murmured. "I want to remember everything."

"The first one?" she questioned.

"Yeah, the first one, because I owe you at least two more. One for an apology, one because I love that beautiful pussy of yours and one because you make my dick so hard I can barely see straight."

She drew in a ragged, needy breath, her nipples pebbling against the silk of her blouse and silently turned to lead me to her room.

It was bathed in the golden light of early evening, casting Cassidy in amber shadows as I slowly undressed her. I unfastened each button of her blouse with deliberate care, my knuckles grazing against the soft skin beneath. Each newly exposed inch of skin received my focused attention—a kiss here, a gentle touch there. I traced the delicate lace edge of her bra with my fingertip, watching goosebumps rise in my wake.

"Cold?" I asked, my voice low.

"Not even close," she breathed, her pupils dilating as I slid the blouse from her shoulders.

I lowered my mouth to the curve of her neck, right where it met her shoulder, relishing in the taste of her, a hint of perfume and salt. "You taste even better than I remembered," I murmured, tracing my tongue along her collarbone.

Her hands tugged at my shirt. "Too many clothes."

I stepped back enough to pull my shirt over my head in one fluid motion, tossing it aside. I drew in a ragged breath as she ran her palms over the planes of my chest. My heart beat a steady rhythm as her warm hands caressed the ridges of my muscles.

"God, I missed touching you," she whispered. Her thumb circled my nipple, and I couldn't help the groan that escaped me.

I unhooked her bra, sliding the straps down her arms. The sight of her breasts, flushed and perfect, almost brought the animal out in me that wanted to devour her, but my desire to take our time was more powerful. "Beautiful," I breathed, cupping their weight in my palms.

When I lowered my head to take one nipple into my mouth, Cassidy gasped, her fingers threading through my hair. I swirled my tongue around the sensitive peak before lightly grazing it with my teeth.

"Gunner." She arched into my touch, her fingertips tightening.

I stepped back just enough to help her out of her remaining clothes before quickly shedding my own, discarding them into a pile at our feet, before gently guiding her backward to the bed.

"Lie down for me, sweetheart," I said, my voice rough and full of the pain I was feeling in my balls.

She complied, moving to the center of the bed, her honey-gold skin glowing in the fading light of the room and I followed. Crawling over her but pausing to press kisses up her inner thigh.

"What are you—" Her question cut off with a sharp intake of breath as my tongue found her center.

I took my time savoring her taste, making her gasp and moan, as she pulled me closer by my hair. When I added two fingers as well, her thighs began to tremble.

"Don't stop," she begged, one hand slapping onto the mattress and fisting the comforter. "Please Gunner."

I increased the pressure and pace, driven by the erotic, sinful sounds coming from her parted lips until she finally came apart, crying out my name. Pride swelled in my chest that I'd brought her that pleasure so before she'd fully recovered, I moved up her body, positioning myself between her thighs.

"Look at me." I commanded.

Her whisky eyes, hazy with pleasure, locked onto mine as I slowly pushed inside her. The feeling of her tight heat surrounding me was almost too much.

"Fuck," I breathed, struggling for control. "You feel incredible."

Her legs wrapped around my waist, pulling me deeper. "Move," she urged, her nails digging into my shoulders.

I started with slow, deep thrusts, watching her face, memorizing every flicker of pleasure. When her mouth opened on a gasp, I knew I'd hit just the right spot.

"You like that, do you?" I asked, angling to hit it again.

"Oh my God, yes." Her words were hurried like if she didn't tell me I might change the pace or the position.

I didn't, though, I kept the same punishing rhythm, fighting to hold back my own release until I felt her tightening around me again. "Come for me sweetheart," I encouraged, sliding a hand between us. "And make it fucking loud."

My finger had barely touched her before her second orgasm ripped through her, triggering my own and I buried my face in her neck as I came. Her name was a prayer on my lips as we clung to each other through the aftershocks, neither of us willing to let go.

As our breathing gradually slowed, I rolled to my side, keeping her close against my chest. My fingers tracing lazy patterns along her spine, committing every curve to memory.

"Stay with me," Cassidy breathed as I moved above her.

Her eyes locked with mine, heated and earnest asking me for far more than just this moment.

"Always," I promised, sealing the vow with a kiss that felt like coming home.

"You know what I was thinking about this morning?" I asked, my voice a low rumble filled with desire for my incredible woman.

"Hmm?"

"Those emerald waves that you love. The land rolling toward the mountains like it knows exactly where it belongs." My arms tightened around her. "That's how this feels, like finding where I'm supposed to be."

Cassidy smiled against my skin, pressing a kiss to my chest right over the beating pulse of my soul. "Then maybe we should explore this territory a little more thoroughly," she suggested, her hand sliding down my stomach with unmistakable intent.

My body immediately responded to her touch. "I thought you'd be tired," I said, my breath catching as her fingers wrapped around me.

She raised herself up on one elbow, her eyes dancing with mischief. "You're the one who promised to fuck me three times, cowboy," she reminded me, shifting to straddle my hips. "And number two is going to be my gift to you."

"So, I still owe you two more after this?" I asked, a smile touching my lips.

"Oh yeah, absolutely."

As she sank down on me, taking me deep inside her again, I knew with absolute certainty that I was falling in love with this woman. And the way she moved above me, her eyes never leaving mine, I dared to hope that she felt the same.

Willow – Taylor Swift

CHAPTER 41
Cassidy

I had done something that I'd never done in my life. Something I would never do again. Did I feel ashamed? A little, maybe. Did I feel guilty? A little, maybe. Would I go to hell for it? Probably not. Was it worth it?

"Oh my God, Gunner," I gasped as he pulled out of me. "I think you've broken my vagina."

Yes it was oh so worth it!

"Is that what you said when you rang in sick today?" He smiled against my lips before moving them to my neck and gently sucking on it.

"No, I told Suki I had the stomach flu. What was your excuse to Nash?" I swatted him away. "And don't give me a hickey, I don't look good in a turtleneck."

"I didn't have one. I just messaged Mikey with some instructions and said I'd be back after lunch."

My heart sank, the disappointment real. "You're not staying in bed with me all day?"

Gunner groaned and wrapped an arm around my waist, pulling me to him. "I'd love to, sweetheart, but I have a new horse coming in this afternoon and Dick Hazel is coming for an update."

"Who's Dick Hazel?" I rested my cheek on his chest and ran my finger up and down his sternum, all the while marveling at the hard ridges of his hard muscles.

"He's a client and a pain in my damn ass. He tried to undermine me with his horse's training, and it put him back weeks." He sighed deeply. "It's one of the things Charlie and I argued over."

"Have you heard from her since she left?" I moved to trace a faint scar just above his hip bone. "What's that?"

"I fell from a tree when I was seven or eight, had four stitches but luckily it wasn't serious." Reaching for my hand he linked our fingers together as I continued to run my finger along the raised skin. "That is entirely too distracting. What was the other question?"

I giggled and dropped a kiss to his shoulder loving that his smell would now be on my sheets again. "Have you heard from Charlie?"

"Yeah, she messaged to let me know she'd got home okay. I was worried about her driving a U-Haul all by herself, but she just had too much stuff to ship apparently. She lived in three rooms above the stables, how much stuff can one woman have." He lifted his head from the pillow and looked over toward my shelves stuffed with books, cosmetics and purses and chuckled. "Yeah, maybe I get it."

"Imagine if I had more room for more stuff?" I joked. "Oh, and a beautiful kitchen island."

Gunner's gaze snapped to mine, and something shifted in his expression. It looked like longing or maybe hope as his hand came up to tuck my hair behind my ear. "Yeah, imagine that," he whispered.

A little while later, after a lazy breakfast of eggs that Gunner cooked, and my cinnamon rolls of which he devoured three, we were driving over to the ranch. I'd suggested that I follow in my car, but he'd insisted that I ride with him. And, apparently, I was staying for the weekend.

"I need you with me, sweetheart, so don't even think about arguing." Gunner had said, while thrusting into me from behind when I was supposed to be washing the breakfast dishes. How's a girl supposed to say no to that?

As we drove back from town, Gunner's hand reached for mine across the console. He lifted it to his lips and kissed it before placing our linked fingers between us, his thumb tracing patterns on my skin while he hummed along to the radio. It was casual but intimate and felt significant somehow. Like it wasn't just desire between us but something deeper. Something that felt like belonging.

When we pulled up outside the house, he leaned over and gave me a soft kiss. "Fuck I missed you," he said when he pulled away. "Stay, I'll get the door for you."

So, I stayed, quietly stamping my feet like an excited toddler as I watched his big body swagger in front of the truck before leading me inside.

"Well, hello," Lily said, grinning, as we walked through the door hand in hand. "I see you made up."

"Yep." Gunner let go of me and held up my overnight bag he was carrying. "I'll take that to my room then go and do some work."

As I nodded he leaned in for a hard, closed mouth kiss, one hand at the back of my head, igniting another fire within me. When Lily cleared her throat, I let go of his biceps and stepped back, breathless.

"See you later," I said, sure I had heart emojis in place of my eyes.

"I'll be back after lunch," he replied, then paused, his expression shifting to something softer, more uncertain. "Unless you want me to stay away longer? Give you some space?"

The fact that the confident, self-assured cowboy was suddenly concerned about crowding me made my fingers tingle and my knees feel weak. I reached up to trace the worry lines between his brows.

"Don't you dare stay away," I whispered, pulling him in for another kiss. "I've had enough space for three years."

He smiled softly, saluted me and said, "Yes ma'am," before disappearing up the stairs.

After a few seconds of watching his perfect ass, I turned back to Lily unable to contain the smile that seemed to have bloomed from somewhere deep inside my chest.

"And why aren't you at school?" my friend and colleague asked, folding her arms over her chest, her gaze narrowed on me, the weight of my expectation hanging in the air between us like the static before a storm.

"I have the stomach flu," I replied in a small voice.

"You don't have to talk like you actually do." Lily barked out a laugh. "I'm not going to snitch on you."

"I do feel bad about it," I confessed. "I've never ever skipped work before."

"You've never ever made up with a Miller brother before, and if Gunner is anything like Nash I'm guessing there was a lot of sex involved." Her lips quirked into a mischievous grin. "You should have just said your vagina was broken."

"That's what I said!"

As we both burst out laughing, my guilt dissipated a little.

***

The kids had gone to bed and the rest of us were around the dining table, discussing the camp and what our next steps should be when we got our next meeting with Nate Jenkins .

"We're all agreed, then?" Nash asked, looking at each of us in turn. "If he doesn't agree to an initial and then regular environmental report then we don't take the sponsorship or investment."

We all nodded and gave our verbal agreement.

"We also request a stretch of rewilding between the development and our land along with the nature trail." He looked at Lily when he said this, seeing as both brilliant ideas had been hers.

"And if he says no?" Wilder asked.

Nash's gaze turned to Gunner. "Your call, seeing as it's your house that will be closest to it all."

I blinked and turned my eyes in the same direction as Nash. Gunner hadn't ever mentioned a house. I'd just assumed that the brothers would always live in this house. Together like they'd always been since their battle with their father had begun, since Nash came home from college.

Gunner caught me watching him and cleared his throat. "Me and Wild are having houses built, once we've got the camp and the wedding venue sorted."

"Imagine it," Wilder said with a wink at me. "You'll be able to be as loud as you damn well please."

"Wild, shut the fuck up now," Gunner growled and turned back to me. "I apologize about my stupid idiot of a brother."

"What?" Wilder exclaimed. "I was talking about having your music loud. It's you with the dirty mind, *brother*."

It did sound quite appealing, though, I had to be honest. I loved this house with it's fun and noise and general chaos, but alone time in his huge bed out on the outskirts of the land where no one could hear sounded perfect. If we were still a couple by then, of course. Not being a couple was something I didn't want to consider, so pushed it to one side.

"The point is," Nash said with a heavy hint of irritation, "you're the one who will have to look at the factory from your back windows."

When Gunner turned to me and asked, "What do you think, sweetheart?" I almost choked on the air that rushed from my lungs.

"M-me?"

He gave me a cocky grin, one that told me he knew exactly what he'd said. And knew exactly what my reaction would be. "Yep, you."

What did I think about it? I mean how often would I be looking out of the back windows of the house? The odd weekend or maybe longer during school break. The idea of me living there permanently flitted around my brain, like it was a possibility. Me and Gunner making a home together? No, it was far too early to be considering that, as beautiful an idea as it was.

"I think you should insist on it," I finally managed to say. "Maybe ask him to plant some established trees or hedgerow at the very least." That would be what I'd want to look out on…if it was my home.

Gunner nodded. "I agree. Let's stipulate that, too."

"And the wedding venue?" Lily asked. "Are there any stipul—" she stopped talking and looked over Gunner's shoulder to the doorway. "Bertie, baby, what's wrong?"

We all turned to see Bertie, mussed from sleep, her little shoulders heaving with tiny sobs.

Nash and Lily were out of their seats and to her within seconds. "What's wrong, munchkin?" Soft and coaxing he dropped to his knees and brushed his daughter's hair from her face.

"I had a bad dream," she said through her cries, rubbing her eyes.

She'd just reached ten years old but standing there it was clear she was still a little girl, no matter how emotionally expressive she was for her age.

"Hey, it's okay," Lily added soothingly. "Like you said it was just a dream."

Bertie's eyes went to Gunner as she heaved out a tattered breath. "I thought you'd been hurt Uncle Gunner." She started to run to him and immediately he also dropped to his knees from his chair, his arms open wide.

"I'm fine, Bertie girl. See, I'm all good." He gathered her up and swallowed her in an embrace, kissing the top of her head and squeezing her tight. "It was just a bad dream."

I watched his expression transform. The confident, sometimes cocky cowboy melted away, replaced by something so tender it made my throat tight. His large hands, the same ones that could break a wild horse or gently bring it peace, smoothed over her hair with a delicacy that seemed impossible from such a big man.

He moved back onto his chair as Bertie wrapped her arms and legs around him, gradually becoming calmer the more Gunner pacified her. My breath stalled, because it was probably the most beautiful thing I'd ever seen and in that moment I could see him with a child of our own, patient, protective and completely devoted. The vision hit me with such clarity and longing that I had to look away, afraid my face would reveal too much.

"Want me to take you back up?" Gunner asked once Bertie had stilled in his arms. "I can read to you until you fall asleep."

Damn there went my ovaries.

Bertie lifted her head and screwed up her tiny features in a frown. "I can read you know. Probably better than you seeing as you only ever look at horse magazines."

Nash's chuckle was filled with relief as he moved back to his chair, his hand moving to stroke Lily's long, blonde hair as soon as she sat too, making it clear that she was *his* cornerstone for peace.

"Very true," Gunner agreed. "But I did go to school, you know. Admittedly my teacher wasn't as pretty as yours, but I went." He winked at me and then dropped a kiss to Bertie's forehead. "How about I make up a story?"

"Oh, he's real good at that," Wilder offered, reaching for his bottle of beer. "Hey, that hurt."

I looked at Gunner who was throwing his brother a dirty stare as he got up, Bertie still in his arms. Already displaying the kind of father that he would be one day.

"I'll be back."

As he passed Lily, she ran a hand down Bertie's calf covered in cotton pink and white stripe pajamas, while Nash stood and gave her a quick kiss to her cheek.

"What's the betting he falls asleep with her," Wilder said as the door clicked shut.

And he was right, when I padded into Bertie's room twenty minutes later, Gunner was fast asleep. His feet were hanging off the end of the twin bed, one hand behind his head while the other arm was wrapped protectively around a sleeping Bertie. As I watched them, I felt something shift inside me. It wasn't the flutter of attraction or even the warmth of affection. It was a bone-deep realization that resonated through me like the first notes of a familiar song. I knew then that I wasn't falling in love with Gunner Miller, I'd already gone. Hook, line and sinker. The knowledge didn't frighten me as it should have. Instead, it felt like finding something that I didn't know I'd lost. It was exciting and wonderful, if not a little terrifying. It was absolutely right.

Everybody Hurts - R.E.M.

CHAPTER 42
Gunner

The noise was horrific. A high-pitched screech wailing like a wounded animal caught in a trap.

"Gunner, what is that?" Cassidy sat up as I jumped out of bed and grabbed my jeans from the floor.

"I have to go, sweetheart. It's the fire alarm!" Panicked blood rushed through my veins, urging me forward.

Cassidy threw back the covers and dropped her feet to the floor. "My clothes, where are they?"

"No way, I want you to stay here safe." I pulled a t-shirt over my head at the same time as shoving my feet into my boots. "It's at the stables."

"I'm coming." Her tone was no nonsense, and I didn't have time to argue with her.

As I pulled the bedroom door open and rushed onto the landing, Nash and Wilder were already there. Nash was fully dressed while Wilder was hopping on one leg pulling on a boot.

"The fire department should already be on their way," I yelled as I ran down the stairs in front of my brothers. "The ranch and stable hands know the drill."

The three of us ran down the stairs and out of the house as fast as we could toward the stables. My heartbeat was thudding, fear screaming through me as huge orange flames licked against the night sky from the direction of the stables.

"Wilder, you head to the paddock and get the gate open so I can herd the horses in that direction," I yelled over my shoulder. "Nash, you come with me and help get the horses."

"What about me?"

Cassidy was running alongside me pulling her hair up into a ponytail. I stopped and grabbed hold of her arm.

"Sweetheart, please go back to the house."

"No." She jutted out her chin. "Now get moving and tell me what you need me to do."

I grabbed her hand and pulled her along with me. "You swap with Wilder." If I couldn't keep her safe at the house I could at least keep her away from the fire. "When the horses come your way, keep well back. They'll be spooked as it is, and I do not want you getting trampled by them." The idea made me feel like I might puke. "Promise me, Cassidy."

"Okay, okay, I swear." As soon as I let her go she ran away in the direction of the paddock.

"I'll come with you two." Wilder ran up beside me. "I'll steer them toward the paddock and make sure Cassidy is safe."

"Thanks, Wild. I appreciate it."

When we got to the stables the sight was petrifying. Our fire process had already started with the ranch hands working on the fire with extinguishers and the fire hose we had permanently fixed up to a hydrant. The far end of the stables was engulfed in flames and the guys were already bringing horses out of the stables, the ranch horses that were pretty much bomb proof, but the fire was creeping steadily toward the horses still in there.

"I need to get to the other horses," I told Nash as the sound of squealing animals pierced the air. It was shrill and horrific.

"No point me telling you to wait for the fire truck is it?" Nash asked.

"We don't have time. Wild, can you help the guys move the ranch horses to the paddock? Nash come with me." As we rushed toward the stables Mikey came out leading Mother's Pride by a rope. "How many left in there?" I cried over the noise.

"Another four and Ariel." His eyes were wide with fear because he knew how much that horse meant to me. "She's in the end stable, boss."

Right next to the partition wall on the other side of the fire.

For a split second, I saw Mom again, her gentle smile as she brushed Ariel's mane, telling me how this horse would outlive us all. How she was special. The memory vanished as quickly as it came, replaced by desperate urgency. "Fuck!" Without thinking about it I ran into the stable desperate to get to my mom's horse. "Mikey get that horse to Wilder and then come back and help Nash with the rest."

"Just point him toward the paddock, Mikey," Nash called over his shoulder. "We can round them up later if we have to. We just need to get them away from here."

"Okay." Mikey slapped the horse's ass and yelled at it to run.

"I'm going in for Ariel," I announced.

"Boss, be careful."

The heat inside the stables was like being in the pit of a furnace. Blistering and red with choking smoke creeping like a poisonous cloud into the air. The stench of burning wood and hay filled my nostrils, mixing with the sharp scent of fear-soaked horse sweat. My lungs burned with each breath, my eyes watering and narrow. I pulled my shirt collar up over my mouth, knowing it would do little against the thickening cloud, but needing to keep moving forward. The bitter taste of smoke coated my tongue despite the makeshift barrier and, as I ran toward Ariel's stall, all I wanted to do was cover my ears from the horrific noise that was screaming from the scared animals. I had to get to Mom's horse, though, I had to save her.

Behind me I heard Nash unbolt each stall and yell at the horses to get them moving. He was right, the best thing to do was to let them loose and then just herd them to safety. The worst that could happen was that they'd end up loose on our land.

The heat pressed against my back like a living thing, searing through my t-shirt as I pushed forward, almost at Ariel's stall when I heard a loud crack. It startled her and caused her to rear up, kicking her front legs against the door. As she bashed hard against them a splintering sound had me looking up. The partition wall started to gape open like a newly inflicted wound, getting wider as shards of wood started to splinter and drop onto Ariel. The screech she made was horrifying.

"Gunner!" Nash's yell came just as a beam cracked above me and fell into the stall.

"Ariel!" The scream didn't sound like it was coming from me. It was someone else. Someone watching the horror unfold. It was too loud, too terrified to be me. I couldn't move, my legs felt leaden even though I desperately needed to move. If I didn't, I would be gone with her, but I couldn't leave her. I had to still try even though I knew it was impossible.

Rushing to the stall I reached for the bolt but pulled my hand back as the heat burned my palm. Pulling my t-shirt over my hand I reached for it again. There was another crack above me. For a surreal moment, everything seemed to slow. The roar of the fire dimmed in my ears, and I could see every detail with crystal clarity; the sweat on Ariel's coat catching the orange light, the smoke particles dancing in the air, the pattern of the flames consuming the wooden beams. Then reality crashed back in. When I glanced up I knew my time was done, and the image in my head wasn't of my own life flashing before my eyes—it was of Cassidy. Her whiskey-colored eyes crinkled at the corners as she laughed, her hand reaching for mine like she had just hours ago.

Stand By You - Rachel Platten

CHAPTER 43
Cassidy

All I could see from the distance was black, billowing smoke and flames of deep orange and blue whipping up against the inky blue sky. Each flame that rose sent a shiver of fear through me. Not just fear but bone wracking horror at the sights and sounds coming from the area of the stables. From my perch on an old tree stump to avoid being trampled, I watched as horse after horse charged into the paddock. A couple ran beyond it, but one of the stable hands who was with me told me not to worry. We were surrounded by thousands of acres of Miller land so they would be safe enough. Honestly, they were the last of my worries, all I cared about was Gunner, but there was no sign and with each passing minute my anxiety grew tenfold. It clutched at my throat, strangling me with its icy fingers.

When I heard the sirens of fire trucks I turned my head in the direction of the house to see two engines careering towards us.

Thank God.

Looking back toward the stables I could see that the flames had got higher, the smoke thicker. As the trucks screeched past me I stopped breathing, every ounce of hope seeping away as a couple more horses ran into the paddock without any men following. I knew Gunner and I knew he'd be fighting the fire. Fighting to save his pride and joy, his work and dreams and I was petrified.

Another horse, a straggler, ran in, and I was thankful it was a big enough space to take them all, especially when I saw Songbird protecting Gypsy, her foal, against the fence. We didn't need a crushed foal or a horse fight to add to the enormity of the chaos and destruction.

When I heard running feet coming my way, a jolt of optimism shot through me. It was Mikey, though, his face and clothes blackened from the smoke and disaster of the night.

"That's the last of the horses," he called to the stable hand as he pushed the gate closed. "I'll look for the others when it gets light." He turned to me and held out his hand. "Here, let me help you."

"Gunner?" I asked, ignoring his help and jumping down.

Mikey didn't answer me with words, but his eyes shifted in the direction of the devastation.

"No," I gasped as my feet took me on the road to my worst nightmare.

"Miss," Mikey yelled, his feet pounding behind me. "Cassidy. Miss. Turner, he wanted you to stay safe."

Ignoring him I carried on, my legs pumping, my lungs screaming at me to take a breath, but I couldn't not until I found him. My Gunner. My cowboy.

When I reached the stables it was pure bedlam. Men were dousing flames on anything that had caught fire from the sparks, the fire crews were hooking up their hoses to the ranch's hydrant and Wilder was being held back by a fire fighter as he fought and kicked to get away from him.

My heart stopped like an old clock; its springs uncoiled, making it useless. "Wilder, where is he?"

Wilder whipped around in the fire fighter's arms and tugged at his hair. "They're in there, Cassidy and they won't let me in."

I looked over his shoulder at the stables to see the roof had partially collapsed and the fire was spreading rapidly. No one was stopping me from going in there. I instantly ran toward the burning building pushing past Wilder who held out an arm to grab me.

"Get her," someone yelled behind me. "Jack, grab her."

Whoever Jack was I didn't give a damn. I had to get to Gunner. I had to try and save him. The heat was scorching as I got closer and the smoke denser and clogging, the acrid smell of burning wood and something else, something terrible, filled the air, but I didn't care. I was almost there when a hand grabbed my arm and jerked me back.

"No way." A man's arm came around my waist, clasping me tight against their body.

"I need to find him."

"Let me go you fucker." Wilder clearly had the same idea as me.

I continued to fight to get free when I heard Wilder scream out a curse. Dread snaked itself into my blood making it as cold as ice as I whipped my gaze back to the stable. I thought I would pass out with relief as Nash and Gunner stumbled out of the cloud, blackened by the smoke, coughing and spluttering as they held onto each other.

Wilder and I ran to them both reaching them at the same time and dragging them into our arms.

"Baby," I sobbed. "Are you okay?" Gunner bent over, his hands on his knees as he retched and hacked. I gasped when I saw the palm of his right hand, the skin angry and blistered. He held it slightly away from his body, a reflex against the pain that must have been excruciating even through the shock and grief.

"You fucking idiots," Wilder yelled. "How could you?" He had his hand on Nash's back as he bent at his middle, too. "What the hell were you thinking?"

"Ariel." Gunner sounded like he was sobbing, as I felt my heart shatter into a thousand pieces. "Mom. Ariel." It wasn't just Ariel. It was his mom. It was every memory he still held onto like it could keep her close. Losing Ariel must have been like losing the piece of her he could still touch.

He sank to the floor, like his legs couldn't hold him any longer, like they were made of cooked noodles. I went down with him, gathering him into my arms as he wept for his lost horse. For his mom. Over Gunner's shoulder, I could see Nash was leaning heavily against Wilder, his breathing labored and a nasty gash running across his forehead. His eyes met mine briefly, filled with pain and something else—guilt, maybe, that they couldn't save Ariel. He gave me a small nod before dropping his gaze back to his brother who was quietly sobbing in my arms.

Around us, the ranch hands had fallen quiet, the only sounds were the distant hiss of water on flames and Gunner's ragged breathing. Everyone's expressions were a mixture of shock and solemn respect. Mikey pulled his hat from his head and held it against his chest, while others averted their eyes from their boss's rare display of vulnerability. These men who'd seen Gunner as unshakable were witnessing the depth of what Ariel had meant to him. I did all I could do and let him cling to me.

I had no idea how long we were there, but someone eventually put a hand on my shoulder and gave it a gentle shake.

"Miss, we need to get him to the hospital. He's probably inhaled a lot of smoke."

I turned to see an EMT looking cautiously at Gunner. To my left I saw Wilder move to one side to let another take a look at Nash. When I tried to pull away, Gunner clung tighter to me.

"Baby, you need to let me go. You have to go to the hospital."

"Ariel," he whispered, tears tracking through the grime on his face. "I couldn't save her, Cassidy."

His normally bright, happy eyes were full of pain and grief, and I felt it in my own bones, wondering if he'd ever fully recover from what he'd lost tonight.

"I know, baby, I know." I stroked his face, hoping it was giving him some comfort but not sure it was or could.

The EMT gently eased his arm under Gunner's shoulder. "Sir, we need to get you up now." Gunner's legs trembled as he tried to stand, and I slipped my arm around his waist, feeling him lean into me as if his usual strength had been consumed by the fire along with everything else. Each step toward the rig seemed to cost him, his body suddenly heavy with exhaustion and grief.

"Go with them," Wilder said. "I'll go and talk to Lily and then come back here to check on everything." His tone was commanding, no nonsense and not to be questioned, so I nodded and got into the back with Gunner and Nash, desperately clinging onto the hope that Gunner had only lost his beloved horse in all the ruin of the night. As the rig doors closed behind us, I looked at Gunner's ash-streaked face and swore silently to myself that whatever came next, the physical recovery, the rebuilding, the grief, I wouldn't let him face it alone. Some losses cut deeper than others, and I recognized the wound of this one. It wasn't just a horse he'd lost tonight, but a piece of his past, a connection to his mother that could never be replaced.

Fix You – Coldplay

CHAPTER 44
Gunner

The antiseptic smell of the hospital couldn't mask the pungent scent of smoke that seemed to have seeped into my skin. It clung to my clothes and hair, a bitter reminder of the night's devastation and pain. Each breath felt like sandpaper against my raw throat, and my muscles ached with the bone-deep fatigue that came from pushing past every limit. The bandage on my hand felt too tight, too clean against skin that still seemed to burn with phantom heat. My clothes, some dark blue scrubs, scratched against my skin, a constant reminder that everything familiar had been stripped away in the inferno.

The nurse who'd dressed my burn, told me she was gone to get some pain killers. Not sure how a couple of pills could ease the agony in my damn chest, though. It wasn't just the torture of losing Ariel, it was how she died, in pain and terrified. There was fear and sadness in her eyes, like she knew we were about to be parted. All those years of being buddies were over. That connection to mom was gone and my soul felt bleak, with jagged pieces of pain stabbing, tearing raggedly at my skin.

"Hey."

The soft voice drew my gaze from the tiled floor. It was Cassidy. My fingers gripped the edge of the gurney, my knuckles going white.

"You should go home and get some sleep," I told her. The words felt bitter on my tongue, bitter and dry, yet there was nothing inside me that wanted to change them. I didn't have the energy to pretend that I felt okay and that everything would be alright.

"Not going anywhere," she told me, pushing her hands into the hoody she was wearing. I hadn't seen it before so figured someone from the hospital must have given it to her.

"I can get a lift home with Nash." Turning from her I looked at the eye chart on the wall not able to meet her gaze, the woman I was in love with. Yep, there was no denying it no matter how much I tried to tell myself, and her, that I was still only falling I was completely gone. Even knowing that I still couldn't look at her or find the words, so I carried on reading the mix of letters and numbers.

I'd reached the third line from the bottom when she finally spoke.

"I know you're hurting, and I don't mean your hand."

Her voice was quiet and strong, measured, like the nightmare we'd just experienced hadn't touched her. Yet, looking into her eyes told me a different story. Whiskey pools stared back at me, soft and shining with unshed tears. Understanding and sympathetic. Love.

She took a breath and continued. "I won't allow you to shut me out, though, Gunner. Grief is something we've both experienced before and we'll deal with this together."

"No one died," I snapped back.

"But Ariel did, and she was your horse, your friend." She stretched her neck and unzipped the hoody, blowing out her cheeks. "She was your connection to your mom. Don't tell me it doesn't matter," she said quietly. "Because we both know it does."

Her words landed like a physical blow, not because they were cruel, but because they were true.

She shrugged off her hoodie, draping it over the gurney. "God, it's stuffy in here." Despite her complaint, goosebumps pebbled her arms. She nodded toward my bandaged hand. "What did the nurse say? Did she give you care instructions?"

The clinical question was an olive branch, a way forward that didn't require either of us to bleed any more than we already had.

"Keep it clean, clean dressing every day, Tylenol for the pain and don't pop the fucking blister. I can deal so like I said you can go home. You have the Uber app, right? Best organize one for yourself."

Her cheeks blew out and her nostrils flared revealing her frustration. "I'm not going anywhere, no matter how much you act like a huge dick to me, so suck it up cowboy."

Reaching out for a chair, she dragged it to her and sat down with a bump.

"I guess I can't force you to leave," I mumbled out.

"Nope you damn well can't, so don't even try."

And that, it seemed, was that.

Once I'd been given all clear for my lungs and a printout of care instructions for my burn, I was free to go. Just like she'd said, Cassidy stayed with me the whole time. Quietly taking everything in while she observed from her seat in the corner.

"You manage to speak to Wilder?" I asked Nash as we both signed our insurance forms.

"Yeah, the fire's out and the horses are safe bar a couple of stragglers, but Mikey is going to look for them at first light." His gaze lifted to mine. "I'm so sorry about Ariel man." His Adam's apple bobbed on a big swallow. "I know how much she meant to you, how much you loved her, but I couldn't let you do it, you know that right?" Nash's pen hovered over the form his hand suddenly unsteady. "I thought I was going to lose you in there," he admitted, his voice dropping to a rough whisper. "When that beam came down and I couldn't see you…" He cleared his throat, blinking rapidly. "Don't ever make me have to tell my kids that their uncle's gone, Gun. I couldn't bear it." The rare crack in my older brother's armor made my chest tighten. He'd always been the strong one, the steady one. "I couldn't let you do it."

Images of me desperately trying to get to Ariel, made my blood run cold. The look in her eyes would haunt me forever more, but seeing Nash so shaken rattled something deeper inside me.

"I know. You were right to pull me out of there." He'd have killed himself saving me if he'd had to and that was not an option. "How did you manage to get Lily to stay home?"

He chuckled which led him to start coughing, looking anxiously around for a nurse, adrenaline tearing through my body. "I'll get someone."

My brother shook his head. "I'm okay. Seriously, Gun, I'm fine. As for when I get home that's a different matter. I think Lila will finish me off for not letting her come here. She'd already called her mom to come and stay with the kids. Cal and Ella are there now, apparently. Oh, and Cal said he's got a few of his hands coming over first light to help with the cleanup."

I inhaled slowly, ignoring the ache in my lungs. In moments like this, the tangled web of people who'd come together around us felt like armor, the kind you don't know you need until everything's literally burning around you.

"How's Lily holding up?"

Nash's expression tightened. "Hearing her cry on the phone…" He rubbed a hand across his mouth, the gesture erasing whatever he'd been about to say. "She thought I was lying about being okay. Thought I was worse off than I was letting on." His eyes met mine. "I imagine Cassidy wasn't much different."

I raised a brow. "More determined than anything."

"Not when I saw her." He dropped his pen onto the form and pushed it back across the nurses station. "She was inconsolable."

"She came in to see you?"

"Nope. The nurse left the door to my examination room open, and I saw her. Folded in on herself crying." He slapped a hand on my shoulder. "Seems like she might really like you, little brother."

Cassidy then appeared around the corner with a bag of my clothes, making my heart jump as warmth wrapped itself around me. It was comfort, it was happiness, it was love. It was me needing to make another huge fucking apology.

Heavy – Linkin Park ft. Kiiara

CHAPTER 45
Gunner

In the Uber on the way back to the ranch, I held Cassidy's hand trying to convey my regret without words. Words would be used when we were alone. Her head lolled against my shoulder as she slept for the greatest part of the journey, only stirring once we pulled up in front of the house.

"Sweetheart." I gave her a gentle shrug. "We're home."

Stirring, she yawned and rubbed her eyes. "The ranch?"

"Yeah, the ranch." Despite what I'd said at the hospital, I didn't want to be far from her. "Let's get inside."

The three of us stepped out into the cool early morning. It was still dark with a faint hint of the moon through the clouds, and the smell of smoke lingering on the breeze. My whole body shivered as I trained my eyes on the house, not wanting to glance in the direction of my beloved stables. I didn't want to see any of the devastation or think about Ariel's body being there, alone in the dark, charred remains of what should have been her safe place. A familiar whicker caught my attention, and I gasped, thinking for a moment it was her. I heard it again, daring me to look in the direction of the temporary paddock, I realized who it was. Dream Maker stood at the fence, ears pricked forward, watching us. The rescued racehorse who'd once been so skittish, so mistrusting of humans, pawed at the ground as if impatient for my attention. I took a step toward him but at the last moment lost my nerve and stood, still as a statue, watching him. His head went up and he called out to me, as if telling me that he understood my reluctance, but everything would be okay. Something in his gentle acceptance broke through the numbness. This was why I did this, not just for the ghosts of horses past, but for the ones who still needed me. Dream Maker held the promise that not everything was lost.

Nash slapped a hand on my back, clearing his throat. "Come on, let's get inside."

We hadn't even reached the bottom step of the porch before the door was pulled open and Lily came barreling out and threw herself at my brother. They didn't speak but she just clung on, her arms and legs tight around him as he brushed a hand down her long, blonde hair. It felt wrong watching their private moment of relief and love, so I guided Cassidy past them and up into the house.

The light was on in the lounge, so I walked us there knowing that I needed to thank Calvin for the help of his men and for Ella for supporting Lily in the long wait. The warmth from the fire and the glow of the lamp was comforting after the sterile harshness of the hospital. Instantly the noise in my head quietened, if only a little.

Home.

"Oh, thank goodness," Ella gasped, rushing forward. "We were so worried about you both." Giving her a one-armed hug, I kept a tight hold of Cassidy who I could feel flagging at my side.

"Calvin, thank you, for the offer of your men."

The older man shook his head. "It's the least I can do." He cleared his throat. "I arranged for Markus Gruber to get his excavator over here to dig the grave."

We were ranch men, we worked long hours in hard conditions, were used to losing animals, accustomed to having to euthanize or rehome our horses when they retired, but the look in Calvin's eyes was something I'd never seen before. It was sympathy and sorrow.

"If you tell me where you want her to be buried, I'll personally see to it first thing."

Glancing at the clock on the mantel, I shook my head. "You've done enough, Cal. Thank you, but I'll do it. It's four a.m., you guys should get some sleep for a few hours."

"We're staying over and I'm going to help you whenever you're ready." There was no trucking with him that was clear, so I nodded.

"You look out on your feet, honey," Ella said, cupping Cassidy's cheek. "You both do. Why don't you go up? Give me the bag of clothes and drop what you're wearing outside the door. I'll get them laundered for you."

Bed did sound good, if only so I could be alone with Cassidy and hold her, because I wasn't sure I would sleep. There were too many images flashing around my brain.

"You okay with that, sweetheart?" I asked the tiny brunette at my side.

"Yes, I think I could sleep for a little while. We need to help with the cleanup, though."

"You don't." No way was she getting out of my bed until she'd had a good eight hours of sleep. "There are plenty of people to help out."

There was that determined jut of her chin again, and I managed a small smile despite the darkness surrounding me.

"Okay, but first you need some sleep. We both do."

Those eyes, the color of Macallan, told me that she knew it was unlikely that either of us would rest easy, but she nodded anyway.

A noise in the hallway took our attention and as we turned Nash walked in with Lily still clinging to him like a baby monkey.

"Oh Nash," Ella whispered, propelling herself toward him and wrapped him and her daughter in an embrace.

"Hey, Ella. Thanks for coming over."

"I wouldn't be anywhere else but with my baby and my grandbabies."

"Is Peggy okay?" Nash asked, shifting Lily further up his big body. "Being left at the house alone?"

"She's fine. I called her to tell her you were on your way home. I'll go home and get her later today; she wants to cook for you all. Her famous meatloaf."

"Sounds good to me." He rubbed his hand up and down Lily's back. "I'm going to get Lila to bed, you sorted for somewhere to sleep?"

"They're in the guest room," Lily said, lifting her head from his shoulder. "There's towels in there too, Mom."

"Don't worry honey," Ella replied. "We can take care of ourselves. You all get up to bed and we'll wait for Wilder."

"He's not back yet?" I somehow expected him to be asleep upstairs, but I should have known he'd be waiting for us if he was home.

"Where is he?" Nash moved to put Lily down, but she wasn't going to let him go and clung on tighter.

"He's fine," Calvin informed us, holding up a hand. "He came back here about a half hour ago, but Mikey was a little concerned about Songbird and Gypsy being in amongst all the other horses, so he had a quick slug of coffee and went back out there."

Instantly my blood ran cold. Gypsy was the first of my breeding program and I didn't want to lose another horse I cared about.

"I need to get down there and see—"

"Gunner, buddy, it's fine." Cal placed his hand on my chest. "She was just getting nervous about her foal around the other horses. Mikey said she was starting to stamp so wanted Wilder's agreement to move her."

"Where are they moving her to?"

"The winter barn is empty," Nash suggested.

"That's what Wilder said. He went down there to fence an area off for them while Mikey and Benny got them from the paddock."

My shoulders slumped and my legs began to tremble as the weight of more sorrow lost its focus.

"I think you need to rest," Cassidy said, tugging on my hand.

Exhaling, I nodded because she was right, I needed to at least try.

Once the door of my room clicked shut, Cassidy and I both let our steadfast resolve disappear. We simultaneously sighed and collapsed onto the bed; our fingers still entwined. Our bodies were exhausted and our emotions wrung out. The bedside light caught the dark smudges beneath Cassidy's eyes, etched deeper than I'd ever seen them. Her hair, usually so soft and shining, was dull with ash and smoke. There was a streak of soot still marking her jawline despite the hours we'd spent at the hospital and the tears that she'd evidently shed. She'd been through hell for me tonight, standing strong when I needed her, and only now did I see the toll it had taken. Yet there was no complaint, no martyrdom in her exhaustion, just the quiet determination that had become as familiar to me as my own heartbeat.

"I'm sorry I was a dick to you at the hospital." As my eyes searched her face, my fingers traced the outline of her brows and then down the center of her cute, upturned nose. "You didn't deserve it."

"No, I didn't, but I understand why you said what you said. You're grieving, you've lost an important part of your life and in the most horrific circumstances."

My throat was dry and constricted as the ball of mixed emotions lodged itself there. "She didn't get to live her best life." My bottom lip trembled as I thought about the beautiful mare lying with a tarpaulin over her in the charred debris of the stables. Memories pierced through of me riding her across our land, letting her have her head as she raced us to the edge of the horizon. Of me rubbing ointment into her legs when she started to get arthritis, of buying her the best apples and the biggest carrots and even sugar cubes for a treat. She'd been my constant since I was eight years old.

"She did live her best life, baby," Cassidy replied, her tone soothing as her eyelids fluttered with sleep. "You made sure of that."

"I feel like I failed her. I should have saved her."

Instantly Cassidy's eyes flashed open. "No, you couldn't. You would have been killed, too. Nash said it was too late before you even got in there."

Thinking back, my brother was right, she was already trapped by the time I tried to open her stable door. The wall was already alight, the beam was already set to fall.

"I always stabled her at that end because it got less wind if the doors were open. There was less noise for her and that's what got her killed. She was all I had left of my mom. Now they're both just…ashes and ghosts in my memories."

When Cassidy's fingers swiped at my cheeks, I realized that it was tears she was wiping away. Tears of pain, grief and exhaustion.

"It was a terrible accident. You can't have known. All you can do is remember that she knew she was loved, always."

"A couple of days after Mom died," I started, trying to keep my voice steady. "I went out to the paddock at dawn. Just me and Ariel." My fingers twisted in Cassidy's hair as I took a deep breath. "I'd talk to her—not Ariel, Mom—tell her about my day, about Nash being a closed-up ass, about Wild trying to make stupid jokes one minute and then being too quiet the next." I swallowed, fixing my eyes on Cassidy's whisky-colored pools, thinking how expressive they were. "I never cried, though. Figured someone had to stay strong, even if I didn't feel it. Pretty stupid really. Being strong isn't about breaking, it's about how you put yourself back together." My breath was whisked from my lungs, as Cassidy held my face in her hands. Soft and gentle. "And now Ariel's gone, that's what I have to do. Think about the good she brought to my life and move on as best I can."

Cassidy was right, that beautiful horse had known love, every single day since she was four years old and Mom had brought her to the ranch. Whenever she saw me, she would nicker and flick her tail around, it even looked like she was smiling at me at times. We loved each other. She was my support animal of sorts.

"It sounds like she was incredible and got you through so much."

I nodded. "More than I realized. The hardest of days."

My throat tightened as I remembered the day after Mom's funeral, the day I did I let the strength ebb away and allow the grief to take over. Ariel had nickered softly when I appeared, pushing her velvety muzzle against my tear-stained cheek as if she understood. I'd buried my face in her mane and sobbed until I had nothing left, her steady heartbeat against my palm the only thing keeping me anchored. She'd stood perfectly still, not flinching once, like she knew exactly what I needed. Just like Mom would have done.

"I'm going to rebuild in brick," I told Cassidy, because that was what I needed. To focus. To put myself and the stables back together. "I thought I was doing the right thing, keeping it traditional, but look what happened."

"Again, a tragic accident, but I agree it's an opportunity for you to do something new and forward thinking. Tie it into the camp maybe?" She sounded unsure, like maybe she shouldn't be mentioning it.

"We will," I told her, steadfast in my promise. "We'll build something great that people will talk about, will want to emulate, will be desperate for their horses to be trained at."

"Good." Cassidy gave me a sleepy smile and pursed her lips. "Kiss and then sleep."

I gave her what she wanted because it was getting that I couldn't deny her anything any longer. She was too defiant to let me anyways.

Unbelievably, once we got under the covers, I did sleep. For four whole hours I slept a heavy, dreamless sleep with my girl in my arms the whole time.

Delicate – Taylor Swift

CHAPTER 46
Cassidy

Three days after the fire, the ranch house was finally empty of well-meaning visitors. Not that they hadn't been welcomed but I could see that Nash, Gunner and Wilder were feeling the strain of being hosts and being pleasant when all they wanted to do was move forward with the rebuild and find out how the fire started. Mrs. Wright had given Lily and me a leave of absence for a week after she found out about the fire, so I could stay close to Gunner. She'd been so supportive it had brought a lump to my throat; I wasn't even aware that she knew about me and Gunner. The whole town had been nothing but brilliant, bringing food, offering shelter for the horses, manpower for the cleanup. Even Brad Jenkins had offered to help and his relationship with the Miller brothers wasn't the best.

Everything was too quiet, though. The ranch, the stables, there was no humming, no chatter or laughter. Just the wind slipping through the trees and the sound of Gunner's breath, shallow and anxious.

Today, we were alone in the house. Wilder had gone to Telluride for a meet up with some old high school buddies while Nash had taken Lily, the kids and Dorcas to Denver for a couple of days. He wanted to get them away from all the misery for a while, particularly as Bertie kept going over to Ariel's grave and bursting into tears. Gunner had buried her under a Gambel oak tree in a pasture on the far side of the winter barn. Her favorite spot apparently. He'd insisted on digging the grave himself with an excavator that Calvin had arranged, and only allowed Nash, Gunner and Mikey to help take her there because he couldn't manage it on his own. The sight of him on the back of a trailer with his hand stroking her covered body had been horrific and heartbreaking.

Each day since he'd seemed a little brighter, but there was still a heaviness to his shoulders, a stoop to his normally ramrod straight posture. A dimness in his beautiful chocolate pools that I wasn't sure would ever leave. Especially as he didn't want to talk about Ariel and the fire but keep the agony inside. He'd even ripped off the bandage on his hand, arguing that all it needed was fresh air. I was desperate to help him and was just grateful that he wasn't shutting me out and had agreed to a lazy day. Most of the cleanup was done and as soon as she heard what had happened, Tally said yes to the job and offered to man the office for the day, reading all the training records to get up to speed. It had taken a lot of persuasion, but Gunner had finally agreed, on the promise that she called him if necessary.

He had now gone missing, though, and I had a sneaking suspicion he was answering emails.

"Babe, where are you?" I called to no response as I padded through the house. The kitchen was empty and silent, but for the sound of the clothes being washed in the laundry. Toys were piled inside Billy's playpen and Bertie's reading book was on the table making me smile. Devastation was outside yet inside all seemed normal. Life carried on. The beauty of this family was pulling together through adversity and the more time I spent with them, the more I wanted to be a part of it.

It was as I pondered the future that I heard a sound up the stairs, so headed that way.

I found Gunner in the shower, water pounding against his skin like rain on steel. His massive frame was hunched slightly, hands braced against the tile, muscles coiled with barely leashed tension. He needed me and I needed him, so I undressed quickly and quietly. He didn't turn when I stepped into the steam, just let out a breath that was more growl than sigh.

"I'm not good company right now," he rasped, his voice hollow as it echoed off the white tile.

"I don't want good company," I said softly, my body already aching. "I want *you*."

When he turned, the look in his eyes nearly dropped me to my knees.

No softness. No hesitation.

Just dark, raw *hunger*.

"You sure? Because I'm not in the mood to be gentle today, sweetheart."

I stared him dead in the eye. Determined. "Absolutely certain."

He stalked toward me like a predator, and I didn't flinch. I *offered*. My body, my trust, my everything.

He backed me into the cold tile, his hands already on my wrists, slamming them above my head.

"This what you want?" he growled, voice tight with restraint. "Because I'm about to ruin you."

"Yes," I whispered. "Do it."

His mouth crashed onto mine, hard, biting. There was nothing gentle in the kiss. Just teeth and tongue and the bruising kind of need that makes your heart race and your knees weak.

"You want rough, baby?" he asked, lips dragging down my neck. "I'll give you rough."

"Gunner," I gasped, but it came out like a moan.

He grabbed my ass and lifted me effortlessly, slamming my back against the shower wall. His cock, hard and hot, pressed between my thighs, and I hooked my legs around him on instinct.

"Hold on," he warned.

He drove into me in one brutal thrust that knocked the breath out of my lungs. It wasn't slow. It wasn't careful. It was *everything*. The weight of grief, love, anger, and lust poured into every punishing stroke.

"Fuck," he snarled. "You take me so goddamn well."

I clawed at his shoulders, needing *more*, and he gave it. Gave it like he needed to bury himself so deep I'd never forget what we were. What *this* was.

His hands gripped my hips hard enough to bruise, slamming me down onto him again and again until I couldn't see straight.

"You're mine," he panted against my throat, teeth scraping the skin. "Say it."

"I'm yours," I choked, loving the way his control frayed with every word I gave him. "Yours."

He bit down, not too hard, just enough to make me cry out and that did something to him. His hand came up to my throat, fingers wrapping around the column of my neck, not squeezing but claiming.

"You like this, don't you?" he asked, voice hoarse with arousal. "Being taken like this. Like you're my good little woman."

I whimpered, so turned on I couldn't breathe. "Yes. Fuck, yes."

His rhythm turned savage, relentless, primal, the kind of fucking that scraped every nerve raw and set it alight.

"I'm gonna break you in half," he groaned, "and you're gonna thank me for it."

I was already thanking him, with every ragged moan, every time I tightened around him. He shifted, angling his hips, and hit that spot so perfectly I screamed.

"Gunner, I'm…oh God…"

"No," he barked. "Not yet. You wait. You come when *I* say."

He pulled out abruptly, spinning me around to face the wall before I could protest. I was still reeling when he kicked my legs apart and slammed back inside, this time from behind.

The new angle was brutal and perfect.

One hand tangled in my hair, yanking my head back, the other gripping my hip so tight I knew I'd wear his fingers for days.

"You like being used like this?" he growled into my ear. "Like a good little toy for me to fuck?"

"Yes," I cried. "Use me, please."

His fingers slid through my desire, rubbing rough and fast. Unyielding and just what I needed. How I liked it. "You're gonna come so hard you forget your own name. You're gonna scream mine until the whole goddamn town knows who you belong to."

"I'm yours," I sobbed, aching, frantic, lost in him.

"Come for me, Cassidy. Now."

I shattered.

Violently. Completely. My whole body convulsed around him as pleasure detonated through me, my cry echoing off the tile.

He followed with a roar, jerking into me hard, emptying himself with one last vicious thrust.

He held me there, chest to my back, both of us trembling in the aftermath. I could feel the moment his dominance melted, replaced by that quiet, aching tenderness only *I* ever got from him.

He kissed my shoulder, softly this time, his breath shuddering.

"Too much?" he asked, pulling out slowly, reverent now. "Did I hurt you?"

I turned in his arms, cradled his face between my palms. "You healed something I didn't know was broken."

Relief flooded his expression. Then he kissed me, soft, lingering, with none of the desperation from before. Just love. Raw and real.

Skin still tingling, heart still full, he whispered, "The only thing that settles me lately is the sound of your voice. I don't know how to be without you now."

"You don't have to be," I whispered back, kissing the curve of his jaw.

Later, tangled in the sheets, Gunner traced lazy circles on my hip, his other hand curled around my back like he still couldn't let go.

The contrast from the storm in the shower was jarring in the best way.

Here was the other side of him, the quiet, steady kind of love that came not in words, but in gestures. The kind that stayed.

"I love you," he whispered into the silence, like a secret he'd kept too long.

My heartbeat thudded, breath catching. "Not falling?"

He shook his head slowly. "Not falling. *Gone*. Head over fucking heels, Cassidy. There's no coming back for me."

I pressed a kiss to the center of his chest, right over the place I knew his heart beat strongest.

"I love you too," I whispered, my voice shaking with truth.

"I know," he said with that cocky little smirk. "Hard not to, with a dick as beautiful as mine."

I burst out laughing, full and unfiltered. It felt like something broke open in me. Something healing.

When he laughed too, I knew we were okay. We were *more* than okay as we held onto each other, the sound of joy filling the room.

"Oh, I have something for you," he said after our laughter died down. "Wait there."

He got out of bed and moved his gloriously naked body across the room to his closet and opened the door, taking something out. When he turned around he had a box in his hand. The box he handed me wasn't just any laptop, it was the exact model I'd talked about during a casual conversation with him the week before.

"Gunner," I gasped. "That's for me?"

His eyes shone with excitement but there was a blush to his cheeks. "I know you're having problems getting your laptop fixed, so I thought…"

Looking down at the box my stomach swooped like I was on a rollercoaster. "Baby this is just too much." It was top of the range, and I knew exactly how much it would have cost him. "I can't accept it." Tears pricked my eyelashes at the level of generosity and thoughtfulness.

"Yes you can." He placed his hand on top of mine on the box. "You deserve it, and I want you to have it. Take a look. I charged it up and created a temporary password for you."

"What is it?" I asked, lifting the lid on the box and marveling at the sleek silver laptop inside.

"Gunner is a sex god," he announced with a crooked smile. "The e's are the number three and the I is a number one."

Shaking my head with amusement I keyed it in, watching as the screen came alive.

When I saw what he'd already installed my throat went tight. Teaching software that I'd mentioned wanting, specializing in math applications and a folder labelled 'Camp Curriculum'. Holding my breath, I clicked into it to find a template based on my scattered notes. He'd been listening to every word, even when I hadn't realized.

"Gunner," I whispered, breath catching in awe. "This is incredible."

"Glad you like it." When I leaned in for a kiss, he met me halfway, his lips soft and sure.

Pulling back, emotion rose like a swell in my chest at his generosity and thoughtfulness. The way he always saw what I needed before I did. "Thank you," I breathed

He gave a small, almost bashful smile, exhaling slow and steady. "My pleasure, sweetheart. I wasn't sure how you'd take it…thought maybe you'd be mad. I just wanted to give you one less thing to worry about."

His honesty hit me right in the chest. A beautiful gesture and he'd been afraid it would upset me. Maybe once it would have. But now…

"You know," I said, brushing my fingertips along the line of his jaw, "I used to think being strong meant doing it all alone. Holding everything together. Taking care of everyone else and proving I was fine."

He met my gaze, waiting.

"But now," I continued, voice low, "I've realized you don't have to keep holding on to the pieces that don't fit anymore, not just to keep other people happy. You can let them go. Make space for something new. And you don't have to do it alone either. Sometimes the bravest thing is letting someone help you see what those new pieces could be."

I leaned in, kissed his cheek.

"You give me that bravery, cowboy. That belief that someone will still love me even when things get hard, when I need them the most."

He didn't say anything, just lifted the laptop from my hands and put it carefully on the floor. Climbing back into bed he wrapped me in the arms that said everything and tapped his bare chest. "Come on back here where you belong."

Damn he was cute and hot, a lethal combination. Happily, I snuggled up against him, putting my head back, listening to the comforting steady beat of his heart.

"I'm so sorry about Ariel and the stables, baby," I whispered. "I wish I could get her back for you, get it all back."

There was an extra thud of his heart as he swallowed. "We're going to rebuild it all, sweetheart," he finally said, pressing a kiss to my lips. "Together."

His arms tightened around me, and for the first time since the fire, I felt him truly relax. Whatever came next, we would face it side by side.

***

The morning light filtering through Gunner's bedroom curtains felt different somehow. Softer. More golden. Or maybe it was just that everything felt different after last night.

I lay on my side, watching Gunner sleep, his dark lashes casting shadows on his cheekbones. His arm was still wrapped around my waist, even in sleep unwilling to let me go. The memory of his whispered "I love you" echoed in my mind, sending warmth cascading through my chest all over again.

But with the warmth came something else. A flutter of panic that made my stomach twist.

Had I told him too soon? Did he mean it, or was it just the heat of the moment, the emotion after the fire?

I must have tensed because Gunner's eyes slowly opened, immediately finding mine.

"Morning, sweetheart," he murmured, his voice rough with sleep. "You okay? You look like you're thinking too hard."

Heat crept up my neck. "Just...processing."

He shifted onto his side to face me fully, his thumb tracing lazy circles on my hip. "Processing what?"

"Last night. What we said." I bit my lip. "I don't want you to feel like I rushed you into anything or—"

"Hey." His hand cupped my cheek, stopping my rambling. "Look at me." When I met his eyes, they were steady, certain. "I meant every word, Cassidy. Did you?"

The simple question cut through all my spiraling thoughts. "Yes," I whispered. "I meant it."

"Then what's got you all twisted up?"

I took a shaky breath. "I've never said that to anyone before. Not like that. Not and meant it the way I mean it with you."

Something soft and wondering crossed his features. "Never?"

"Never." I felt exposed, vulnerable. "And it scares me a little. How much I already need you."

Gunner was quiet for a moment, his fingers threading through my hair. "You know what scares me?" he said finally. "How right this feels. Like I've been waiting my whole life for you to say those words." He pressed a gentle kiss to my forehead. "I love you, Cassidy Turner. Not because I think it's what you want to hear, not because of great sex, but because you're you. Because you challenge me and see me and make me want to be better."

Tears pricked my eyes. "I love you too. So much it makes my chest ache."

"Good ache or bad ache?" He was smiling now, that crooked grin that made my heart flutter.

"Definitely good." I leaned in to kiss him softly. "The very best kind."

Rise Up – Andra Day

CHAPTER 47
Gunner

The weather was getting warmer, but there was a breeze, which meant even a week after the fire, there was still a hint of smoke in the air. Things on the ranch were almost back to normal, not that it had ever stopped being busy, but the cloying depression everyone had been feeling was slowly ebbing away.

Gradually, we were healing, but if anything at all good had come from the fire in the stables, it was me and Cassidy. We were tight. Like the real deal, couldn't stop grinning, couldn't keep our hands off each other in love. She'd been my rock throughout it all, determined that we were going to push through it together. I'd never thought of myself as someone who needed much. A full day's work, a few beers at the weekend and my family safe. That had always been enough.

But Cassidy?

Watching her trust me with her soft parts, with her whole damn heart... it wrecked me in the best way. I'd spent years being the one people leaned on; Nash, when he was heartbroken over Lily, and Wilder when he was too young to handle losing our mom. I'd forgotten what it felt like to be needed for *me*, not just my strength, but my *softness*, too.

Cassidy saw that in me. She *wanted* that in me.

And for the first time in my life, I didn't want to keep moving. I wanted to stay still, right here, and build something real. Lasting.

With her. For me. For us.

She was standing next to me now, quiet as we watched Marcus Gruber and his crew wrap up their first day breaking ground on the new stables.

"I'm just glad that he was able to fit us in," I said, wrapping an arm around her, pulling her closer. "The winter barn isn't ideal."

"How long is it going to take?" she asked. "Did he say?"

Nash, Wilder and I had agreed that the new stables should include everything we needed for the camp. Even if the camp ended up being delayed, which looked likely seeing as Nate Jenkins still hadn't got back to us about a second meeting.

"A month, maybe six weeks. Depends, when his plumber is available." Each stall was going to have its own faucet and water trough, plus we'd decided on the addition of the showers, like the illustrations that Cassidy had come up with. We were also adding a cool down area, double stables for mares and their foals and a damn walking machine of all things for rehabilitating horses. The sort of thing that would have been good for Ariel.

After a moment of heavy silence, Cassidy reached up on my tiptoes to kiss my cheek.

"I know you're thinking about Ariel."

I swallowed back the emotion, looking out toward the remnants of the stable. "Keep hearing her." My voice was rough, barely above a whisper. "In my dreams, I keep hearing her call for me."

"Oh, baby." Cassidy hugged me tighter.

"The logical part of my brain knows she's gone. Knows there was nothing I could do." Exhaling, my whole body shuddered with the memory. "But the rest of me…the rest of me feels like I failed her. Like I broke the promise I made to Mom to take care of her."

"But you did," Cassidy's voice broke as tears tracked down her cheeks.

I reached out a thumb to gently wipe them away, hating that my pain had become her pain, too. "Hey, sweetheart, don't get upset, it's going to be okay."

"But I hate that you're dealing with this. That you lost her." Her chest heaved on a ragged sob as she leaned into me.

"Me too, but at least I had her for all those years," I said, stroking her hair. "And it'll get easier. Mom used to say let the bad go, a little bit each day until it's light enough to throw away. And that's what I'm going to do," I kissed her softly, "with your help, if that's okay."

"Of course. Even when it's heavy, you give some of it to me to carry."

"I don't want to burden you too much." I winked at her. "You already have to deal with my huge di—"

"Do not finish that sentence." She gifted me with a beautiful smile, swiping away the last of her tears. "You are not a burden. That's what love is, Gunner. Sharing the weight when it's too much for one person."

I studied her face, memorizing every single detail for eternity. "How did I get so lucky?"

"We both got lucky," she whispered as I pressed a kiss to her temple.

Dropping my forehead to hers, I breathed her in, relishing every single second of her.

"Hey boss."

I turned to see Tally walking toward me, her auburn ponytail swinging behind her. She had a bounce in her step, all the time, a continual ray of sunshine around the ranch. Makeup free but always with perfectly manicured nails, usually blood red, she was not exactly what I'd been expecting. The main thing was she was great at her job and had fitted in well. Too well with some of the idiots we had working for us. It was rare I ever saw any of the ranch hands, yet since Tally had started to work for me at least one of them had popped by daily over some ridiculous notion or other. She was desperate to learn, though, and had made it quite clear to all of them that she wasn't interested in any workplace romance.

"You okay?" I asked her.

"Yes, great. I've just been working with Momma's Pride." She gave me a flash of perfectly white teeth. "He's doing so well. Hi Cassidy." She pointed to the guys digging for the foundations. "They started then?"

"They sure did." I straightened my spine, determined to push away the misery for the joy. "You finished for the day?"

"No. I'm going to do some work with Devon, the gray mare."

I pulled my phone out and checked the time. "Tally, it's gone six, knock off for the day."

She was staying in our guest bedroom until the stables were finished but then we were building her a small cabin adjacent to the office. The idea that someone could have been above the stables when they set alight had scared the life out of me. I knew a cabin could just as easily go up in flames, but I didn't want to take any risks. Besides which, I knew Charlie had done it, but who wanted to live above the stench of horse shit.

She shrugged. "I don't have anything else to do."

I knew she was avoiding going back to the house. Not because we hadn't made her welcome because we had, she just felt like she was encroaching on our privacy.

"Ruby has left us dinner, and if you're not at that table at six-thirty with the rest of us Bertie will not be happy."

Glancing over her shoulder and then back to me, she shrugged. "If you're sure. I'm happy to—"

"Tally, go get ready for dinner."

"Okay."

As she skipped away, Cassidy reached up on tiptoes and kissed my cheek. "You're a good boss, you know that."

"I do my best." My grin turned to a frown when I saw Wilder and Nash stalking toward me, both with expressions as black as thunder. "What the hell is wrong with these two?"

My brother's strides were long, their feet stomping angrily on the yard.

As they reached me, Wilder thrust an envelope at me.

"What's this?" I asked, moving my arm from around Cassidy and taking it from him.

"The fire report," Nash bit out, running a hand through his hair.

I opened the envelope and took out a stack of papers. "And?"

Wilder's nostrils flared as he inhaled slowly, thrusting his hands to his hips. "It's fucking arson, Gun. Someone set fire to our stables and when I find out who, I'll kill them."

Cassidy gasped as my fingers gripped the edges of the paper looking down at the words in front of me. The paper trembled in my hands as I scanned the report. The words jumped out at me" 'deliberate ignition'… 'accelerant used'… 'point of origin identified'. My vision blurred, rage and disbelief battling for dominance.

"Arson?" The word sounded strange in my head, like it was someone else saying it. "How do they…what did…shit." I looked over to the beginnings of our new stable block having no idea what to think.

"They found gasoline traces," Nash said, his voice unnaturally controlled. "The other side of the wall to Ariel's stall."

Cassidy's hand found mine, squeezing tight. "Were there any witnesses? Security cameras?"

Wilder shook his head. "Nothing. The cameras we had were destroyed in the fire, but they didn't pick anything up before that."

I felt dizzy, like the ground beneath my feet was shifting. Ariel hadn't just died in an accident. Someone had deliberately set that fire, knowing horses were inside. Knowing they would suffer.

Looking at Nash and Wilder I didn't think I'd ever seen them look as angry.

"My family was in the house." Sounding dangerous, barely audible over the wind Nash's hands curled into fists at his sides, knuckles bleaching white. "My entire world. If they had—" He cut himself off, turning away sharply.

I placed a hand on his shoulder, feeling the tremor running through him. My gaze drifted to the ranch house in the distance, and a cold, sick dread pooled in my gut as reality crashed down. This wasn't just about Ariel or the stables. We could have lost everything. Everyone.

"The sheriff is coming by tomorrow morning," Wilder continued. "They're treating it as a serious crime, not just property damage but animal cruelty."

"Do they have any suspects," Cassidy asked.

Nash and Wilder exchanged a look that sent a shiver through me and my stomach rolling. She'd been asleep in my bed that night. She'd been out here helping with the horses. What if she'd been hurt or worse.

As a breeze ruffled the papers in my hand, I turned to Wilder. "What aren't you telling me?"

Nate sighed. "Sheriff thinks it might be connected to the development dispute. Some kind of intimidation tactic."

"J-Jenkins?" The name felt like acid on my tongue.

"No way of knowing," Wilder bit out. "Could be someone working for the development company, could be someone with a personal grudge against us."

I looked over at the foundations being dug for the new stables. What should have been a moment of hope, rebuilding from tragedy, was now tainted by the knowledge that someone had deliberately done this to us. To me.

"I want the security upgraded," I said, my voice sounding distant to my own ears. "Cameras, motion sensors, the works. And I want someone watching the horses at all times until we figure this out."

Nash nodded. "Already on it. I've got Ray setting up a rotation with the hands."

Cassidy's arm slid around my waist, her warmth anchoring me when I felt like I might fly apart with rage. "We'll find out who did this," she promised quietly.

"And when we do?" Wilder's question hung in the air.

I folded the report and slid it into my back pocket, my mind made up. "When we do, they'll learn exactly what it means to mess with the Millers."

A breeze kicked up, carrying away the last traces of smoke and bringing with it the scent of freshly turned earth from the construction site. Whatever came next, whatever battles we would have to fight, one thing was certain was that we would rebuild. We would rise from this stronger than before.

Whoever had tried to burn us down would regret the day they struck that match.

Turning to my brothers, my blood boiled with anger and determination. "Just promise me one thing?"

"What's that?" Nash asked.

"When we found out who did it, let me be the one to kill the bastard."

Fight Song – Rachel Platten

CHAPTER 48
Cassidy

Sheriff Jackson's cruiser rolled down the driveway, away from the house, his hand out of the window tapping a rhythm on the door like he didn't have a care in the world. Like he didn't have an arsonist to catch. From the porch I watched as the brothers stared after him. Three, tall, broad, uptight cowboys, stiff as boards.

"Do you think he had any idea who did it?" Lily asked, coming to stand beside me, Billy balanced on her hip. He was spinning the wheels of a plastic car, totally oblivious of the gravity of the situation.

"I've no idea," I sighed, wrapping my arms around myself despite the warm morning. "But somebody deliberately killed Ariel and nearly killed Nash and Gunner too."

The thought made my blood run cold all over again. I could have lost him that night. Lost everything before we'd even had a chance to truly begin.

"I can't stand the idea of what might have happened," Lily whispered. "If I'd have lost him…again."

I linked my arm with hers and pulled her closer. She was my best friend but in the last few months we'd become more than that. Sisters almost with our mutual love of one of the Miller brothers.

Bertie appeared in the doorway behind us. "Momma is Daddy talking to the police about the bad person who hurt Ariel?"

Lily and I exchanged a glance. They'd tried to shield Bertie from the worst of it, but not only was she smart, there was a horse sized grave under a tree that she insisted on visiting almost every day.

"Yes, baby," Lily answered carefully. "The sheriff is going to help find who did it."

"When they do, can I kick them in the shin?" Her little face was serious and determined. "I mean Uncle Wilder said to kick him in the nu—"

"No!" Lily put a hand over her daughter's mouth. "I think we'll forget Uncle Wilder's advice and let's just leave it to Daddy and your uncles, okay, baby."

Despite everything, I couldn't help but smile. It was good to have some brightness amid the fear and sadness.

The men began walking back toward the house, and I could tell from Gunner's stride that the meeting hadn't yielded much. His jaw was set in that stubborn way that meant he was containing his frustration.

As they reached the porch, Nash lifted Bertie into his arms and dropped a kiss on Billy's head and then one to Lily's lips. He breathed them all in, his eyelashes shuttering closed for a beat. It had all taken its toll on him that was for sure.

"Hey sweetheart." Gunner's hand went to the small of my back, drawing me close. "You okay?"

Nodding, I stroked his face, searching his eyes. "Anything?" I asked.

"They're looking at everyone who might have a grudge against us," he said, keeping his voice low.

"That's a damn long list," Wilder muttered moving toward one of the rocking chairs.

"Language." Bertie chimed, watching us all with keen interest.

"Hey, munchkin," Nash said, setting her down. "Why don't you go and see if Ruby needs help with lunch? I think she was making those cookies you like."

"Adults are so boring," she said with a heavy sigh. "I'm just glad cookies were the bribe." She skipped away singing about blessing a beautiful hide, the front door slamming behind her.

As it did, Nash continued. "They're looking into anyone connected with the development who might have wanted to send us a message."

"The sheriff asked for the names of anyone we've had conflicts with," Gunner added. "Which means they've got nothing solid."

"I mean I gave them Dad's name," Wilder quipped from his perch on the rocker. "But he didn't think it was a great lead."

"Joking apart, it's the kind of thing he'd do." Nash moved to lean against the balustrade of the porch, reaching out for his son. "He did poison the creek for his own ends, so it's not a stretch to think he'd set the stables on fire."

"Is there any footage at all, you know from security cameras of nearby properties?" Lily asked. "Or traffic cameras?"

"Nothing," Gunner's frustration was palpable. "The closest camera is at the main road, too far to catch anything useful." He took my hand and pulled me to another of the chairs, sitting and then patting his lap for me to sit in.

"The new security system is being fitted tomorrow," Wilder said. "I know it doesn't find who did it, but it's something."

When Nash's phone started to ring, Lily took Billy from him so he could get it from his pocket. He pressed the screen. "Yep…fantastic…I'll tell him but I'm sure it's okay…yeah, okay, thanks for that." When he pushed his phone back into his pocket he turned to Gunner. "That was Markus. He says they're ready to pour the first concrete for the foundations. He's going to wait until tomorrow to let the ground settle. You okay with that?"

"Sure, no problem," Gunner replied, snaking his arm around my waist.

"He also asked if, while the excavator is here, you want to start on the foundations for the camp building?"

The boys had decided that instead of using the existing barn a new building would be built for the kids camp. They'd employed an architect who had come up with a design that made it look as rustic as possible while being as safe as possible.

"Damn right I do," Gunner said firmly. "I'm not letting whoever did this think they've won anything."

"The hands still on rotation watching the place?" Nash asked.

Wilder nodded. "Twenty-four seven. Nobody's getting near them."

"Good." Gunner's hand found mine, squeezing it tight. "I need to check on Dream Maker before lunch. Tally said he's been even more skittish since the fire."

"I'll come with you," I offered.

"I'll keep your lunch warm if you're not back," Lily added.

Gunner patted my leg, urging me up. "We'll be back in time and don't worry guys, we've got this."

As we walked away from the house toward the temporary paddock, I could feel the tension radiating from him. "Do you think it's connected to the development?" I asked quietly.

He shook his head. "Who knows, sweetheart. They had to know starting it in the hay would be most effective, but they also had to know that just the other side of the dividing wall were horses."

"But who would do that? Knowing that the horses would probably be killed?"

"And that's what keeps me up at night," he admitted. "It had to be someone who either knows the layout and doesn't give a shit about the horses, or someone who doesn't know the layout so had no idea."

"It wasn't hard to see that there were stables attached to it, though. Even someone who'd never been here before must have known that. They'd have heard the horses, surely." A chill ran down my spine at the idea that they did what they did knowing there were living creatures there.

"Yeah, sweetheart, it's evil, right." He blew out his cheeks, disbelief in his eyes. "I'm finding it hard to understand this damn world more and more."

With the warm smell of hay and hints of the sun in the air we walked to the paddock, and I was surprised to see Dream Maker had been separated from the other horses.

"Why is he in here alone?" I asked as Gunner picked two apples from a bucket on our side of the fence.

"Tally did it this morning. She said he's getting spooked at sudden movements and sounds. The changes we've had to make seem to have affected him more than the actual fire." He sounded almost defeated, but I knew it would be momentary because he was a strong, stubborn man. "It feels like we're back to square one with him rebuilding the trust we'd established."

As we slowly approached, Gunner bounced the apple from his forearm and into his hand a couple of times before holding it out to Dream Maker.

"Hey, Dreamy, there's my good boy," he murmured, his voice gentler than I'd heard it all day. "You're doing so great. That's it. You're such a brave boy."

Watching him with Dream Maker, the tenderness in his touch, the patience in his eyes, revealed everything his swagger tried to hide. He was a good man who just wanted to love and be loved. A man who was gentle, kind, and compassionate. A man who made me realize that our future was all about second chances and starting over. Despite everything we were all learning to trust again, to rebuild what had been lost.

Dream Maker nuzzled Gunner's palm for more treats, and for the first time in days I saw a genuine smile. It didn't reach his eyes completely, but it was a start.

"I was thinking," I said cautiously, "about the camp."

Gunner looked over at me, his expression guarded. "What about it?"

"What if we don't wait for the stables to be finished? What if we start smaller, with just a few kids? Lucas and maybe two or three others?"

He leaned his hip against the fence, letting Dream Maker nuzzle his nose. "We don't have the facilities yet though, sweetheart."

"We could use the old hay barn for now," I suggested. "I know you didn't want to use it for safety reasons, but short-term it might be a good place to start testing our program. Work out any kinks before we go bigger."

Gunner was quiet for a moment, his hand stroking Dream Maker's nose in a rhythmical way that seemed to calm them both.

"We'd need to adapt our plans," he said finally. "Safety would be our priority so no overnight stays for now." He breathed in, straightening his spine. "Non-negotiable."

"Of course," I agreed. "But maybe this is exactly what we all need right now, something positive to focus on."

Dream Maker nudged Gunner's shoulder as if offering his own endorsement of the plan.

"Can I think about it?" Gunner asked, but I could see his mind was already working through the possibilities. "It would be good to have something to look forward to, though."

We stood in silence for a moment. The three of us, Gunner, me and a horse who'd been through his own trauma and was still finding his way forward.

"Whatever happens," I said, slipping my around his waist, "whoever did this, well, we'll get through it together."

He turned to me and the intensity in his eyes took my breath away. "You know what's strange? As terrible as this has been, I've never felt more certain about what matters." He tucked a strand of hair behind my ear, his focused gaze finally dropping to my lips. "About you. About us."

"Is that your way of telling me again that you love me?" I teased gently.

"Haven't I told you about five times a day, every day since the first time?" He narrowed his eyes and gave me a playful smirk. "Need me to punctuate it with my dick each time, because I can if you want me to."

"You are so bad, but I do like your thinking." The kiss I gave him was quick because anything longer would make me desperate for more, and we had lunch to eat. "Maybe try that later. 'I love you sweetheart, here's my dick'."

I thought that my impression of him was pretty good, but Gunner clearly found it amusing. His loud bark of a belly laugh made Dream Maker pull his head up startled.

"Shit, sorry Dreamy." Gunner whispered against his neck. "It's okay buddy."

I handed Gunner my apple and let him give it to the horse. He clearly trusted him and if anyone could turn this horse around then my cowboy could.

"That was a terrible impression of me by the way," he said, watching Dream Maker stroll away. "But to answer your question, being certain about us means I'm never letting you go." His voice was rough with emotion. "Fire, arson, whatever else comes our way, none of it changes that."

As his lips met mine, I felt that familiar warmth spread through me. Beyond us, the foundation for the new stables was taking shape, tomorrow the concrete would begin being poured and it all felt like a fitting metaphor for what we were building together. Something solid and lasting, meant to endure whatever storms might come.

As for whoever had tried to destroy what Gunner loved? They would learn what I already knew; you don't mess with a Miller and walk away unscathed.

"There is one thing that all this has changed," he said as he took my hand.

"What's that?"

"I think maybe it's changed me." He was quiet for a moment, the gravel crunching under foot as he started to walk us away from the paddock. "I thought about what it would have been like had you been in danger. It made me realize something."

I tilted my head to look at him. "What?"

"That I don't want to waste time being careful. Being scared." His fingers found mine in the darkness. "The camp, us, this life we're talking about building, I want it all. Even if it's risky. Especially if it's risky."

"Even if there's a great hulking development next to it."

He laughed softly. "Especially then because," there was steel in his voice, "because whatever we build, whatever life we create together, will be bigger and stronger than whatever they can throw at us."

I was quiet for a moment, processing. "When you say life *we* create together?" My heart hammered against my ribs. "What would it look like?"

He turned to face me fully. "It would be a life with no holding back. To go all in with me, even knowing it might get messy."

"And what would 'all in' look like?" My mouth felt like sandpaper, as tentative thoughts whirled around my heart.

"Taking risks and lasting instead of protecting ourselves against the possibility that it might not be."

I thought about all the ways I'd held pieces of myself back in the past. All the safeguards I'd built without realizing it. The way I never gave myself fully.

"I've always been too scared," I admitted. "In the past."

"Me too," he said simply. "But I'm more scared of missing out on this because we're too afraid to try."

I leaned against him, breathing in his familiar scent. "What if we mess it up?"

"Then we'll figure it out. Together." His lips pressed against the top of my head. "What do you say, sweetheart? Ready to trust us?"

I thought about the fire, about how quickly everything could change. About how precious this was between us. How he made it more valuable.

"Yeah," I whispered. "I'm more than ready for us."

Titanium – David Guetta ft. Sia

CHAPTER 49
Gunner

The idea that pouring concrete into a huge hole would be interesting was a little weird. Of course, we had to be there, but the other dozen people I wasn't sure. There was Calvin, Ella and Peggy, our friend Deacon who owned the feed store, Shane and Felicia who owned the lavender farm along with a handful of ranch hands and stable hands including Mikey and Tally. Everyone was standing around, waiting expectantly, like something great was about to happen.

It was, in the sense that it was the start of something new and exciting.

A fresh start as we literally rose from the ashes.

The smell of smoke had ebbed away and now there was only the faint aroma of charred wood from the old stable door that was propped up close by, covered by tarpaulin. It was one thing that had survived the fire, and I was insistent that it was used in the new stables. Me and my brothers had our names carved into it and trashing it would feel like throwing away part of our legacy. It might have been a new start for us, but it was good to keep some of the old, too.

"It's a big day, boys," Calvin said, wrapping his arm around Ella's shoulder.

"Sure is," Nash replied. "You excited for your new stables, guys?" His smile at Mikey and Tally told me he was just as thrilled.

"I mean I didn't spend any time in the old ones," Tally replied, "but I've seen the plans. It's going to be incredible." Her hands were shoved into the back pockets of her jeans as she looked over to the team waiting to start. "I just feel honored to be a part of it all."

The eagerness shining in her eyes was catching because seeing her made me desperate for us to get going, to start working together. To fulfil all our ambitions.

"It's sad the old stables have gone, though," Mikey added. "But not much we can do about that." He nodded at the new security cameras around the yard. "I'd like to see them try again, though."

"If I ever get hold of the basta—"

"Gunner," Nash growled, his eyes moving in the direction of his kids.

"Let's forget about them for today," Shane said, slapping my back. "Just remember your mom would be proud of you boys.

The three of us exchanged a look, a mixture of sorrow and pride. Shane was right, she was always telling us how everything we did was incredible, but it clutched at my chest that she wasn't here to see what we were starting. Admittedly, it hadn't come about for the best of reasons, but maybe we could take a positive from it; the new, state of the art stables were just the beginning of a brand new future.

"We ready to go?" I was anxious to get started. It was time to move on and leave the sadness of the last week behind us.

"Hey, Bertie, you think we should bury something in the concrete?" Wilder asked, his hair blowing in the breeze as he held his Stetson at his side.

Shit he was just too easy. "You maybe," I replied.

"I vote Wilder," Nash cried at the same time.

"Dicks," he muttered. "I was thinking of some sort of time capsule if you must know."

"I think that's a great idea, Uncle Wilder," Bertie cried, clapping her hands excitedly. "Can we Momma, can we?"

Lily gave Wilder a tight smile. "We're a little tight on time, baby. They're about to pour."

"We can do something really quick," Wilder offered. "I have a tin box we could each grab something from the house." He breezed over to Markus who was talking to the guy operating the machine pouring the concrete. "Hey, Markus, can we delay for say twenty to thirty minutes?"

"Sure, we should be okay, right, Eddie?"

Eddie nodded. "Twenty is the max. I don't want it going off."

"We can manage that." He turned and gave us all a thumbs up. "Let's go guys. Get something for the time capsule."

"Okay, let's go." He gathered Bertie up and grabbed Lily's hand. "We have twenty minutes."

"Honey, give Billy to me," Ella offered. "You'll be quicker without him."

As Lily led a toddling Billy to his grandmother, Wilder jumped excitedly on the spot. "Come on people, come on."

It was typical of Wilder, to have an idea and expect everyone to run with it. What was also typical of him was to have the most thoughtful ideas that we would all be grateful for in the end. I had a feeling that this might be one of them.

As I followed Nash, his family and Wilder back to the house, I wished that Cassidy was there. She had gone back to work that morning; in fact, she'd gone back to her apartment the night before and I'd hated every minute that she was gone. I also hated that she wasn't here to add something to the capsule because as far as I was concerned she was now a part of this place. She was a part of its future. She was my future. So, as I wandered back to the house, I took out my phone and called her knowing she would be on lunch.

"Hey, sweetheart."

That beat before she answered me was always filled with excitement. The anticipation of her sultry tone, the wonder of what she might say.

"Hi, baby. This is a pleasant surprise."

Yep, sultry and sexy and I was already halfway to a stiff dick and now was not the time. I adjusted myself and carried on walking toward the house.

"Have they laid the concrete yet?" she asked. "Jenny Evans stop running."

"I'm sorry, I forgot you were on lunch break supervision. I'll be quick."

"It's okay." She giggled softly. "You're a good distraction. So, tell me, what can I help you with?"

It was my turn to laugh. "Oh, there's plenty you could help me with sweetheart." She gave a little moan on the other end of the line, and my erection grew a little more. Loosening my stride, I smiled as Jamie, one of the ranch hands, passed me. He was too engrossed in something on his phone to notice what was going on South of my belt. "Wilder had this stupid idea of burying a time capsule in the foundations."

"That's a brilliant idea!"

"What is it with you and Lily pampering to that boy?" Shaking my head I started up the steps of the porch, noticing the two colorful pots full of flowers that Lily had put there. They were new and a good addition, bright and pretty like life was starting to be again. "The point is we have about fifteen minutes to find something to put in it and I was wondering whether you had anything here that I could put in for you?"

There was a beat of silence followed by a sigh that I recognized as her 'God I love you cowboy' sigh.

"Sweetheart?"

"You want to put something of mine in there?" There was that sigh again.

"I love you, too, sweetheart."

Chuckling, I pulled open the door and wandered inside the house only to have Bertie barrel into me.

"Hurry Uncle G, we don't have much time."

She had her arms full of stuff including a toy clown which gave me the willies. "Good choice, short stuff." I pointed at the clown. "I'll be five minutes I promise."

"Okay, see you back there." She ran away yelling, "Daddy, Momma hurry."

"She sounds better, how's she doing?"

"I think this time capsule thing of Wilder's has helped." I started to climb the stairs, and I had a light bulb moment. "He did it again, didn't he? We thought he'd come up with a stupid idea when all along it was for Bertie."

"He did." Cassidy's laugh lightened my soul. "And on the nightstand next to your bed there's a beaded bracelet that I made when I was about fifteen. Oh, and there are some white lace panties in the drawer you set aside for me."

"You want me to put those in?" I pulled up just outside my room, my mouth dropping open. "Sweetheart there is no way that—"

"I don't mean for the time capsule," she whispered, so soft and sexy that I felt the honker making a reappearance. "I was thinking you could maybe wrap them around yourself next time you know…"

Full on hard, I cupped myself and groaned.

"You're cranking." The laugh down the line was loud, dirty and addictive.

"I do not fucking crank, do not believe Wilder, the little shit." Grabbing the bracelet from the nightstand, which was next to her glasses that she used when she took her contacts out, I pulled open the drawer. I whispered a curse when I saw not only white lace panties, but a red thong and the matching bra that I knew didn't quite cover Cassidy's nipples. Her fuck me bra. "You are one dirty girl," I told her.

"Just something to remember me by when I'm not there." She giggled. "Tell Bertie I'll bring her some work over this evening, and I hope the time capsule, and concreting goes well, baby."

"See you later and bring enough clothes for the weekend, but Cassidy."

"Yeah."

"No panties."

Before she could answer I ended the call, grabbed the photograph I had of me, Mom and my brothers along with an old keychain I'd made in high school. It was a wooden horseshoe, and I'd made it for a girl I liked. I then caught her eating with her mouth open and decided to keep it. I'd used it for years until about a year ago when the ring snapped, and it fell off my keys.

"Gunner, hurry." Wilder's head was popping around my bedroom door, his eyes wild with excitement. "We don't have long."

"I'm coming, I'm coming ." I followed him down the stairs, grinning at Nash as I met him on the landing and then went back to place my precious items in the time capsule. Grateful for my past and excited for my future.

Unstoppable – Sia

CHAPTER 50
Cassidy

The morning was cool with a pale sun in the sky as the gentle noise of the cattle, interspersed with the shouts of ranch hands herding them into pens, could be heard on the breeze. It was a hive of activity as Rosie, the vet, started the annual check of the herd.

"Damn he's magnificent."

"Yeah," I sighed, dreamily.

Lily and I turned to each other, and both barked out a laugh, clearly spellbound by two different Miller brothers as they stood on the bottom bar of the examination pen, one each side, maneuvering cows in, muscles hard and toned as they worked in unison with each other.

"Wow."

We swung around to see Tally. Her hat clutched against her chest, her mouth open, she stared out toward the boys. I followed her gaze, and it was pinned to Wilder and Glenn, one of the younger ranch hands, wrangling a calf between them. Wilder was roping its front legs while Glenn was at the back.

"You okay?" I asked her with a smirk.

She didn't answer but simply nodded, entranced by one of the boys.

"Think she's been bitten by the Miller bug?" Lily whispered from the side of her mouth.

"Maybe or could be Glenn."

We turned back to the boys and watched for a few seconds, when Wilder whipped off his hat and wiped his brow with the back of his hand, I heard a little gasp.

"Wilder," Lily and I said at the same time with a giggle.

Tally inhaled and blew out her cheeks. "Anyway, sorry to bother you, but there's someone here to see the guys. Ruth asked me to let them know as I was coming over here. She didn't want to leave him alone in the office."

"Did she give a name?" Lily asked.

"Yes." She grabbed one of her braids and started to run it through her hands, looking nervous, clearly affected by the youngest Miller man. "Nate Jenkins."

My eyes went wide as Lily turned to the activity with the herd. "I should let them know." Immediately her fingers went to her mouth, and she gave a shrill whistle. Nash's head shot around and when he set eyes on his wife a smile lit up his face.

"What's up?" he yelled over the noise.

She cupped her mouth with her hands. "Nate Jenkins is here."

The smile slipped from her husband's face as he tapped Gunner's shoulder to alert him. He said something to him, and both jumped down from the side of the pen, heading toward Wilder.

Within seconds all three brothers were heading our way having been replaced by other ranch hands.

"Hey, sweetheart." Gunner leaned in and gave me a quick kiss before turning to Tally. "Where is he?"

Tally startled her attention away from Wilder. "Oh, yeah, sorry. He's in your office." Ruth didn't want to leave him there alone so asked me to divert here on the way to the pool."

"Thanks, Tally. We'll get over there," Gunner replied, turning to his brothers. "Wonder what he wants."

"No idea, but I guess we'll soon find out." The jut of his jaw told me he was ready for a fight. "And if I get any inkling that he knows about the fire you better hold me back."

"Try and keep it cool, Wild," Gunner warned. "We don't need you on a murder charge."

"He's right," Nash said, his hand reaching for Lily's. "Now let's go. You too, Cassidy. It's your project, too."

***

When we walked through the door of the office, the atmosphere immediately turned icy. Wilder's eyes were dark and narrowed on the man sitting in the visitor chair drinking a mug of coffee. Dressed in a suit with a crisp white shirt, he looked entirely out of place in the office with its half wood walls and wooden floors, the rancher coats hanging on the door and the smell of hard work and muddy boots that the boys had brought in with them.

"What are you doing here?" Wilder asked, immediately on the attack.

Nate blinked slowly. "I heard about your fire and wanted to check whether there was anything I could do to help."

Ruth pushed her chair back, gaining Gunner's attention. "Shit what time is it?" he asked.

"Three. I need to go pick Lucas up from his play date. Is that okay?"

"Absolutely. I didn't expect you to be here today anyway, just because we were working." Taking Ruth's jacket from a hook by the door he passed it to her. "I'll see you Monday after you've dropped Lucas at school."

The conversation felt paused mid-sentence until Ruth said her goodbyes and left, but as soon as the door closed behind her all eyes were back on Nate

Jenkins.

"So, you heard about the fire?" Wilder asked, his tone more than a little accusatory. "Even though you've been in Europe for weeks."

Nate nodded. "I got back late last night and was told this morning."

"And who told you?" Wilder's arms folded over his chest as he leaned closer, like he was about to torture him for more information.

"My friend is a contractor, and he knows your contractor, Markus."

Standing, putting his mug on Gunner's desk, slowly and deliberately, he didn't strike me as a man who was hiding something like arson. He had a quiet, confident presence and even in the chair he'd held himself ramrod straight. The fact that the man wore a suit and shirt on a weekend said a lot.

Wilder, though, he was not so calm. He had a bee in his bonnet about the idea that Nate Jenkins was to blame for the fire, and it was obvious from his fisted hands that he wasn't going to let it go. When he opened his mouth to say something else, Nash beat him to it.

"So, you'll know how devastating it's been and that we decided to totally rebuild the stables."

Nate nodded, a solemn expression falling over his features. "I was sorry to hear you lost a horse."

My gaze immediately went to Gunner, with my pulse thudding loud in my ears. He'd been lost and grief stricken for days about Ariel and was slowly coming through the pain. I didn't want Nate's comment to set him back, so I was relieved that he gave a small smile.

"She was my horse," he said, his voice strong and level. "She was the best and if I find out who did it, I'll kill them with my bare hands."

"Definitely not an accident then?" Nate asked, a hint of question on his brow.

Wilder scoffed. "Like you didn't know."

"Wild," Nash growled in warning.

"What is it that you're trying to insinuate?" Nate asked.

The calm, professionalism dropped for a beat as he gritted his teeth and stared at each of the brothers in turn.

"I'm a businessman," he said, brushing something off the sleeve of his jacket. "I'm not a thug who needs to resort to underhand tactics to get what

I want."

"What *you* want." Wilder's fingers gripped the edge of the desk as he leaned his upper body forward. "What about us? What about our land, the plans we have here for the kid's camp? What about the wildlife that your development site, the one that *you* want, is going to displace?"

I looked at Gunner, trying to gauge how he was going to react to what Wilder had said. Would he add his own opinion or take on board Nash's desire to stay cool. His eyes met mine and he gave a small nod that felt like an affirmation that between us all we had it—we would be okay. We would see our way through everything to achieve our dreams. Just being in the room with them all, being part of the conversation made me feel wanted and part of a family again.

"Which we have an idea about." I aimed my comment at Wilder, giving him a cue if he wanted it.

"Which is?" Nate asked.

"I think we're here to listen to you," Wilder added. "But we have some stipulations on whether the development goes ahead or not."

"Is that so?" Nate looked amused. "And what are they?"

"We can get around to that," Nash added. "

"There was another reason why I wanted to see you. Not just to offer my sincere apologies."

Wilder pushed up from the desk and moved to stand next to his brothers, as he did Nate took a step closer to them.

"I'd like to increase my sponsorship for the kid's camp, which you should think of a name for so that you can start marketing the place." He shoved his hands into the pockets of his pants and rocked on the balls of his feet; a relaxed stance that I wouldn't have expected from him.

"If you're looking for a gold star then I reckon Lily and Cassidy have kids in their classes who are way ahead of you."

Nash gave a frustrated sigh and turned to Wilder. "Wild, can we just hear what Nate is offering and then we can decide. The fire is being investigated, and we *will* get to the bottom of it."

"I'd also like to make an offer there, too," Nate added. "I have a guy I can ask to investigate it for you."

"The fire department is working alongside the Sheriff and the County Police Department," Gunner told him. "What makes you think your guy can find anything different?"

Nate narrowed his eyes and was silent for a beat, like he was considering his answer carefully. "Let's just say he has ways and means available to him that the authorities don't."

"Criminal ways and means?" Gunner asked.

"No." Nate shook his head, a categorical denial. "He stays on the right side of the law…just, but rest assured he will get you the answers that you need."

"Not the ones you need?" Wilder asked, still poking that stick.

Nate, to his credit, gave him a smile. "I like your tenacity and the fact that you're not afraid to voice your opinion, but I can promise you the fire was not my doing. Now, would you like to talk to me about those stipulations you have?"

He looked at each of us, like he was the teacher, and we were the kids lined up in front of him. Yet, we were the ones who needed answers.

"I think that's a good idea," Lily said. "But how about we go over to the house and do it over food. The kids are at my mom's for the night and Ruby has made us a lasagna. We could have an early dinner, Nate, if you'd like to stay."

"I'd like that," he said without pause. "It would be good to hear it over some good food."

I wasn't sure we'd get any answers from him today, but at least it was a start.

Count on Me – Bruno Mars

CHAPTER 51
Gunner

Watching Cassidy help Lily to prepare the meal earlier had brought a warmth to my heart that I didn't want ever to leave. Watching them both was like watching my mom and Felicia all those years ago. Felicia had started as an employee running the lavender farm with Shane, but they had soon become friends, giggling and gossiping as they prepared dinner.

Now it was time to start a new era with new opportunities and dreams, and I was more than ready for it. All we had to do was wait for Nate Jenkins to finish reading through our new stipulations and agree to them.

Wilder restlessly bounced his leg up and down as his hand gripped a tumbler of whiskey. It was Dad's best Pappy Van Winkle twenty-three year old family reserve, a remnant of his overspending of the money he stole from us over the years. It was good but it didn't have that rich hue of Macallan, the same color as Cassidy's eyes.

"Well?" I asked as Nate placed the document back on the table.

He studied the papers for a second and then placed a flat palm on it. "I'm willing to meet those stipulations. In fact, I think they're great. Believe it or not I'm a big environmentalist and wildlife lover." He tapped the papers with his pointer finger. "The idea of the rewilding alongside a nature trail is something I might consider for future developments. I think both will complement the camp well."

I looked over at my brothers to try and figure out their reaction to Nate's response. Nash was his usual calm, possessed self while Wilder was…fuck, Wilder was grinning, and it wasn't one of his 'mass murderer who'd just killed his tenth victim' type of grins.

"It was Lily's idea for the rewilding and the nature trail," Nash told him, smiling proudly at his wife.

Nate nodded and grinned. "Maybe I need to employ you for future development designs."

"Oh no." Lily shook her head as her fingers wrapped around the stem of her wine glass. "I'm quite happy teaching, thank you."

"What about the reports?" Wilder asked. "The regular environmental reports, do you agree with them?"

"I do. Could you meet me halfway and say half-yearly instead of quarterly." He held up a hand when Wilder took a breath to speak. "But I will increase the remediation fee if we fail to produce the report, or it signposts any issues. Shall we say an extra twenty percent?"

My head whipped around to watch my brother's reactions. I was met with the wide eyes of Nash and the narrowed eyes of Wilder. No matter what the shape of their eyes, it was clear they were both surprised and in agreement.

"Okay. That's a start," I replied. "It doesn't alter the fact that there's a meat packing factory going to be overshadowing our home."

Nate steepled his fingers under his chin. "About that. Plans have changed. Much to the anger of the owner I've told him that his factory is no longer a part of my development."

"Say that again," I requested, putting a hand on Cassidy's thigh.

"I'm no longer building the meat packing plant. I listened to your views, read your report, read Sandra O'Neil's report and I agree that despite all the measures and processes that I planned to incorporate, the plant would be far too detrimental to the land and the area. It's not something I've done before and not something I'll be doing again."

"So why do it here?" Nash asked.

Nate raised an eyebrow. "Let's just say there was some pressure put on me by the County, but I've realized it doesn't fit my brand," He gave a quiet chuckle. "Besides, I don't like it when people think I can be bullied. And I certainly can't be bought."

Well, that pretty much confirmed what we'd thought about someone being paid to pass the plans for the development of the land.

"Where's it going to be now?" Cassidy asked.

"That is Jim Westlake's problem, but it won't be in Sundance County." He chuckled softly. "It appears that my father was not happy about the factory either and as an ex journalist he still has friends in the business. So, apart from anything else, I do not need that sort of publicity and neither does the County."

Even though he was grinning, I got the feeling that maybe there was a hint of truth in his joke. It seemed like he had a whole load of responsibility on his shoulders, because heavy was the crown despite the bank balance it brought with it.

"What are you building there instead?" Wilder asked. "More houses?"

"Actually, that is up to all of you." He placed his hands on the table and then spread his gaze around each of us. "I thought maybe extending that piece of land to the ranch. You could then consider having those classrooms that you mentioned as a future development for the project. Perhaps a small movie theater? I know you mentioned an outdoor one but this damn Colorado weather, hey."

Cassidy gasped and instantly I could see excitement shine in hers and

Lily's eyes. It would be their own little school, and I could imagine them, their heads together, discussing what they needed and what they could teach there. Pictures of her leaving my bed to go to work in our mini-school at our camp made my blood heat with want. It was different than the desire to get her naked in my bed, it was more a constant nagging in my veins, so insistent that it felt like it was clawing at my skin. But I'd learned my lesson—only if that was what she wanted.

"What do you think, Lila, Cassidy?" Nash asked.

"What's the alternative?" Lily asked.

He shrugged. "A petting zoo?"

Wilder was the first to burst out laughing and it was so big and so loud, I almost shit my pants. "I like it," he wheezed out in a laugh.

"We could do both." Cassidy's voice was tentative, but there was a hint of longing there, too. "Some chickens, a goat, grow some vegetables."

I drew in a breath when I saw her eyes shining because I knew she was thinking of her childhood home. The life she'd loved growing up, the life her foster siblings had enjoyed the safety of. Talking about the chickens and goats, her eyes had lit up with the memories, and I just wanted to hug her, feel her joy. I could suddenly see her so clearly—barefoot in the summer grass, teaching a group of kids how to collect eggs, our own children among them someday. The image felt so real, so right, it nearly stole my breath. I reached across under the table, finding her hand and linking our fingers together. When she looked at me, surprised, I gave her hand a gentle squeeze. *I see you*; I tried to tell her without words. *I see the life you miss, and I promise we'll build it together.*

"I think that would be a great idea," I reinforced, staring into her eyes like there was no one else in the room. That whatever made her happy made me happy, even if I had to wash the fleet of cars that Nate Jenkins undoubtedly had every day for the rest of my life. I turned to Nash and Wilder. "I vote we do both, we can put money aside for it. Maybe forgo the horse's showers."

"I'm not sure you understand," Nate said. "It's all on me. It's the least I can do after turning your lives upside down with site traffic and noise for the next few months."

"Really?" Nash asked.

"Yes, really. I'd like to gift you the land, pay for the building, sponsor the camp, find out who set fire to your stables and wash the dishes after such an incredible meal." He slammed his hands down on the table. "And hopefully all of that means you'll trust me from now on."

"Can we though?" I asked. "Businessmen don't usually give away millions of dollars without an angle."

"I get your concerns," he replied, nodding. "I'd feel the same."

"You can understand why we'd be wary, though?" Nash sat back, dark eyes studying our guest. "It feels like a big turn around."

"I do get it, and I promise you all my intentions are good. I believe in the environment. I believe in community, and I believe in family." He leaned forward and looked each of us directly in the eye. "That's why I believe in what you're doing here and why I want to help." I heard him exhale slowly placing flat palms on the table. "So, do we have a deal?"

Nash pushed out of his chair and offered Nate his hand across the table. "I think that's a deal." He looked at Wilder and I in turn. "Do you agree?"

We both nodded and I personally let out a breath of relief when the two men shook on the agreement. A handshake for the future. When Cassidy's fingers found mine under the table I didn't think anything would feel that good.

"And the name?" Nate asked. "Any ideas? I can start marketing if you do."

Nash cleared his throat, pulling all our gazes to him.

"I thought maybe… Emily's Promise."

Wilder inhaled sharply, while instant tears pricked my eyes.

"Your mom's name," Lily whispered.

"Yeah," Nash said, his throat bobbing. "I think it fits."

He was right, it did. She'd always promised we would have a good life, and looking around the table, I knew she'd been right.

Hands To Myself - Selena Gomez

CHAPTER 52
Cassidy

It had been a week since Nate Jenkins had made us his offer, and it had brought an air of optimism to everyone. It was Spring break, and Gunner was determined that I was spending it on the ranch. He said it was a great opportunity for us to plan for the camp, but I had a feeling it was more wanting me in his bed every night. In fact, I couldn't remember the last time I'd slept in my own bed, even before school took a break. On the days that Lily went into school we drove in together, otherwise I drove in Gunner's truck because he said it was safer than my car. I loved how protective he was of me, even if it wasn't necessary, because it had been a long time since I'd had that.

"Hey, babe."

As I pushed through the door of the office, Gunner's face lit up. He turned his chair away from his desk, stretched out his legs and stuck his pen between his teeth, his eyes grazing my body from the bottom to the top. All with a sexy smirk that had heat pooling in my belly.

"You look beautiful." He patted his lap. "Fancy taking a perch here for a while?"

"And where's Ruthie?" I asked, taking a step closer and glancing over at the empty chair.

"Got a couple of days off, you know being Spring break, she's catching up on some chores while Lucas is here." He raised an eyebrow when I opened my legs and moved closer to straddle him. "Want me to lock the door?"

"I don't know, cowboy, do you think we should?" I ran a finger down the center of his chest and the idea of what was underneath his shirt made my fingertips buzz with anticipation.

"I don't know, I quite like the thrill of maybe being caught...let's leave it unlocked." His mouth went to my ear, his teeth nipping at the lobe. "Now that's decided, what do you prefer?"

"Prefer?" I reached down to pull his shirt and undershirt from the waistband of his jeans. "Not sure I understand."

"That I fuck you on my desk, Ruthie's desk or in this chair. Which will it be?"

I shrugged. "Not sure I mind." I reached for his belt buckle, it was big and heavy, not unlike his very pretty dick. "Or maybe we try all three." It was a statement. A bold statement but I would never get enough of him. Could never get enough of him, even though we'd already had lazy sex at five-thirty that morning before he'd left me to get to work.

"Oh, Miss. Turner," he murmured, dropping his arms to the sides of the chair as if giving open access to him. "I think we can manage all of the above."

"Chair first," I breathed out.

The chair creaked beneath us as I settled into his lap, the heat between us building with each passing second. My fingers worked quickly at the buckle;

the heavy metal warm against my skin as I pulled it free.

"Easy, sweetheart," Gunner whispered, his voice rough with desire. "We've got all day."

"I know it's a thrill, but someone could come in at any time." And patience wasn't one of my best traits. Not when his hands were sliding up my thighs, pushing my dress higher to discover what waited for him.

"Christ, Cassidy," he groaned when he realized I was wearing a tiny thong. His calloused fingers traced delicate patterns against sensitive skin, pushing under the lace of my underwear finding me already slick with anticipation. "Were you thinking about this when you got dressed this morning?"

"Maybe," I admitted, my breath catching as his thumb circled just where I needed him. "Or maybe I just like being spontaneous."

His mouth found my neck, teeth grazing lightly as two fingers slipped inside me, curling in that perfect way that had me gasping his name. "I'll never get tired of hearing that sound," he murmured against my skin.

Working his jeans open, I freed him from the confines of denim, feeling him hot and hard against my palm. The way his breath hitched when I stroked him made my belly swoop with want.

"I need you," I whispered, shifting to position myself above him.

His hands gripped my hips, guiding me down slowly until we were perfectly joined. For a moment, we stayed still, foreheads pressed together, sharing the same breath.

"You're everything," he said, eyes locked with mine as I began to move.

The office filled with the sounds of our breathing, the creak of the chair beneath us, my soft moans as he matched my rhythm. His hands were everywhere, tangled in my hair, skimming my breasts, gripping my hips to guide me faster.

Just as I found my rhythm, Gunner reached behind him and grabbed his black Stetson from where it hung on the back of his chair. With that cocky grin that made my heart race, he placed it firmly on my head, adjusting the brim so it sat just right.

"There we go," he drawled, his voice thick with desire and amusement. "You know what they say, sweetheart..." His hands gripped my hips tighter as I moved above him. "Wear the hat, ride the cowboy."

The combination of his words and the possessive way he looked at me wearing his hat sent heat spiraling through me. "Is that an order, cowboy?" I breathed, picking up my pace.

"It's a promise," he growled, his eyes dark with want as he watched me move above him, his hat on my head marking me as his.

When I was close, trembling on the edge, he suddenly stood, lifting me with him. Without breaking our connection, he carried me a few steps to his desk and set me on the edge.

"I want to see all of you," he said, pushing papers carelessly aside. He leaned me back until I was spread before him, vulnerable and wanting.

With deliberate slowness, he unbuttoned my dress, exposing skin inch by inch until I was practically begging. When he finally moved again, it was with renewed intensity, his hips driving forward as his mouth claimed mine in a kiss that left me breathless.

"Look at me," he commanded softly as he felt me tightening around him. "I want to see you come apart for me."

Our eyes locked as pleasure crashed through me, *his* name a prayer on my lips. He followed moments later, *my* name a rough whisper against my neck as we clung to each other.

For what felt like an age we struggled to catch our breath, papers scattered around us and clothes in disarray, he pressed a tender kiss to my forehead.

"I think that's one desk down, one to go," he murmured with a wicked smile that promised our morning was far from over.

After round two on Gunner's desk, we decided it might be disrespectful to use Ruthie's and so felt maybe we were finally satiated for a while. I was just pulling my hair into a messy bun with the spare band I kept on my wrist, when the office door burst open, and Tally came bustling in red cheeked and breathless.

"Boss, quick," she cried. "You need to come and see this, quick." She noticed me and waved. "You, too, Cassidy."

Gunner frowned and caught my hand as he moved to follow Tally outside. The three of us jogged across the yard toward the training paddock. Bertie and Lucas were having some riding lessons with Mikey, and I internally screamed with fear wondering if something bad had happened.

"Tally what the hell is going on?" Gunner asked her, reading my mind.

"Just wait and see." She grinned which eased the throbbing rush of blood in my veins.

As we rounded the corner the sight pulled us both to a stop. Breathing deeply, Tally turned to us with a huge, expectant grin.

"What do you think?" She threw her hands to her hips and pulled her shoulders back, hugely proud.

And she should have been, because there was Dream Maker trotting around the ring with Wilder on his back, not just Wilder but Bertie was sitting in front of him. Following behind was Mikey leading Lucas on Christine. It was Dream Maker, though, that our eyes were pinned to. The horse who didn't even like to be looked at was walking happily with two people on his back.

"Fuck me, Tally," Gunner said reverently. "That's incredible." He turned to me, excitement and pride in his eyes. "Look at it, sweetheart."

"That's amazing. Tally, you're so clever."

She blushed and looked down at the floor, kicking at the dirt. "It was Wilder who finally persuaded him to let him get it on his back."

Gunner shook his head. "No, Tally, it's all you." He turned to her, putting a hand at her elbow. "Wilder wouldn't be doing that without the work you've been putting in for these last weeks." He tipped his head toward her and raised an eyebrow. "It's not the end, though, he still needs a lot of work. He can be a temperamental ass, and I don't mean my brother."

"I know, boss." She flicked one of her braids over her shoulder. "But I can spend a little time enjoying this, can't I?"

The chuckle beside me came deep from his chest. "Yes, you can enjoy your moment."

As Wilder came back in our direction Gunner beckoned him over and led us closer to the fence.

"How's he feel?" he asked, letting go of my hand to take a packet of mints from his jeans' pocket. He took a couple out and passed them on his palm to Dream Maker.

"He's such a good boy, Uncle G," Bertie gushed.

"Yes I am," Wilder quipped.

He winked, not at us, but at Tally. And for a split second, the swagger dropped just enough to let something real shine through.

Lord help whoever finally tames that cowboy. They won't just get his charm. They'll get his whole damn heart.

"Wild, think you could put your ego to one side for a minute and tell me what you think about Dreamy." Gunner rolled his eyes.

"Hey, Miss. Cassidy, so nice to see you." Bertie gave me a finger wave as she tried out the name we'd agreed she could use for me when we weren't in school.

"Hi Bertie." I grinned seeing as we'd already eaten breakfast together. "Nice to see you, too."

"Hey Miss. Turner." Lucas was thriving since he'd started riding lessons and his mom had been working at the ranch. His clothes were always clean, he was bright eyed, happier and had put on a little weight. Ruth was never without a smile these days, and it was all thanks to Gunner. The man I loved. The man I wanted to spend every minute with, here on this ranch.

Looking around at the mountains in the distance, the lush green paddocks, Songbird and Gypsy nuzzling gently while the noise of the ranch carried on around us. I knew that this was where I wanted to be. These people were who I wanted to be with. Gunner was who I wanted to be with.

"Hey," I said, giving him a nudge. "How do you feel about expanding those classrooms and the academic components?"

Two lines appeared between his eyes. "What do you mean?"

I led him away from the paddock, not wanting the kids to hear what I was about to say.

"Sweetheart?"

"I was thinking about the classrooms and how we want to use them to teach ranch work."

"Yeah," Gunner said, his expression one of confusion.

"How would you feel about expanding our idea?" He opened his mouth, so I held up a hand to stop him. "What about offering lessons, making it a school away from home. Lessons alongside learning about the ranch, working on the ranch, doing the nature trails. It would give us more opportunities, a bigger reach maybe. Kids who don't fit in at school or are struggling. What do you think?"

He didn't speak for a moment, his hands hanging loosely from his hips as he watched me closely. Holding my breath, I waited, wondering if I'd overstepped, if I hadn't thought things through properly before saying it out loud.

"So, we give math, English, history lessons, that sort of thing?" he finally asked. "Elementary level?"

Nodding, I remained silent, letting him ruminate on my idea, hoping he'd go for it because now I'd had the idea I desperately wanted it.

"And who would do these lessons?" He pushed his tongue into his cheek, a glint in his eyes as he anticipated my response.

My heartbeat sped up, even the deep breath I took didn't help to slow it down. "Me and Lily?" I know I sounded hesitant but not because I didn't want it to be us, but because *I did*. "Maybe we employ others who can do higher grades."

Any fears I had were soon dispelled by the beautiful smile that I was met with from the man I loved.

"Fucking A idea, sweetheart. I love it."

"You do?"

He moved to pull me into his arms but then hesitated. "What about your jobs at the school?"

The memory of our argument about my commitment to my job came back to me. It made my stomach roll. I'd meant it, I did mean it, I was committed to my job, my career, the kids, but this idea excited me. It filled my blood with fire even though it was a tiny seed of an idea.

"I love the school, and I don't ever want to let Mrs. Wright down but I want this because I know it could make a huge difference and isn't that what we all want to do in the end; make a difference." Gunner took my hand and linked our fingers. "The kids of Silver Peaks have a lovely life and are so privileged in where they live. I know there may be some who don't have the latest phone, or designer sneakers, or get to eat take out every week but it's an incredible place to live." Emotion started to lodge itself in my throat as

I envisaged all the kids that had passed through my class and those still to come. "I also truly believe if there are any kids who are suffering abuse of any kind, there are a whole load of people who would help them, support them, listen to them. I would still be there for them. The whole town would be there for them, but not every kid has that and maybe we could give that to those kids too."

Gunner pulled me closer, running a finger down the center of my nose and then the line of my lips. His eyes stared into my soul, latching on to it and entwining it with his own. If love was all we ever had then it would be more than enough.

"Fuck, sweetheart, I love you," he whispered. "I think it's a brilliant idea and you should do it however you want to do it. Whenever you want to do it. At your pace, in whichever way you think. I'll build you a classroom with the view of the mountains you love and enough space you won't know how to fill it. Whatever you want will be yours, because your work matters, sweetheart. Not just to you and your students but to me too."

If words could turn you to a marshmallow then I was done.

"I don't know how to thank you," I whispered. "Nothing would ever be enough to convey it."

He gave me a crooked grin. "I can think of something."

Laughing I slapped a playful hand against his chest. "You think Lily would be on board?" I asked.

"Too fucking right." He then squinted one eye and gave his head a wobble. "But maybe you should ask her. Let's go do it now."

He kissed the end of my nose and led me back to the house to check whether my best friend was on board with my maybe not so crazy idea.

Good Time – Owl City, Carly Rae Jepsen

CHAPTER 53
Cassidy

It was incredible how far the construction had come on in the last few months. The stables were taking shape, with the interior being started after the weekend. As for the camp building, the foundations had been laid, and the walls were about thirty bricks high so far. Everything was going to plan, and Lily and I were just about finished with our planning session. It was our third one and we were making inroads into how we wanted to run the school side of the camp.

"Flo Jeffreys from the stationery company has offered to give us a forty percent discount on anything we need." Lily grinned and clapped her hands like a little seal. "It's starting to feel real isn't it?"

I relaxed back in the chair on the porch, lifting my face to the Summer sun, letting the heat soak in. Happiness was a strange feeling, you couldn't pinpoint what it was or describe it, but you just knew it was happiness, and that was what I'd been feeling for the last four months. Since Gunner Miller had called me sweetheart and made some incredible, totally fulfilled, promises about his penis.

"How are you feeling about going part-time at school?" Lily asked, pulling her feet up under her butt.

Dropping my gaze to hers, I breathed out. "Okay. Mrs. Wright was good about it, and I know it's what I want, but I'm still nervous."

Lily had been more than on board with the idea of expanding the kid's camp curriculum, but with her usual level-headedness, she suggested we not both leave our jobs until we knew we were on to a winning thing. Of course, I'd pouted for about ten minutes and then realized that she was right; hence why I'd asked Mrs. Wright if she'd be amiable to me becoming part-time and sharing classes with Audrey, who shared classes with Lily. Seeing as Audrey was desperate for more classes it was a win-win situation. I worked Monday through to Wednesday, and Lily worked Wednesday through to Friday, meaning the three of us got a midweek handover and catch up.

"You're bound to be, but take it from someone who knows, I feel more refreshed and invigorated by only teaching three days." She looked over toward the stables. Bertie and Lucas had been spending every day over there since Summer break started. Tally was brilliant with them, and she and Mikey had created a little work schedule for them to keep them occupied. They would eventually become our guinea pigs for the camp, but while construction was still ongoing they were earning an allowance with ranch chores.

"Did you see the kids riding yesterday?" she asked me. "The progress they've made is incredible."

"Hate to break it to you," I grinned, "but Bertie mentioned something about being a barrel racer when she's older."

Lily shrugged. "If that's what makes her happy. And as long as she's allowed to wear protective pads on every inch of her body and an army strength helmet then it'll be fine." A shadow crossed her face. "God, the idea scares the shit out of me, but I want her to be happy and fulfilled and if that's what it takes then so be it." Billy toddled past with a toy horse in one hand and a guitar in the other. "And he clearly is going to be a singing cowboy."

Our laughter was filled with joy and that happiness that was so hard to pinpoint.

Gunner

Watching Tally working with the horses was a lot like watching myself when I first started. On one hand she was eager with a whole host of ideas that she only knew how to put half of them into practice, then on the other hand she was a complete natural. She would benefit from some guidance from someone other than me, which was why I had a surprise for her. A good one I hoped.

"Tally, you got a minute?"

She looked over from where she was watching Benny working a horse that acted like he was lame even though we couldn't find anything wrong with him.

"Hey, boss. What can I do for you?"

"You heard of Jesse Connor?" I asked as she stopped in front of me.

Her eyes widened. "Yeah, of course, who hasn't. He's one of the best horse trainers in the country."

"*The* best," I corrected her. "And he's a good friend of mine, has been since I went to spend time learning from him about eight years ago."

"You trained under Jesse Connor? Wow."

"I know, I feel privileged. It's amazing what that guy can teach you in three weeks."

"I bet." She clasped her hands in front of her chest, and I noticed her nails were bright pink today. That was Tally's thing, jeans, Western boots, a flannel and a Stetson were her regular attire, but her nails were always painted and manicured to perfection. "I hear he's quite hot, too." She laughed loudly, the shyness of her first few weeks completely gone, except for when Wilder was around strangely.

"Yeah, he's a good looking guy," I chuckled. "Anyway, how do you feel about going and spending some time with him on his ranch? Learning from the best."

Her mouth and eyes went wide making her look like that Scream painting. "M-me?"

"If you want. You'll be working alongside Jesse, his brother Caleb and Jesse's daughter Clementine who he's also training up. She's a bit younger at eighteen, but I figure you'll get on okay with her; if you decide to go, of course."

"Yes, yes, yes I'll go," she yelled, jumping up and down before throwing her arms around me. "When do I go?"

Once she extricated herself from me, I was finally able to tell her she'd be going in a week's time.

"Thank you so much, boss," she squealed. "I really appreciate it, but you should know I have learned so much from you already. More than all the other trainers I've worked for put together."

Grinning, I nodded. "I know, I'm pretty awesome, now get back to work."

As she skipped off, Nash sauntered over with Wilder. Nash's face held an impassive expression, while Wilder's was full of fury. He must have been mad because he didn't even glance Tally's way.

"What's up buttercup?" I asked, looking them both up and down.

"Nate just called." Nash thrust his hands to his hips and tipped his head back with a groan.

"He's not removing his sponsorship is he?" I kicked at the ground. "If he's reneged on the deal about the meat packing plant I'll—"

"No," Wilder ground out. "He's found out who set fire to the stables. Well, his guy has."

It was difficult to explain how that statement made me feel, a mixture of anger and something that couldn't be described as joy or pleasure, but there was a certain level of elation. It felt like maybe we would finally get some answers, allowing us to move on toward our dreams, as a family.

"Well?" I braced myself, thinking for some bizarre fucking reason he might say our father's name.

"A developer called Ernie Saint. Nate outbid him for the land," Nash told me.

"The fucking bastard thought if he set our stables alight we'd go against the development, get rid of Jenkins and then Saint would swoop in and take over promising whatever we wanted. Nate said he's well known for his dirty tactics." Wilder's nostrils flared.

"Yeah," Nash added. "He gets the community on side and then once the build is underway changes the plans and goes against everything he promised."

"Did Nate know this when he outbid him?" My chest was heaving with the exertion of not yelling, knowing it would scare the horses.

"Yeah, and as soon as he heard about the fire he had an inkling it might be him but needed to get the proof." Nash put a strong hand on my arm and gave it a squeeze. "I'm so sorry about Ariel, Gun, she didn't deserve to be a victim of some fucking land deal."

The pain of losing Ariel was always there but knowing the reason she'd died made me want to vomit. A greedy, spoiled man who hadn't got what he wanted thought it was okay to take matters into his own hands. He felt that it was acceptable to put us all in danger to get what he wanted.

"You'd better tell me that he's under lock and key because if he isn't I'll fucking kill him."

Nash nodded. "Arrested this morning at four a.m. The cops have all the evidence they need, thanks to Nate's 'man'."

"What kind of evidence?" I asked.

"It's what took the time, but it was a bank transfer for the guy who lit the touch paper. Also, for some reason," Nash smirked, "the guy decided to give himself up. I think there was some gentle persuasion involved. Seems like Nate came good on his promise to help."

I didn't know who I wanted to get my hands on the most, the fire starter or Ernie fucking Saint.

"I know you might feel you've missed out on getting your form of revenge for this, Gun, but this is for the best." Nash's eyes were full of resolve that this was the end of it. "Just think about what you've got with Cassidy and the camp, not what you've lost."

He was right. I knew he was, but I at least needed a few minutes to let the anger flow like hot lava through my veins.

"Any more amazing news for me to digest on this beautiful sunny day?" I asked, glancing toward the office. "I have work to do."

"Wilder found us a new bull and is going to see it tomorrow," Nash offered.

Wilder grinned and nodded.

"That's good news. Anything else?" I asked, sticking my hat back on my head.

"This morning, I did a shit so huge I thought I'd broke my ass," Wilder offered. He grinned like the devil, but there was a weariness under it, like humor was his favorite armor. *Damn, my brother was trouble, but of the best kind.*

"Christ, Wilder." Shaking my head, I turned to leave. "You're a fucking animal."

I did my best not to laugh until I was in my office, because despite everything, the fire and losing Ariel, my shoulders felt a whole lot lighter.

When the door swung open I was surprised to see Nash again.

"What?" I asked. "Can't stand being apart from me, now?"

He chuckled and closed the door behind him. "Just wanted to check on you."

"Why? We just spoke out there."

"I know, but I've got a sense that there's something going on with you." He pulled out a seat and sat down, running a hand through his already messy hair. "I know the fire took a lot from you, not just emotionally, but you seem restless."

The creak of my chair as I shifted was the only sound as my brother waited for me to respond. Staring at me until I cracked.

"It's about Cassidy," I finally admitted.

My chest sank with relief that I was finally going to acknowledge my concerns. I'd thought if I didn't voice them they wouldn't exist, but what I wanted was too big to go into it lightly. It was a decision that I needed to be completely at ease with, even if Nash's response wasn't what I wanted to hear.

"I thought things were good with you two?"

"They are. Incredible."

"So what's the problem?"

I slumped in my chair. "I want to ask her to move in with me. Into the house I'm going to be building, but our house before then. I know since the fire she's practically moved in anyway, but I want to make it official."

Nash shrugged. "If you want my approval then you've got it. If you want my consent then you don't need it."

My stomach clenched at the idea that all my dreams might not be ready for fruition. I wanted it all…now. I was impatient to start my future.

"What if it's too fast? What if she's not ready? What if—"

"Gun," Nash's voice cut through my spiraling. "How long have you been together?"

"A few months."

"And how long have you been in love with her?"

I thought about it. Really thought about it. "Probably since our first date to the restaurant at the farm." I chuckled. "I mean I've been in lust with her for three years if that counts."

"Yeah, your hate for each other was kinda like angry foreplay." He rolled his eyes. "Which means you're sure that this is what you want."

"Dead sure." The answer came without hesitation. "I can't imagine my life without her anymore. Don't want to."

Nash leaned back in his chair, studying me. "Then what are you really afraid of?"

I was quiet for a long moment, trying to put words to the tangle of emotions in my chest. "What if it's still too soon? What if she says yes but doesn't really mean it? What if she's just going along with it because things are good right now?"

"Didn't you say you had this conversation a while back, right after the fire?"

"Well, yeah, but she might have changed her mind." The possibility pressed heavily on my shoulders.

"She give you any indication that she has?"

"No." My response was so positive I had to wonder why we were having this conversation.

"And you haven't?"

"No. She makes me want things I never thought I wanted. A real home. Kids someday. The whole damn thing."

"Sounds terrifying." He gave me the smirk of a man who already had all of that and loved every second of it.

"How did you know? With Lily. How did you know she was ready for everything?"

"When you've spent ten years apart and there's still that pull for both of you then I guess it's obvious. But leaving it that long is not recommended. If you know, you know—time is irrelevant." His gaze turned to the window, probably across the ranch to the house where his whole world was. "To be honest I knew Lily was the one the minute she walked into that classroom when we were sixteen years of age. When she came back I knew why I'd never made a future with anyone else. Thankfully, she felt the same."

"But *how* did you know that?" I pressed.

He tapped his chest. "In here."

My hand instinctively moved over my heart, feeling the steady glow of deep rooted happiness that settled there.

Nash stood up, clapping me on the shoulder. "Take her to the place where you want to build your dreams. Whether that's where you're going to build the house, the camp, or even if it's just somewhere you envisage spending time with her. Show her what you're offering and then trust her to know her own heart and you to feel it with yours."

I nodded, knowing exactly where that would be. "The North pasture, where I want to build."

"Perfect." Nash grinned. "And Gun? Stop overthinking it. That woman is crazy about you. Anyone can see it and don't forget my wife is her best friend," he grinned, "and she is terrible at keeping secrets after I've given her an orgasm."

As he left the office, I felt the last of my nerves transform into anticipation. Nash was right. It was time to start building the life I wanted.

With her.

At Last – Etta James

CHAPTER 54
Cassidy

The morning had started well, an orgasm courtesy of Gunner followed by Nash's pancakes. They had become a weekend staple for me, seeing as I'd spent every one of them at The Last Creek Ranch since Summer break had started.

We were almost in August, and the Colorado weather wasn't letting us down. It was hot but thankfully the humidity made it a whole lot easier. Naked sleeping was a must, but then when you slept next to Gunner Miller it was a must anyway.

And just like that, thinking about him manifested him as he wandered into the kitchen

"You ready, sweetheart?"

The sight of him almost had me spitting out my coffee. He was wearing chaps, gloves, his hat and his sleeves rolled back, revealing his deep veined forearms. I'd thought he'd looked hot and sexy peeking up at me from between my thighs earlier, but it was nothing compared to how he was looking now.

"Close your mouth," he said with a smirk. "You're drooling."

"I'm not sure you should be allowed to walk around like that." My thighs squeezed as heat pooled in my belly. Would I ever not want him?

"Just being my normal self. Admittedly, it's a pretty awesome normal self but it's just me."

The ego I once found obnoxious now amused and turned me on in equal measures. I'd learned that it was often a barrier to his insecurity and his need to be liked. His desire to be loved. Seems it worked on me.

"Why are you dressed like that? As awesome as it is." My eyes moved up and down his body, finally settling on the bulge between the worn, soft, brown leather.

"Some of us have been working while others sleep in."

After waking me in his own special way, Gunner had, like he said, gone to help with the branding of a new herd of cattle they'd recently bought to replace some that had gone to the butcher. I didn't want to think too much about it, but that was the circle of life on a ranch, and I'd have to get used to it.

"Are you leaving them on for our ride?" I asked. "Because I wouldn't be averse to it, cowboy." Getting up from my perch at the kitchen island, I sauntered toward him, wondering whether we could get to the horses via the bedroom.

"Want me to?" His arm snaked around my waist as he slammed me against him, his hips pressing against me and the leather glove he wore warm against my back.

"Yeah, I think I like them."

The way he looked at me made me heat up from the inside, not just because it was a look that said he wanted to devour me but because it was full of reverence and devotion. Love.

"Do you know how fucking beautiful you are?" he asked, running a gloved finger along the apple of my cheek. "Stunning."

"I'm not wearing any make up, so I think I've looked better." A swipe of mascara and a little lip gloss was all I'd bothered with knowing we were going riding.

"You're always gorgeous," Gunner replied on a swallow. "But like this, your hair up in that damn messy bun, smiling and satisfied is when you're the most beautiful."

His words, the honesty in his tone brought tears to my eyes. It brought a light to my soul.

"I love you," I whispered.

His eyes searched mine for a second before he said, "I fucking love you, too, so much. I have no idea how I missed you for those three years."

I shrugged. "Shit happens, baby, but we're good now."

An enormous smile full of sunshine filled the room. "Too fucking right, sweetheart. Now, get that sweet little ass of yours outside, I have somewhere I want us to go."

"Where?"

He tapped my nose. "Wait and see. Now hurry."

"I'll be right there." First I wanted to watch *his* sweet little ass as it left the room.

***

We'd taken a slow ride out to what Gunner had told me was the North side of their land. It had taken over an hour to get there, pausing every so often for him to point out a bird, a plant, or a point of interest on the land. We also stopped at the creek for the horses to drink, giving us time to sit and talk about the camp, our childhoods and our work. The air was warm but with a hint of a breeze making the sun feel like a balm against the skin.

"Have we done a full circle?" I asked. "I recognize that tree."

"Sure have. We came the real long way round; I just wanted to watch those hips roll on that horse for as long as I could." Chuckling, he pulled Peanut, his horse, to a stop and dismounted. "You need help getting down, sweetheart?"

"I can do it." I gave him a little side-eye which had him chuckling. "I'm not totally useless."

"Oh, there is nothing useless about you, believe me." He wiggled his eyebrows suggestively. "Now get down so I can show you what I brought you out here for."

With a little struggle, that Gunner kindly ignored and that made me realize I wasn't as flexible as maybe I thought I was, I got down from Stevie handing her reins to him to tie with Peanut's.

Turning three hundred and sixty degrees, I held my hands up. "I don't see anything other than lots of land and that beautiful old tree." To the East the main house, the stables and the barns weren't too far in the distance, just under a mile maybe, but far enough that it felt like we were totally alone and free from anyone's gaze. Every other compass point, though, revealed nothing but wide open space, those rolling emerald waves that I loved.

"You know that Wild and I are having a house built in the future, once we get settled with the camp, the wedding barn and the development site?" He took a deep breath, looking down at the grass beneath his feet. "I picked a place near to the stables."

"Seems logical." I understood why he'd want to be near to the horses, especially after the fire.

"Yeah, a small two-bed with open plan living was what I was thinking." He scratched the back of his neck and looked up at me through his lashes. "But I've changed my mind."

"Is this why you wanted to show me here?" I asked, taking another turn. "Because I agree it's the perfect spot. It'll be beautiful, Gunner, and you can still see the stables and you'd be there in minutes."

"I spoke to Nash and Wild and we're going to continue the drive from the front of the house, around the back of the stables out to here." Gunner pointed where the drive would run, moving alongside me as he did. "I mean I can walk or use the ATV, but I wouldn't expect you to, especially in the winter."

I frowned. "Well, that's a lovely thought, but don't go to a lot of expense for a new track for my benefit. When I visit I won't mind a walk." I felt a tickle at the back of my throat, that pessimism of always being the one left behind still lingering in my heart. The truth was I didn't want them to go to the expense when one day Gunner might decide I wasn't who he still wanted.

"That's the thing, sweetheart," he said softly. "I don't want you to just visit." His hands lifted to cradle my face as his eyes bore into my soul sending a delightful shiver down my spine.

"W-what do you want?" I didn't dare to think what his words, along with bringing me here might mean. My heart felt like it was beating outside my body as I watched Gunner looking completely at ease with whatever decision he'd made. What he was going to say to me next.

"I want you to live here with me." His arm circled my waist, pulling me against the solid warmth of him. "This isn't a proposal." One finger lifted in playful warning, though his eyes remained serious. "Trust me, when that happens, it'll make this horse ride look like a trip to the grocery store."

My breath caught somewhere between a laugh and a sob. "It would be beautiful." The words came out whisper-soft, while something deep and fundamental shifted inside me. After years of temporary—temporary homes, temporary relationships, temporary happiness—I'd found something that might actually last.

"Duly noted," Gunner whispered, his mouth close to my ear. "So, what do you say, Miss. Turner, how do you like the idea of living here? Laying down roots to match those of that huge tree because I've been thinking about this house." His voice softened, eyes fixed on the horizon as if he could already see walls rising from the earth. "A wraparound porch facing west, perfect for watching the sunset paint those mountains. Built-in bookshelves next to a stone fireplace for your collection." His fingers traced absent patterns against my back. "That kitchen island you've mentioned, big enough to bake dozens of cinnamon rolls while I make coffee and try not to distract you." He brushed a strand of hair from my face, his voice growing softer. "I've been thinking about a room facing east, where the morning light comes in perfect for your desk by the window. You can grade papers or plan lessons for the camp kids there while watching the horses in the pasture. And there's this spot in the back perfect for that vegetable garden and the chickens you miss from your farm. Maybe even that goat you keep talking about."

His thumb traced my cheekbone as he continued, "And upstairs...well,

I've planned for at least three bedrooms besides ours. For our kids someday. I can already imagine them running down to the stables, learning to ride just like you did. Like we'd teach them together."

He paused, swallowing hard. "I want to build a life with you, Cassidy. Morning coffee and evening rides. Christmases by that fireplace and summer nights on the porch. Fighting about whose turn it is to do the dishes and making up after. All of it. Everything. With you."

I didn't hesitate. Why would I, for something that sounded so perfect? "I would love it, more than anything. It would be magical."

"Just what I thought," he said before pulling me to him.

His mouth found mine with a tenderness that slowly transformed into something deeper, more consuming. The warm summer breeze swirled around us, carrying the sweet scent of wildflowers and sun-warmed grass. His gloved hands cradled my face with a gentleness that belied their strength, the leather warm against my skin as his thumbs traced the line of my cheekbones.

I melted into him, my hands finding their way to his chest, feeling his heartbeat strong and steady beneath my fingertips. The world narrowed to just this moment, the heat of his body against mine, the soft rustle of grass beneath our boots, the distant nickering of the horses.

His kiss tasted of promise and possibility, of mornings yet to come and evenings yet to share. When his arms wrapped fully around me, lifting me slightly off the ground, I felt weightless yet anchored all at once. This was what belonging felt like, this perfect fusion of passion and tenderness, of desire and trust.

The kiss deepened as he ripped off his gloves and tangled his hand in my hair, releasing it from its messy bun so that it cascaded down around my shoulders. The contrast of his rough fingers against my neck sent shivers cascading down my spine. I could feel his smile against my lips as he registered my response, the quiet sound of satisfaction rumbling from deep in his chest.

When we finally broke apart, breathless and flushed, he rested his forehead against mine. His eyes, dark with emotion, held mine with such intensity that I felt seen in a way I never had before. Fully, completely, with all my flaws and strengths laid bare and cherished equally.

"I've been waiting my whole life for you," he whispered against my lips. "Even when I was too stubborn to know it."

Then in the whisper of the breeze, I was sure I could hear the gentle whinny of a horse and hoped it was Ariel giving me her approval, too.

Gunner

As we walked into the house, hand in hand, everyone was there waiting expectantly. Wilder the idiot was bouncing on the balls of his feet, like he was waiting for me to reveal the secret to eternal life.

"Hey, you two," Lily said, her eyebrows almost disappearing into her hairline.

"Have a good ride?" Nash asked, heaving Billy over his shoulder making the little guy giggle as he hung upside down.

"Did you do the thing, Uncle G?"

Trust Bertie to be the only one to spit it out.

"I did the thing and asked Miss. Cassidy to live in my new house with me."

"And?" Wilder asked. "Am I going to be the only single pringle in the house?"

'You were the only damn single pringle anyway," Nash scoffed, dropping Billy and catching him by the ankles in one slick movement making him chuckle even louder.

"And you know what, I'm more than fine with that," he muttered. "All that googly-eye shit. I don't need someone to knock me on my ass to stop me adopting stray cats and journaling."

I just chuckled. "It'll happen one day," I grinned at Cassidy, "believe me."

Wilder turned to me, one brow raised. "Maybe. But I feel sorry for the poor woman who catches me, I'm a lot of cowboy to handle." He paused. "And a whole lot more underneath."

"Someone shut him up," Nash groaned and addressed Cassidy and me. "What's happening before the house is built?"

Cassidy wrapped her arm around my waist at the front, her right hand still in mine, cocooning me in her love. With her tucked against me it felt like there wasn't anything we couldn't achieve together.

"She's moving in here." I looked at each of them in turn. "If that's okay with all of you?"

"It's going to be so good," Lily cried excitedly. "Wine Wednesday will be so much better now we can both just stumble up to bed when we've had enough."

"Hey," Bertie yelled, "did you ask Miss. Cassidy to marry you or not?"

"Munchkin," Nash warned.

"But I thought that's what the horse ride was for?" Pouting my niece crossed her arms over her chest. "I thought I was going to be a flower girl again. Like I was for you and Momma."

I ruffled her hair. "One day short stuff, but when I do ask Miss. Cassidy, to marry me I'll be asking her during something better than a horse ride."

She looked at me wide-eyed, an expression of total horror. "What the heck is better than a horse ride you fool!"

"Bertie!"

"Munchkin!"

"Way to go Bertie girl, he is a fool."

"You sure you want to be a part of this family one day?" I asked Cassidy, brushing her hair from her sun-kissed face. "It's a bit crazy at times."

She took a breath before a serene smile appeared on her face. "Absolutely, you fool."

I took her mouth in mine for a slow kiss, letting every ounce of my love for her feed into it. Telling her silently that ours was going to be a love of the ages. We would live on this ranch with our family, bring up our children here and we would be happy. There would be ups and downs, tears of sorrow and joy, happiness and sadness but the foundation of it all would be love. She would have the love of a stubborn man who almost didn't get the sweet because of his stupid misconceptions of her. Cassidy Turner was more than I deserved yet I still had her. I believed she was a gift from another beautiful woman who I'd loved, the one who was giving me life for a second time, and I would always be grateful.

"Okay," Wilder said above the noise of my incredible family. "Who else thinks Gunner is a fool, or is it just me and Bertie?"

I thought about smacking him around the back of the head, but he was right, I was and was thankful I'd woken up just in time.

Glory Box – Portishead

BONUS CHAPTER

Cassidy

Three years earlier

It was too hot, and all I could smell were sweaty kids, sun-warmed asphalt and over ripe, uneaten lunches. Kids shrieked, cars idled, and parents jostled for the prime spot to see their child emerging from school. Roll on next semester when we'd have a more organized pick up line.

I stayed where I always did on the fringe. Half in the shade of the large overhang, half watching the chaos to make sure every child got picked up.

Lucas Keller's backpack had a broken zip, and I wasn't sure it had one more week left in it before the end of the school year. The game of football he and the other boys had been playing with it at lunch break hadn't helped. I bent down to help him with the zip after he'd lost half the contents outside my classroom. I adjusted the weight, so it didn't dig into his shoulders. He just rolled his eyes like it was fine, desperate to get to his dad who was waiting with his usual disgruntled demeanor.

"There you go," I murmured, smoothing his hair down. "You're ready to go without losing half your stuff."

He gave me a half-smile and sped away across the grass to his dad.

And that's when I saw him.

Leaning against the hood of his truck like a Marlboro ad that had grown up and developed a more judgmental stare.

Gunner Miller.

Of course he was here. It was his day to pick up Bertie. I knew because even though she wasn't in my class, Bertie Miller could out-talk a talk-show host. Which meant I knew that Tuesday and Thursday were the day her uncle, the silent and infuriatingly attractive Gunner, showed up like clockwork.

He didn't see me.

He never did.

Not that it really mattered. Not really.

Because no matter how much I told myself he was too arrogant, too vain to be even vaguely interesting, he still made my stomach twist every time he showed up. Which wasn't fair or convenient.

I could have been totally wrong about him, but he looked like the kind of man who only liked his horses for company. Horses and cattle. Yet somehow I just knew he was also the kind of man who would be on time for dinner and hold the door open for you while calling you ma'am. There was something else, though, something in the way he watched the world, like he was always holding something back. Like he had more to say but couldn't be bothered— as I said, horses and cattle.

He probably thought of me the same way. Or worse, he thought I was like a cafeteria menu, bland and avoidable.

Fine. Like I cared.

Liar.

I turned my eyes away before they could linger too long. Before he could catch me watching and not react. No reaction would be worse than complete indifference. Like I was just another face in the sea of parents and teachers.

Probably wasn't his type anyway. If he even had a type. Just a pity my interest in him was growing exponentially every damn week.

Then Bertie launched out of the building, backpack bouncing, hair desperate to escape the confines of the braid her dad made a decent go of. As he saw her Gunner pushed off his truck and opened the back door for her, like it was his prime job on this earth.

They exchanged words and he smiled. It was rare and knocked the wind out of me for a second.

I stepped further back into the shadows, swallowing the weird twist in my chest and telling myself that it didn't matter that he had no idea that I existed.

It was just another day. Just another man who I had a crush on. I clearly needed to get laid.

None of it mattered.

Yet I still couldn't stop wondering what a date with him would be like.

MORE FROM SILVER PEAKS SERIES

Want to find out who takes Wilder's heart? Then check out The Sapphire Ocean. Let me tell you, she may take his heart, but *he* will steal *yours*! Available on Amazon or click on the links

THE SAPPHIRE OCEAN

mybook.to/TheSapphireOcean

Out 1st December 2025

Sign up for a SO Pre Release Pack

https://forms.gle/Rn59Sk7XK9dh8TN97

SILVER PEAKS PLAYLIST

Listen Now on *Spotify*
https://tinyurl.com/Silver-Peaks-Playlist

NIKKI'S LINKS

If you'd like to know more about me or my books, then all my links are listed below.

Website:
www.nikkiashtonbooks.co.uk

Instagram
www.instagram.com/nikkiashtonauthor

Facebook
www.facebook.com/nikki.ashton.982
Ashton's Angels Facebook Group
www.facebook.com/groups/1039480929500429

Amazon
viewAuthor.at/NAPage

TikTok
https://www.tiktok.com/@nikkiashtonbooks

nikki ♥
ashton x

Printed in Dunstable, United Kingdom